INSPECTOR KIRBY AND HAROLD LONGCOAT

....

A Northumbrian Mystery

Ian Martyn

www.martynfiction.com

Copyright © 2017 by Ian Martyn.

All rights reserved. No part of this publication may be reproduced, distributed or transmitted in any form or by any means, including photocopying, recording, or other electronic or mechanical methods, without the prior written permission of the publisher, except in the case of brief quotations embodied in critical reviews and certain other noncommercial uses permitted by copyright law. For permission requests, please contact via www.martynfiction.com

Ian Martyn
www.martynfiction.com

Publisher's Note: This is a work of fiction. Names, characters, places, and incidents are a product of the author's imagination. Locales and public names are sometimes used for atmospheric purposes. Any resemblance to actual people, living or dead, or to businesses, companies, events, institutions, or locales is completely coincidental.

Book Layout ©2013 BookDesignTemplates.com

Ordering Information:
Quantity sales. Special discounts are available on quantity purchases by corporations, associations, and others. For details, contact via www.martynfiction.com

Inspector Kirby and Harold Longcoat. Ian Martyn - 1st ed.

Contents

Dedication

Acknowledgements

Chapter One

Chapter Two

Chapter Three

Chapter Four

Chapter Five

Chapter Six

Chapter Seven

Chapter Eight

Chapter Nine

Chapter Ten

Chapter Eleven

Chapter Twelve

Chapter Thirteen

Chapter Fourteen

Chapter Fifteen

Chapter Sixteen

Chapter Seventeen

Chapter Eighteen

Chapter Nineteen

Chapter Twenty

Chapter Twenty One

Chapter Twenty Two

Chapter Twenty Three

Chapter Twenty Four
Chapter Twenty Five
Chapter Twenty Six
Chapter Twenty Seven
Chapter Twenty Eight
Chapter Twenty Nine
Chapter Thirty
Chapter Thirty One
Chapter Thirty Two
Chapter Thirty Three
Chapter Thirty Four
Chapter Thirty Five
Chapter Thirty Six
Chapter Thirty Seven
Chapter Thirty Eight
Chapter Thirty Nine
Chapter Forty
Chapter Forty One
Chapter Forty Two
Chapter Forty Three
Chapter Forty Four
Chapter Forty Five
Chapter Forty Six
Chapter Forty Seven
Chapter Forty Eight
Chapter Forty Nine
Chapter Fifty
Chapter Fifty One

Author's notes
About the author
Also by Ian Martyn

To the county of Northumberland where I was fortunate to spend my formative years. If true magic exists anywhere in the world then it's here amongst its wild hills, magnificent coastline and castles.

Acknowledgements

As always to my wife Catherine and my sons Daniel and Jonathan who continue to believe in my writing. Neil Kirby and John Horton who always read those early versions. This time also Chris Seaward whose enthusiasm for this book has given me so much encouragement. Jaqui Thake who is still correcting my sometimes novel and original use of the English language.

To all those who've read my books and expressed their enjoyment of them, thank you, it's what keeps an author going.

"Kirby was never one to dismiss someone on the grounds they felt things "didn't feel right". In his experience things not feeling right often led to things not being right. It didn't feel right to him either".

ONE

....

Inspector Kirby glanced at the Journal newspaper that someone had left on his desk while he'd been in the loo. They had even, needlessly, ringed the headline in red pen, "GOSFORTH GODDESS GRABBED, Lilly 'Medussa' Johnson was taken into custody at her home in Regent Avenue along with thirty-seven snakes stolen from pet shops and private collections". There was a picture of him leading Lilly towards a police car. He had his head down. Someone had drawn a speech balloon coming out of his head with the words, "Oh hell, why me?" inside. Lilly was dressed in a long white gown, blonde wig and tiara. She was smiling for the cameras.

Kirby frowned, the Super wasn't going to like that. Glancing at the clock his frown deepened. With a sigh he turned back to the screen and the accusing blink of the cursor. It was nine o'clock, he'd been in for two hours and achieved two-fifths of sod all. Sometimes he felt that writing the report was harder than solving the crime, especially with the crimes that came his way.

He pushed back his sleeves and readied his right index finger for another go at stabbing the keyboard. He looked around the office and wondered about a cup of coffee. He dismissed the thought as just another way of putting off the onerous task. Back to the screen. He swore. The last sentence he'd written was all in caps. Why the hell did they have to put the caps key so close to the 'A'? There were a few sniggers as he cursed at the screen. He swivelled his chair to the left. 'Tell you what, Sergeant, I'll dictate and you type.'

Sergeant Vendatelli glanced at his fellow officers who were now all very intent on their own screens.

Kirby shook his head. 'Don't worry, Sergeant, you might struggle with some of the longer words.'

'Er, thank you, sir.'

Kirby knew that the younger members of the force liked to call him "Old School Kirby" or just "Old School" for short. And yes, when it was an option he did prefer to use pen and paper. Also, he called a phone a phone rather than a mobile. What's more, his "rang" rather than play the theme from his favourite song. If it had have done, his choice would no doubt have provoked even more comments. Anyway, Louis Armstrong singing "What a Beautiful World" didn't seem appropriate for a copper.

He wasn't a complete techno Luddite. He did admit computer age policing had its uses; only you couldn't solve crimes by googling and tweeting. He still believed coppering was ninety percent slog, ten percent inspiration and ten percent perspiration. And yes, he did know that was one hundred and ten percent.

He also knew those same youngsters considered him a bit of a loner. He didn't meet the others down the pub after work. He didn't do the social club and avoided, if at all possible, any activity that included the words "team building" in the title. To his way of thinking, if you couldn't feel part of a team as a copper with half the world against you then plodging around, in January, in Kielder Forest, knee-deep in a freezing cold stream, trying to build a bridge with a few sticks and bits of rope was not going do it for you either.

Kirby saw himself as an ordinary police inspector trying to do his job in the way he knew worked best for him. That's not to imply he thought a police inspector's job was in any way ordinary. By most people's standards it was anything but ordinary. He'd seen some extraordinary things, and often things most sane people would never want to see.

However, the downside of being viewed by some of both the junior and senior ranks as somewhat eccentric was that he ended up with the cases that leaned towards the stranger end of the spectrum of police work. The cases other officers avoided. Which meant, as with this case, he was presented with the problem of reporting the facts while not getting himself hauled up in front of the Super for "sensationalism". The Super took a dim view of "sensationalism" as it tended to find its way into newspapers, and newspapers being newspapers the result was rarely complimentary. He glanced back at the Journal, even United's latest, miserable performance was preferable to the headline.

The Lilly "Medusa" Johnson case had already had its share of press coverage. Over a period of three months there had been fifteen reports of snakes being stolen from pet shops and private collections in the area. Rumours were rife that it was Animal Liberation or even some strange – foreign, of course – cult. The papers loved it. They, lacking much imagination in Kirby's opinion, had referred to them as the Snake Men, as in: 'Slippery Snake Men Strike Again' or the 'Snake Men Crimes are Addering Up' and 'Snake Men Bring Hissteria to the Snake Community'.

It turned out, to the disappointment of the local press, the culprit wasn't a fanatical group or exotic cult. It was one Lilly Johnson, who lived in a two-bedroom terraced house in Fawdon. They did cheer up however when they found out she liked to call herself Medusa, insisted her house was a temple and had erected two, two-storey, polystyrene Doric columns on the front of it. A fact that didn't seem to register as strange enough to report those who lived nearby. The headline was only the start. Inside there was a two-page spread of interviews with Lil's neighbours and an artist's impression of Lil appearing down the shops in full regalia, a long, white gown with a gold, snake-shaped tiara on her blonde and curled locks. As for the neighbours, if anything those of a certain age had seen her originality and level of eccentricity as something to aspire to.

When interviewed, Lil's defence was that she was above the laws of men and refused to accept the validity of anything from mere mortals. Although Kirby noted that didn't seem to extend to the tea and chocolate Hobnobs they kept supplying her with, which she insisted on calling her 'ambrosia'.

On digging, Lilly had 'history', as the police liked to put it, having been responsible for a series of more than thirty burglaries in the 1980s. The papers had then dubbed her Diamond Lil on account of her only taking jewellery, most of which was found stuffed into drawers and cupboards in her then small flat off Gosforth high street.

He was wondering about how to describe Lil without being "sensationalist" when the phone rang. 'Kirby.'

'Ah, sir. Would you happen to have an hour to spare?'

'Why, Sergeant?'

'It's just something's come up and none of the other officers can be spared at the moment.' Kirby knew that was Desk Sergeant Caruthers speak for, 'It's a bit weird and I don't think anyone else will want to take it'.

He was about to say, 'Neither can I', when he glanced at the screen. So instead he said, 'Fine, give me the details.'

It was mid-August and the air was already warming up as Kirby made his way out to the quiet and largely middle-class suburb of Jesmond with its red-brick Victorian streets. Seeing a patrol car he turned down the next side street, parked and made his way back onto Osbourne Road. 'So what have we here then, Constable?'

'Shoes, sir.'

Kirby peered at the ground. 'Well done, Constable, eight out of ten for observation.'

The Constable raised a questioning eyebrow.

'You omitted the colour,' Kirby said looking down at the pair of flat pink ladies shoes. Canvas by the look of them. What in his younger days might have been called "sandshoes" or "pumps" by his dad. 'Anything else?' he added. The shoes had been left but not abandoned, sitting as they were neatly side by side.

'Er, we thought we'd wait for you, sir.'

'I bet you did,' Kirby mumbled. 'OK, do we know whose they are?'

'They're Sarah's,' a girl behind him answered. The constable looked relieved. 'Sarah Cooper's, I know because they're brand new. She only bought them yesterday. It was the pattern that attracted her. Said she'd never seen anything quite like them before.'

Kirby hunkered down to give the shoes a closer inspection. The girl was right, stitched into the canvas was an intricate pattern in varying shades of pink and purple that seemed to swirl in front of his eyes, to the point where he had to look away.

'And you are?' Kirby said standing up and turning to the girl.

'Susie, Susie Summer.'

'And how do you know Sarah, Susie?'

'I'm her friend and flatmate.'

Susie was about the same age as his own daughter, Anna. She had reddish hair and was dressed in jeans and a plain white T-shirt. She had a bag slung over one shoulder. A student, he presumed, although it wasn't term time. Then again his daughter had gone back to York early to help with a dig. Although he suspected it might also have something to do with being bored at home. He smiled at Susie and picked one of his preferred open, opening questions. 'So tell me what you know, Susie.' He didn't like to guide people too much to begin with. It could be quite surprising and revealing where a story wandered and he could always drag them back if he had to. He glanced down at the shoes, which were still lined up at the edge of the pavement, as if waiting for their owner to return. Or, it occurred to him, ready to cross the road to the bus stop on the other side.

'Sarah left the flat at about 8.20 to catch the 8.32 bus to uni. She poked her head round my door as she left, said she wanted to get to the library early so she could have the afternoon to herself. I slept in a bit and was walking to the bus stop when I spotted the shoes. I called Sarah's mobile but it went to voicemail. I then phoned the library. They looked around, however she wasn't there. Hadn't been seen.'

'She wouldn't have taken another pair of shoes with her?'

Susie shrugged. 'Then why leave these new ones here?'

'Yes quite.'

'Sorry, I was worried. Sarah and I are very close and this is going to sound silly, it just doesn't feel right. So I called the police. I hope that was OK?'

Kirby was never one to dismiss someone on the grounds they felt things "didn't feel right". In his experience things not feeling right often led to things not being right. It didn't feel right to him either.

'Yes, of course,' Kirby said. Normally the station wouldn't bother until someone had been missing for over twenty-four hours unless there were suspicious circumstances. Did a pair of shoes count? However, together the shoe thing, a single girl and Susie's insistence, he presumed had persuaded the experienced Desk Sergeant that an exception should be made. 'Quite right,' thought Kirby. He smiled at Susie again. 'She may well just turn up or call. We hope she does. Better to be safe though.'

He stared down at the shoes as if willing them to tell him something. It looked as if Sarah had simply stepped out of them and continued her journey. Yet that wasn't right. The shoes were both laced up good and tight. Another puzzle. *Why couldn't life be simple?* People always assumed that as a detective you lived for puzzles. Well he didn't. Solving crime should be straightforward. The burglar caught with a bag marked "swag" in his hands, "You got me bang to rights there, guv, and no mistake." Case solved.

Kirby shook his head. Why would someone unlace their shoes, remove them, lace them up again and then line them up at the side of the road? Or, for that matter, why would anyone attack someone, then carefully take off their shoes, lace them up again and place them at the side of the road? He put the last theory in his mental wastebin. Even half-braindead commuters would have noticed a young girl being attacked or forcibly abducted at the side of the road in broad daylight. Although they might not have reported it, of course. However, someone would have filmed it, put it up on Twitter or Facebook or whatever was trendy this month in social media. He poked the shoes with his pen. They didn't get up and run off. He frowned. *What now?*

'Do you have a recent picture of Sarah?'

Susie took out her mobile and flicked through her photos. 'Will this do?'

Kirby took the phone. In the picture were two young girls who appeared to be having a good time – a "selfie". On the left was Susie, on the right was a girl not unlike her. She was holding up a glass of what looked like white wine and smiling.

'Sorry, it's all I've got with me. I upgraded recently. I'll have a better one on my laptop.'

'No, that's fine for now. Er, Constable.'

'Yes, guv.'

'Do whatever you do to get a copy of this picture and then get on to the bus company. Find the driver. See if he noticed her getting on his bus in just her, er, socks.' He glanced at Susie, who shook her head. 'Bare feet.'

'Bluetooth?' Susie asked the Constable, who got his own phone out.

Kirby watched the two perform what to him might as well have been magic. 'Does Sarah often take this bus?'

'Sometimes,' Susie answered. 'Says she likes to see where she's going, rather than stare at nothing on the Metro.'

Kirby nodded then turned back to the constable. 'Maybe the driver'll recognise her.'

'Sir.'

'Oh and while you're on, find out where it stops and what businesses are nearby so we can check if anyone else saw a girl with no shoes get off.'

'Sir. No shoes, sir. Right away.'

Kirby didn't look at the constable as he was giving the orders. He didn't want to see the barely-hidden smile that suggested they were wasting their time. However, he'd been a detective long enough and no, it definitely didn't feel right.

'Hmm,' he mused to himself. 'Tell you what, Susie, let's go to the college just in case she's turned up or someone's seen her.'

'Sure.'

Kirby turned to the patrol officer. 'Constable, before you go on your merry way, call the station and have a WPC, preferably WPC Barker, meet me there.'

Yes, sir. Er, whereabouts?'

Kirby looked at Susie.

'The Robinson Library?'

'Got that, Constable?'

'Sir.'

Stepping back to the kerb some smartarse had put a square of crime scene tape around the shoes. The two patrol officers avoided his gaze. He was about to harangue them for wasting precious police resources when something on the other side of the tape to the shoes caught his eye. It was just a stone, well not just a stone, it was smooth, more what he thought of as a pebble than a stone. Bending down he picked it up. It fitted into the palm of his hand. It looked and felt like an innocuous pebble, however to Kirby's mind it didn't belong there. He tossed it into the air once, then stood still and put it into his pocket.

'Shall we?' he said to Susie.

TWO

....

'Sorry, Susie, take me through it again,' Kirby said, pulling out onto Osbourne Road, more for the sake of avoiding the 'police car silence' than a belief he was going to gain any new insight. 'She hadn't done anything like this before?' he asked when she'd finished.

Susie shook her head. 'No.'

'And she seemed alright to you when she left?'

'Guess so. I only saw her for a second.'

'And you say they're new shoes, bought yesterday?'

'Yes. She got them from a little shop on Clayton Road. Mystique, I think it's called. It's become a favourite of hers recently. They sell lots of quirky stuff. Not my sort of thing although Sarah seems to like it. D'you think that's important?'

Inspector Kirby nodded slowly while tapping on the steering wheel. He hadn't a clue whether it was important or not. It was his detective brain working on its own, then connecting to his mouth without his conscious mind having any say in it. 'Maybe,' he said. 'Nowhere else she might be? What about parents, grandparents?'

Susie shook her head. 'Her mum's not around. Her dad works in town. He's something big in Bertrands. You know, that construction company. Always jetting off all over the place. I've a number for him if you want it?'

'Thanks, remind me when we get to the library.'

Turning into the university car park, Kirby watched with some amusement as a uniformed man in the security kiosk glanced towards them, knocked something over, then jumped up, jamming a cap on his head. You didn't need to be a lip-reader to understand what he was saying. Kirby pressed down for his window.

The shouted words, 'you can't come in here without a permit!' preceded the man as he emerged from the kiosk, red faced and wiping at his trousers with a handkerchief.

Kirby held out his warrant card. 'I think you'll find I can.'

The man squinted at the card as if trying to come up with a reason why it didn't count. He gave up and stomped his way back inside the kiosk. The barrier rose.

'Thank you ever so much,' Kirby called in an over-cheery voice as they drove through. He glanced across at Susie who was grinning. 'One of the few perks of being a copper.'

Outside the library, the WPC was waiting.

'Susie, this is the excellent Constable Shirley Barker. Constable this is Susie Summer.' The two women shook hands. 'Did the boys tell you what's going on?'

'Yes, sir.' She glanced across at Susie who was studying her feet. 'Bit early though isn't it, sir? I mean…'

'Yes, I know what you mean, Constable. However, the girl left her shoes.'

'Shoes, sir, yes. Er, perhaps she didn't like them? Or she had some others with her.'

'Susie?' Kirby said.

Susie looked up from the floor. 'She loved them, they were new. And no, I don't believe she had any others with her. Why would she?'

'Indeed,' Kirby said. 'Why would she. Constable?'

Constable Barker shrugged.

'And they weren't simply abandoned. They were laced-up and placed neatly side by side. That strike you as a bit odd?'

Constable Barker raised a finger as if about to argue. Seeing Kirby's eyes focused on her, she lowered the finger. 'Yes, sir. Odd.'

Kirby smiled. 'Good, I'm glad we agree.'

Constable Barker gave him a "well, you're the boss" look. 'So why are we here, sir? I thought, Miss Summer had already phoned.'

Kirby nodded. 'Crossing 'i's and dotting 't's. Detail Constable. What am I always telling you?'

'The Devil's in the detail, sir.'

'And speaking of the Devil, what would the Super say if by some remote chance she was here?'

'Ah, I'm with you, sir.'

'Good.'

The door swished open and the three of them entered the reception area.

'Constable, why don't you and Susie have a look around for yourselves? Ask anyone if they've seen Sarah? I'll try reception.'

As the two women wandered off, Kirby approached the desk. He coughed. The receptionist looked up and Kirby produced his warrant card. She blinked but didn't smile. Whatever irresistible atmosphere it was that libraries possessed kicked in and Kirby dropped his voice to a whisper. He took his phone out. 'We were wondering if you've seen this girl this morning?'

'Sorry?' the woman said leaning forward.

'We were wondering...' The woman leaned forward again. Sod it, Kirby thought. He raised his voice. 'We were wondering if you've seen this girl this morning?'

'Shhh, please, this is a library.'

Kirby glanced around and concluded that the only thing he might be disturbing was the sleep of two students at the nearest table, who had their heads down resting on their arms.

Kirby leant down and forward with the phone in front of him. He kept his voice at the same level. 'Well?'

The woman took a step back as if the power of his voice was too much for her. She glanced at the two sleeping students who hadn't even twitched. 'Er, no. Sorry, Inspector. I do recognise her. She's a regular visitor and a nice girl from what I can tell. I've been here since just after eight, with the exception of a couple of short breaks. She turned to the woman at a desk behind her. 'Joan?' The woman looked up. 'Joan, did this girl the inspector's looking for come in while you were on reception?' Joan joined them and studied the picture on Kirby's phone. She shook her head. 'No.'

'Thank you, ladies,' A few minutes later Constable Barker and Susie returned. 'Anything?'

'No,' they said at the same time.

Kirby glanced around the room, his gaze ending up back on the two sleeping students, one of who was now snoring softly. 'So, Sarah hasn't been in the library this morning, with or without shoes?'

Leaving the library, Kirby loosened his tie and undid his top button. A small concession to the warm day to come. 'So where now?'

'The department?' Susie suggested.

'Sorry, Susie, I never asked what you and Sarah are studying.'

'We're both doing archaeology.'

'Really? My daughter's doing archaeology at York.'

Susie nodded. 'I thought about York. But I wanted to stay local as Mum's on her own.'

'Hmm,' Kirby said. 'So where's archaeology these days?'

Susie pointed to her right. 'It's over in the Armfield building.'

Kirby set off in the direction she indicated. 'Well, well, still in the good old Armfield.'

'You know it?'

'Yes. I did zoology there, over twenty-five years ago.'

Barker came alongside him. 'Really, sir?'

Kirby glanced at her. 'Yes I know, Constable, amazing, isn't it, a copper my age with an education?'

'Sorry, sir, didn't mean it like that.'

Outside the Armfield, Kirby paused and looked up at the imposing facade and the main tower with its turrets.

'We going in, sir?' Barker asked.

'Yes, sorry, Constable,' Kirby said as they approached the doors. 'Takes me back, that's all.' Walking across the stone floor of the entrance foyer, towards the rather grand main staircase, his echoing footsteps brought back more memories as they. Even the vague musty smell with a hint of polish and formalin was as he remembered.

Constable Barker looked around. 'Very nice. A bit wasted on students thought isn't it, sir?'

'I think, Constable, that the Victorians believed learning was worth celebrating.'

'If you say so, sir.'

In the archaeology department there was no sign of Sarah, nor had anyone seen her since the previous afternoon.

'That it then, sir?' Barker asked when they were back outside, this time in the quadrangle at the back of the building.

Kirby took in the scene that had changed little since his day. 'We'll call in at the Union while we're here.'

Susie shook her head. 'She wouldn't have gone in there at this time of day. Too many possible distractions.'

Kirby smiled. 'We'll try anyway. Met my wife Jeanie there at the end of our first year.'

Kirby strode ahead and Constable Barker fell in alongside Susie. 'Just so you know, the inspector lost his wife a few years back.'

'Ah.'

Walking down the "Quad", retracing familiar steps towards the students union, memories came tumbling back into Kirby's mind. The faces of friends he'd lost touch with long ago. His palm tingled as he relived the thrill of holding hands with Jeanie in those first few weeks together. That was the trouble with memories, they hid themselves away, and then when triggered, they would emerge to snag you in nostalgia. Things you didn't even remember remembering would pop into your head from so long ago. They walked through one of the two arches, then over the road to stand in front of the red brick union building. Kirby stopped below the steps leading up to the main entrance. He hadn't stood here since his student days. He remembered the first time he'd bumped into Jeanie, literally. It was June, the end of the summer term. He was walking up the steps with a group of friends when one of them pushed him. He'd stumbled into her, making her spill the half pint of lager she had in her hand.

'Oi, watch it, you big oaf,' had been her first romantic words to him. He'd apologised and, being a well-brought-up young man, he'd offered to buy her another drink. He smiled to himself, the fact that she had the biggest blue eyes he'd ever seen, and was wearing a low-cut T-shirt, had nothing to do with it of course. She'd followed him in. 'In that case I'll have a pint.' He'd grinned at her, she had smiled back and that was it, smitten. Well at least he was. She had taken a bit more convincing.

'Sir?'

'Sorry, Constable. I was miles away. Or rather twenty-five years or so.'

Inside, they put out an announcement over the Tannoy for Sarah or anyone who had seen her that day. Neither Sarah nor anyone else came forward. However, Kirby insisted on looking around. The men's bar was still called the men's bar, which surprised him in this more PC age. The decor had changed but the smell of stale beer took him back. He stared across at what had been their favourite corner, for no good reason other than he and Jeanie had always sat there. He could see her now on their first date. As he went to the bar, she was giggling with her friends while they studied him.

On what had been "level six" in his day he remembered the late nights, getting drunk and what had passed for dancing.

'That it then, sir?' Barker asked when they were in the lobby again.

'Yes, Constable, I think so.'

With a last look around and a nod to the ghosts in his head, Kirby walked out of the front doors and back down the steps. He glanced back, half expecting a twenty-year-old Jeanie to come running after him as she had done so often, usually with something he'd left behind. He took a deep breath and returned to the present.

'You OK, sir?'

Kirby cleared his throat. 'Er, yes, Constable. You take Susie home will you?' He turned to Susie. 'I never asked, where do you and Sarah live?'

'We share a flat – 35 Eslington Terrace, near the Metro station.'

'I know it. Sorry, isn't it a bit upmarket around there for a student flat?'

Susie smiled. 'It's her dad's. He owns a few, I think. I give Sarah the rent. She calls it our good-times fund.'

Kirby nodded. 'I'll go and see her father, if he's around,' he said to Constable Barker

'Sir.'

'And Susie.'

'Yes, Inspector?'

'Perhaps you'd come down to the station and give a full statement?'

'Gladly.'

'Thank you. Tell you what, before that, why don't you take Constable Barker here back to your place? Let her have a look at Sarah's room.'

Sarah glanced at the Constable, who smiled back. 'Of course.'

'Oh and Sarah's dad's number?'

Kirby wrote the number on the back of one of his cards. He then let the girls wander off before drifting back to his own car, the memories still rolling through his mind. That's the trouble when you're young, he thought, you don't know how lucky you are sometimes. Then he thought about some of the kids he came across in the course of his job and revised that to - most don't know how lucky they are.

The thoughts of young people returned him to Sarah. So she hadn't been where she'd said she'd be. Nothing unusual in that. A girl was allowed to change her mind, or so his wife had always told him. Without her shoes though? Then putting a hand in his pocket, his fingers closed around the pebble. A second thing that didn't feel right and Kirby didn't believe in coincidence.

Driving through the barrier, he waved a cheery hand out of the window to the man in the kiosk. 'Many thanks again!'

THREE

....

Kirby parked his car then walked back on to Grey Street with its imposing stone buildings, built by people who, it seemed to Kirby, must have been rather certain of their place in the world. To his right, was old man Grey himself keeping an eye on the city from the top of his monument. Kirby sometimes wondered how much of an honour it really was to have a statue of yourself erected so that pigeons could then crap on your head. It occurred to him that it might be a bit of a metaphor for life.

A hundred yards or so in the opposite direction he came to a large brass plaque which announced that these were the offices of Bertrands Construction, Est. 1927. Through a gleaming brass-and-glass revolving door, the reception area was all polished wood with marble tiled floors and a smell of beeswax, something his mum had always been fond of using. Kirby glanced up at three large portraits of Charles Bertrand and his two sons, Edward and Joseph, all looking every bit the well-to-do entrepreneurs. On a low dark-wood table were copies of a glossy brochure titled, The History of Bertrands Construction. Very impressive, he thought. What they didn't tell you of course was in the late Sixties Joseph had run off with the nanny to become an ageing hippy in California, and Edward had narrowly escaped jail after being linked with T Dan Smith in the early Seventies.

A well-made-up and manicured receptionist behind yet more polished wood smiled at him. 'Can I help you?'

He showed his warrant card. 'I'm here to see Mr Cooper.'

'I'll see if he's in and able to see you,' she said, reaching for the phone.

'He is and he can,' Kirby said heading towards the lift. 'Which floor?'

'Er, six.'

As the doors closed, he heard. 'There's a police inspector on his way up. I tried…'

When the doors slid open, a man was standing there. He was wearing suit trousers, but no jacket or tie. His top button was undone and his sleeves were rolled up. He held out his hand. 'John Cooper.'

Kirby shook it. 'Inspector Kirby.' Several pairs of eyes poked above waist-level, grey dividing screens.

John Cooper smiled. 'You haven't told me what all this is about, Inspector.'

'No,' Kirby smiled back. 'In your office, perhaps?'

Mr Cooper glanced around. 'Of course, this way.' The eyes followed them. Approaching the office a young woman looked up from her desk and smiled.

'Can we get you a coffee?' Mr Cooper asked.

'Thank you. White no sugar.'

'Julie, would you mind?'

'Of course not. And you John?'

'Please.'

Kirby decided he liked the man. The company may appear traditional and stuffy however John Cooper wasn't. The plaque on the door read "Finance Director". The office itself was in the corner of the building with views down Grey Street and High Bridge. 'Very nice,' Kirby said, looking out back up towards the theatre which stood there doing its best to look like an ancient Greek temple with its impressive columns and portico.

'Thank you. Seat?' Cooper said pointing to a leather sofa and chair on either side of a low table rather than the formidable-looking desk. They sat, Kirby in the chair, and the door opened.

'Thanks, Julie,' Mr Cooper said taking the coffees and handing one to Kirby. 'Can you make sure we're not disturbed?'

'Of course.'

'So, Inspector?'

Kirby smiled. 'I would tell you not to worry. However, I'm here so you will. It's about Sarah, she's...'

'Is she in trouble? Hurt? What's happened?'

Kirby held up both hands. 'Please.'

Mr Cooper sat back and then forward again.

'It appears she's gone missing.' Again he held up a hand. 'Only this morning. It may well be nothing.'

'Yet you're here, so you don't think it's nothing.'

'We're just being cautious. We were contacted by her flatmate, Susie.' Kirby relayed a succinct account of the facts, what Susie had told him and the visit to the university. 'So I wanted to ask if there is anywhere you think she might have gone or anyone she might have gone to?'

'Without her shoes?'

'Her mother perhaps?'

Mr Cooper sat up straighter before lowering his gaze and shaking his head. 'Her mother? No. We don't know where she is, even if she's alive.' The clenching of a fist told Kirby all he needed to know about what Mr Cooper thought of Sarah's mother. 'So, no, Sarah has no interest in her mother.'

'Sorry, I have to ask. Are you sure? It might be natural for Sarah to wonder about her. Do you think she might have tried to contact her?'

Mr Cooper's fist clenched again and his face reddened as he looked away from Kirby. 'No, definitely not. She wouldn't.'

'You seem very sure about that. Her mother might have tried to contact her.'

Cooper glanced out of the window again, and took a breath in an obvious effort to control his emotions. He turned back to Kirby. 'Sarah would have told me. We… we have an understanding. That woman is… is…'

'I'm sorry, Mr Cooper. Please…'

Mr Cooper gave a small apologetic smile as he let his head sag. He nodded and whistled a breath through his teeth before looking up. 'I understand what you're saying, Inspector. You see, Sarah's mum left when Sarah was two. We've never seen her or heard from her since. She's never contacted us or shown any interest.'

'Left?'

Mr Cooper shook his head. 'Ran off, to be more precise. With a magician of all people.'

'Magician?'

'Yes, Mephisto he called himself. He became quite big in the States for a while. However, if you look him up, nothing's been heard of him for ten years. Marianne neither.'

'And you never tried to contact her?'

Again there was the clenching of the fist. 'No, she'd made it quite clear she wanted nothing to do with me, us.'

Kirby nodded. 'Please go on. You were saying about when she left.'

'Well, I guess me becoming an accountant was all too normal, boring for her. When we met, I was a bit wild. My parents had died in a car crash when I was ten and my grandparents couldn't control me. Didn't do uni. Had a band, drugs, parties. All very rock and roll. Marianne fitted right in, she was wilder than any of us. A true free spirit. She had, I dunno, what you might call charisma. With her doing the talking, we even got a recording contract.'

'Then you became an accountant?'

Mr Cooper laughed. 'I know what you mean. We discovered our agent was ripping us off so someone had to look at the figures. I found I had a head for it and then Sarah came along and the rest, as they say, is history. I guess it wasn't what Marianne was looking for.' He shrugged. 'But leaving your own daughter like that?'

'And family?'

'Marianne?'

'Yes.'

Mr Cooper shook his head. 'Don't know. She never mentioned any. Our wedding was a few friends that's all. If I tried to talk to her about it she changed the subject. Didn't seem important.'

'Hmm, do you have a photo of her?'

Cooper shook his head. 'Not here. At home somewhere, althjough that's going to be nearly twenty years ago. As I said, if you go on the net you'll find the odd one a bit more recent.'

Kirby nodded. 'Well, I think that's all for now.' He stood and moved towards the door. Cooper followed. 'We will, of course, keep you informed. And if you hear from Sarah, or anyone who calls about Sarah, you will let us know, won't you?'

'Of course,' Cooper said, reaching for the door knob. He stopped. 'Wait, you think someone might have taken her? Why?'

Kirby put a hand on Mr Cooper's arm. 'No, no, it's just police speak. We have no reason to believe that.' He opened the door himself. 'I'll show myself out.'

Outside the building, Kirby took out his phone. 'Ah Constable, where are you?'

'Still at the girls' flat, sir.'

'Where's Susie?

'In the kitchen making me another cup of tea.'

'Good for her. So?'

'Nothing much, sir. Sarah's room's a bit untidy, a few clothes and stuff on the floor. Open text book on the desk with a few pages marked. Photos of her and friends on a pinboard, that sort of thing. One of a guy about your age, sir, somewhere hot. Her dad, I guess.'

'Not one of anyone looking like they might be her mum?'

'Er, just a second… no, sir, not that I can see.

'And nothing out of the ordinary?'

'No, sir. All very young girl, studenty, if you get what I mean. Nothing to indicate she was going to do a runner anyway.'

'OK, you can fill me in back at the station. And Susie? You two getting on alright?'

'I sat down and had a chat with her for bit when we arrived. Seems a nice kid. Loves her mum, who lives on her own up the coast. Concerned about her friend. I don't think she's hiding anything.'

'Well done, Constable.'

'Oh and sir. I did get her to call Sarah's mobile again. It went straight through to the mail box. I told her to say to call her, say it was urgent but not why. Also, that she didn't mention us at this point. Hope that was right?'

'Yes, perfect. Thanks, Shirley.'

Kirby liked WPC Shirley Barker. She was good with people. They trusted her and she knew how to ask the right questions. She also knew how to use her policing brain. Not a collection of attributes one always found in the average copper. He looked up. John Cooper was staring out of his sixth-floor window, no doubt wondering where his daughter was. Kirby wondered where she was too. He was happy that Cooper was genuine. Sarah's mother, Marianne, on the other hand was a loose end and he didn't like loose ends. And despite what Cooper said, what girl wouldn't be interested in her mother? Or, for that matter, what mother wouldn't be interested in her daughter?

FOUR

....

Back at the station, Kirby grabbed a coffee and headed for his desk in the corner of the open-plan office. At one time he'd had an actual office with blinds at the windows, as in all the best police dramas. It was, as in all the best police dramas, 'In my office now, Constable!' Then draw the blinds and put the wind up junior officers. Ah, the good old days. Now he had to book a room and schedule a meeting if he wanted a "little chat". That gave them far too much warning.

A head popped over a screen. 'Guv?'

'Yes, Sergeant.'

'The Chief wants to see you.'

'Wonderful. Any news from the two lads yet?'

'Which ones, guv?'

'The ones who were at the scene where the girl was reported missing.'

'Ah, no one's seen nothing, guv.'

Kirby tutted. 'Anything.'

'Sorry?

'No one's seen…' He shook his head. 'Never mind. Listen, I want you at that bus stop near where the shoes were found, between four and six, when most people'll be returning from work. Show them the picture. Someone must have seen something.'

Sergeant Jones huffed. 'Isn't it a bit soon for all this, guv? She's probably just gone off with a boyfriend for the day.'

Kirby thought of the pair of pink shoes at the side of the road as if waiting patiently for Sarah to return. 'No, Sergeant. It's a young girl gone missing. If she turns up all rosy-cheeked, coy and smiling, then great. Until then, we keep looking, if that's alright with you?'

'Sir.'

Kirby picked up his mug and headed off towards the chief's office. He still had one, of course. All those new touchy-feely ideas of "all in it together" and "we're all just one big team" only went so far.

In the corridor Constable Barker was coming the other way. 'Ah, sir, I've got Susie downstairs for her statement. Do you want me to wait for you?'

'Yes please. I've got to see the Chief and then perhaps we can touch base before we talk to her. In the meantime, have a go at googling, or whatever, for Sarah's mother Marianne. Apparently she ran off with a magician called Mephisto.'

'Mephisto?'

'Yes, I know. Just see what you can find.'

'Sir.'

Kirby knocked on the door.

'Enter.'

Kirby smiled to himself. Who said "enter"? He bit back the temptation to reply 'Yes, milord'. Instead he opened the door and asked the expected question to which they both already knew the answer. 'You wanted to see me, sir?'

'Yes, Jonah. Please sit.'

Kirby resisted tugging at his forelock as he perched on the hard, wooden chair while the chief steepled his fingers and leant back in his one-off, special, ergonomic, leather one. Apparently, it was essential for his back. He never explained what it was about his back that made it essential, you were just expected to nod in sympathy whenever he mentioned it, as if it was an old war wound, which it wasn't. The chief took a deep breath then looked at Kirby over the desk. He pursed his lips while appearing to be in deep thought. He was playing the waiting game. People hated silence, so they tended to fill it. However, Kirby was also good at this game. He smiled and waited back.

Eventually the chief frowned. 'So this girl?'

'Sarah.'

The chief gave a slow, solemn nod. 'Sarah.'

'Yes, sir. She's missing.'

Another nod. 'Missing.'

'Yes, sir. Missing.'

'Missing...' the chief said, drawing out the word.

The chief wanted Kirby to volunteer the whole story because that way you were often given answers to questions you hadn't asked. However, Kirby was good at that game as well and for now, because he had no real answers, he didn't want to give the chief too much to work on.

'Missing,' the chief repeated yet again.

Kirby waited some more. It was beginning to feel like a Monty Python sketch.

The chief shifted in his seat, then leant forward, drummed his fingers on the desk and caved in. 'Surely it's a bit soon to be mounting a full-scale missing person's investigation? How long has she been missing?'

Kirby looked at his watch. 'About four hours. And it's hardly full-scale. Just me and Constable Barker poking around.'

'Yes, well, still a bit soon. She might have gone off with a boyfriend or something.'

'Without her shoes?'

'Shoes?'

This time Kirby felt he'd had enough of playing the game. 'Yes, sir. They were left at the side of the road.'

'Perhaps she didn't like them? Or they were deficient in some way?'

'They were new, pink and although I'm no real judge of these things, rather pretty. What's more, they weren't discarded, they were lined up neatly and the laces were tied. Which forgive me, sir, you have to admit is a bit odd.'

At the word "odd" the chief sat up. He'd seen enough of Kirby's cases to know that things that started as "odd" had a habit of becoming "weird", and weird led to places that he hated to have to explain to the super. However, Kirby knew the chief had also been a decent detective in his day. The chief's nose twitched. 'Very well. Yes, a missing girl, can't be too careful.'

'No, sir, exactly.'

Kirby threw out his now cold coffee and refilled his mug. He found Constable Barker sitting, bent over, nose close to a screen. He perched on the edge of her desk. 'Bad posture, Constable. It'll catch up with you when you're older. Look at the Chief – has to have special chair. We wouldn't want that now, would we?'

Shirley laughed. 'No, sir, quite.'

'Where's Susie?'

'Er still in the waiting room, sir. She's been there a while. Shall I go and get her?'

'In a minute. I'm sure I've read somewhere that it does young people good to be bored once in a while.'

'I think that's to do with little kids and playing, sir.'

'Oh well, found anything?'

'Just started really. Yes, there was a magician called Mephisto and he had an assistant called Marianne. Did quite well in the States apparently, a few TV shows an' all that. Then about ten years ago, they seem to have disappeared from the scene. Nothing, zilch.' She swivelled the screen around. 'There are a couple of publicity shots.'

In the first was a man of around, what, forty? Balding, with what was no doubt supposed to be an all-knowing and mysterious smile. To Kirby, he looked smug. In the next was a woman, a striking woman who could have been anything between twenty-five and forty. She had long wavy red hair and the darkest eyes he'd ever seen. The resemblance to Sarah's photo was obvious, however this face was harder, sharper. The face of someone who was very sure of themselves.

'Wouldn't fancy tangling with that one,' Shirley said.

Kirby studied the face again. 'No, I think I agree with you there, Constable. 'Hmm…' The eyes peering out of the picture seemed to be studying him.

'Shall we go and see Susie?'

'Yes, why not?'

FIVE

....

Susie sat in the waiting room of the police station. Constable Barker, Shirley, had said she wouldn't be long, although looking at her watch, that was nearly an hour ago. She had thought she quite liked Shirley, now she was less sure. She puffed out her cheeks. She was bored, bored, bored. She should have brought her iPad or a text book. She had so much catching up to do on her summer dissertation. She hadn't thought she'd be waiting so, so long. There was a large notice, outlined in red, telling people to turn off mobile phones. Susie had complied immediately. She'd thought about turning it on again to see if anyone was missing her, or trying to message her – Sarah even? However, she imagined if she did turn it on they'd somehow know and a policeman would come and order her to, 'Turn it off, or else!' So now that possible source of entertainment was a dead weight in her pocket, reminding her even more of how bored she was.

A door opened and she looked across, hopeful that the waiting might be over. Nope, just another policeman. He didn't even look her way as he strode out of the station, through the door beyond which her life would start up again. She went back to being bored. She had already given names and characters to the faces she could see in the much over-painted and peeling walls. She'd had them having conversations. Two had embarked on a romance, split up, got back together again and were now thinking of getting engaged, to be married next summer. Although they were already living together, of course, much to the disapproval of her parents. Susie decided she had better stop there, while some of her sanity remained intact.

She must have read every crime-prevention poster five times. She was now an expert. She knew how not to invite pickpockets; how to make her flat less attractive to burglars and where not to walk alone at night. She wished she was doing crime prevention at uni instead of archaeology, then she'd be bound to get a first.

'Susan?'

Susie looked up from studying her fingernails. Only her mum called her Susan.

Shirley Barker was smiling at her. 'Sorry to keep you waiting. If you'd like to come this way,' she said, lifting the hinged section. Susie followed the constable down a bright corridor and into an interview room.

'Thanks for this, Susan. Have a seat.'

Susie sat. 'Susie, please.'

Susie sat on the wooden chair at one side of a scratched and stained plastic table. Shirley Barker sat opposite and smiled. 'Susie then. Thanks again for waiting. The Inspector got held up.' she said putting two tapes in a machine. 'Don't worry about this, it's standard procedure.'

At that point, the door opened and Inspector Kirby entered the room. He smiled at Susie, pulled out a chair and sat at an angle to the table.

'Inspector Kirby has now entered the room,' Constable Barker said. 'Now a few formalities to start with. You are Susan Summer, sorry Susie Summer, currently living at 52, Eslington Terrace, and you're a student at Northumbria University?'

'Yes, except I'm at Newcastle University, not Northumbria.'

'Ah, yes, sorry.' Constable Barker nodded and made a few notes. 'Tell me, how do you know Sarah Cooper?'

'We met in freshers' week. We're on the same course, archaeology, and have been the best of friends ever since. After the first year, we've been sharing a flat.'

'And still friends,' Constable Barker said, smiling.

'Yes, I know. Doesn't always go like that. But Sarah's one of the nicest people you could wish to meet.' Susie stopped as a tear ran down her cheek. Constable Barker produced a box of tissues from somewhere under the table and put them in front of Susie. She took one. 'Sorry,' she said, sniffing.

'No need to be sorry. This must be very distressing for you.'

Susie nodded and blew her nose.

'So how did she seem to you in the weeks and days before today?'

'She was fine, happy, the usual Sarah. A bit worried about having to tap her dad for more money, however that's all part of being a student. Happens every term, and her dad doesn't seem to mind that much.'

Constable Barker nodded. 'Boyfriend?'

'She did have,' Susie said. 'Roger. It finished about three months back.

'Roger?'

'Roger Walton. He's doing engineering.' Susie glanced across at the inspector who was listening but not saying anything. 'It wasn't a problem or anything. She wasn't mooning around the flat in her pyjamas all the time, eating ice cream, or anything like that. As she put it, the relationship had run out of steam, kind of petered out really. She and Roger are still friends.'

'And Roger saw it like that?'

'Roger? Yes, of course.' Susie leaned on the table. 'You can't think Roger would have anything to do with Sarah going missing? They both moved on, it was nothing dramatic.'

Constable Barker smiled. 'I'm sure you're right, but we have to ask. We need to cover all angles.'

Susie nodded. The constable asked her what she knew of Sarah's home life, did she have another boyfriend, any admirers or anyone hassling her on social media? Had anyone been hanging around outside the flat who they didn't know? Had she mentioned anyone, anything? After an hour, Shirley Barker rose from her seat. 'Well I think that's about everything.' She looked across at the inspector. 'Boss?'

Inspector Kirby leant forward. 'Do you know anything of Sarah's mother?'

'Only that she left them when Sarah was very young and that she and her dad haven't seen her since.'

'Does she ever talk about her?'

Susie shook her head. 'No, not really. Once or twice when she's heard me speaking to my mum, she's said something like, "It must be nice to have a mum". Then she's got her dad, and I think they're very close.'

'Do you know if she's ever tried to find her mother?'

'I don't think so. Once she showed me a picture of her mum that's on the net from about ten years ago, that's about it.'

'So she's not tried to contact her and her mother hasn't been in touch?'

Susie shook her head again. 'Not that I know of.'

Kirby nodded. 'Thanks. And no one's been hanging around outside the flat? Or anything else that didn't feel right to you?'

'Feel right?'

'Yes, you know. You can't quite put your finger on it, but…'

Susie shook her head. 'Sorry, nothing I can think of. Only that the shoes were there, of course.'

The inspector looked across at Constable Barker and shook his head. She then smiled at Susie.

'If we have any more questions, we'll get back to you,' the constable said getting out of her chair and holding the door for Susie. 'Thank you, you've been very helpful,' she added, although Susie couldn't see how anything she'd been able to tell her could help in finding Sarah.

'Are you alright for getting home?'

'Yes, thanks. I might do a bit of shopping since I'm in town.'

Outside, Susie glanced up at the sky. Threatening, dark clouds were rolling in from the west. She groaned. It looked as if they might have a thunderstorm and there she was in just a T-shirt and thin jacket with no umbrella. That made her mind up, to abandon the shopping trip and go straight back to the flat. She quickened her pace and headed for the metro in Central Station. Before she arrived, there was a crack of thunder, which made her shudder, and raindrops the size of marbles started to hammer on to the pavement. Susie ran the last twenty yards, however by the time she got inside, her hair was wet and the shoulders of her jacket looked as if they were of a darker pink material to the rest of it. Inside, she headed for Costa Coffee, ordered a latte and then sat at a table on the concourse.

Taking her first sip, she thought about the day. Not quite what she'd been anticipating when she woke up and Sarah had poked her head around the door. She tried to remember Sarah's expression in that second or two.

Inspector Kirby had asked if anything hadn't felt right. She tried to recall Sarah's tone of voice. No, she'd been her usual cheery self. And what about the days before? Again nothing came to mind. She took her phone out of her bag.

'Hi, Mum. It's me.'

'Oh hi, love. You alright?'

'Me, yes. It's Sarah though. I think she's gone missing and I'm worried about her.' She relayed the story, finishing with: 'I called the police. It didn't feel right. It seems a bit silly saying it, although the Inspector said I was right to do so.'

'Yes, dear, you were. And never just dismiss things that don't feel right.'

'That's what the Inspector said.'

'Really, what's he called?'

'Kirby.'

There was a moment's silence on the other end.

'Mum, d'you know him?

'No, no, I don't think so, dear. Anyway, they're taking it seriously then?'

'Yes, seems so. That's where I've been,' Susie laughed, despite the situation. 'Helping the police with their enquiries. Sorry, Mum, sounds such a cliché.'

Susie's mum chuckled with her. 'Yes it does a bit. Was there anything in particular they were interested in?'

'Well, they wanted to know if she's been in touch with her mum.'

'Oh.' Again there was a moment's hesitation. 'And has she?'

'As I told them, not that I know of. She talked about her a couple of times, you know, wondering about her, where she was that sort of thing. And she showed me an old photo online. It's only natural, right?

'Hmm…'

'Mum?'

'Sorry, dear. And there's nothing else? No one hanging around?'

'Mum, you're beginning to sound like the police. No, why?'

'Oh, a silly mum asking silly questions that's all. Perhaps it's living out here in the sticks, or I've been watching too much TV.'

Susie knew her mum wasn't silly and didn't ask silly questions. 'Mum?'

'Nothing, dear. As you say, it's only natural for a girl to wonder about her mother.'

Susie recognised her mother's tone of voice that was meant to mean "I don't want to worry you", yet it did quite the opposite. She decided not to pursue things further, storing it away for another time. Perhaps when they were together. 'Guess so. Well, I'd better go, Mum. Maybe I'll come home for a few days soon.'

'OK love, that'd be nice. Call me if you hear anything. Well, call me even if you don't. Well, you know.

'Yes, Mum. Bye.'

SIX

....

Kirby waited for Constable Barker to return from escorting Susie to the front door of the station. 'Well, Constable?' he said as they were wandering back to the office.

'Susan or Susie rather?'

'Yes.'

'Nice girl,' Constable Barker said, shrugging her shoulders. 'As I said before, I'm sure her concern for her friend is genuine and I think she's telling us everything she knows. Or at least I don't think she's deliberately hiding anything. I'm certain she's on the level.'

'Yes, so am I.'

'And the father?'

'Genuine too. He got quite upset when I mentioned Sarah's mother. Then again she had run out on them when the girl was only two years old.'

'And she hasn't been in touch?'

Kirby shook his head. 'Not according to Cooper. Said she'd made it clear she didn't want anything to do with them. Although that could of course mean anything to do with him. He's hardly going to be impartial when it comes to talking about her.'

Barker nodded. 'So we keep trying to find the mother?'

'Definitely.'

'What about the ex?'

'Yes, why don't you go and talk to him?'

'Sir.'

Back in the office, more paperwork had appeared in his in-box and the report on Diamond Lil still needed completing, without sensationalism of course. However, the picture of those pretty little shoes lined up at the side of the road kept popping into his head, as did thoughts of his own daughter who was about the same age. He looked up at the clock, three-thirty. 'I'm off,' he said to Sergeant Jones. 'I'm going to call in at that shop in Clayton Road, see what I can find out about those shoes, for what it's worth.'

'Are you sure you want to do that on your own, Guv,' Jones asked.

Kirby hesitated, what piece of station humour was coming next? 'Why?'

'I wouldn't want you to get all tied up. I'd feel a right heel if that happened.' Jones's head disappeared below the level of his screen as he sniggered.

Kirby waited for his head to pop up again. The look on his inspector's face told Jones he wasn't impressed. 'Yes, well don't forget I want you at that bus stop soon, showing everyone who gets off Sarah's picture and asking if they saw her, or anything unusual, this morning.'

'Really, Guv?' Jones complained.

'Yes really,' Kirby said walking towards the door and pulling on his old tweed jacket with the patched elbows. He paused, then looked back at Jones as if he'd just thought of something. 'What's more, it'll be good for your soul.'

Kirby pulled into an empty space on Clayton Road, outside a dry cleaners, and walked back to the little shop Susie had mentioned, Mystique. The sign over the window was written in such a way as if to give the impression the word was riding a wave, with the letters getting smaller towards the end. Susie had said it sold a lot of quirky stuff, and looking in the window, to Kirby's mind, confirmed she was right. There was an eclectic mix of vintage clothes and scarves draped over tatty old chairs. One of the chairs had a price tag that made him regret getting rid of those he'd thrown out a few years ago. Then on a low table there were books on vampires, druid practices and other subjects that could be classed as quirky, or even weird. Some he guessed were novels and others had a look that suggested the authors wanted you to take them seriously. There were also a number of crosses and weird figures on chains that he supposed were charms, along with other objects that meant nothing to him.

Kirby entered to the sound of a tinkling bell, the old-fashioned sort, which was attached to the door on springy bit of metal. Inside the shop it smelled of what he hoped was only incense. The place was a jumbled riot of colour. In one corner were a couple of rails full of vibrant patterned dresses and flamboyant floppy hats. In another were shelves of books and what some designer home style magazines might refer to as "objets" including a few Buddhas, the largest of which was draped with a selection of beads. He wondered if Buddha would approve.

A thin young woman in a floaty, emerald-green, full-length dress emerged from the back room with a mug of, what judging from the aromas that preceded her was, herbal tea. Wrapped around her head, keeping her hair back, was a scarf in the same colour as the dress. Numerous bangles on her wrist jingled as she moved. If this was the Sixties, he might have pigeon-holed her as a hippy. She glided towards him. Her eyes looked him up and down and a shiver of uncertainty passed across her face as if she'd never seen a middle-aged man in tweed before.

'Good afternoon, how can I help?' she said in a low voice that sounded as if it came from far away.

Kirby began to wonder what was really in the tea. He took out his warrant card. He held it up and smiled. 'By answering a few questions.'

'Oh, of course.' Her voice had now risen in tone and returned to the here and now, which gave him more hope he might get sensible answers.

'And you are?'

The woman seemed to have to think about it. 'Jane. But I like to be called Titania.'

'Of course you do,' Kirby muttered.

'Sorry?'

'Nothing.'

Jane's or rather Titania's gaze drifted towards the ceiling and her hand fluttered in front of her face. Her mouth opened as if she was about to say something, then closed as her eyes glazed over.

Kirby waited, then decided if this conversation was going to go anywhere, his normal tactics weren't going to work. The onus was on him. He smiled. 'So, er, Titania. It's about a young girl I believe is a customer of yours.'

'Young girl?' Jane wafted the limp hand in front of him. 'We get many discerning girls visiting our emporium.' The voice had drifted away again. Perhaps he'd got his hopes up to soon.

'I'm sure you do.' He took out his phone. 'This girl.'

The eyes focused and the voice normalised again. 'Oh, yes, she's in here often,' Jane said. She paused and her eyes glazed over again. It was if her mind didn't like to be tied down for too long. 'A singular young lady. She has a definite affinity for our unusual style and tastes.'

It reminded Kirby of trying to listen to pirate radio as a kid. At the time, he'd imagined the coming and going of the signal was due to the ship bobbing around on the water. He had the urge to try and tune Jane, or rather Titania, in, or find a better frequency. Her eyes drifted around the shop and a half smile was forming on her lips.

'Yes, well,' Kirby said waving the phone to get her attention back on him. 'Have you seen her recently?'

'Yes, only the other day, I think.'

'Could it have been yesterday,' he added while she was back in the room.

'Yes, come to think of it, I believe it was.'

'Did she buy anything?'

The woman put a finger to her lips. Her eyes were heading towards the ceiling again and he could see she was slipping away.

'Well?' he asked, adding a little sharpness to his tone.

Her eyes widened as if surprised he was still there. 'Oh, yes. A pair of pink canvas shoes. Lovely design on them. Just come in. Would you like a pair…?'

What! He was losing her again. 'No, thank you.' He flicked at the screen and pushed it towards her, forcing her to focus. 'This pair?'

This time Jane jumped as if he'd startled her. She put a finger with dark purple nail polish on his arm. The bangles jingled. She smiled and leant towards him so that she was that fraction too close. 'Oh naughty, inspector. You knew all along. I've seen the shows. You're testing me.'

Kirby fought the urge to back out of the shop. 'So you did sell her these yesterday?'

'Yes. Late afternoon I think. No, I'm sure of it, late afternoon.' She paused. 'Although, it could have been nearer mid-day. I'm sorry, I'm not very good with time.'

'No matter.'

Excellent,' she said tapping his arm, and much to his relief, stepping back. 'Is that all?'

I wish it was. He decided to battle on. 'Is this your shop?'

'My shop...?' she said, halting mid drift this time.

'Yes. Is it yours? As in, do you own it?'

'Goodness no. No, no, no... No head for figures, you see. I'm told I'm very good with the customers though.'

'I'm sure you are.'

Jane beamed at the perceived compliment. 'Ah yes, a detective, you'd notice.'

Kirby pressed on while he still had her attention. 'So who is the owner?'

'Mary.'

'Mary?'

'Yes, Mary.'

'No, I mean what about her surname?'

'Surname?'

'Yes, the one that comes after the Christian name or names. You know the family name.'

Jane smiled as if pleased with herself. 'Oh yes, I know what a surname is.'

Kirby wondered how some people survived, how they remembered to eat, or even breathe. 'So, Mary who?'

Jane let out a little giggle and a painted finger touched his sleeve again. 'You know, I don't know.'

'You don't know your employer's surname?'

The hand wafted in front of him with its accompanying bangle music. 'No, it never came up. Didn't seem relevant, if you know what I mean?'

Kirby puffed out his cheeks. 'Do you have an address for her? On your contract perhaps?' he asked, more in hope than expectation.

Jane blinked at him several times as if he'd just asked what she thought of the Large Hadron Collider and Higgs Boson particles.

This time the hand waved to encompass the whole shop. 'You see, inspector, Mary and I are well... of a similar vibe, you might say.'

'Similar vibe,' he repeated.

She smiled. 'That's right. So the need for contracts and surnames aren't important.' She put her finger to her lips again, which moved in silence, as if the actual words had got lost somewhere after leaving her brain.

Kirby waited a couple of seconds. 'You were telling me about Mary.'

Back in the room. 'Was I?' Jane extended a finger towards him and then, thankfully, retracted it. 'Oh, yes. Mary's what you might call a strong woman. When we talk about a contract or working times or time off, I always come in determined to put my foot down, to be strong. Then somehow I end up doing what she wants. My boyfriend says I'm weak. He hasn't met her, you see. It's not like she's a bad person or anything, just...'

'Strong.'

'Yes... yes, that's it.' The now vague smile suggested he was losing her once more.

'One more thing before you go.'

'Me? Go?'

'Do you know when she'll be back in?'

Jane placed a hand on her hip and frowned. 'Funny you should mention that, but…'

'No,' Kirby finished for her.

The smiled remained.

'I suppose it's not important when you're of the same vibe.'

'No, quite.' Jane said starting to rearrange a few scarves on the table next to her. She looked up and for a second seemed surprised to see him. 'Oh, er, sorry. Will that be all, inspector?'

'Yes, thank you, er, Titania,' he paused, before adding in time-honoured police speak, 'for now'.

Leaving the shop, Kirby wondered if in some way the woman was acting, or in this case, overacting. Pretending perhaps, keeping something back. As a detective you had to be good with 'pretending'. It was almost part of the training, both as a practitioner and as an observer. In many ways he thought it would be a better course for a young copper than team-building. Then, thinking about the shop and Jane, he didn't believe anyone would be that obvious, or that good. Still it might be worth having another go. He took a deep breath, if he had any more questions for her, he decided he'd send Shirley next time. His mind was mulling it over as he was about to set off down the street back to his car. Distracted, he almost fell over an old lady who was blocking his path.

'Sorry, madam,' he said and tried to step around her. She moved back into his path. He made to go the other way and she nipped in front of him again. He had to admit she was nimble for her age.

'Er, excuse me, madam,' he tried again, refusing to believe the thought that popped into his head that an elderly lady in a grey cardigan was trying to mug him, in Jesmond. In other parts of the city maybe.

'No,' she replied, which wasn't the response he'd been expecting.

'I'm sorry?'

She fixed him with a stare. 'Will you stop skipping around for a minute like a demented goat and listen.' He was about to reply along the lines that he was in a hurry and that he never acted like a demented goat, when her eyes made direct contact with his. Those eyes gave him no choice but to stay where he was. As an experienced detective, he could read eyes better than most, and these had such stories to tell. 'You looking for a girl who's gone missing.' It was a statement rather than a question.

'How do you know?'

'Never mind that. Not important. You need to see Harold Longcoat.'

'Harold Longcoat?'

'That's what I said, wasn't it, sonny boy?'

Sonny boy?

'You're Inspector Kirby.' Again it was a statement rather than a question. He searched his memory, which was excellent for faces, this one wasn't there. He would have remembered those eyes if nothing else.

'You know me?'

The old woman's face moved a few inches closer to him. It only struck him later that those eyes were on the same level as his, whereas when he first saw her he was sure she was a good foot shorter than him.

'I named you, didn't I?' she said. 'For a detective you ask some stupid questions. But enough of this. Harold Longcoat. The corner shop on Eskdale Terrace.'

Before he could ask anything else, he was looking down at grey hair and the grey patched cardigan as she turned and shuffled away from him, blending in with all the other grey-haired and grey-cardiganed ladies out on Clayton Road that afternoon.

Harold Longcoat?

SEVEN

....

Kirby reached his car with his mind turning over the encounter with the old lady. She knew him? However, he'd occasionally had his photo in the paper and given the odd talk around the place so there was no reason she couldn't know of him without him knowing her. One thing was for certain, he was sure he would have remembered her if they'd met before. *What was it she'd said? She'd named him. What was that supposed to mean?* More riddles. He glanced at his watch, put the keys back in his pocket and decided to heed that old police adage, "if in doubt follow your nose". And Eskdale Terrace wasn't far away.

Kirby entered the shop to the sound of another tinkling bell. It was a standard corner shop, moderately stacked with a range of food and household goods, the kind that people ran out of and couldn't be bothered to go all the way to the supermarket, or into town, for. It smelled faintly of polish, disinfectant and peppermint. Tucked away in corners, as if forgotten, were random items from decades ago, the sort of things he hadn't come across since childhood, such as red step polish, Brasso and mothballs.

At the end of the aisle, an elderly man in a grey cardigan was intent on stacking a few tins of beans onto a shelf. Grey seemed to be the in colour for the elderly of Jesmond this season. Kirby watched as the man shuffled down the aisle towards the back of the shop. He waited for a few seconds, still wondering quite why he was here. Well, he was here so…

'Can I help you?' came a voice from behind Kirby.

Kirby's heart leapt. 'Jeeze, do you practise that? he asked spinning around.

The elderly grey-cardiganed man, who had a slight stoop, was smiling at him.

'Harold?' Inspector Kirby asked.

The man raised his eyebrows in response.

'Harold Longcoat?'

The man looked Kirby up and down and narrowed his eyes. 'Who wants to know?' he said.

'I do, why?'

'And who are you when you're at home?'

'Why the suspicion?'

'Why not? Can't be too careful these days.'

Kirby tutted. This was turning into the opening for some old B-movie detective story. He produced his warrant card. 'Look, do you go by the name of Harold Longcoat?' he asked, sticking with the genre.

'Might do.'

Kirby growled and waved the warrant card. He'd never liked the way old B-movies portrayed the police force. It was always some smartarsed, down-on-his-luck private investigator who solved the crime. One that he would have seen through in the first five minutes. He played the waiting game.

'Alright, yes. I am sometimes known as Harold Longcoat. Before I say any more, tell me, who gave you that name?'

'Why, do you have others?'

The shoulders inside the grey cardigan shrugged. 'I'm simply known as Harold around here, that's all. The Longcoat bit is only used by a few people.'

Kirby parked the idea that Harold was a criminal mastermind with a series of aliases. To the best of his knowledge, they didn't tend to hang around in corner shops in old grey cardigans, although he had to admit it would be one hell of a cover. 'An old lady whose eyes hold more history than the local library.'

Harold scowled. 'It's closed.'

'What?'

'The library, it's closed. Damn shame if you ask me.'

'I didn't ask you.'

'You mentioned the library.'

Kirby shook his head and blew out his cheeks. *What is it with elderly people? Why don't conversations go in the direction they're supposed to?* This was now morphing from B movie to Ealing comedy. 'Never mind the library,' he said. 'The old lady?'

The old man nodded and looked Kirby up and down. 'She talked to you, sent you to me?'

'That's right and since I'm a good copper I don't simply dismiss things old ladies tell me. Although I'm beginning to wish I had. Anyway, I'm here.'

Harold straightened a jar of jam on the shelf next to him and then took a breath, as if coming to a decision. 'Edna, she's called Edna.'

'Well, finally we seem to be getting somewhere,' Kirby said, picking up a can of mushy peas and checking the sell-by date. When he turned back, the man – Harold – seemed to be a good six inches taller than when he'd first seen him. What's more, the person he'd assumed was about seventy now looked no more than fifty. This all disturbed him more than the fact that he'd been looking for someone called Harold Longcoat. He prided himself on how he observed things that other didn't, how he saw through charades, attempts to deceive and the pretenders, even if they hadn't written the course yet. However, he'd been completely fooled by this one. He handed Harold the can, buying himself a little thinking time.

'You want this?'

'No, it's out of date.'

'Is it really?' Harold said and put it back on the shelf.

Kirby decided to let it go. A missing girl was more important that an out of date tin of peas. 'So who is Edna, or you for that matter, and why is she implying you know something about a missing girl?'

Harold ignored the questions. 'Have you got a picture of the girl?'

Kirby took out his phone, and after a few seconds cursing and flicking, he showed it to Harold. 'Her name's Sarah Cooper.'

'I didn't know her name. She comes in here sometimes. Nice girl, polite.'

'Is that it?'

'And Edna sent you?'

'We've already been through that.'

The taller, younger Harold, hesitated. Kirby let the silence develop.

Harold frowned. 'The trouble is, you lot don't listen. We've tried before.'

'Which you lot?' Kirby said. It was something that irked him, especially as it was often said by those who had something to hide. 'People who wear tweed? People who wear sensible shoes?'

'The police.'

'Well, we can't listen if people don't talk to us. So come on, Harold, humour me.'

'Edna said that did she? That I'd know something about a missing girl?'

'Yes!'

Harold nodded. 'Why don't you come into the back?' he said turning and heading past the counter and through a beaded curtain, which clacked behind him.

Kirby followed, ignoring the grey-cardiganed, master-criminal idea that popped back into his head and the thought Edna might be there with a gun in her hand. Maybe he'd been watching too much TV.

He clacked through the curtain. No Edna, only Harold pulling out a chair for him.

Kirby sat back in the scuffed old chair Harold had offered him and studied the man for a second or two. No, he didn't like it when people pretended to be something they weren't, it generally indicated they were up to no good. One for later. 'So you know something about this missing girl?'

Harold scratched his head. 'Is that what Edna actually said?'

Kirby searched his memory. 'No, not exactly. She told me I was looking for a missing girl and that I should come and see you.'

'Ah.'

'Does that make a difference?'

'Yes.'

Kirby put both hands on the old wooden table and leant forward. 'Then please enlighten me, Harold Longcoat.'

Harold shuffled in his seat. 'Er, well, things are not quite as they may appear.'

Kirby huffed his annoyance. He was getting tired of what he felt was Harold beating around a whole shrubbery of bushes. 'You don't say. In this job I find they seldom are.' He held up his hand to stop Harold interrupting. 'Don't tell me, you and this Edna are part of the master criminal group known as the Grey Cardigan Gang?'

'No.'

'It was a joke.'

Harold twitched his mouth into a smile, then studied his fingernails. 'I know. It's just the truth will seem a whole lot stranger than that and harder to believe.'

Kirby arched an eyebrow. 'Oh really? I'm a copper, Harold, I've seen lots of strange things.' He fixed Harold with one of his best stares. 'So try me.'

Harold shrugged in a "you asked for it" sort of way. 'We're guardians.'

OK, granted he hadn't been expecting that one. 'Guardians of what? Jesmond high street? Great, a grey cardigan vigilante group.'

Harold ignored the sarcasm. 'This is not going to make much sense.'

'Well at least you'll be consistent with the rest of my day.'

Harold shrugged. 'Guardians of the divide.'

Kirby drummed his fingers on the table. He could see that Harold was not deliberately trying to wind him up. However... 'Yes, I agree that doesn't make much sense. Now look, I'm losing patience. If you have information, I need to know. I've got a missing girl. It was only this morning, yet my convoluted subconscious mind believes that because she left a pair of new pink shoes, laced-up, at the side of the road, something is not right. My conscious policeman's mind is battling with all that. It's also not that enamoured with me listening to an old lady on the street telling me to find you, that you profess to be called Harold Longcoat and that you are pretending to be something you're not. So you see my dilemma?'

'Er, yes.'

'Good. Now I'm prepared to give my subconscious mind the benefit of the doubt for now. However, I can see where my conscious mind is coming from.' Kirby stood. 'So if you insist on talking in riddles we can continue this down the station.'

Harold straightened up, becoming even taller. He glanced around the dusty shelves as if looking for guidance from the spare supply of baked beans and toilet rolls, then up at Kirby. 'That won't help, believe me. Please sit down. I'll do my best to explain, and when I do you'll understand my hesitance.'

'Go on,' Kirby said, lowering himself back into the seat.

'OK, although I tell you now, you're going to struggle with this.'

Kirby looked into Harold's eyes, seeking clues as to what he was dealing with. What he saw was the same intensity, the same dramatic intelligence he'd glimpsed in Edna's. Those eyes made you believe. 'All right, I'll tell my conscious mind to pipe down for now. So?'

'You said this missing girl was called Sarah Cooper?'

'Yes.'

'Well if Edna has sent you to me it's because there's every chance she's not in this world.'

Kirby felt his heart beating in his chest. 'You mean she's dead?'

Harold held up a hand. 'No, sorry. No, that's not what I mean.'

Kirby shook his head. 'What then, she's not in Newcastle, not in the country?'

Harold took a deep breath. It seemed he was finding it as difficult to explain as Kirby was to understand. 'No, I mean she may be in another world. As in on the other side of the divide.'

Kirby opened his mouth to speak, however there were no coherent words forming in either his conscious or subconscious brain.

Harold continued. 'I'm not sure how else to put this. She's not in the world that you and I are currently in. Where she is it's not the twenty-first century. It's a world that's more like the sixth century BC.'

Kirby felt that all this nonsense about capped his day, topped his week and was heading for his all-time top three with designs on making it to the number one spot. What had started as strange was becoming bizarre to say the least. This was the last time he was going to listen to his subconscious. He rose from the table again. 'Well, Mr Longcoat or whoever you are, be grateful that I've got better things to do at the moment than charging you and Edna, if that is her name, with wasting police time.'

Harold reached out and grabbed his arm. Kirby tried pulling away. Harold wasn't letting go. 'Please, Inspector.

I'm telling you things that we don't normally share with anyone. However, I'm telling you now because if I'm right, you're going to need our help and not only with a missing girl.'

Kirby stopped pulling. Harold's eyes were pleading with him.

'Hear me out. Edna approached you because she saw something in you. A mind that might be open to possibilities that are beyond the ordinary. And you wouldn't be here if you hadn't seen something in her that you believed. She did this because things are stirring that could affect the whole of this land – Newcastle, Northumberland and beyond.'

Kirby shook his head. 'What things? I…'

Harold stared up at him. 'Look at me. Really look at me and if you don't like what you find then by all means go. Then Edna and I, and others, will have to do what we can on our own as we've done before.'

Kirby looked into the man's eyes. He'd come across more than a few people who were, shall we say, on the borderline of sanity and beyond. What he saw convinced him that Harold was firmly his side of the line. There was a weight and truth in the man that Kirby didn't see every day. Even the most innocent of people had things to hide, things they'd rather you didn't know. As a copper, you had to winkle them out. Yet here was a man offering him everything and this time it was Kirby who wasn't sure he wanted to know.

Harold had let go of his arm, so he was free to leave. Instead he sat down. He closed his eyes for a second, then opened them again just to check if he was dreaming. He wasn't. On impulse he reached into his pocket and took out the smooth stone that was begging to be stroked. He put it on the table. 'Does this mean anything to you?'

Harold looked at it but didn't touch it. 'Where did you get it?'

'It was on the ground near Sarah Cooper's shoes.' He shrugged. 'It... I felt it didn't belong.'

'It must have been dropped. It's a contact stone. It allows people to find each other when they're separated.'

Kirby pushed it with the tip of a finger so it rolled over. 'It's a pebble.'

'You said it didn't belong. It doesn't. If it was simply a pebble you wouldn't have picked it up, kept it and be showing it to me now.'

He nodded. Harold had a point. 'So what you're saying, it's like GPS?'

Harold laughed. 'Nothing so crude. I suppose it's sort of like a homing beacon. Although it's more than that. In the hands of the right person it can lead them to people or places they want to be. It can tell them what's happening to others with compatible stones.'

'So, assuming I believe you,' Kirby said, adding the caveat to help with his own feelings of sanity, 'someone might know it's here?'

Harold shook his head. 'No, someone does know it's here and also, more than likely, who it's with.'

Kirby focused on the stone and ran a hand through his hair. From anyone else, what Harold was telling him would seem like the ravings of a lunatic. The problem now for Kirby was that he was starting to believe him.

EIGHT

....

'Comfortable, Mephisto?'

Marianne watched Mephisto opening first one eye, the green one, followed by the blue one. It took a second for them to focus. When they did, they darted from side to side as if his first thought was to leap off the garden seat he was lying on and make a run for it. However in his current manifestation that wouldn't be cool, would it?

'Hello, Marianne. Finally tracked me down then?'

Marianne smiled and watched as Mephisto, despite himself, squirmed. 'Oh, I've known where you are for a long time, Mephisto. You're not the only one who can do disguises. Thought I'd let you suffer a while, that's all.'

Mephisto licked a paw then stroked an ear, feigning indifference. 'It's hardly suffering. I quite like it, having someone pampering me. And all I have to do is give a little affection occasionally.'

'And pose for the camera.'

'Ah.'

'Those eyes are a bit of a giveaway. And you never could resist an audience. Although I ask you, Youtube?' Funny she thought, how her instinct was to pick him up. She resisted, it suited her to be looming over him.

The tip of Mephisto's tail flicked up and down as he avoided her gaze. 'So, Marianne, I'm guessing since I'm not writhing around in agony, or even dead yet, there's a reason for your visit, other than revenge.'

'Revenge, hmm,' Marianne placed a finger to her lips as if thinking about it. She watched the hairs on his neck stand up and his eyes widen in fear. Then as he was finding it difficult to breathe she eased the pressure and grinned. She stroked his ear. 'That's so you know I haven't quite forgiven you.'

'It didn't mean anything.'

She gave his throat another squeeze. Her voice hardened. 'It did to me.'

He breathed again and this time kept quiet.

Marianne smiled and let her tone ease. 'How could you? A doe-eyed little receptionist with all the backbone of a limpet. I would have thought that was beneath even you, Mephisto.' Marianne placed a finger under his chin, forcing him to look into her eyes, something she knew he would normally try to avoid. She felt the weight of his head and watched as his eyes glazed. 'It was her I felt sorry for.'

'You nearly killed me.'

'Yes, only nearly though.' She flicked her finger and Mephisto's head bounced off the wooden slat. She heard his teeth clack together and took satisfaction from the pain in his eyes. 'A moment's sentimentality got in the way.'

Mephisto hissed and flexed his jaw. 'So why now, Marianne?'

'I have a use for you.'

'Oh, what is it this time, power? Lands?'

'Both of course.' She cocked an eyebrow. 'What else is there?'

'And as usual you need others to do your fighting for you.'

'Naturally.'

'So who is it this time?'

'Sisillius.'

'Again?' Mephisto laughed, at least he did until he couldn't breathe again. 'Sisillius,' he repeated in a hoarse whisper. 'Come on, Marianne, we've been there twice before. Anyway, what do you need me for?'

Marianne scratched Mephisto's head, which produced an involuntary purr. 'Oh, they're hardly enlightened times and you know Sisillius and his men. All muscles and macho. Taking orders from a woman, or at least directly from a woman, is a stretch too far for their meagre intellects to cope with.'

Mephisto shook his head. 'I'm sorry, Marianne, but it didn't work last time. He's got too many enemies and not enough friends and that proved too much even for you. Which is why, if you remember, that first time, we had to do a runner and ended up here, with me peddling my skills alongside tricksters and frauds. While you, for a while at least, tried your hand at the twentieth-century version of domesticity.'

Marianne waved a hand in the air. 'Yes, that was a mistake, I admit, even if it was fun to start with. It's amazing how soon they lose their sense of adventure in this world. How narrow their ambition becomes.'

'I think that's because they have laws, Marianne.'

'Yes, well last time we almost succeeded.'

Mephisto nodded. 'Except, and I hate to bring this up, Marianne, you weren't strong enough to hold on to all that power.'

Marianne resisted the urge to grab Mephisto by the scruff and shake him. 'It wasn't all a waste of time and I admit it taught me a lesson.' She smiled. 'It's different this time. There's my daughter.'

Mephisto started to laugh again, then checked himself. 'I'm sorry, Marianne. You left when she was what, two?' Don't tell me you've suddenly found a mothering instinct?'

Marianne snarled her annoyance but left it at that. 'Small children are of so little interest and so needy. However, she's a grown woman now.'

'I know, I see her around. Looks like her father.'

Marianne pursed her lips. 'Perhaps, however she's still my daughter. And I see her too.'

Mephisto's eyes widened. 'Oh Marianne, that's ambitious even for you. You do know Harold's still around, and Edna?'

'Of course I know.' She sniffed her contempt. 'The old meddler, I look forward to dealing with him. As for Edna...' she shrugged. 'Anyway, I've planned for them to be a little distracted.'

Mephisto was nodding. 'Two of you?'

She had him. 'Think of it.'

'Your daughter though, Marianne. That really is playing with fire.'

She grinned. 'You know me, darling, I don't burn that easily.'

This time Mephisto grinned back. 'OK, give me a little time to tidy my affairs.'

Marianne looked around the neat suburban garden. 'What affairs? Oh, I get it, you want to say goodbye in your own special way, don't you? Ever the showman.'

'A day or two, that's all.'

'Tomorrow.'

NINE

....

Kirby woke. The birds outside were annoyingly cheerful and as usual the pigeons were clomping up and down the gutter with their clogs on. His mind was churning. While asleep, his subconscious had failed to come up with anything, or at least anything sensible. Not surprising, his conscious mind reasoned, since he was being asked to accept that there was another world accessible from this one and vice versa. Stranger still was that yesterday, when he'd been with Harold Longcoat and looked into the man's eyes, he had believed it. He sat on the edge of his bed and looked across at the dresser and a photo of Jeanie taken seven or eight years ago, before... well before. It was in Cornwall and it was raining. She was smiling at him with that 'who cares' smile she had. He smiled back. 'Well, Jeanie, what d'you reckon?'

'Just go with it, Jonah, just go with it. Trust your instincts.'

He nodded, she was always right. He smiled again, even when she was wrong.

While dressing, he turned the facts, if you could call them that, over in his head, trying to give his conscious mind a go this time. He was fastening his shirt when he realised his phone was ringing. It was in the kitchen where he'd left it on charge. He ran down the stairs wondering quite why he did that when he could always call them back. He took a breath. 'Kirby.'

'You been running, sir?' It was the duty desk sergeant.

'You know me, Sergeant, five miles every morning. Healthy body, healthy mind and all that.'

The Sergeant hesitated. 'Er yes, sir. Sorry, I...' Kirby could hear the cogs turning, wondering if he was being serious or not.

'Never mind, what is it?'

'Ah, then, you're not on your way in yet, sir.'

'Well deduced, Sergeant. We'll make a detective of you yet. So?'

'Well you know you wanted me to let you know of anything that came to our attention in Jesmond?'

Kirby's heart sank to somewhere near groin level. 'Yes...'

'Well, sir.' The hesitation that followed spoke volumes.

'Go on, Sergeant. You've got this far.'

'Er, there's a cat that's disappeared.'

Kirby's heart bobbed part way back up. 'And you phoned me about a missing cat?'

'Ah ha, no. No, sir. Not missing. I mean, I had the same thought until I saw the evidence.'

'Evidence?'

'Video, sir. It literally disappeared in front of the owner's eyes. There's a couple of Constables there now.'

Kirby glanced at the calendar to make sure his life hadn't fast-forwarded to April Fools' Day. It wouldn't have been the first time he failed to notice. No, it was still August.

'You still there, sir?'

'Text me the address.' Despite the so-called "evidence" it was probably some dotty old lady. He hoped it was some dotty old lady, however given everything else that was going on… 'Oh and Sergeant.'

'Sir?'

'If this is simply a missing cat, you'll be pounding the streets for the next week looking for it.'

'Sir.'

Kirby parked outside the typical suburban semi; 1960s he guessed by the large floor-to-ceiling windows, not that he was any architectural expert. Two constables were there talking to the elderly owner. As he got out of the car, one of the officers who he recognised as Constable Bains ambled over to him.

Bains touched a finger to his helmet. 'Mornin', sir. Sarge thought this was right up your street.'

'I'll bet he did,' mumbled Kirby.

'Sorry, sir?'

'Nothing, Constable,' Kirby said. 'So what've we got?'

The constable flipped open his notebook in the manner that constables of a certain level of experience felt was required to impress a senior officer. He then lapsed into constable-on-duty speak, a peculiar form of the English language unique to the lower ranks of the police force. 'Well, sir, the elderly lady,' he pointed with his pencil, she smiled back. 'One Mrs Tanner, eighty-seven, widow of one Arthur Tanner, deceased now these fifteen years on account of him being in the army and never getting over it, was out minding her own business, taking advantage of this here warm spell by tending her plot when her cat, one ginger Tom called Napoleon…'

'Napoleon?'

Bains frowned at having his monologue interrupted. 'Yes, sir. The cat's name is Napoleon. Is that important?'

Kirby shrugged. 'Unusual, that's all. Bit dramatic. What's wrong with Tiddles?'

'Quite, Tiddles. If I may continue, sir?'

'Go on.'

'Where was I?' He glanced at Kirby but didn't say, "before I was rudely interrupted". 'Ah, yes. One ginger Tom called Napoleon and her favourite gnome, garden variety, one Mr Pickles, upped and disappeared.' Constable Bains licked a finger and with a flourish continued his performance by turning the page. 'Apparently, sir, said ginger Tom is easy to identify on account of him having one blue and one green eye. At the time I am given to understand that Napoleon was lying, no sorry, basking, on the plate that said gnome, Mr Pickles, holds in front of him. The lady said, let me get this right, sir. "I was looking straight at them and they just went, poof, right before my very eyes. And I've not been at the sherry if that's what you're thinking, young man."'

'And did they, Constable?'

'Did they what, sir?'

'Go poof before her very eyes?'

'Ah, I see what you're getting at. My first thought as well, sir. That she's turned her back and some little ne're-do-well has half-inched said gnome, which according to Mrs Tanner is a bit of a collector's item and worth a bob or two, startling Napoleon who has then simply scarpered. And being an elderly lady, no disrespect intended, and perhaps not quite the full shilling, she's got a bit muddled.'

'Something like that, Constable. However, I believe there's a "but" coming. Which is why I'm here?'

'Yes, sir. Although,' Constable Bains paused, which made Kirby suspicious of what might be coming next, 'Wayne here wondered if we shouldn't be calling the gnome office first.'

Kirby gave the constable nine out of ten for delivery on account that the constable's lips didn't even quiver as he said it. He only lost a point due to a single twitch in the left eye. The constable continued. 'Although I thought it might be more one for gnomicide, sir.' This time he failed to hide a satisfied smirk.

'Yes, thank you, Constable, I get the picture. Now if we can carry on without the puns.'

'Sir.' Bains half turned. 'Wayne, lad, get over here with Mrs Tanner's iPhone.'

Wayne, who appeared to Kirby to be about fourteen, except that the waistband of his trousers was thankfully at an acceptable height and not showing the make of his underwear, ambled over holding out said iPhone.

'Show the inspector, lad,' Constable Bains ordered.

Wayne flicked at the screen and up popped the face of a rather scary-looking gnome. It had rosy cheeks and the paint was peeling from its nose, which gave it more than a passing resemblance to Alex Ferguson about to explode at some half-witted footballer. As the picture panned out, said gnome, Mr Pickles, was holding what at times obviously acted as a birdbath. However, given the hot weather had dried out and was now an impromptu resting place for said cat, Napoleon. At this point the voice of Mrs Tanner could be heard. 'Come on, Napoleon, say hello to all the lovely ladies and gentlemen.' The cat opened its eyes, one green and one blue, and uttered a single meow when, literally "poof", they both disappeared complete with the "poof" sound affect. And just in case there was any doubt, a small puff of smoke rose from where they'd been.

'See what I mean, sir?' said Bains. 'Poof!'

'Poof indeed, Constable,' Kirby said staring at the picture of where the cat and gnome had been only moments before. 'Poof indeed. Hmm… clever editing?'

Bains shook his head. 'Don't think so, sir. And Wayne reckons he could tell.'

'I takes the videos, Pet, to put on Facebook and YouTube,' came a loud voice just behind Kirby's left ear. He managed to keep his surprise to a twitch, while Wayne ended up juggling with the phone as he tried not to drop it. It seemed that Mrs Tanner had glided undetected around and behind them in a way that only the elderly can. Kirby suspected it was a secret shared only by the elderly and was one small way of getting their own back on the rest of society.

The three of them turned.

'Really?' said Kirby.

'Social media, sir,' Bains whispered, leaning towards Kirby.

'Yes, thank you, Constable, I do know what social media is. It's what you constables use too much and sometimes gets you into bother.'

Bains straightened and reddened before glaring at Wayne who was now grinning. 'Won't happen again, sir.'

'Never mind,' Kirby said. 'Well that's a help for us, Mrs Tanner. Thank you.'

'Yes, Napoleon has quite a following.'

'I'm sure he does,' Kirby said. 'Napoleon? That's an unusual name for a cat.'

Mrs Tanner beamed. 'I know. Inspiration, I calls it. I think that's why people likes to see him, sounds grand. That an' his eyes. He just wandered into my kitchen one day and made himself right at home. And when I was stroking him there was something about him that said Napoleon.'

'Nasty little bugger then?' Bains suggested.

'Sergeant!'

'Sorry, sir.'

'Really, Mrs Tanner?'

'Yes, you can see him most days, Inspector. People consider a cat with one green and one blue eye to be lucky, you see.'

'Not perhaps for Napoleon though,' Bains muttered.

Kirby ignored the comment and looked at Wayne, noticing various holes in his ears and nose that no doubt sprouted rings and studs when he was off duty. 'Er, can you fax, er, send, er e-mail…'

Wayne smiled at having succeeded in letting a senior officer dig a small hole for himself. 'Got your mobile, sir?'

Kirby handed over his phone.

Wayne sniffed, whether in contempt or disappointment that it was not some archaic brick, was hard to tell. 'A four, sir. Ooh nice case,' he smiled. 'Is it real leather?'

'Just do it, Constable.'

'Sir, I'll bluetooth it now,' Wayne said, and a few seconds later handed the phone back to Kirby.

'Well, I think I'm done here,' said Kirby, already knowing where he was going after he'd checked in at the station. 'I'll leave you two to placate Mrs Tanner,' he added, smiling at Constable Bains. 'Perhaps you can get Wayne to make her a cup of tea?'

'And what shall I tell her we're doing about Napoleon, sir?'

'Tell her, he and Mr Pickles are now part of an ongoing investigation.'

TEN

....

Kirby wandered towards his desk eating a croissant he'd bought at the service station on the way in, dropping flakes of it across the floor. While placing what they insisted was a small latte – they didn't do a simple white coffee – on his desk, across the floor Sergeant Jones popped his head over the screen. 'Morning, Inspector.'

'Sergeant. Anything from your bus stop vigil?'

'You mean, sir, apart from a possible cold on account of that so-called summer shower that turned into a thunderstorm?'

Kirby wiped the last of the croissant from his lips with the brown paper napkin he'd been holding it in, succeeding in scattering more flakes, this time on his piles of papers. He took a sip of coffee as the sergeant blew his nose for dramatic effect. 'As you know, Sergeant, the health of junior officers is one of my top priorities. Which is why I'm always advising you, when out and about, to wear sensible clothes and shoes appropriate to the prevailing and predicted weather conditions. So just because you choose to ignore that advice, don't think you can skive a day off with a sniffle. So, yes, apart from that?'

'Nothing, sir. Or at least nothing helpful. One girl, a Sophie Wilson, did remember seeing the young lady standing there as the bus pulled up. Apparently, they don't speak, they're just on nodding terms, seeing as they've only been taking the same bus as each other for about a year.'

'Yes, yes.'

'Well, it seems Miss Cooper just stood there, didn't get on.'

'And that was it? She didn't look like she was in trouble, being held, threatened?'

'No. Miss…' Sergeant Jones blew his nose again, then consulted the piece of paper in his hand. 'Miss Wilson did say she saw a group of three or four teenagers in grey hoodies "hanging around", as she put it, close by.' The Sergeant handed Kirby the piece of paper on which his report was printed.

'Well, we can't go around picking up kids for hanging around.'

'Hoodies?'

'Nice idea, Sergeant, however, we'd have half the teenagers in Newcastle in here if we started doing that. Although, they might have seen something. Follow it up, will you, see if you can find them?'

The Sergeant looked out of the window at the grey clouds that were gathering over the city.

'The forecast says it's going to be warm and sunny,' Kirby said as Sergeant Jones disappeared behind his screen again. 'Tomorrow,' he added in a whisper.

The shop bell tinkled. Kirby looked down the aisle and Harold was there in full grey-cardigan disguise. Harold looked up and smiled. 'Ah, Inspector, can't keep away from all my bargains then?'

'Not quite, Harold. I've got something to show you.'

'Oh?'

Kirby dug the phone out of his pocket, entered the pin number, then entered it again while Harold tutted. 'I thought given our conversation yesterday that you might be the person to help me with this,' he said, pushing the phone in Harold's direction.

Harold took it. 'Delphiniums. Sorry, couldn't tell you what variety. Not my specialist subject. Now if it was old English roses I...'

'What?' Kirby said snatching the phone back. 'Bloody thing,' he added, as the latest share prices appeared from nowhere. 'Got a mind of its own.'

'Give it here,' Harold said, taking it back. 'What am I supposed to be looking for?'

'A video of a cat and a gnome.'

'Why?'

'You'll see.'

'Fine,' Harold said squinting at the phone and flicking through the screens. 'You should upgrade to the 6, bigger screen.'

'Everyone's an expert,' mumbled Kirby.

Harold studied the video and his eyes widened. 'Oh, I see. Poof.'

'Poof exactly. So, does this mean anything to you?'

'Hmm.'

'Hmm?'

Harold played the video again and then handed back the phone to Kirby. 'I have an idea and it's not one I like. So if it's all the same to you I'd like confirmation from an expert.'

'And there's an expert in cats that disappear and go poof while they're at it?'

Harold smiled. 'Yes, and luckily for you I know the man and he happens to be in town.' Harold glanced at the old clock on the wall whose ticking and tocking seemed to grow louder as it was scrutinised. 'And if we get a move on we might catch the performance.'

'What performance?' Kirby asked, but Harold was already heading out of the shop. Outside, Harold stopped as if having a sudden thought. 'Got your car, Inspector?'

'No, I flew here. Why?'

'Quicker that's all. We could walk, although I wouldn't want us to miss it.'

Kirby pointed to his Ford Focus. 'And where are we going?'

'The University Theatre.'

'And what're we going to see?'

Harold grinned. 'Oh, I would hate to spoil the surprise.'

Kirby shook his head. 'Would you indeed,' he said pulling out on to Osbourne Road. In a couple of days of outrageous surprises what was one more?

Entering the theatre foyer, Harold hung back with his hands shoved into the pockets of his cardigan, doing his best to look aged and innocent. Kirby found himself behind four elderly ladies in the queue to pay.

'So why are we here?' Kirby asked when Harold had shuffled forward to join him.

Harold pointed to a poster. "The great Geraldo," it read. "You won't believe your eyes. One week only, matinee Thursday."

'It's Thursday,' Harold said by way of explanation as they reached the desk.

'That's one full and it's half-price for your dad,' the receptionist said. 'So, fifteen pounds, in all, love.' Kirby glanced back to Harold who had shrunk back into the cardigan, which now looked a couple of sizes too big for him.

'Do you need any assistance?' the receptionist asked, nodding towards Harold.

'You don't know the half of it,' Kirby muttered.

'Sorry?'

'Nothing,' Kirby said, pushing Harold ahead of him. 'Come on, Pops.'

'I think that might count as fraud,' Kirby said sitting down.

'Oh, come on,' Harold said. 'I might not be registered as a pensioner but I'm a few hundred years older than this lot.' He looked around. 'Well most of them anyway,' he added.

Kirby stared at Harold. 'You're joking, right?'

'About what?'

'Your age.'

Harold smiled and produced a bag of Maltesers. He offered them to Kirby.

'And what's the expiry date on these?' Kirby asked. He held up a hand. 'No don't answer that,' he added taking a handful.

The lights dimmed.

'Ah, just in time,' Harold whispered.

A man in traditional magician garb of top hat and black cape with a red silk lining walked onto the stage pushing a tall cabinet, also black, with strange, oriental?, gold and red lettering all over it. He opened the front and back sections and walked through. With a theatrical flourish he closed them, back first, then front. He waved his white-gloved hands in a sinuous fashion before opening the front door again. A woman in a long white dress stepped out and curtsied as a ripple of applause circulated the theatre.

'He always opens with that one,' Harold said, which earned him a shush from behind.

Kirby watched what he thought of as your standard magic show, although he was no expert. At one point during a card trick, the man behind Harold said, 'Bet that was up his sleeve,' to the woman next to him, which caused Harold to crunch hard on a mouthful of Maltesers and mutter, 'Idiot.'

After the show, when everyone else was filing out, Harold led Kirby to the front and a door to the side of the stage marked "No Entry, Staff Only". He turned the handle then tutted.

'Locked?' Kirby suggested.

Harold turned it again and this time it opened. They continued down a narrow corridor to another door with a faded star on it. Scrawled on a Post-it note was "Geraldo".

Harold knocked.

'Come in, Harold,' a deep voice said and the door opened. A man sat with his back to them. Kirby looked around, the man was alone, or at least he was before they joined him. He glanced at the door, presuming it was some sort of trick. However, the last day or so gave him reason to doubt. He decided not to ask.

'Been a long time, Geraldo,' Harold said.

'Indeed, Harold,' Geraldo said. 'And are you going to introduce me to Inspector Kirby?'

'He likes to show off,' Harold said to Kirby. Geraldo smiled and inclined his head.

'Can I ask a question?' Kirby said.

'Ask away.'

'Why the fumble?'

Geraldo sniffed. 'Tell him, Roberto.' As he spoke, a pair of long, white and pink ears rose from inside the top hat, which was resting on the dressing table.

The rabbit rested it paws on the rim and looked up at them. 'Because although they come to see magic they still want to believe that it's really all sleight of hand and trickery.'

Kirby pinched the back of his hand, nothing, this wasn't a dream either. The door thing Kirby could accept, however, he had to admit the rabbit was good. The rabbit winked at him before turning to Harold. 'To what do we owe the pleasure?'

'Show him,' Harold said.

Kirby continued to stare at the rabbit. *Surely not?*

'The video, Inspector.'

'Er… yes, right,' Kirby said, taking out his phone and entering the pin. He frowned at it.

Harold held out his hand. 'Oh, give it here.'

'You should try the six,' Geraldo said taking the phone from Harold. 'Bigger screen.'

'So I've been told,' Kirby said.

Geraldo studied the video then showed it to Roberto who nodded. 'Mephisto,' he said, handing it back to Harold. 'He's been out of circulation for ten years or more.'

'The gnome?' Inspector Kirby asked.

Geraldo tutted and glanced at Harold who raised his eyes to the ceiling in sympathy.

Geraldo smiled as one might do to someone you thought to be a little simple. 'The cat, Inspector. I'd recognise those eyes anywhere.'

'I thought it might be,' Harold said nodding. 'I knew you could confirm it though.'

'And the gnome?' Kirby asked again, because he was beginning to appreciate that in the worlds of Harold and now Geraldo things were rarely as they appeared. And if the rabbit could talk, who knows?

'Well, I'm no expert,' Geraldo said. 'German perhaps, although could be Swiss, early twentieth century. Worth a bob or two I'd say.'

Everyone's a comedian, thought Kirby. 'Simply a garden gnome though?'

'Ah,' Geraldo said. 'I see what you're getting at. Yes, Inspector, this time just a gnome of the decorative garden variety.'

Kirby nodded. 'Lucky then that Mrs Tanner was filming him.'

Geraldo shook his head. 'Oh, I don't think so, Inspector. I take it the lady posts these videos of her precious cat, what did she call him?'

'Napoleon.'

Geraldo laughed. 'Oh yes, how appropriate. I take it she posts them on YouTube or something?'

Kirby took the phone back. 'And Facebook apparently. She seemed very up on her social media.'

'Oh she would be,' Geraldo said. 'Very Mephisto, loves an audience, the bigger the better. As for taking the gnome with him and the little puff of smoke, all very theatrical if a little over the top in my opinion.'

'So,' Harold said, 'he's announcing his return?'

Geraldo nodded. 'So it would seem.'

'Return?' Kirby asked.

'Yes,' Geraldo said, drawing out the word. 'Which is interesting. You see Mephisto's been in hiding on this...' he glanced at Harold, who nodded. '... this side of the divide after falling out with his former paramour. What these days you would call partner.'

Harold smiled. 'Not a lady to get on the bad side of.'

Geraldo and Roberto chuckled. 'No, exactly,' Geraldo said. 'Marianne's not one to tangle with lightly.

'Marianne?' Kirby said.

Harold frowned at Kirby 'Yes, why?'

'The missing girl's mother is called Marianne. Ran out on her and her father when she was two.'

'Harold?' Geraldo asked.

Harold grabbed Kirby's phone back and flicked at the screen. He found the picture of Sarah and Susie, and zoomed in on Sarah for Geraldo and Roberto to look at.

'She does have something of a look of her,' Roberto said. Geraldo nodded.

'Why do I feel this is not good?' Kirby said.

'So what do you reckon?' Harold said to Geraldo, ignoring Kirby.

'Mephisto and Marianne, points to one thing for me.'

Roberto twitched his whiskers. 'Sisillius.'

'Again?' Harold said. 'Didn't work out last time.'

'But now with a daughter,' Geraldo said. 'And of this world?'

Harold nodded. 'Oh Edna's going to love this. They didn't exactly part on good terms last time they met.' He narrowed his eyes. 'Hang on. And you two just happen to be around?'

Geraldo glanced across at Roberto, who ran a paw over one long white ear. 'Three days ago we were playing Whitby when Roberto felt a disturbance.'

Kirby held up his hand. They continued to ignore him.

'It's the whiskers,' Roberto said.

'On the same fault line,' Harold filled in.

'Exactly,' Roberto said. 'So we thought we'd better come north and see what's what.'

'And there happened to be a slot?'

Geraldo inspected a fingernail. 'One of the Dupreis sisters went down with laryngitis. Apparently she's quite prone to it; all those cigars.'

'And you're sticking around?'

'As the poster says, here all week.'

'You care to fill me in?' Kirby said on getting back in the car with Harold. 'I know it may seem trivial to you,

Geraldo and Roberto, however, I am supposed to be in charge and there is still a missing girl.'

'Yes well, let's get back and I'll make you a cup of tea. I think you might need it.'

ELEVEN

....

'So, any news on Sarah?' Harold asked as they were leaving the car park.

'Bit difficult if she's not in this world, as you put it.'

'Ah, yes. Did anyone see anything?'

Kirby glanced at Harold. 'Like what?'

'Anything.'

Kirby shook his head. 'Not really. Had my Sergeant asking around. However, it's amazing how people can look without seeing. Some did say they'd seen a group of teenagers hanging around near the bus stop, but that's all.'

'Teenagers?'

'Yes, you know, bigger than children, smaller than adults, well some of them anyway. Grey hoodies, crotch around the knees and arse hanging out of their jeans, that sort of thing. Talk in grunts and look at the floor when you speak to them.'

'Yes I know what teenagers are. I get them in the shop from time to time.'

'Trying to nick stuff?'

Harold smiled. 'Not from me. These teenagers, all in grey hoodies you say?'

'I think so.'

'With the hoods up?'

'Of course.'

'Hmm.'

'Hmm?'

Harold sucked his lip pausing, then drumming his fingers on the dashboard before glancing across at Kirby.

Kirby could feel another test of sanity on its way. 'Come on, out with it.'

'Goblins,' Harold said.

'Goblins?' Kirby repeated, feeling he was failing the test.

Harold tutted to himself. 'Could be, makes sense.'

'Goblins?' Kirby said again, this time pulling the word out as if it was reluctant to leave his lips. He stared across at Harold. 'Goblins? And that's supposed to make sense?'

'Watch it,' Harold said, pointing at a red light. Kirby hit the brakes so hard it had them both straining against the seat belts.

'Like me to drive?' Harold asked as he rubbed his neck.

'You drive?'

Harold shrugged. 'Why not?'

'No,' Kirby said as the lights changed. He took a deep breath to steady himself. He gripped the wheel a little harder. 'So, go on then, goblins.'

'Simple little fellas. Shortish, keep themselves to themselves and communicate mainly in grunts. Always fighting with each other.'

'Like teenagers then.'

Harold smiled. 'So stick them in hoodies, who'd know?'

'What and then send them to abduct a girl at a bus stop? In Jesmond? On a Monday morning?'

Harold pursed his lips thinking about it. 'Possible, if you had one of the brighter ones leading them.'

'Not like teenagers in that case. Anyway, how'd they get here?'

'A gateway.'

'I thought you were guardians or whatever of those things?'

'Can't be everywhere. And it's not unknown for new ones to pop up.'

Kirby shook his head. 'Great. Just dandy.'

They drove the rest of the way without speaking while Harold whistled what Kirby later realised was "Raindrops keep falling on my head". It seemed to him Harold might be enjoying all this, a bit of a break perhaps from the mundane life of a Jesmond backstreet shopkeeper. Whereas Kirby felt as if his brain had filled up its daily, no weekly, quota of strange things to think about and that it couldn't cope with much more. However, another part of his grey matter, where the coppering part was housed, was still fighting to understand. They turned on to Clayton Road and then took a right.

'Er, this isn't it, Inspector?'

'Yes it is.'

'My shop's further on.'

'We're not going to your shop, Harold,' Kirby said pulling into the car park of the Collingwood Arms. 'I've a feeling I'm going to need more than a cup of tea.' He took out his phone. 'Ah, Constable where are you?... Excellent, let me buy you a drink... On duty, I know, well just this once. I think it might help... Yes, Constable, it is like that.'

'A Constable?' Harold asked.

'Yes, WPC Shirley Barker.'

'Er, is that good idea? The fewer who know and all that.'

'Humour me, Harold,' Kirby said opening the pub door. 'If I'm going mad, I don't want to be on my own. And if I'm not, I think I'm going to need someone to remind me from time to time.'

It was a relief for Kirby to walk into the normality of a pub in the late afternoon. The dim lighting and the smell of beer were a balm to his frayed senses.

'Hiya, Harold,' the barmaid greeted them.

Harold nodded. 'Nancy.'

Kirby raised an eyebrow at Harold but didn't ask. After all, it must be Harold's local and even a man who came from another world must fancy a pint every now and then. 'What're you having?'

'The IPA, thanks.'

'Three pints of the IPA, please. Oh, and a couple of bags of plain crisps.'

The barmaid smiled as she reached up for the glasses. 'Coming up, pet.'

They took the drinks and the crisps to the benches and tables that ran along the front of the pub. Kirby chose the one at the far end furthest away from the two other groups that were there.

Kirby's trained brain went into automatic analysis mode. In the opposite corner were a group of what looked like academics, the older, balding one, in a creased linen jacket and the other two in T-shirts and jeans with holes at the knees. They were hunched over a document, pointing, gesticulating and occasionally laughing in that "ha, ha, would you credit it" sort of way. Next to them were five office types, three men and two women. They had no doubt decided to knock off early and make the most of the sunshine. The three men were in their shirtsleeves, ties loosened and top buttons undone. One of the women was nursing what appeared to be a small lemonade with both hands, as if for comfort, while the other was sipping a glass of white wine. White wine woman was flirting with the man next to her, leaning in close then slapping him on the arm at whatever he'd suggested.

It all seemed so normal. He envied them. It was a warm late summer afternoon and they were sitting outside enjoying a drink, blissfully unaware of all the disturbing things he was being told. And he knew there was more to come. Then wasn't that always the policeman's lot?

That's what coppers did, protect everyone else from the things they didn't want to think about.

Harold sipped at his beer. 'I prefer cheese and onion myself,' he said, helping himself to a few crisps which were laid out on the packet Kirby had split open. 'Since we're waiting, what's your first name? Can't keep calling you Inspector.'

'You can call me Kirby.'

Harold raised an eyebrow. 'Must have a first name?'

'Alright, it's Jonah. But only my mother calls me Jonah.'

'Nothing wrong with Jonah. It's a good name, an old name.'

'And you, Harold, what are you supposed to be, Celt?'

Harold put his pint down and stopped mid crisp. 'Celt? British please, ancient British as your archaeologists like to call us. Or even worse, Iron Age, as if somehow they weren't people. Huh, everyone seems to think being Celtic is just so cool. I could tell you a thing or two about the Celts...'

'Sorry, only asking,' Kirby said, realising he'd touched a bit of a raw nerve. To his relief Constable Barker appeared in the doorway. He held up a hand and she wandered across. She looked at Harold as she sat down. Kirby pushed a pint of IPA in her direction. She stared at it for a second, then shrugged and took a sip while still studying Harold.

Very good, Constable, Kirby thought, wait to hear what's volunteered before asking your questions.

Kirby downed a good quarter of his pint and licked his lips as he glanced from Shirley to Harold. 'Now, Constable, this is Harold. You can think of him as a consultant, an expert in his field. Or at least the nearest we've got to one.'

Harold frowned above the glass at his lips.

Shirley smiled briefly at Harold then turned to Kirby. 'Sorry, sir, no disrespect and all that, why do we need an expert for a missing girl? And an expert in what?'

'Both excellent questions, Shirley.' Kirby put down his pint so he could hold her gaze. 'However, I want you to listen to what I'm about to tell you without comment, understood?'

Shirley paused and sipped at her pint again, glancing at Harold, then giving Kirby a suspicious sideways look. 'Yes, I'm sure I can manage that, sir.'

Kirby held an index finger in the air. 'Right, hold on to that. Because what I'm about to tell you will test that ability.'

Shirley narrowed her eyes, but said nothing as Kirby started his story. At the mention of another world she put her pint down. Her jaw dropped when it came to the stones. Kirby was impressed – so far she hadn't tried to interrupt. However, the Mephisto episode caused a bark of disbelieving laughter when Roberto was mentioned. Kirby paused and raised his eyebrows. The laughter subsided and

Shirley took a long draft of her drink instead. She was in mid sip at the mention of goblins, which had her wiping dribbled beer from her jacket as Kirby finished.

'Well done, Constable, a commendable effort in the circumstances. So?'

'I…' Shirley paused and gazed into the bottom of her now empty glass as if looking for answers. She burped and clapped a hand over her mouth, her eyes wide in surprise. 'Sorry, sir, don't normally drink pints and certainly not that fast.' She burped again. 'Pardon.'

Kirby smiled. 'Granted.'

Shirley shook her head. 'I don't know, sir. I really don't. I think I'm still waiting for the Hobbits, Elves and Gandalf to make an appearance.' On saying the name Gandalf she stared across at Harold.

Kirby shook his head. 'No, Constable,' then he too looked across at Harold. 'Or at least I don't think so.'

This time Harold shook his head and tutted. 'Damned Tolkien.'

'So what now?' Shirley asked.

Harold shook his empty glass.

Kirby stood and took Harold's glass from him. 'Constable? Half perhaps?'

'Well, sir, I am on… oh what the hell, thank you, sir. And make it a pint if that's OK?'

'You two getting to know each other each other?' Kirby said returning with two more pints of IPA and a Coke for himself. 'Driving,' he explained as Harold looked at him.

'Turns out we've met,' Shirley said. 'I'd kind of forgotten until he told me where his shop is. I used to live just around the corner. He kept selling me stuff I didn't intend to buy.'

'Harold?'

Harold tried to look innocent. 'I don't know what she means.'

Kirby shook his head. 'So come on, Harold.' He glanced across at Shirley. 'What's going on? My priority is the missing girl. And on one level the rest is just... just a distraction. However, this distraction involves things I don't like the sound of, threatening things. And when I hear of things becoming threatening I start to get a little upset. So then, as a copper, if I feel people aren't helping me or I feel they're holding back I begin to use phrases like "obstructing the police", "withholding information" and "we can continue this down the station".'

Harold sipped at his second pint as if considering his words. Kirby employed the waiting trick and Shirley joined in. It's hard not to fill the silence.

'Fine,' said Harold after a few seconds. 'You accept that there's another world sort of connected to this one?'

Kirby glanced across at Shirley and nodded. 'Let's assume we do.'

'And you're happy with the idea of goblins and magic and the like?'

This time Shirley managed not to spill her beer.

'Not exactly happy with it,' Kirby said. 'But go on.'

'So what do you need to know?'

Kirby could see the indecision in Harold's eyes. For the first time since they'd met he seemed unsure. He waved the arm that wasn't holding his glass to take in the road, the pub and the other groups of people. 'Look around, Harold. Tell me what you see.'

Harold shrugged. 'Folks having a drink, enjoying themselves in the warm weather. The pub, houses, a few trees, a blue sky, fluffy clouds. Oh and some dark ones coming in from the west. Reckon it might rain later.'

Kirby nodded. 'Right, what you might class as a bit of normality, at least for the vast majority of people. With the possible exception of the warm weather, after all this is Newcastle. Agreed?'

'Sure.'

Now Kirby looked around, taking in the people, the pub, the trees, the sky, the gathering clouds and then back to Harold. 'Well, this is my world. And as a policeman it's my job to ensure these good people can continue to enjoy it. So, Harold, the answer to your question is everything you know. You are going to help me join the dots, is that understood? Because if not I'll start using those phrases I mentioned earlier.'

'You might struggle with the charge sheet.'

Kirby put his drink down, leaned across the table and narrowed his eyes. 'I've been doing this a long time, Harold. I'll find something. Or maybe I'll get health and safety to check out that shop of yours.'

Harold's fingers drummed on the bench as Kirby leaned back, waiting. He glanced at Shirley who was smiling. 'OK, but you're not going to like it.'

'We don't have to like it,' Kirby said patting his chest. 'We're coppers remember. We get paid not to like things.'

Harold took a breath. 'Well Sisillius, as I've said is, for want of a better word, a king, who has ambition that goes way beyond his ability. He was defeated some time ago and since then has kept himself to himself. Although, now it appears he's on the move again and I'm thinking he's been put up to it this time. Someone is making him promises.'

'This Mephisto?'

'Last time I reckon Mephisto couldn't handle it, which is why it failed. A bit all-show-and-little-substance that one. This time I'm guessing it's Marianne who's taking the lead.'

Shirley put her drink down and leaned forward. 'You mean Marianne as in Sarah's mother?'

Harold nodded. 'The real power. One wild child, that one.'

'So why does she need Mephisto?' Kirby asked. 'I thought you'd said they'd fallen out?'

Harold shrugged. 'The world of Sisillius is what these days you might class as a bit male chauvinistic. My guess is Marianne just wants him to be the acceptable mouthpiece.

'And I take it none of this is good news?'

Harold shook his head. 'No.'

Shirley waved a hand in front of them. 'Whoa, let me catch up here. This world is supposed to be what?' she asked, 'our past?'

Harold shook his head. 'Only sort of. More like an alternative past.'

Shirley leaned back and smacked her forehead with the heel of her hand. 'Well that's alright then. I mean an alternative past, why didn't you say before?'

'Take your time, Constable,' Kirby said. 'Pause, breathe.'

Shirley closed her eyes for a second, took a deep breath then opened them and breathed out slowly. 'Sorry, sir. Thank you.'

'That's alright, Constable.'

Shirley smiled across at Harold. 'So changes there can't affect what is happening here, now. I mean it's our past right?'

Harold scratched his head and glanced at them both. 'Yes and no.'

'Go on.'

'Well your history is your history, it's happened. Changes there are not going to alter it. Although if they did you wouldn't know of course because that would now be your history, if you get what I mean?'

'Not really. Tell me then, why we should be concerned with what goes on there?'

Harold finished off his beer and glanced around as if expecting another one to magically appear. 'It's all a question of balance,' he said, waggling a hand from side to side to emphasise the point. 'The two worlds rub up alongside each other and although it may not directly be your own past it can have an effect. Things travelling between the worlds have an impact, even if you don't realise it at the time.'

'Such as?'

'Those riots a few years ago. That was the last time, when Sisillius and Mephisto let their avarice get the better of them. With Marianne's help they tried to suck the magic out of this world to use in theirs.'

Kirby kneaded his eyes with his fingers before glancing at Shirley who was gripping her glass so tightly Kirby was afraid it might shatter in her hands. He took his own advice and breathed. He focused on Harold again. 'Okaayyy. So you're telling me those riots of a few years ago were down to magic?'

Harold smiled. 'Well, to be more precise, the removal of magic. As I said, it's all a question of balance.'

'But you're here,' Shirley said. 'So is this Edna and Geraldo and the rabbit, what's he called, Roberto. Then if

I'm to believe you, there's these goblins. Does all that not have an impact on the balance?'

Harold nodded then shook his head. 'A little. Think ripples in the ocean, they don't do any real harm. What they're trying to do is cause waves. Big magical ones.'

Kirby had his elbow on the table, hand supporting his head as if all this information was weighing it down. 'Magic? I'd like to say I don't believe in magic.'

Harold helped himself to the last of the crisps. 'Doesn't matter what you choose to believe, it's there and here.' He moved a hand over the table. 'In your 21st-century world it's thin, spread out so it has little effect. However, that just means in the other world, if they want to get at it, they have to take it from over a large area and that…'

'Upsets the balance,' Kirby said.

Harold grinned. 'Exactly.'

Kirby nodded towards Harold's empty glass. 'Another?'

Harold nodded. 'Wouldn't say no.'

'Constable?'

Shirley looked at her half-full glass and burped again. 'Sorry. Better not.'

Kirby stood and grabbed Harold's glass. 'So what about Sarah Cooper, Marianne's daughter?'

'Ah. Edna and I reckon being Marianne's daughter she's old magic living in your world, even if she doesn't know it. That's what they're looking for, a seer, a diviner, a conduit, if you like. Think of her as a lightning rod for the magic in your world.'

Kirby shook his head. 'She'd use her own daughter?'

'Especially her own daughter.'

TWELVE

....

'You wouldn't think it, would you, sir?' Shirley said watching Harold enter the front door of his shop. The bell tinkled a greeting. 'I mean a corner shop and the grey cardigan and all. It's…it's…'

'All so normal,' Kirby finished for her.

Shirley shook her head. 'I'm sorry, sir, I'm struggling. Do you believe all that?'

Kirby set off and turned on to Clayton road. 'So where do you live, Constable?'

'Not far from Bridge Street in Wideopen, sir.'

'I'll drop you off.'

Shirley pointed back over her shoulder. 'Er, I should really go back to the station. Things to do.'

Kirby kept driving in the same direction. 'Go home, Shirley. Crack open a bottle of wine, put your feet up and watch some trash on the telly and let your subconscious have a go at this. If there's a problem, blame me.'

Shirley grinned. 'I'll take that as an order then, sir.'

'Excellent.'

Kirby watched the young constable's grin fade and lines appear on her brow. He didn't have to be a mind-reader to know what she was thinking about.

Shirley turned to him. 'Sorry, sir, you didn't answer my question.'

He smiled. 'I know. What d'you make of Harold?'

Shirley nodded and puffed out her cheeks. 'Difficult. One minute you think he's just some slightly dotty old geezer in a grey cardigan and then the next time you look at him he's six inches taller, straight-backed and those eyes, it's like... it's like they've seen more than you could ever imagine.'

'Exactly and this Edna woman, grey cardigan and the same eyes if not more so. It's as if you can't not believe them. And of course I did meet Geraldo and Roberto.'

'The talking rabbit.'

Kirby sucked in air. 'Yes, I know. You had to be there.'

Shirley laughed. 'I wish I had been.' She pointed to a bus stop a hundred yards ahead of them. 'Here'll do, sir.'

Kirby pulled over. 'Remember, wine and telly.'

Shirley smiled as she got out of the car. 'Will do, sir.'

As Kirby drove the rest of the way home he knew he hadn't answered Shirley's question. It was as if he didn't want to admit it to himself. He did wonder if he should have involved her in the first place. But then part of being a good copper was knowing when you couldn't deal with something on your own. Many a nearly good copper had got into serious trouble one way or another dealing with things on their own. And Shirley was good. Others by now would be hiding behind walls of disbelief and scepticism, whereas she was prepared to give her instincts a go. With a mental sigh he pulled into his drive.

Opening his front door he still half expected to hear, 'That you, Jonah?' It had always made him smile, who else could it be at the time he got home? If he mentioned it, the usual reply was, 'Wouldn't you like to know?' He bent down and picked up all the leaflets and junk mail and put them unopened on the recycling pile. *Why do they bother?* He wished he could do the same with the brown envelope, a tax reminder. That went on the 'to be dealt with' pile.

In the kitchen, Kirby slung his jacket over a chair and removed his tie. Jeanie was still everywhere, pictures, mementos of past holidays, a pottery little girl with ducks at her feet that she'd had since a child. All those feminine touches, as she liked to call them. He took a bottle of beer out of the fridge, carried it through to the lounge and sat down. Then with a grunt and a sigh he got up and went back to the kitchen for a bottle opener. Returning to the sofa he took a sip from the bottle, turned the telly on and flicked through the channels, soap, soap, documentary on… the police force. Forget that. He flicked to Sky, maybe there was some footy. *Man Utd, why was it always Man Utd?* Ugh, and it wasn't even live. He turned the telly off and gazed instead at a photo of Jeanie on the mantelpiece. As always, she smiled back at him.

'What d'you make of it, love?'

'Have you eaten?'

Smiling to himself he went back into the kitchen to see what was in the freezer. He couldn't be bothered to cook. Ah yes, wrapped in foil was half a lasagne his mother had made him bring home last time he'd seen her, perfect. He looked at the oven and shoved it in the microwave. He could almost hear the tutting. 'So?' he said as he sat down again and looked at her picture.

'Talk to your mum.'

'After I've eaten,' he said. Jeanie had always got on well with his mum even if she reckoned she was a bit weird. He suspected his mum played on it. She was the seventh child of a seventh child, which in her world meant she had "the sight". Not that he ever really understood what "the sight" was. It was just something she quoted whenever she said something a bit strange, which was fairly often.

Five minutes later, having put the empty plate in the dishwasher, he picked up the phone. 'Hello, Mum.'

'Hello, dear. You alright?'

'Yes why?'

'Oh a feeling that's all. You know.'

The sight, Kirby said to himself and sniggered.

'What's funny?'

'Nothing, Mum. Thought I might pop over tomorrow after work, if that's OK?'

'Yes, dear. Do you want something to eat?'

'Er, not sure what time it'll be.'

'Not to worry. I'll do something that won't spoil.'
'Thanks, Mum.'
'Then you can tell me all about it. Bye.'
'Bye.'
Tell me all about it?

THIRTEEN

....

Sarah Cooper opened her eyes, although at the time she didn't know her name was Sarah Cooper, nor did she even register that her eyes had been closed. Her mind refused to work beyond what was in front of her at that particular moment. It was dark, well not quite as she could see dim outlines of... she didn't know what.

She half expected to see people feasting in a hall. Her mind was stirring again and had decided to throw in a memory of the last thing she'd been aware of before being wherever she was now. Having located one memory, her brain seemed pleased with itself and went looking for more. A picture of the hall formed in her head. It was a large room, no building, built of wood. It had weight and not just the physical kind. It carried its age and importance, it held its head high, walked tall in its surroundings, at least that was the impression it had left her with.

The lighting there was also dim, but not as dim as it was here. There had been a large fire in the centre. Most of the smoke drifted out through a hole in the roof, although some failed to make it and billowed around the rafters in thin clouds, looking for eyes to sting. There were also burning torches in sconces around the walls, which added more to the smoke than the light. It had all made her eyes water. Not that the other occupants of the hall seemed to notice. She assumed they must be accustomed to it. They were sitting on benches at crude wooden tables eating and drinking, with the aim, it appeared to her, to eat and drink as much as was humanly possible. As a result they were shouting, singing and grabbing at the women who served the food and drink. Some of the women were expert in dodging the grasping hands. Some responded with playful slaps which earned roars of approval from those sitting next to the recipient. Others welcomed the attention to the degree that behind those at the table were several couples, well, coupling.

Dogs snarled and fought over food that was dropped or thrown at them. Sarah was also sure she'd heard the rustling of small creatures in the rushes that covered the floor. The smell was the other thing that registered in her mind at that point. Besides the smoke, there was the roasting meat, mixed with the odour of sweating, unwashed bodies and spilled ale. Part of her felt she should have been disgusted by it all. She wasn't, it had all seemed perfectly normal.

At the far end, sat on a raised area at a polished table and in a chair with a high back, had been a large man, an important man; a man with a thick beard, matted hair and eyes that were small, dark pits under bushy eyebrows. The back of his chair was ornately carved with winged beasts. Creatures that looked to Sarah like dragons, made up the arms. That man laughed loudest of all, banging the table with a huge fist, causing plates to jump and ales to spill. However, it wasn't him who drew the eye, who demanded attention, who filled the room with their presence. That was the silent woman next to him who occasionally bestowed a knowing smile on those around her. She picked at her food and sipped at her drink. She was tall and slender, in contrast to all the masculine muscle that surrounded her. She had long, dark auburn hair flowing over her scarlet dress, cut low at the front, displaying her ample charms. The eyes of the men flickered in her direction, although none dared linger. Her own eyes were large and dark. And when she turned her attention to Sarah, it felt as if she was seeing into her very soul. After studying her for several moments, the woman had smiled, waved in her direction and Sarah had, well, stopped being there. And now she was… here. Part of her brain suggested these memories should be disturbing, even frightening. However, another part found them reassuring.

During the time she'd been reliving this strange experience, the sky had lightened, dawn she presumed. The smoke in the room had been replaced by a thin mist which hung and swirled as it lifted, leaving behind glistening droplets on the moss and cobwebs that decorated the rough stone of the walls that were now visible. Above her, there were gaps where windows might once have been. Above that was the sky. She could make out the jagged outline of the top of the walls. Wherever she was, it required more than a little maintenance. 'A project' they'd have called it on the TV. She reached out and touched the stone closest to her. It was damp and slick with algae. She rubbed the green slime between her fingers as she considered where she might be.

She had no idea. From overhead came the raucous call of a herring gull, and there was a tang of salt in the air. On the coast then. The more she recognised, the more awake she became. Sarah shivered, she was cold; coldest of all were her feet. She looked down, no shoes. Her bare feet were wet with the morning dew which had formed on the sparse grass that was growing in the middle of wherever she was. She turned and in the wall that had been behind her was an entrance, or for her, an exit. She pulled her long cardigan tight around her as she wandered out and into what promised to be a pleasant morning. The sun was rising. She had the thought it must be summer and indeed the sun already seemed to be warming the air. She stood in its comforting glow for a few seconds, crossing her arms and rubbing her shoulders before picking her way across a field, taking care not to step on thistles or nettles. She was greeted by the cawing of crows and the raised heads of sheep as she disturbed their cropping at the tufts of coarse grass. They looked up at her, some bleating their annoyance. After a while she paused and turned. She now remembered who she was, Sarah Cooper. She also recognised where she was, for the building was

Dunstanburgh Castle, or at least what was left of it these days.

Sarah had no inkling as to how she had got here or what those memories that still poked their fingers into her conscious mind were all about. The thought they might be a dream didn't even occur to her. They were memories, she was sure of that, and again something told her not to worry. It would all make sense in time.

Since it was Dunstanburgh, Sarah knew that a mile or so down the well-trodden path, along the coast leading south, must be the little fishing village of Craster. It was a place she associated with eating ice-cream and sitting outside the Jolly Fisherman pub with a beer while staring out across the North Sea. At least it would be Craster if this was the Dunstanburgh she knew. Those recent memories were giving her reason to doubt. She glanced back at the castle. It looked like Dunstanburgh. She knew it well, even as a child it had been one of her favourite places to visit. She had always been drawn to it. Somehow, touching its ancient, damp, weathered stone had provided a much needed anchor to her life.

She set off along the grass path that had been flattened by numerous feet. Glancing out across the rocky shore the early light sparkled on the calmest of seas. She couldn't remember ever seeing the North Sea so still, with only a hint of a wave and the thinnest line of white foam where sea met shore. Small, grey birds were skittering from pool to pool, eating whatever small birds ate. Ten minutes later, a neat row of terraced cottages came into sight that she knew led down to the harbour.

Entering the village, a stout woman of middle years was coming the other way. She was the picture of what you expected a woman to look like in a fishing village, even down to the apron and the headscarf. The woman stopped and stared at her. 'Do you know what time it is, pet?'

'No,' Sarah replied.

'It's a quarter to six, love.'

'Oh.'

For a moment the woman, standing hands on ample hips, seemed lost for words. 'And you in just jeans, a T-shirt and cardy.'

Sarah pulled the cardy around herself again. 'I know.'

Then the woman noticed her feet. 'And no shoes!' she exclaimed. 'You poor dear. At this time in the mornin' an al.'

'Ah, yes,' Sarah said. 'I'm not sure how that happened.'

'So where have you come from, pet?'

Sarah pointed back along the path. 'Just now, the castle. Before that…' she shrugged.

The woman took her by the arm. 'Ee, I'm sorry, pet, here's me rabbiting on and you standing there all cold and with no shoes. Tell you what, why don't you come in and warm yourself up?' she said, pointing to the door of the cottage they were standing outside. A climbing rose covered the small porch. 'I'm Pauline by the way.'

'Sarah.'

'Well, Sarah, coming?'

'If you're sure?' Sarah said.

'Of course, pet,' Pauline said opening the gate and nudging at Sarah's arm so that she started down the path which was bordered by more roses. Inside, Pauline led Sarah to the back of the cottage and into a warm kitchen. She pulled out a chair and placed it in front of the Aga. 'Now you sit yourself down and get warm.' She took a small towel from the rail in front of the Aga and handed it Sarah. 'For your feet, pet.'

'Thank you.'

While Sarah sat drying her toes, Pauline was already filling the kettle. 'Expect you'd like a cup of tea?'

'I don't want to put you to any trouble.'

'Oh, no trouble, dear. And how about a bit o' breakfast while I'm on?'

Sarah hesitated for a second. The mention of food triggered the realisation that she was ravenous. 'Yes, thank you. I am feeling a bit hungry.'

Pauline took a large frying pan off a hook and placed it on the Aga. From the fridge, she took three rashers of bacon. They were soon sizzling away and giving off that unique, enticing aroma that only frying bacon can achieve. Sarah's stomach grumbled in anticipation.

'Now, while you're eatin' I'll just make a phone call if that's' alright wi' you?' she said pouring Sarah a mug of tea. 'It's me nephew, Colin. He's a Constable in Alnwick.

Nice boy, married a farmer's girl from Longframlington. Expectin' their first bairn now they are. Ee, you know, it doesn't seem five minutes since he were a bairn himself. Anyway, I just think you should speak to someone, pet.'

Sarah looked up through the rising steam from the mug she was cradling in both hands and nodded.

Pauline cut two thick slices of bread and buttered them before plating up the bacon. 'I'll make that call,' she said, as Sarah began making herself a bacon sandwich. As she tucked in she could hear one side of the conversation.

'Yes, I know, a young girl... about nineteen, twenty, I'd guess. Couldn't believe it, a quarter to six and just jeans, a T-shirt, cardy and no shoes.... Hmm, what, pet... eating a bacon sandwich, poor girl's famished... Yes, yes... Oh, don't worry, I'll be fine. She seems a very nice girl, polite y'know, like she's from a good family... I know, pet, but I can just tell. She seems a little lost that's all... No, no, I think she's all there. As I said, seems a bit lost, that's all. Yes, bye pet.'

'Very good,' Sarah said, smiling and holding up what was left of her sandwich as Pauline came back into the kitchen. 'Thank you.'

'No bother, pet.' Pauline said, wiping her hands down the front of her pinny. 'Now, Colin said he'll be right over. Thinks it might be best if they had a little chat with over you at the station. They'd like to make sure you're alright and then they can see about getting you home. How's that?'

Sarah nodded her acceptance and finished the sandwich.

FOURTEEN

....

Overnight Kirby's subconscious had been working away and one thing it reminded him of was that whatever else was going on, or was supposed to be going on in this world or other worlds, he still had a missing girl on his hands. There again, if he was to believe Harold, which reluctantly he did, she wasn't anywhere it would be possible to find her. He could hardly send a bunch of bobbies clomping around in their size nine boots to do house-to-house or hut-to-hut, or whatever, in a world that was two-and-a-half thousand years removed from this one. He smiled at the picture it conjured up. 'Excuse me, sir, but do you have a licence for that there sword? No? In that case I'm afraid I'll have to ask you to accompany me to the... to the... Sarge!' No, perhaps not.

His subconscious mind had also been musing on Harold and his revelations. He'd accepted that Harold and Edna were not wind-up merchants. Let's face it, if you're intent on winding up a policeman you'd come up with something a lot more believable than the story they were telling him. Then there was the Geraldo and Roberto double act and of course the disappearing cat. The sensible part of his brain wanted him to stick his fingers in his ears and shout 'La, la, la,' until they all went away. However, as a copper, if you only went with was what sensible you'd never get anywhere. The world was far from sensible. You only had to watch the news to realise that.

As he chewed on his toast and sipped his coffee, Jeanie's picture was looking at him. 'Remember, Jonah, you always find a way.' He tried to hold on to that thought as he drove to the office.

Hearing a sneeze from the other side of the partition, Kirby decided he needed some cheering up.

'You're in early, Sergeant. Well done.'

He was answered with more sneezing and a bout of nose-blowing which sounded like a baby elephant playing in a water hole.

'So how did you get on looking for the Grey Hoodie Gang?'

Sergeant Jones raised his head into sight. 'It… it… it…' another sneeze this time followed by a long sniff.

'Well?' Kirby asked in what he hoped was a lull.

The sergeant blew his nose again. 'It rained.'

Kirby smiled. 'Really? I could have sworn the forecast was for sunshine all day.'

The sergeant gave him the "I don't believe you, but I can't be bothered," look. 'A few people said they'd seen them hanging around.'

'Doing what?'

'What teenagers do, sir, being pointless.'

'Hmm, anyone get much of a look at them?'

'Not really on account of the hoods and them staring at their feet all the time. Oh, just a minute I did get one description from someone who got a bit of a glimpse.' The sergeant sniffed, then shuffled the papers on his desk. 'Ah, here it is, and I quote, "The wind blew the little devil's", you'll appreciate there's a small edit there, sir.'

'Yes, yes.'

'"… the little devil's hood back for a second and he looked a bit of a rum'un and no mistake. The sort of kid only a mother could love, if you know what I mean?"'

'Well that should narrow it down, Sergeant.'

'That's what…' The sergeant's phone rang. 'Aha, yes, he's here.' He glanced at Kirby. 'Yes I'll tell him.'

'Tell me what?'

'They think they've found your missing girl.'

'Where?'

'She's with the local plods in Alnwick.'

'Alnwick? They're sure? Last time, remember, they thought they had that missing lad from Gateshead. Only they'd picked up a girl on a day trip to the castle who'd sneaked off for a sly fag.'

'To be fair, sir, it's not always easy to tell. She did have short dark hair, and her name was Jo.'

'As in Johanna, Sergeant. And I would have thought the school uniform might have given them a clue.'

'Hmm, anyway, it seems this one matches the photo.' Seeing the look on Kirby's face he decided to hedge his bets, 'So they say. And her name is Sarah.'

'Not Simon?'

'Er, no, sir. Oh, and she was found without her shoes.'

Kirby nodded.

'Tell them I'm on my way.'

'Yes, sir. Oh and sir, nearly forgot, the Chief wants five minutes.'

'Now?'

'I don't think he does any other sort, sir.'

'Hmm.' Kirby's shoulders sagged a little. He gave the red-nosed sergeant a hopeful half smile. 'No chance you could have actually forgotten rather than nearly forgotten.'

The sergeant blew his nose. 'Sorry, sir.'

'You alright, Jonah? You look a little peaky.'

'Fine, sir. Just a bit of a disturbed night that's all.'

'I know what you mean.' The chief's eyes dropped to his desk and he started shuffling papers in that annoyed, purposeless way people have when they feel the need to rant. 'I've been telling the wife for months we need a new mattress. Does she listen to me? It's just...' He glanced up and paused, as if remembering where he was. 'Well, yes, quite. Anyway, this case, the missing girl. I hear she's been found.'

'Looks that way, sir.'

'Good, good,' the chief said, fiddling with a pen. 'Where is she?'

'Alnwick.'

He stopped fiddling and fixed Kirby with a stare. 'And they're sure this time? Her parents knew the Super you know. Played golf with him or were in Rotary with him. Well, something like that.'

'So I heard, sir. But yes, I'm pretty sure.'

The chief relaxed a little and leant back in his special chair. 'So, case solved then?'

'Well, we still don't know how or why she was taken.'

'Taken? Sure she didn't just decide to go off for the day? Young girls and all that. A boy perhaps?'

'Without her shoes, sir?'

'Well, I'm sure there's a perfectly logical explanation.' The chief smiled a smile that said, 'There WILL BE a perfectly LOGICAL explanation'.

Kirby had been here before. 'Perhaps, sir, and of course we are exploring every possibility.' The chief's smile remained fixed. Kirby scratched his ear. 'Er, however, there's some other stuff that I believe might be connected with her going missing.'

The smile faded and the chief hunched his shoulders, shrinking in his chair a little as if he already knew and was afraid of where this might be going. 'You said stuff, Jonah?'

'Yes, sir.'

They were now in familiar territory where the chief had to balance his curiosity and his need to know what was going on with the knowledge that he might be called upon to explain it all to the super at some point. The chief waggled his fingers as if thinking about doing some more paper-shuffling. 'OK, Jonah, let's get this over with. So, weird?'

Kirby signalled with both palms raised.

'Very weird?'

He signalled again.

The chief's own hands were now on the desk caressing a pile of papers. 'Extremely weird?'

Kirby signalled higher, again.

The chief started shuffling paper. 'Jonah, we don't go above extremely!'

'I think we might do now, sir.'

Paper started falling on the floor. 'Well, keep me... let me... good luck.'

'Thank you, sir.'

Kirby walked out of the office and closed the door. The WPC looked up. 'Did I hear paper hitting the deck?'

'I'm afraid so, Jane.'

She started to get up. 'I'll get the tea then.'

He glanced back at the door. 'I think you'll need the chocolate Hobnobs too.'

As he was making his way to his car, Kirby called Shirley Barker. 'Where are you, Constable?'

'Er, just about to leave home, sir. Sorry, I'm a bit late. Afraid I took your advice.'

'Yes?'

'You know, sir, about opening a bottle of wine. The trouble was I was the only one drinking it.'

'Never mind, Constable. I'll pick you up. They think they've found the missing girl.'

'Who, sir?'

'The boys in Alnwick.'

'Alnwick?'

'Yes, Constable, a trip out. How exciting is that?'

'Wonderful, can't wait, sir. See you in a bit. Where you dropped me last night?'

'Fine.'

Driving through Gosforth high street Kirby peered down Henry Street where he'd first come across Lily "Medusa" Johnson, then plain old Diamond Lil. That had been plain weird, alright turning very weird. Now he needed to add something above "extremely weird" to his definitions' list. Somehow, "very, extremely or unbelievably" didn't capture what he was feeling.

'I'm sorry, sir,' Shirley said after she'd fastened her seatbelt. 'However, I'm still struggling with all of this.'

'Good.'

'Sir?'

'I'd be more worried if you weren't. Struggling means questioning everything and that's what we've got to do.

Then when we've eliminated everything that doesn't fit, whatever's left, no matter how improbable, must be the answer, right?'

'If you say so, sir.'

Kirby had to admit that despite the conclusions his subconscious had come to while he was asleep, his conscious coppering mind persisted in trying to suggest more normal explanations. His conscious and subconscious were still arguing as he sped along the A1 dual carriageway past Stannington and on to the Morpeth bypass. Eventually he told them both to shut up.

Heading past the slip road down into Morpeth always evoked memories. It was where Jeanie had loved to go to do a "bit of shopping". She wasn't one for the big centres; said she could wander around them for hours and never find what she wanted. She'd always drag him into the small department store, Rutherfords, where "if he was good" she'd buy him a coffee. He never quite figured out how she could go in for a jacket or a skirt and come out with a cushion or table mats. Sometimes he'd leave her mooching about while he wandered around the town or along the river.

'You alright, sir?'

'Sorry?'

'Just you looked miles away.'

'Yes, something like that, Constable.'

Kirby opened the window, breathed in the fresh air, pushed the memories aside and turned his attention to the scenery he never tired of.

'Beautiful isn't it, Constable?'

Shirley glanced across to the purple of the Simonside hills in the distance. 'Guess so. Although I'm more of a city girl.'

Kirby sat up straighter as he sucked in another breath. 'Take my advice, put on a pair of boots and get out there. Clears the mind.'

'I'll take your word for it, sir.'

Fifteen minutes later, past the Hog's Head Inn, Kirby pulled off the A1 and made his way to Alnwick police station; a rather stern-looking brick building with, he thought, pretentions of grandeur. Just what a police station should look like, in his opinion.

Inside, the Desk Sergeant looked up from his crossword and greeted him. 'Morning, sir. Welcome back.'

'Thank you, Sergeant. This is Constable Barker. I believe you have our missing girl, or at least you think you have?'

The sergeant put down his pen and coughed. 'Er yes, sir, we're sure this time.'

'So who found her?'

'Well, sir, it was Constable Cuthbertson. Or at least he collected her.'

'Uh huh, and is the Constable in?'

The srgeant pointed to a door a few metres along. 'In there, sir. Should be making me a coffee.'

Kirby and Shirley entered the small kitchen area to see a tall constable with his back to them and the sound of a spoon clinking in a mug. 'Morning, Constable.'

Constable Cuthbertson turned around, holding a mug of steaming coffee. Kirby took it from him. 'Thank you Constable, very kind. I'm sure Constable Barker here would love one as well.'

Shirley grinned. 'Thanks.'

'Right, sir,' Cuthbertson said before turning back and getting two more mugs from the draining board.

Bright lad, Kirby thought. Didn't miss a beat. 'So you found her then?'

'Sarah?' Cuthbertson said as he let the kettle boil again and spooned in the coffee.

'Yes, Sarah.'

'Well, it was actually me aunty who found her, sir. The girl was wandering along outside her cottage in Craster at six in the morning. And seeing as she was looking lost and in just jeans and a T-shirt with no shoes on an' all, and Auntie Pauline being a decent sort, she invited her in to warm up like. Said she could see there was no harm in her.'

'Good for her. Then she called you.'

'Sir.'

'So which direction was she coming from?'

Cuthbertson handed Shirley a coffee. 'The castle, or at least that's what Auntie Pauline thought. Her cottage is at that end of the village, you see.'

Kirby nodded. 'And have you interviewed her?'

'No, sir. Thought I'd leave that to you.'

Of course you did, Kirby thought. Not the sort of report you want to write. He studied the constable who maintained a look of innocent helpfulness under the inspector's gaze. *Well done, Constable, you'll go far.* 'So where is she?'

'Second room on the left.'

'Thank you. Now I expect the Sergeant will want his coffee.'

'Er, yes, sir. Thank you, sir.'

Kirby opened the door, allowing Shirley to enter first, to find Sarah sitting, facing a wall. On her feet, looking a little out of place on someone of Sarah's age, were a pair of blue, what he believed were called "mules", complete with pink feathery pompoms, no doubt donated by Auntie Pauline. Sarah didn't turn or show any other indication that she knew they were there. It was as if she were watching something no one else could see. Given how this case was developing, it wouldn't have surprised Kirby if she was.

Kirby sat opposite. 'Hello, Sarah. I'm Inspector Kirby and this is Constable Barker.'

Sarah's eyes flickered across their faces for a second before losing focus again. *So at least she knows we're here*. Kirby nodded towards Shirley, hoping the constable would seem less threatening to the young girl.

Shirley smiled. 'So, Sarah, you were at the castle?'

'Castle.' Sarah said in a flat voice devoid of any intonation.

'Yes, Dunstanburgh.'

'Dunstanburgh.'

Shirley glanced at Kirby, who shrugged. 'Do you remember how you got there?'

'Dunstanburgh.'

'Yes, Dunstanburgh.'

Sarah's eyes focused for a second and a faint smile touched her lips. 'Nice lady gave me a bacon sandwich.'

'Yes, that was nice of her. Now can we get back to the castle, Sarah?.'

'Dunstanburgh.'

'Yes. How did you get there?'

'Men.'

Perhaps we're getting somewhere.

Shirley leaned forward a little. 'Now…'

'Big men, beards, big beards, beer.'

'They got you drunk?'

'Big men, big beards. Smoke, smell.'

'And they took you to the castle?'

'Dunstanburgh. Hurt my eyes.'

'They hurt your eyes?'

'Dunstanburgh.'

'Yes, Sarah, Dunstanburgh.'

'Dunstanburgh.'

Perhaps they weren't getting anywhere. Kirby put a hand on Shirley's arm. 'I think we'd better get you back, Sarah,' he said.

He turned to Shirley. 'Let's arrange for a car to pick you up when we get to the hospital and then you can take a little trip up to the castle.'

'Me, sir?'

'Yes, Constable, I know, two excursions in one day. How exciting is that?'

'What am I looking for?'

'Anything, Constable. Have good poke around. Should be a nice day. A little walk, fresh air and all that.'

'If you say so, sir. Personally, I always thought fresh air a little overrated, especially when it contains water.'

Shirley stood and placed a gentle hand on Sarah's arm. 'Come on, let's get moving shall we?' Sarah stood and let Shirley guide her out of the station and into the back of the car. On his way out, Kirby stopped at the desk.

'Sir?'

'Give the folks up at Dunstanburgh a call, will you, and tell them to keep it shut for the day.'

'Dunstanburgh?'

'Yes, you know, the castle, big thing made of stone. I don't want the public trampling all over it until we've had a chance to poke around.'

'Yes sir.' The sergeant said, making a note on his pad. 'Castle… made… of… stone,' he muttered as he wrote.

Kirby ignored the ritual Desk Sergeant sarcasm. 'Oh, and see if you can spare a Constable to go over there and make sure no one goes inside until…. No, tell you what…' He turned to Shirley. 'Why don't you go over there now and have a poke around, see what you can find? Perhaps talk to the lady who found her. I'm sure they can spare Constable Cuthbertson to give you a lift and then bring you back into town.' He raised an expectant eyebrow at the Desk Sergeant.

'Sir.'

On the way back, Sarah gazed out of the window, saying nothing, clearly back to seeing things no one else could see, Kirby thought as he glanced at her in the mirror. *What are you seeing, Sarah? What did you see?* He guessed she was back in Dunstanburgh, at least whenever she was asked a question that's how she answered, 'Dunstanburgh'. Except for one occasion, just as they passed over the river Coquet, when he noticed her smile. 'Not alone,' she said.

'Remembered something, Sarah?'

'Dunstanburgh.'

Kirby radioed ahead to say he was taking Sarah to the Freeman hospital and could they let Mr Cooper know.

When they arrived Mr Cooper, a doctor and a nurse were waiting for them.

FIFTEEN

....

Mr Cooper rushed over and pulled Sarah to him. Sarah allowed herself to be hugged, but didn't hug him back. 'Where've you been, darling? We've been so worried about you.'

Sarah stared into the middle distance. 'Dunstanburgh.'

'Dunstanburgh? What about Dunstanburgh, Sarah? Did they hurt you?'

'Dunstanburgh.'

'Mr Cooper,' Kirby said, interrupting on the grounds that he felt this could go on for some time.

Cooper turned his head towards Kirby while still holding on to Sarah, who remained passive in his arms. 'Is she hurt? What's she told you? What's wrong with her?'

Kirby raised a hand. 'Please, Mr Cooper, it seems Sarah's not saying much at the moment. He took Cooper's arm. 'Why don't we let the doctors have a look at her? We don't believe she's been physically harmed, however they can make sure.' Cooper glanced across at the nurse, who smiled in return. He nodded, then relinquished his hold on Sarah.

The nurse stepped forward and put an arm around Sarah's shoulders. 'Why don't you come with me and we can make you comfortable?' She led a passive Sarah into the hospital with Cooper following a few steps behind. Kirby touched the doctor's arm, who being well-versed in these things, hung back.

'What do you think?'

'Traumatised, shock, at first guess. As you say, nothing physical. We'll have a good look at her just to be sure.'

Kirby handed the doctor one of his cards. 'And can you let me know if she says anything peculiar, anything funny?'

'Funny?'

'As in strange.'

'Strange?'

'Yes,' Kirby said, tapping the card the doctor was now holding away from his body in the tips of a finger and thumb as if it might be infected with something contagious. 'Don't worry, you'll know when you hear it.'

The nurse guided Sarah into a single room and the doctor followed.

Kirby stopped at the door. 'Mr Cooper, why don't we leave them to it? And perhaps I could ask you a few questions?'

Cooper glanced at the doctor.

'She'll be fine with us, Mr Cooper.'

Kirby led him back down the corridor to a small visitors' waiting room he'd spotted.

'Why was she in Dunstanburgh?' Cooper asked as Kirby closed the door. 'How did you find her? Who took her there?'

Kirby held up both hands to stop the wave of questions. 'Why don't we sit down and I'll try to answer some of your questions, and then you can answer some of mine.'

'But I don't know anything. It makes no sense to me.'

Kirby smiled. 'No perhaps not, however, please humour me. I'm a policeman, asking questions is what we do. And sometimes people know things without knowing they know things, if you get what I mean?'

'If you say so.'

They sat near the window. Cooper perched on the edge of the seat and played with his wedding ring.

'You still wear it?' Kirby said, pointing to Cooper's left hand.

Cooper stopped fiddling and looked down at the ring as if he hadn't realised what he was doing. 'Yes, I... what has that got to do with anything? I thought it this was about my daughter?'

Kirby smiled in apology. 'Nothing, I'm sorry. You're quite right. I have a daughter about the same age, so I can imagine a little of how you might feel.' He gave Cooper a brief account of how Sarah was found by "Auntie" Pauline and what little Sarah had told them. 'So you see, we're presuming she was at or in the castle because of where she was found and the direction she was coming from. And of course the fact that she keeps saying Dunstanburgh.'

'Did she say anything else?'

'She mentioned men with beards. Oh, and smoke and beer.'

'What? She was in a pub? The beards, do you think it was a group of bikers?'

Kirby shook his head. 'No, I don't think so.'

'It makes no sense.'

'I know. Let's give her time. See what else she might remember.'

'So, she was abducted?'

Kirby hesitated. 'We don't know that. It's possible she made her own way there and then something happened that has led to her being confused. Is there any reason she might have gone to the castle or the area? Do you have any relatives around there, or someone she knows?'

Cooper shook his head. 'No, I've no relatives there. Mine are all from Durham.'

'What about her mother?'

'Marianne, no. I've no idea, she never said.' Cooper ran a hand through his hair and glanced out of the window before taking a deep breath, calming the agitation Kirby could sense rising in him. 'I told you she didn't reveal anything about her past. So Sarah couldn't have had anything to do with them.'

'My apologies, Mr Cooper, I have to ask these things.'

Cooper nodded. 'I'm sorry. It's just Marianne… anyway Sarah knows nothing about any family Marianne might have. Neither of us do.'

'Yes, quite. So there's no reason for her to go there?'

Cooper sat back and shook his head. 'No, other than she always loved the place as a child.'

'Really?'

Cooper smiled. 'Yes, it was her favourite place to go for a picnic. We'd park in Craster then walk along the headland. She'd always run on ahead, couldn't wait to get to the castle. I even took out membership every year. You couldn't drag her away. You know, young girls and castles, fairy princesses and all that. She always did have a vivid imagination about such things. Then one day she just stopped wanting to go.'

'Oh, when?'

'She'd have been about thirteen, fourteen. One day she announced she didn't need to go any more. I suppose it's all part of growing up. The dolls go away and make-up starts appearing, that sort of thing. In the end I think I missed it more than she did. You know, daddy's little girl and all that.'

Kirby nodded. 'Yes, I know all about that. And she's been herself recently?'

'How do you mean?'

'You've not noticed anything different in her, change of mood?' he shrugged. 'Anything that struck you as odd about her?'

Cooper pursed his lips as he thought and then shook his head. 'Nothing really. I think she's happy. Her and Susie are good friends. I haven't seen much of her lately'she seems to be working hard. I've taken her out for the odd meal and she's been chatty, loving her course. She did break up with a boyfriend not long ago.'

'Roger.'

'That's right, Roger. I never met him. Although she didn't seem too bothered by it. You don't think…'

Kirby shook his head. 'No, we've no reason to believe this is anything to do with him.'

'Oh good. Then I'm sorry, Inspector, I don't think there's much else I can tell you.'

'No, that's been helpful, thank you,' Kirby said. 'Well, if you do think of anything…'

Kirby glanced into Sarah's room as he made his way out of the hospital. She was lying on the bed in a hospital gown and the doctor was poised with a syringe in his hand. Kirby shuddered, even though he didn't consider himself squeamish. He could watch those fly-on-the-wall hospital documentaries without flinching and he'd seen a few dead bodies in his time. Yet when it came to needles or even the thought of needles, it made the ends of his fingers go numb. He paused and Sarah turned her head in his direction. 'So what have you seen, Sarah?' he wondered. 'What do you know that you can't tell us, or aren't willing to tell us perhaps?' She smiled. It was a smile that made him shudder in the same way the thought of needles did. It was a smile that didn't belong on the face of a young girl.

Back in the car park, Kirby decided it was time to visit Harold again.

SIXTEEN

....

Shirley followed Constable Cuthbertson out of the station to the car.

'I'm Colin, by the way,' Cuthbertson said after he'd negotiated the streets of Alnwick and they were heading for the coast road.

'Shirley.'

'So what's he like then, Shirley?' Colin asked.

'Who?' Shirley said, playing dumb as she watched the countryside from the car window. Living around Newcastle you could almost forget this side of Northumberland existed; fields, woods, hills, rivers. She'd heard it was the least populated county in England, however that didn't mean anything until you left the city. Maybe the inspector was right. It did sort of call to you to get out there, feel the grass under your foot, smell the flowers, stand in a cow pat and all that. She turned back to Colin and smiled. 'Sorry. Yeah, he's alright. Sarky at times, but then he's an inspector. Bit of a loner sometimes as well, not a great mixer. Perhaps why he gets some of the weirder cases.'

'Like what?'

Shirley told him about the Lily Johnson case.

'Oh yeah, Medussa. I saw that in the Journal. Bet the top brass loved that one. You on that?'

'Nah. Other officers side-stepped the case. Kirby got to the bottom of it though. He sees through the crap somehow.'

Colin nodded. 'And this one? An Inspector comes all the way out of town to drive a girl back who's only been missing a day?'

'You don't want to know.'

'Go on.'

'No really, I mean it. You-do-not-want-to-know!'

'So multinational drug smugglers? Diamond heist? Plot to take over the world?'

'In Alnwick?'

Colin rounded a corner and braked hard. In front was a group of cows that were being herded across the road. He wagged a finger in front of him. 'Come on, give me a break. This is what constitutes excitement around here.'

Shirley watched the docile creatures which were in no hurry as they plodded and chewed their way towards the farm buildings. 'You know I said the Inspector gets all the weird cases, right?'

'Yeah.'

'Well he has this scale. There's weird, then there's very weird and extremely weird.'

Colin raised his eyebrows. 'So don't tell me this is extremely weird?'

Shirley flapped a hand above her head. 'Off the scale.'

He whistled through his teeth. 'Funny you should say that. My Auntie Pauline, who found the girl, has been saying there's been some weird things going on.'

Shirley sat a little straighter and looked at Colin. 'Just weird?'

Colin shrugged. 'Dunno. I mean one of the fishermen with new waders has the curtains twitching in Craster. Then this is my Auntie Pauline. Plays on the dotty-lady-living-alone-in-a-little-village bit. But e's all there, if you get what I mean? Not much gets past her.'

Shirley met the gaze of one of the cows as they cleared the road. 'I look forward to meeting her.'

'D'you want me to take you right up to the castle?' Colin asked when they were a few miles from Dunstanburgh.

'No, why don't we park at your Auntie Pauline's and walk along. It's a nice day and Sarah must have come that way, so you never know.'

'Sure.'

Colin pulled up outside a terraced cottage. A woman was in the garden on her hands and knees, weeding between the neat rose bushes. Shirley presumed this was Auntie Pauline. The woman stood as they got out of the car, and wiped her hands on her flowery apron. 'Hello, pet,' she said coming to the gate.

Colin greeted her with a kiss on the cheek. 'Hi, Auntie Pauline, how you doin'?'

'Oh, you know me, pet, mustn't grumble.' She glanced across at Shirley. 'This'll be about that young lass then?'

'Aye, Auntie. This is Constable Barker from Newcastle. We're going to have a look round up at the castle and then we thought we might have chat with you, if that's OK?'

'Of course, pet. I'll have the kettle on.'

'So what are we looking for?' Colin asked as they set off.

Shirley shook her head. 'Dunno. Anything. Anything that looks out of place or doesn't look like it should be there.'

'Or weird,' Colin added, waggling his hands in the air.

'You're getting the idea.'

It struck Shirley that the last time she had walked the mile or so from Craster to Dunstanburgh had been on a school trip over ten years ago. When you had all this on your doorstep you took it for granted it would always be there. The sound of the sea breaking over the rocks and the smell of seaweed brought it all back. That day all those years ago had been much like this, warm with a hint of a breeze off the sea to take the edge off the temperature. One of those days when you could never imagine it ever being cold or rainy again.

She smiled at the memory of all the friends who had been so much a part of her life at that time. She, Ellie and Janet regularly met on the last Friday of the month for a few drinks and she kept in touch with some of the others, however, that was about it. She'd held hands with Peter Brown. They'd snogged up at the castle when they were out of sight of the teachers. Her smile faded. Three years ago she'd arrested him in the Bigg Market for drug-dealing. She'd hardly recognised him; he was thin and unkempt with lank greasy hair, an addict himself. Being a copper had a habit of doing that, spoiling things.

'You alright?'

'Yeah sorry, just thinking. Anything?' she asked.

'Nothing unusual.' Colin shook his boot. 'Unless a high number of sheep droppings count?'

Shirley laughed. 'Let's put it this way, I'm not bagging them up.'

They were met at the castle by one of the wardens. The hunched shoulders, frown and hands rammed into the pockets of his green gilet announced his feelings on being made to keep the place closed in mid-summer. 'How long's this going to last, huh?' he asked, ramming his hands even harder into his pockets, in case they hadn't picked up on his annoyance. 'People aren't happy, you know. I keeps having to turn them away and they don't like it.'

'I don't know,' Shirley said, pausing, hands on hips and making a dramatic scan of the area around them. 'It's a possible crime scene.'

The man's expression lightened, he stood straighter and took his hands out of his pockets. 'Oh well in that case,' he said, hurrying off down the path to where another warden was talking to a group of, Shirley presumed, disappointed tourists. He made shooing motions with his hands. 'Come on please, keep away. This is a crime scene... what? No, sorry, all I know is it's a crime scene.'

'Is it?' Colin asked.

Shirley shrugged. 'I don't know, it might be. Anyway,' she said, pointing to the warden who was now flapping his arms at three more people ambling down the track. 'It's keeping him happy and off our backs. Always a good one that.'

Colin laughed. 'I'll make a note.'

Shirley walked around the building, or what was left of it, trying to imagine what it must have been like seven or eight hundred years ago. Horses, men in armour perhaps? Then, thinking of Sarah, she amended that to men with beards in armour. The again, that's what you always thought of in places like this, not the miserable ordinary people doing all the crappy, ordinary jobs that kept somewhere like this running. A shiver broke her thoughts. She'd wandered into the shade of one of the great stone walls. High above her head was a small opening in which a seagull was sitting looking down at her. 'Don't you dare,' she said. The gull took off, squawking, and she shivered again. It wasn't cold, more a feeling of being cold than actual cold. She leant against the stone. 'Constable?' she called.

Colin appeared around the corner. 'You called, mi'lady?'

'Yeah, very funny. What d'you make of this?'

What?'

'This stone. Touch it. Does it feel warm to you?'

Colin leant across. 'Maybe. Perhaps the sun's just moved off it.'

'No, it's going the other way, and feel the one next to it. I'd swear that's colder.'

Colin shrugged. 'So?'

'Oh, I dunno. Perhaps I've been around Kirby too much. Keep looking.'

Shirley touched the stone again and the others around it before walking back around the front of the castle and through the main entrance. Inside, the left-hand tower was cool and damp, moss covering much of the walls that loomed above her. Other plants were growing out of gaps between the stones and pigeons, and crows flitted from roost to roost. All as you would expect from an ancient, ruined castle. She crossed to the other tower, which was much the same with its precarious-looking point of stonework jutting above the rest. By now her eyesight had adjusted to the relative darkness of the interior and she could admire the handiwork of the masons in the walls that were still standing, despite all those hundreds of years, the castle's exposed position and everything the North Sea could throw at it. In the far corner, something caught her eye. 'Colin,' she shouted.

'Where are you?'

She turned to the tower's entrance. 'In here.'

'Where's here?'

Shirley tutted. 'The right-hand tower as you look at it from the entrance.'

'Gotcha,' Colin said as he appeared.

'There,' Shirley said, pointing to the wall. 'Tell me I'm not imagining that?'

'What?'

'That,' she said, slapping him on the arm and then holding both her own arms in front of her to take in a section of wall about three feet wide. She moved them up and down. 'See, the stones, no moss or plants or anything. Like it's been cleaned.'

'Oh yes. I can see it now. My eyes have adjusted. So what?'

'What do you mean, so what? It's not right, is it?'

Colin shrugged.

'Some help you are. This is proper detectoring, this is.' Shirley took out her phone and snapped a couple of pictures. Putting the phone back in her pocket she reached out and touched one of the stones, then grabbed Colin's left hand and held it there.

'Ooh, he said.

'Yes, ooh indeed. Well?'

'I can feel something, like a vibration.' He put his ear against the stone. 'Or more like a rhythmical beating, like... like horses?'

'Exactly!'

'It's faint, going away.' He leant back and turned to Shirley. 'Hey, you haven't got an iPod on or something, have you? You know, playing let's have some fun with the country plod?'

Shirley slapped his arm in response.

'Stop doing that, will you.' He smiled. 'That could constitute bullying, you know.'

Shirley slapped him again and pointed to the stone. 'No, it can't, we're the same rank. Anyway, don't try and tell me that's normal or perhaps the vibration from the waves.'

'Could be the waves, I suppose…'

That earned him yet another slap. 'I said, don't tell me that.'

Colin rubbed his arm. 'It's not the waves.'

'Thank you.' She pushed him towards the entrance. 'Come on now, let's go and have that cup of tea with your Auntie Pauline.'

Colin grinned. 'And cake.'

'Sorry?'

'She always has cake.'

'Unusual, pet?'

'Yes, Auntie. Anything out of the ordinary.'

Pauline pushed the plate of cake towards Shirley, frowning as she thought. 'Go on, pet, it needs to be eaten.'

Shirley helped herself again to the irresistible Victoria sponge. 'Thanks. You know, anything that just doesn't feel right.'

Pauline scratched her head and then straightened her apron in her lap. 'Anything?'

'Honestly, anything.'

Pauline glanced at the floor. 'Well, you're going to think me a strange old bizzum. No, I couldn't.'

'Please, Pauline.'

Pauline glanced at Colin and then held Shirley's gaze. 'It's that castle,' she said. 'It's always been like an old friend, you know. There all me life. You're going to think I'm daft, I even talk to it sometimes, tells it things. Recently though, in the evenings when I'm tending me garden, it's… it's… like it's looking at me funny. Not the same. Sends a shiver down me spine, it does.'

'Sorry about that,' Colin said when they were back in the car.

'What?'

'Auntie Pauline and that stuff about the castle. I think she spends a bit too much time on her own. Mam's tried to get her to move nearer to her but she won't leave the village.'

Shirley shook her head and raised a hand. Colin flinched. 'Talk like that and I'll slap you again.'

'You don't believe all that, castle looking at her strange and what not, d'you?'

Shirley laughed. 'A few days ago, maybe not. Listen, the Inspector wouldn't dismiss it. He never ignores people's feelings on things. Reckons there's things that can't be put into words and when we try, it comes out all funny. But that doesn't mean you shouldn't take it seriously. Your Auntie Pauline's lived there all her life. If anyone's going to have a feel for the place, it's her. Maybe it's her subconscious knows something's not quite the same.' She shrugged. 'Something like that anyway.'

'I stand corrected, ma'am.'

'Good.' She smiled. 'And the cake was great.'

'Always is.'

SEVENTEEN

....

Kirby parked his car and wandered around the corner into Clayton Road. He'd decided he needed a little fortifying before he could go through another few rounds with Harold. Walking along, he studied the mix of trendy shops either side of the road. In the news recently there had been a number of pieces about "gentrification" of places like Jesmond, and he guessed this is what they meant. Young city types moving in and doing up the old housing. What they wanted from their local high street was different to those who had lived here all their lives. These new young people had money. They didn't want your basic carrots-and-King-Edwards green grocer and mince-and-pork-chops butcher. They wanted an Italian deli, a specialist grocer which had all those fancy ingredients you saw on those Saturday morning cookery programmes and a butcher who could supply them with pheasant, quail and Barbary duck. Kirby crossed the road between a large Mercedes and a white soft-top BMW and headed towards the coffee shop opposite. Gold lettering on the window announced it was "Relax".

Inside, at the window end, were leather sofas and chairs that were so low they looked a bugger to get out of for anyone over the age of forty. Towards the back were what appeared to be a random, eclectic mix of old tables and chairs that he knew would have been carefully chosen. On the walls were the quaint pictures of "old Jesmond" to remind those who remembered them that they too were old. On one wall was a bookshelf with a notice, "Bookswap Corner - feel free to take and then why not bring one of yours?" Behind the counter was a large chalkboard, 'Jan and Jon welcome you. Why not try this week's special blend? Ask about our delicious gluten-free range.'

On one side, sitting in the sofas, were two groups of thirty-something mums with babies and toddlers. Parked beside them was a range of aspirational buggies that looked more like child-sized, four-wheel-drive vehicles. On the other side, keeping a respectful distance, were three younger women, girls with young children. He guessed by the foreign accents they were au pairs. At the back were three sets of older Jesmondians, one or two giving their large bowls of latte and cappuccino suspicious looks. He knew how they felt; finish all that and at their age you'd be going to the toilet all morning

'So what'll it be?'

Kirby looked up at the array of coffees on offer. 'Er, regular latte, please.'

'Excellent.'

'No wait, can you make that a flat white?' he said as if he wasn't sure such a thing existed. His mother, who seemed to have studied these things, had told him that he would prefer a flat white as there tended to be less of it. She knew that all the hot milk in a latte left him feeling slightly nauseous. 'Maybe you're becoming lactose-intolerant,' she'd said as if she'd been studying that as well. As far as Kirby was concerned, people only became intolerant to something after they'd read somewhere that you could become intolerant to it.

'Cool, coming up. Regular or special?'

'Sorry?'

The young woman, he presumed Jan, smiled. 'Our regular blend or this week's special?'

'Er regular.'

'Milk?'

He'd presumed a flat white came with milk. 'Er, yes.'

Her smile suggested that for Jan, who looked in her twenties, this wasn't the first time she'd had such a conversation with an older person. 'Whole, semi-skimmed or soya?'

'Whole, no semi, please.' His mum had also told him he should switch to buying "semi" some time ago, telling him it would be better for him.

As Jan disappeared behind a cloud of steam, Kirby wondered just when ordering a cup of coffee had become so complicated.

'Anything to eat with that?'

'No thank you.' He did quite fancy something to eat, only he didn't want to waste the rest of the morning going through what he suspected might be another protracted question-and-answer session around gluten and other potential dietary oddities.

Kirby took the carefully selected non-matching cup and saucer and headed towards the older folk on the grounds that if you wanted to hear the ins and outs of what was going on in the area, they were the ones who would know. Some of the women would have had sixty or more years practice in minding other people's business, all simple neighbourly concern, of course. Judging by the fine array of grey cardigans, Edna would have fitted right in.

Kirby chose a table near one couple, who were either sitting in companionable silence or had just run out of things to say after many years together. The woman was staring with some concern at the considerable amount of froth in the bottom of her cup. She had been brought up in a generation who cleared their plates, who abhorred waste. Yet no matter how much she tipped the cup, the foam refused to leave it. In the end, she gave up, hiding it under a napkin in case anyone thought she was being less than thrifty.

Kirby sipped at his flat white. Mum was right, it was stronger and with less milk than a latte, although like most trendy coffee shops, it could have been served a little hotter in his opinion. He smiled to himself, feeling he could now do the whole trendy-coffee-shop thing with added confidence. 'Flat white, please,' he practised. 'Sorry, oh yes semi, thank you. What? Gluten-free? Thank you, I'll take two in that case.'

'Did you say something, pet?' the lady in grey next to him asked. He hadn't realised he'd been practising out loud.

'Sorry, not really.'

'Oh,' the lady said, sounding a little disappointed.

Kirby had made contact. 'Tell me, if you don't mind me asking, have you lived around here long?'

The woman smiled. 'No I don't mind, pet, and the answer's all me life. I remember when there was proper shops on this road. When peas was peas and not petit pois. This used to be a proper cobblers, you know.'

Kirby nodded in sympathy. 'What about the corner shop on Sanderson's Road, d'you know it?'

The lady shuffled her seat around as if warming to the idea of a bit of conversation. The man who Kirby presumed was her husband didn't move and kept his gaze on one of the pictures as if finding things in it others couldn't see. 'Harold's?' Oh yes, I know Harold's. Been there for as long as I can remember. Me mam used to take me in there when I was a bairn. It was just the same. I guess it was Harold's dad back then, although from what I can remember, Harold looks just like him. The shop hasn't changed much either.'

'Been there a long time then?'

The lady glanced at the man next to her and tutted before carrying on. 'I'll say so. Me mam said it was there when she was a nipper. That's staying power, that is. These days they're here and gone before you know it. One minute it's a deli and the next it's a fancy hairdressers where they want forty quid for a set. I ask you, forty quid! They must think we're made of money. An' us on our pensions an' all. Well…'

'Harold's?' Kirby said, trying to take hold of the conversation again while she drew breath.

'Sorry, pet. Oh aye, Harold's. They should do one of those whatsit programmes on them. You know, where they dig into your past and find your great, great grandad was a murderer and the like.'

'Who Do You Think You Are?'

'Pardon.'

'The TV programme.'

The woman gave a little laugh. 'Aye, that's it. Been there for generations, they have.'

That's how it worked Kirby thought. People looked and saw what they expected to see, not what was actually there. You came across it all the time as a copper. 'Yes, thank you.'

The old lady focused on his jacket. Kirby glanced down and brushed off a stubborn croissant flake.

'You from the university as well, pet? Interested in local history?'

Kirby felt his detecting antennae twitch. 'No, why?'

'Oh it's just that there was a young fella in here the other day asking about Harold's. I was a bit suspicious at first, wondered if he was trying to buy it. Y'know, one of them there property developers you see on the telly. Then he said he was from the university, part of his studies. Tall he was, with long hair, which made sense. Too old for it though, I guess it's being with all them students.'

'And what about Mystique?' Kirby said, pointing with his spoon across the road.

The lady expressed her thoughts on Mystique with a shudder and a scowl. 'Been there a while, I'll give them that.' She shook her head. 'I never goes in. A load of old tat, if you asks me. I've thrown out better stuff than they've got, and you should see the prices they're charging for it. The young 'uns seem to like it mind.'

Kirby drained his cup. 'Well, nice to meet you and thanks, I was interested that's all.'

'No trouble, pet,' she frowned at her husband. 'Nice to have someone to talk to.'

Leaving Relax, Kirby glanced across at Mystique. Jane, or was it Titania, was arranging something in the window. She looked across and, on seeing him, stood upright, half raising a hand before stopping as if wondering whether it was wise to wave to a policeman. Kirby nodded in her direction before heading off to Harold's.

EIGHTEEN

....

The shop bell tinkled its welcome as Kirby entered the 1960s' world that was Harold's shop. Perhaps that was its secret. For those who had lived in the sixties, it was a place of nostalgia, and for those born later, it was like some pilgrimage to a mythical time.

'Hello, Jonah,' came a disembodied voice from somewhere deep in the bowels of the shop.

'Harold.'

'Well?'

Kirby jumped, the voice was now behind him. 'Don't do that. Not to a copper anyway.'

Harold stepped around and grinned. 'Good, eh?'

'Impressive,' Kirby said, now feeling sorry for the local youth, a group he rarely felt sorry for, who no doubt visited Harold's shop with deep trepidation. He could imagine the conversation. 'Go round to Harold's, pet, we've run out of soap'. 'Er sorry, Mum, but I really must tidy my room.' Score one to the mums of this world.

'Jonah?'

'Sorry, Harold. Miles away. Anyway, we've found Sarah.'

'Is she OK?'

'Seems to be. No physical harm anyway. I've left her at the Freeman and her Dad's with her now.'

Harold nodded. 'Where d'you find her?'

'Dunstanburgh.'

'Dunstanburgh?'

'Yes.'

'Dunstanburgh.'

'Please, Harold, not you as well.'

'Sorry?'

Kirby shook his head. 'Never mind. I take it that has some significance for you.'

'Might do.'

Kirby picked up the out-of-date tin of peas again and held it, bottom pointing towards Harold. 'Harold! I haven't got time for this.'

Tutting at the threat, Harold scratched the back of his head. 'Come through the back.'

Kirby followed Harold down a dimly-lit aisle, stepping over a box full of tins of "Cats First Choice". 'Someone could fall over that.'

'You health and safety now?'

Kirby grunted, thankful he wasn't, as he thought of how their, no doubt, long list of infringements might go down with Harold.

Kirby sat at the old pine table. Harold reached for a bottle of Camp, peeling it off the shelf where dribbles had stuck it down, and waved at the inspector. 'Coffee?'

'Just had one thanks,' he said, grateful that he had.

'You alright? You're looking a bit peeky.'

'Right as rain,' Kirby said, resting an elbow on the table and his head in his hand. 'Didn't sleep too good.'

Harold huffed. 'I always sleep like a log.'

'Never would have guessed.'

Harold sat opposite Kirby, stirring in five spoons of sugar and watching the bubbles swirl. 'Did Sarah say anything?'

'Not much that made sense. She talked about some men, big men, she said, with big beards and beer. She didn't say they'd taken her or anything. Oh, she also mentioned smoke hurting her eyes.'

Harold nodded. 'You know what I told you about old magic in the world and that in some places the divide between this world and the old world is thin?'

'Yes.'

'Well, Northumberland is sort of on a fault line for these things.'

'And let me guess, Dunstanburgh Castle is bang on that fault line?'

'Yes,' Harold said, levering the top off a battered old biscuit tin with a picture of Blackpool tower on it. 'However, there's more to it than that.'

Kirby waved the tin away. He wasn't sure about accepting anything from Harold where he couldn't check its sell-by date. 'Why am I not surprised? Go on.'

Harold dunked a digestive. 'Well you know the current castle?' he said, pointing his spoon at Kirby.

'Norman, fourteenth-century. Built by the Earl of Lancaster, then extended by John of Gaunt.'

Harold raised his eyebrows in appreciation. 'Yes, well done.'

Kirby had a sudden vision of being back at school and his history teacher walking between the rows of desks with the ruler of retribution in his hands.

Harold tutted.

Kirby frowned. 'What? I wasn't supposed to get that right? Coppers are allowed to have had an education, you know.'

'No, my digestive's broken off in my coffee,' Harold said, fishing around in his mug with a spoon, dredging up soggy biscuit. 'I hate it when that happens. You get all the sludgy bits in the bottom.'

'Make a fresh cup.'

Harold gave Kirby the sort of look he reserved for junior officers when they moaned about hand-writing statements. He then scowled into the bottom of his mug.

'Can we get back to the castle? Some of us have work to do.'

Harold put down his mug with a sigh. 'Well, what people forget is that there was a much earlier Iron Age settlement there. In fact, it had been an important place from the time the first men came to this land.'

Kirby resisted the urge to put up his hand. 'Because of its defensive qualities?'

'No, because of its magical qualities.'

'Why do I wish I hadn't asked? So let me guess. Sarah wasn't here, was she, as in the twenty-first century Dunstanburgh?'

'No.'

'So why did they send her back?'

Harold shrugged. 'Good question. My guess would be that Marianne wanted to waken something within her. She's Marianne's daughter although I doubt Sarah knows much about her. From what you say, her father wouldn't have been too forthcoming and he may also not have known quite who or what Marianne was.'

Kirby half reached for a biscuit, then remembered where he was. 'So what, this was all for some little mother-daughter chat? A chance to get reacquainted and all that?'

'That as well,' Harold said. 'It may have been some sort of test to see if Sarah has what it takes.'

'To act as the magical conduit you mentioned? So how do we know if she has?'

Harold tapped his teaspoon in a little puddle of spilt coffee on the table as he thought. 'We won't until they try to use her. She didn't say anything?'

Kirby shook his head. 'She didn't even mention Marianne.'

'No, she might not even remember. Or of course she could be keeping it from you.'

Kirby frowned. 'I'm pretty good at knowing if people are lying to me.'

Harold smiled. 'With all respect, Jonah, these are not just any people. Think of it not so much as lying, more keeping it from you by keeping it from themselves.'

Kirby tapped a finger on the table. 'Listen, one thing's still bugging me. You reckon Marianne had Sarah taken, right, to wherever it was?

Harold nodded. 'Yeah.'

'So what is it with the shoes? I mean why leave them there at the side of the road all neat and tidy?'

Harold scratched at his ear and sucked in a breath. 'Well, I think the shoes were what would identify Sarah to the gang of goblins. Maybe there was something on them so that they could sniff them out, literally. Good sense of smell, your goblin.'

'Fine, but as I said, why leave them?'

Harold slurped the last of his coffee then frowned as he got to the bottom. He pointed the mug at Kirby with a surprised, "eureka moment" look on his face. 'Calling card.'

'What?'

'That's it.' Harold smiled. 'I reckon Marianne made sure Susie would find them and then report Sarah had gone missing. One way or another that would lead to Edna and me finding out.'

'So?'

'Remember what I said about balance?'

'Yes?'

Harold swept a hand dramatically over the table, almost knocking over the biscuit tin. 'Well that's one reason Edna and I like to keep a low profile. The more we start poking around in magic, the more it starts upsetting that balance.'

'Great.'

'Also, she wants us to know she's back and up to something.'

Kirby shook his head. 'Why? No... don't tell me, balance?'

Harold smiled like a teacher who's just seen the penny drop in a dim pupil.

'Hmm,' Kirby said, frowning at Harold and getting up. 'Where's your toilet, Harold? Too much coffee.'

'Er, through there and on the left,' Harold said, pointing to a door at the back of the room.

The other side of the door, Kirby noticed a long leather coat hanging up. Well that explained the "Harold Longcoat" bit. On closer inspection, he noticed a tear on one side that had been crudely stitched. The sleeves looked like later additions; the leather didn't match and there were other repairs and patches. It had a sheen that suggested regular oiling. It also had a unique smell and not just of oil. It was like a medieval cathedral, a smell that spoke of being ancient, yet not in the sense of decay, more of permanence. It was a coat that demanded some attention from his coppering brain, then he remembered why he was here and headed off to the toilet.

On the way back, with his mind now able to concentrate better, the bulk of the coat struck him as odd. It didn't hang right. He took hold of one shoulder and tested the weight, heavy. A mystery. So he did what police inspectors do and inspected it. Inside, there were a number of pockets of varying sizes. Poking out of one was the top of a small crossbow and in another pocket were four bolts in their own neat little pouch. Pulling open the other side, he discovered three knives. Taking one out, he surmised that they were throwing knives. He knew he should be shocked by the thought of a man walking around Jesmond with enough weaponry on him to start a small war. Like some vigilante pensioner. The weird thing was he'd only been around Harold for a day or so and already this didn't surprise him or worry him as much as he thought it should. Perhaps it was what he'd seen and the revelations of the past few days together with all the talk of goblins and magic. They'd numbed his brain, played with his judgement of what should be deemed normal to the point where medieval weaponry was all part of the picture.

His phone rang, almost causing him to drop the knife. In the two-second juggle to regain control of it, he wondered which would be worse, missing fingers or missing toes.

'That you, Inspector?'

'You were expecting someone else, Sergeant?' he said with bite, replacing the knife and letting his heartbeat settle down.

The Desk Sergeant had known Kirby for years so wasn't fazed by having his question answered by another, terse, question. 'You still in Jesmond, sir?'

'Yes, Sergeant.'

'Well, sir, a burnt body has been found in the Dene.'

Kirby forgot about the knife. His heart rate was up again. 'A body?'

'Ah, sorry, should have said. Not a human body, sir. The Constable reckons more like a monkey.'

Kirby let out the breath he hadn't been aware he was holding. 'And he would know?'

'Well, sir, at least he reckons it's not human. He's saying monkey on account of it having long arms and short legs. However, forensics are on their way just to make sure.'

'Thank you, Sergeant. I'll be there in a few minutes. Oh, and see if Constable Barker can join us there, will you?'

'Sir.'

Kirby opened the door into Harold's back room with the words 'at least reckons it's not human' still in his head. His face fell into an ironic smile. This was too much of a coincidence and he didn't believe in those anyway. The smile was replaced by a frown. After his previous conversations with Harold he suspected this might provide a bit of a challenge for forensics.

Kirby entered the back room where Harold was putting his coffee mug in the sink. 'Come on, Harold, you can come with me.'

'Where are we going?'

'The Dene. They've found a burnt body. The Constable on the scene says it's a monkey.'

'Who burns a monkey? And in the Dene at that?'

'Quite.'

Harold's eyes opened a little wider. 'Oh I see. I'll get me coat.'

'And Harold.'

'Yes?'

'Leave the crossbow behind please. Remember I'm supposed to be the law.'

Harold stared at Kirby for a second then harrumphed as he opened the door to get his coat.

'And the throwing knives,' Kirby called after him.

'Bloody coppers, poking their noses into things,' was muttered from behind the old door. Harold emerged shrugging an arm into the stiff leather coat and with a leather hat on his head.

NINETEEN

....

Approaching the Dene, Kirby's phone rang again.

'Sir, it's Shirley. I'm on my way.'

'We'll wait at the top, near the steps.'

Waiting on the footpath, leaning on the railings Kirby had a long look at Harold and that coat of his. It shrieked old. And then there was the hat that didn't. It was newer, more Australian bush hat. Kirby imagined it with the corks hanging from it and smiled.

'What?'

'So, Harold, the coat?'

'The coat was my father's,' Harold said as if that was the only explanation needed.

Kirby pointed to Harold's head. 'And the hat?'

'The hat was from the John Lewis sale last summer.'

Kirby was trying to suppress a laugh when, to his relief, Shirley appeared. 'How was Dunstanburgh?'

'Nice, sir,' Shirley said, glancing towards Harold.

'Go on, Constable.'

'Sir.' Shirley described the castle and the stones inside the tower.

At the mention of the vibration, Harold sucked in a breath. 'Should have guessed,' he said.

'A gateway by any chance?' Kirby asked.

Harold nodded.

'Anything else, Constable?'

Shirley told them of the conversation with Auntie Pauline. 'Sounds kind of daft, sir. But after everything I've heard recently…'

'Yes, understandable,' Kirby said. He looked at Harold. 'Well?'

Harold's only answer was, 'Hmm…'

Kirby looked towards Shirley and shrugged.

'So what's going on here, sir?' she said. 'Someone mentioned a burnt body?' She glanced at Harold with a "should he be here?" look.

'A body yes, Constable. Apparently not human though'

Shirley hesitated with another glance at Harold. 'Not human?'

'No, the Constable who's on scene is saying he thinks perhaps monkey.'

This time her look towards Harold ended in a frown that said. 'Ah, I see.'

'Exactly, Constable,' Kirby said. 'So I thought if there were two of us we could each vouch for the other's sanity.'

Shirley nodded. 'Nice coat,' she said to Harold as they set off.

'Thanks,' Harold said.

'Not sure about the hat though.'

Kirby grinned.

Talk of other worlds, Kirby thought, as they descended the steps and path down into the wooded valley that divided Jesmond from Heaton. With its steep sides that blocked out the noise of the city all around them, it had always seemed other-worldly to him. Even if it was a sanitised Victorian view of what that might be. Down here you could hear birdsong rather than the revving of engines, and the tranquil trickle of the Ouse burn as it made its way down to meet the Tyne on the Quayside. They passed the petting zoo, which was doing a good trade, it being the summer holidays. Although personally he'd never seen the attraction. For one thing he didn't trust goats; shifty-looking things. Sheep were alright, but if goats were people he was sure they'd be cocky and up to no good. Walking along beside the burn and under the Armstrong bridge, Kirby could see a police officer standing in front of an area cordoned off with yellow tape. It was next to what was left of St Mary's Chapel.

Harold shuddered.

Shirley glanced at him. 'Something wrong?'

Harold studied the old ruin. 'They reckon this was the first church in Newcastle, you know.'

'Really?' Shirley said.

'Yes, well they built it on top of something much older, thinking their god would keep it subdued and they could deny it was there.'

Kirby, who was a step ahead at this point, dropped back. 'And?'

'I've told you, old magic persists.'

'So you say,' Kirby said, as Shirley lifted the tape, letting herself and Kirby through and into the crime scene. They left Harold scowling at a pile of stones.

Kirby mused that on another day it might have been described as a beautiful spot, a small glade next to an ancient chapel, surrounded by tall trees, shaded by their leafy canopy. For those Victorians, somewhere to base romantic poetry on perhaps.

'Nice place,' he said.

'Apart from that,' Shirley said, pointing to a burnt corpse.

'Finished, Hugh?' Kirby asked the man in a white paper suit who was standing, rubber glove in one hand and scratching his head, while another man in a similar suit finished taking pictures.

'Yes,' he said, removing the other soot-blackened rubber glove. He then pulled both gloves inside out and put one inside the other before stuffing them in a bag.

'And?'

'Last night.'

'And?' Kirby wondered what it was about forensics that they needed constant prompting for information, as if they had a finite allocation of words and therefore were reluctant to waste them.

'Ashes are cold.'

Kirby waited

Hugh stared at the body. 'Monkey?'

'Are you asking or telling?'

Hugh focused on the crime scene again. 'Must be.' The pathologist checked the cleanliness of his hand and then scratched his head again. 'Couldn't tell you what sort though. You could get someone out from the Hancock Museum or the university, they might know.'

'Mind if we have look before you bag it up?'

'Be my guest,' Hugh said, before wandering over to join his colleague, who started showing him the photographs he'd taken.

Kirby and Shirley squatted on their haunches, inspecting the burnt circle of grass in the middle of which were the remains, which were equally charred. A small body, human-ish.

'What d'you reckon, Constable?'

Shirley took a breath. 'Well, thankfully not human.'

Kirby nodded.

'Could be a monkey, sir,' Shirley added, trying to sound hopeful.

Behind them was the rustling of tape. 'Sorry, sir, you can't go in there.'

'It's all right, Constable, he's with me' Kirby said, without getting up. As he heard the tread of approaching feet he turned to Harold. 'Well?'

'Hmm, Jonah.' Harold said.

'That'll be enough, Constable.' Kirby said without looking back as he caught the snigger after Harold used his first name. He glanced at Shirley who had her eyes fixed on the remains.

'Sir,' the Constable replied.

Harold took out what looked like a large hunting knife and began poking the bones with it.

'I thought I said to leave those behind.'

'You said the throwing knives.'

Shirley interrupted her study of the body to give Kirby a wide-eyed look.

'Don't ask, Constable.' He shook his head and glanced across at Harold. 'We'll have words later about that.' He pointed at the grizzly scene in front of them. 'However, for now what do you reckon to this?'

'I reckon goblin,' Harold said, just loud enough for Kirby and Shirley to hear. He had another poke with the knife.

'Put it away, Harold,' Kirby whispered. 'This is Jesmond, not the Serengeti. Coppers around here tend to have a natural aversion to something that looks like it could do serious damage to someone else.'

Harold grunted, then complied. The knife disappeared into a pocket in the voluminous coat that Kirby had failed to find back in the shop. 'I still reckon goblin.'

'Goblin,' Kirby said, as if by saying it out loud it wouldn't sound quite as bad as thinking it. It did.

'Goblin,' Shirley said, biting her lip, the look on her face echoing his thoughts. 'I'm now vouching for your sanity, sir.'

Kirby nodded. 'Thank you, Constable, much appreciated. And likewise by the way. Go on, Harold.'

'It happens.'

'What happens?'

'Well your average goblin is not the brightest thing on two short, stumpy legs. So they tend to keep to their own little gang. They feel safer that way, can't handle too much information alone, at one time, as it were. Or too many other goblins for that matter.'

'So?'

'So each gang has its own patch and its own specialisation.'

Kirby puffed out his cheeks. 'What, like kidnapping?'

Harold ignored the question. 'It's all territorial. A bit like those ice-cream wars, you know.'

'What, the goblins sell ice cream?' Shirley burst out before slapping a hand over her mouth.

Harold gave her a stern look.

'OK, so they kill each other?' Kirby said.

'As I said, it happens. And burning them like this is a very visible warning to other gangs.'

'Wonderful,' Kirby said as he stood up followed by Shirley. 'Well this is our patch and I'm not having it, even if they are goblins.'

Harold pushed himself off his knees with a grunt. 'They'll want the body.'

'Who will?'

'The family.'

Kirby glanced at Shirley, who shrugged, then back over his shoulder at the PC who was now half hidden by a tree from which a thread of cigarette smoke was drifting. Somehow he'd never thought about goblins having families. However, in truth, he'd never really thought about goblins much. Then again, why wouldn't they have families and of course that family would want to take care of its own. He sighed and shook his head as the possible ramifications spread out like a google street map on your phone. 'Forensics'll have to bag it up and take it away.'

'Sorry, sir,' Shirley said. 'D'you think that's such a good idea?'

'I don't have a choice,' Kirby said. He thumbed back over his shoulder. 'It's been reported.'

'I could have a word, sir,' Shirley said. 'Me and Duncs go all the way back to college.'

Kirby nodded. 'There's still the pathologist.'

Harold tutted.

'Just a minute, how do you know whose family it belongs to?'

'Don't have to. There are...' Harold paused, 'places.'

Kirby tried his silent technique, although it seemed Harold was learning and this time didn't elaborate. He decided not to push it.

Harold kicked at some burnt pieces of wood. 'You can't persuade them to forget it?'

Kirby laughed, then coughed to cover it. 'What d'you think? Everything these days is in triplicate.'

'Triplicate,' Harold repeated. 'So how are they going to explain it?'

'He's got a point, sir,' Shirley said.

'Ah… yes.' Kirby blew out a long breath and wandered out of the crime scene with Harold and Shirley following. 'Hugh,' he called to the pathologist, who had now removed the paper suit and was packing up his kit. Kirby did his best to adopt a casual-sounding tone. 'A word please.'

The pathologist picked up his bag and joined them. 'You alright, Jonah? You sound a bit strained.'

'You don't say,' Shirley muttered.

'Sorry?'

'I'm fine,' Kirby said, scowling at Shirley, who had taken a sudden interest in her shoes. 'Hugh, this is Harold and the sometimes competent Constable Barker.' Harold nodded. Hugh gave Harold the sort of look that Kirby normally saw when the pathologist was holding a scalpel.

'So what next?' Kirby said.

'Well, I've got a contact in the zoology department at the university; thought I'd let him have a look.'

'Oh that's… that's…'

'Interesting?' Shirley finished for him.

'Yes, quite. Interesting, that's the word. Thank you, Constable.'

'Oh, we wouldn't want you to waste your valuable time,' Shirley said, nudging Kirby with her elbow, adding, 'would we, sir?'

'No, of course not. No, no, not at all.'

Hugh's eyes narrowed with suspicion. 'No, it's no bother.'

Kirby glanced at Shirley, who was staring back at him. He could almost sense her desperate attempts at telepathy, *"do something"*. 'Erm, do you think perhaps you could hold back on that for now. After all, it's not that important. I mean it's only a monkey. It'll just make paperwork.'

One of Hugh's eyes now opened wide. 'Why?'

Kirby read the look on the pathologist's face. It was the one he used himself when he knew someone was hiding something.'

'Can't say right now,' Kirby said, which at least wasn't a lie. He tapped the side of his nose with a finger to emphasise the point.

The pathologist took Kirby by the arm. He leaned in close. 'Can we have a word,' he said, glancing at Harold, 'in private?' He then led Kirby a few yards away from Harold and Shirley who were now taking a great deal of interest in one of the trees.

Still holding on to Kirby's arm, he whispered, 'What's going on here, Jonah? And just who is the guy dressed like he's in a Clint Eastwood movie?'

Kirby tried a smile. 'Oh you mean Harold?'

Hugh didn't smile back. 'Yes, him.'

Kirby pursed his lips and nodded slowly several times while trying to come up with a plausible answer.

'Er, he's a consultant. Er… yes an expert.'

'An expert in what?' Hugh asked, looking at Harold, his eyes running down the patched and crudely-mended leather coat before settling on the grey cardigan underneath with its mismatched buttons.

'It's, er, very delicate.' Then seeing the pathologist's arched and raised eyebrow, Kirby tapped a finger on the side of his nose again and added, 'very, hush, hush.'

'Hush, hush?' the pathologist repeated. Kirby nodded. 'Not a phrase you tend to hear a lot in real life, Jonah. Or have we stepped back into a 1960s' spy thriller?'

Kirby took a deep breath; this wasn't going well. He switched to a look of innocent pleading. 'Trust me,' he tried.

'And, Harold?' Hugh said.

'Yes, and Harold. I'll vouch for him.'

Hugh studied Kirby for a second or two. 'Alright, Jonah, you win,' he paused before adding, 'for now.' The man had been around policemen for far too long.

'They're still taking the body away?' Harold said when Kirby returned to him and Shirley after the pathologist had left.

'Obviously.'

'Do I think that's a good idea?'

Kirby stared back at Harold. He was beginning to think bringing a shopkeeper, guardian or whatever he was along had not been one of his better moves. 'No, of course I don't. However, we've no choice.' He glanced at Shirley for support. She nodded. 'What do you want me to do?

Wait till they bag the body then sling it over my shoulder and say "that's alright guys, I'm sure we don't need to trouble you with this one"?'

Harold tutted. 'No, I suppose not.' He sucked his teeth as he thought. 'Perhaps I could, I dunno, bring in someone else since I'm your expert? Like from another agency?'

Kirby shook his head as he watched the body, now in a black bag, being carried away. 'You've been watching too much Sky Atlantic. And who did you have in mind, Edna?' They both looked at Shirley, who was trying not to laugh. 'I struggled convincing him of you. I think Edna might be stretching it a bit. What d'you think?'

'Hmm, perhaps not.' Harold leaned closer to Kirby. 'Edna likes to keep a low profile,' he added, as if that was the only possible reason not involve her.

'Ah, yes, silly me.'

'Alright, alright,' Harold said, watching the constable gather up the crime scene tape. 'It was only an idea.'

Kirby rubbed his temples and sighed. 'Come on,' he said, and followed the stretcher team and the pathologist back to the road.

'He's right though, sir,' Shirley said as they were climbing the steps out of the Dene. 'If the university boys poke around at that body they'll be heralding some great scientific breakthrough. You know like, "missing link found in Jesmond". Mind you, that wouldn't surprise many…'

'Yes thank you, Constable. I get the picture.'

'Sorry, sir. We have to do something though, don't we?'

'I know, I know.'

'So what?' Harold asked.

Kirby paused and looked from one to the other. 'I'm not sure. I think I'm going to have to have a long talk with Hugh and it's going to cost me a few beers.'

Shirley sucked in a breath through her teeth in appreciation of what that might mean.

'Care to join us, Constable?'

'Er, thanks for the invitation, sir. I think I'm washing my hair this evening.'

'Very wise, Constable. Very wise.'

TWENTY

....

Marianne had watched her daughter climb into the police car outside the little cottage in Craster. No one had spotted Marianne of course. She'd then seen her daughter leave the station in Alnwick with that too-clever-by-half police inspector; the one who was taking the ramblings of the interfering Harold Longcoat seriously. She frowned. That wasn't supposed to happen. She'd wanted Harold and that interfering old bag Edna to know she was around, but working with a policeman who was actually taking them seriously? There was something about him, she felt. it. He'd need to be watched. She sniffed, so what? There wasn't much they could do.

They'd brought Sarah to the Freeman Hospital as she'd expected. She smiled. Modern medicine was clever, new magic. However, she practised old magic and no amount of scanning, probing and analysing was going to help understand that. The inspector had left and finally so had John.

As a youngster, John had been a rebel, wild and unpredictable, and she'd loved that in him. She had fed it, nurtured it. Then when Sarah came along, the world, this world rather than her world had taken over. The need for a house, a mortgage, a steady income, and he'd become like the rest of them. For a while she'd tried to adjust, thinking that perhaps success and money could replace the anarchic adventure that had been their lives before. She had helped him climb the greasy pole. However, all the new cars, fancy kitchens and latest white goods were no replacement for the life they'd had and she still craved. That was the trouble with magic, it was all or nothing and there was little place for it in this world. So if they didn't need it, she'd take it and find a use for it in her world.

Marianne walked through the sliding doors and smiled at the receptionist, who smiled back.

'Can I help you?' the woman asked.

'I'm looking for Sarah Cooper; she was brought in a few hours ago.'

'And you are?'

Marianne focused on the woman and smiled again.

'Of course, let me see.' The woman consulted the screen in front of her. 'Ah, yes, ward 10. Along the corridor, take the first stairs on the right and then just follow the signs.'

'Thank you.'

The woman looked up again. 'Can I help you?'

'No, It's alright, I know where I'm going.'

Marianne walked along the corridor and up the stairs. She followed the signs for ward 10, passing patients, nurses and doctors who stepped out of her way. At the ward reception, a nurse looked up, raised her hand as if about to say something before turning back to the nurse next to her and continuing their conversation. Sarah was in a private room, and outside was a woman police officer. Marianne smiled at her. The WPC stood and opened the door before sitting back down and flicking over the page of the magazine she was reading.

Sarah turned as she walked in. 'Hello, Mother.'

'Hello, dear, they treating you well?'

'This is boring, Mother. They're keeping me in, they say, for checks.' She smiled. 'So if I'm a good girl I might get to leave in the morning.'

'Oh, I think we can do better than that, don't you?' Marianne opened the door to the room. The WPC didn't look up. One of the nurses at the desk glanced at her watch, then jumped from her seat and hurried along the corridor. Marianne held the door for her.

The nurse smiled at Sarah. 'How are you feeling?' she said taking her pulse.

'Fine, I'd like to go home.'

The nurse frowned. 'Well, they want to keep you in a little while to be on the safe side.'

'She wants to go home,' Marianne repeated.

The nurse paused and put the thermometer she'd had in her hand back in its pouch next to the bed. 'I'll get a doctor,' she said.

'Where will you go?' Marianne said as the nurse left the room.

'Dad wants me to go home to him, but I want to go back to the flat.'

'I tell you what, why don't you go back to your dad's for tonight, keep him happy. You know, reassure him everything is fine. Then you can go to the flat tomorrow some time.'

'He'll still fuss.'

Marianne patted Sarah on the arm. 'Leave that to me.'

A doctor entered the room with the nurse and Marianne stood back. 'So how are we then?' he said.

'As I told the nurse, fine and I want to go home.'

'Well, I understand, but we…'

'She wants to go home,' Marianne interrupted.

The doctor glanced at the nurse, his mouth open for a second while playing with the end of the stethoscope around his neck. 'Well, I…'

'Home,' Marianne repeated.

The doctor smiled at Sarah. 'In that case, I'll sign you off.'

'Thank you, Mother,' Sarah said when the doctor and nurse had left the room and she was getting dressed.

'That's alright, dear. What are mothers for?'

Outside the room, Marianne looked down at the WPC. 'You can go now.'

'Thank you.'

'Will she get into trouble? I mean it's not her fault,' Sarah said watching the WPC walk down the corridor.

Marianne put a hand on her daughter's shoulder. 'Perhaps, dear.' She frowned. 'Although, I rather suspect that Inspector Kirby might realise something is not right even if he's not sure what.'

'And what will we do about him?'

Marianne tutted. 'For now, nothing. He's just bumbling around with that old fool Harold. And their bumbling might even be a help.' The arm around Sarah's shoulders gave her a gentle squeeze. 'Anyway, don't worry about that. You go to your Dad's and put his mind at rest.'

'Yes, Mother.'

TWENTY-ONE

....

Kirby was beginning to regret letting Hugh select the venue for their little chat. There again he didn't have much choice. He also knew that Hugh knew that, and that Hugh was therefore going to milk this for everything he could.

Hugh was a bit of a real ale nut; the sort who made drinking sound like a hobby in that they attended festivals, were members of a club, CAMRA, and could never simply go to a pub for a drink. He had bored Kirby before about the merits of real ale, Kentish hops, roasted barley and all that. Not that Kirby didn't like the odd beer himself, and he wasn't averse to drinking what Hugh regarded as a decent pint. It was more that he wanted to drink them, not study them. Also, he didn't regard an evening talking about them as being an evening well spent.

The pathologist had dragged him half way across the city to a pub that was trying hard to look like a pub rather than gastro-pub or a bar. The beers were all written up on a chalkboard with their specific gravity, whatever that is, and their alcohol content, along with a few tasting notes; deep chocolaty aromas and light spice, citrus lingering on the palate, hint of ginger, that sort of thing.

The clientele were doing their best to live up to the image as well. There were far more beards on show than the statistical average for the male population would suggest there should be. Paunches, the aficionado's equivalent of a gym junky's biceps, were displayed with pride; sometimes, but not always fully, covered by T-shirts that proclaimed their love of one brand of real ale or another. And, as if to allay any worries that they might be there just for a drink, there was much tasting of thimblefuls of ale accompanied by swilling in the mouth, nodding and appreciative words before a pint was ordered and drawn with due reverence. The glasses were held up to the light for inspection, sniffed for those floral notes, before disappearing down throats so the whole process could start again.

Kirby had let Hugh choose the ales while he paid. It seemed Hugh was intent on getting full value for the favour he knew he was going to be asked for. The beer kept coming and Kirby lost count of how many or what they were called. He remembered one called something like Cow Dunger which had been alright, and one called Sweet Maids Tipple, or at least he thought that's what Hugh had said. In his opinion, that one could have been dispatched to the toilet without having had to take a detour via his stomach and kidneys. The only other sustenance had been a packet of crisps and something described as a "meat pie".

'A proper pie that,' Hugh said, wiping the gravy from his chin.

The type of "meat" wasn't identified, and after the first bite, Kirby was quite glad. Not that it stopped his fellow aficionados for the evening scoffing them with the same enthusiasm they displayed for the beer.

By nine fifteen, Kirby's eyes were struggling to focus on his watch, and even the large clock over the bar was intent on swaying. He decided he'd had enough and made the excuse that if he didn't catch a bus back to his mum's place in Fawdon by twenty to ten, it would involve a change, not something he felt he could guarantee accomplishing. Even in his current befuddlement, he hated to think what state he might be in if he stayed much longer.

When he picked up the tab, Kirby decided he was in the wrong business. Or at least he did after the barmaid had repeated the amount three times, accompanied twice by his cry of 'How much?'

It seemed that calling it "real ale" allowed you to charge a hefty premium for it. When he moaned to Hugh, the pathologist told him the brewers were artists and the publicans who stocked the beer were the gallery owners where those who appreciated "art" could find it. And that if you wanted "little boy with tear running down face" you could drink the mass-produced rubbish in a trendy bar with all the character of a shopping centre.

Kirby had voiced the opinion that he'd always wondered how a dead cow in a perspex box could be worth millions, which at the time he'd thought was a good point well made, although neither of them could quite understand why. At least the evening had been a success in that Hugh had agreed not to let his contact at the university see the body and to sit on the report until everyone got bored with asking for it.

At the bus station, Kirby kept repeating forty-eight to himself, like some sort of "get me home" mantra. If he stopped saying it he thought the number would leave his brain for good and he'd still be here in the morning. When a forty-eight arrived, he gave a little whoop of joy, feeling very pleased with himself. He got on the bus and, after three attempts, took out his warrant card. 'Pol... pooli, poleesh,' he managed, waving it in the air; an action that almost caused him to miss the step. 'Oopsh.'

'That's wonderful, mate, but you still need cash to travel on my bus.'

Kirby thought about this for a moment, then raised a finger as the memory of going home to his mum's filtered through the fug of his thoughts. 'Ah, yesh. Well ded... dedush... spotted.' He then fumbled in his pocket and took out a handful of cash, allowing the driver to pick out the appropriate amount.

'Where you going?' the driver asked.

'Me mum's.'

'OK, try again. Where does your mum live?'

'Why?'

'Because one fare does not fit all on this bus service. Also, I want to make sure you get off. I don't like the idea of driving around all night with you snoring in the back.'

Kirby smiled and waved a jolly finger in the air. 'Good points. F... Fawdon.'

'Excellent and I'm even going that way. Now you sit down and try not to be sick in my bus.'

Kirby frowned, affronted by the suggestion. He waved what before had been a jolly finger in a more forthright, side-to-side motion. 'No, I can hold glass... hold my... beer, me, yes, hold, never, sick no.' He smiled to himself as he slumped in a seat, pleased that he'd made that point.

'Oi, mate!'

Kirby opened his eyes and raised his head which had become heavier than he could ever remember it being. Not that he was remembering much. He glanced around, then grabbed the back of the seat in front to stop himself toppling into the aisle.

'Yes you, the copper.'

Kirby planted a finger on his chest. 'Me? Waz ser matter?'

'It's your stop.'

Kirby narrowed his eyes trying to force his memory into action. 'My stop?' he asked, trying to buy a little time.

'You're going to your mum's.'

'I am? How... how did... Oh, yesh! Kirby jumped to his feet, which for some reason didn't want to support him, and he sat down again. Bracing himself, he tried again and nodded in satisfaction as he persuaded one leg to move and the other to follow. Finally off the bus, he leant against a garden wall. 'Sank you, ev… eve… so much.' He said as he turned towards the bus that now wasn't there.

'Focus, Jonah,' he said to himself. Taking a deep breath he set off, one hand out in the direction of the hedges, gates and walls, just in case.

At the front door, Kirby poked at the lock with his key, which refused to do what it was supposed to do. After a minute or so, the door opened anyway. He stood back and looked at the key. 'Well, tha's good,' he said, as he wobbled and then steadied himself on the porch wall.

Alice Kirby stood, holding the door. 'You coming in Jonah or are you just going to stand there? I'm watching QI.'

Kirby frowned as he focused. 'Mum? Waz you doin' here?'

'I live here, Jonah. This is my house remember?'

Kirby grinned, giggled, then burped before putting a hand over his mouth. 'Beg pardon.' He giggled again.

Alice raised her eyes to the ceiling, tutting. 'Come on, Jonah, hurry up and get in.'

Kirby focused on the open door, trying to stop it dodging from side to side as he aimed for it. 'QI?' he said. 'Oh, yes. S'on Fridays, isn't it?' he said, trying to sound both interested and aware.

'It's the extended one.'

He screwed up his face as he thought about this. 'What, like the dining table sort of pulled out?' He giggled again, then hiccupped. He placed a hand on either side of the doorframe as he stepped through to stop it moving.

'My god, Jonah, you reek of beer. How many have you had?'

'Hey, I'm… hic, I'm the copper.' He wagged a finger. He narrowed his eyes, then opened them again in attempt to stop his head spinning. 'So I ask zee questions…'

'In that case, I'll answer for you, too many.'

Kirby put a hand on his mum's shoulder, then leant against the wall to stop himself giving her an involuntary hug, which even in his befuddled state he thought she might not appreciate. 'For your information…' He hesitated, then burped again. 'Beg pardon.' He pulled himself upright, doing his best to look dignified. He failed on account of his hair sticking up and not being aware that he was dribbling. He started again. 'For you… your, information,' he said, pausing for emphasis and raising the finger that had finished wagging. 'I've only had one or two.'

'I take it that's gallons?'

'N' anyway, ish not beer. I'll have you know…' He paused, having forgotten where his thoughts were going. In fact his thoughts seemed to have stopped altogether, like a train running into the buffers. He tried again. 'Ah, yes. I'll have you know, I've been… I've been, appreesia… appreeshi… trying real ale. S' not just beer, you know.' His head started to wobble and it took a second or two for him to get it back under control. 'S' mush like wine y'know, all citrus notes and taste of liquor... lisc... lish... liquorice, that's it, liquorice.' He smiled, feeling proud that the awkward word hadn't defeated him.

'If you say so.'

He did say so, but decided at that moment not say it out loud as that required too much effort. Instead, he concentrated on not letting his head fall off his shoulders. He then became aware that his bladder was occupying most of his lower body. 'Mush go... mush go.' He pointed down the hall as another word alluded him. His mum tutted and pushed him towards the downstairs cloakroom.

'Just don't make a mess in there,' she said, as Kirby fiddled with his belt and zip.

'Ish fine, Mum. Don't fuz...fuss. I'm perf... I'm perfecer... I'm OK.'

'Well, I'm going to watch the rest of QI in bed. See you in the morning.'

'Ahhhhh,' Kirby said, then, 'oops,' as he waved a hand in the air. 'Night, Mum.'

Kirby woke up three hours later, slumped on the sofa. At first he wondered where he was, then groaned as the events of the night before filtered slowly back into his brain. All the lights were on, as was the telly in the corner. Some bald geezer was sucking a lollipop. After another few seconds of working out it was an old episode of Kojak, he mumbled, 'I know who did it,' and stumbled off upstairs.

TWENTY-TWO

....

The morning air was cool and welcome as Kirby wandered down the neat suburban road with its redbrick houses and well-tended gardens. A cat sitting on a wall eyed him as he walked past. Given everything that had happened in the past few days, he wondered if it was just a cat. He pushed the thought to one side, on the grounds he already had a headache.

On the corner was a petrol station which now boasted a Marks and Spencer and its very own Wild Bean Cafe. He picked up a bunch of flowers and queued for a coffee, along with several smartly-dressed men and woman no doubt getting breakfast on the run. There was something about petrol stations doing breakfast that made him wonder about the sanity of the world. When asked which coffee he wanted, he resisted the urge to ask for a really wild one or to use his newly-acquired coffee shop skills by asking for a flat white. 'Just a black coffee please.'

On his way back, when the mix of fresh air, car fumes, exercise and caffeine were having some beneficial effect, he pulled out his phone and noticed two missed calls from Shirley and about six from his answer phone. He decided to avoid the message and called her.

'Tried to call you yesterday evening, sir. Guessed you might be in intense negotiation with Hugh.'

'Something like that.'

'Sarah left the hospital last night.'

'I thought they were keeping her in?'

'Well a nurse went in the room about 10pm and she'd gone.'

'Gone? What about the WPC?'

'Er, sorry, sir, Maggie saw nothing.'

'What?'

'That's not all, sir. To be fair to Maggie, none of the nurses or the doctor who signed her out can remember anything either. I talked to the doctor and he confirms it's his signature, but he doesn't even remember seeing her.'

'So where is she?'

'At her dad's as it turns out.'

'Hmm. Pick me up in about half an hour will you, Constable?'

'Sir.'

Back at his mum's, the kitchen door was open and she was already in the garden digging out plants that Kirby assumed were weeds. Someone had once told him that a weed was any plant in the wrong place, so he'd always had a fairly liberal interpretation of what was and wasn't a weed; something that hadn't always met with the approval of Jeanie. His mum looked up as he sat in the garden chair.

'You back in this world then?'

Kirby held up the flowers. 'Er yes, sorry, Mum.'

Alice Kirby wiped her hands on the front of her old trousers as she walked up the path. She took the flowers from him. 'You shouldn't have. To be honest I'm glad to see you getting out and enjoying yourself.'

'I'm not sure I'd call it enjoying myself.'

Mrs Kirby laughed. 'And I have coffee here, you know.'

Kirby looked up and smiled. 'I think another might be a good idea before Constable Barker picks me up.'

'I'll put the kettle on,' Alice said heading into the kitchen. A few minutes later she emerged into the morning sunshine with a tray on which were two mugs of coffee along with several pieces of toast, butter and her homemade raspberry jam.

'Not sure I want anything to eat,' Kirby said with a puff of his cheeks.

'Nonsense,' his mum said. 'You can't go out on an empty stomach.'

He reached for a plate.

'So what's this all about? You were a bit mysterious over the phone.'

Kirby nodded, buttering some toast. 'Do you believe in magic, Mum?'

'What, like that Paul Davids guy who used to be on the telly.'

'Daniels, Mum.'

'What?'

'Daniels, Mum, that was his name, not Davids. Anyway, I don't mean all that trickery, sleight-of-hand stuff.'

'Oh,' his mum said. Kirby could see her expression change. Sometimes she liked to play the little old lady routine. However, Kirby knew that was a front, a way of easing herself through life without upsetting too many people. She reminded him of Edna. He shivered.

'Well I know there's more things between heaven and earth than the police can find.' She smiled at him. 'Your Dad always liked to laugh at my seventh child of a seventh child thing. However, after he passed away I went up the coast for a bit of therapy, I'd guess you'd call it. Met a woman there who convinced me that it wasn't all just silly nonsense.'

'You never told me.'

'Yes, well. You'd have said the same as your Dad. So what're you getting into, Jonah?'

'Not sure, Mum. Let's say I'm coming round to your point of view.'

Mrs Kirby patted his arm. 'You should meet this lady, go and stay. It'd do you good to talk about your feelings and the like. Nice woman, about your age, a widower as well. You'd like her. I could introduce you, she comes…'

'Mum!'

His mum crossed her arms and scowled at him. 'Well, it's about time.'

Kirby didn't say anything. He sipped his coffee. He knew what was coming next.

'It's been a few years now, Jonah. I bet you aren't seeing anyone, are you?'

'I see people all the time mother. Being a copper it's difficult to avoid.'

Alice huffed. 'You know what I mean.'

Kirby gave his usual lame excuse. 'I haven't got time, Mum.'

'Then make time. You're not meant to be alone, Jonah, doesn't suit you. Plays to that morose side of you.'

Kirby smiled and bit into his toast. 'Morose?'

'Yes. And you know Jeanie would agree.'

He nodded. He did know that. They'd even talked about how she didn't want him to be alone in the world.

'How am I supposed to meet someone?'

'What about the internet?'

'That's what Anna says. Keeps threatening to sign me up on Match.com.'

'Sensible girl, takes after her mum. Mrs Dalton met a very nice man through that. Takes her to Whitby and places. Got a caravan at Sea Houses as well.'

'Good for Mrs Dalton. I don't like caravans.'

Just then the doorbell chimed. 'That'll be Shirley,' he said, thankful of the interruption which saved him from further pressing about his absent love life.

TWENTY-THREE

....

Kirby opened the front door, pulling on his jacket. 'Well done, Constable, in the nick of time.'

'Sir?'

'Oh Mother being Mother that's all,' Kirby said, getting into the car. 'Poking her nose into my life.'

'I know the score, sir. Mine's the same, "When are you going to get married". "When am I going to hear the patter of tiny feet". I bought her a kitten, I don't think she was impressed.'

Kirby laughed.

'So where to, sir?'

'I think we'll start with Harold.'

In Harold's shop, Edna was wandering down one of the aisles with a booklet in one hand.

'Oh great,' muttered Kirby. 'The other one's here as well.'

'Other one?' Shirley asked.

Kirby pointed towards Edna. 'She's one of Harold's lot.'

'The old lady?'

'Don't let the old-grey-cardigan routine fool you, Constable.'

Edna scuttled over to them. 'There's two of you then.' She may not have been an old lady in the conventional sense, however it appeared to Kirby that Edna still delighted in playing the part and stating the obvious.

'Very perceptive of you, Edna.'

Edna huffed her displeasure. 'So who's this then?' she asked, turning her attention to Shirley.

'Constable Barker meet Edna.'

He glanced at Shirley and watched as the smile faded from her face under Edna's gaze.

At that moment, Harold appeared from the back of the shop, attracting Edna's attention. Shirley put a hand out to the nearest shelf for support. She turned to Kirby. 'I see what you mean, sir. It's like… it's like…'

'Don't worry, Constable, I know what you mean. If ever there was a lesson in not making a snap judgement of someone, she's it.'

As Harold approached them, Kirby noted that the basket in Edna's hand had Tesco printed on the handle. He pointed to it. 'Thinking of joining them, Harold?'

Harold shrugged. 'No idea how that got there.'

Kirby looked at the other five or six baskets near the door. They all said Tesco on them.

Harold followed his gaze. 'Not my fault if they leave them lying around.'

Edna grabbed Harold's arm. 'Hey, I haven't got all day. You and 'im getting on alright then?'

'His name's Jonah.'

'Who?'

Harold aimed a finger at Kirby. 'The Inspector here.'

Kirby narrowed his eyes at Shirley, who had failed to hide a snigger. 'Never to be used, understood, Constable?'

'Sir.'

'What you mean?' Edna said, turning her mind-burning gaze on Kirby. 'Jonah's a good name. Old name.'

'So Harold tells me.'

To Kirby's relief, Edna returned her attention to Harold, poking him the chest. 'And where've you been? I've been looking for you an' you're never here.'

Harold seemed to shrink under Edna's gaze. He pointed to Kirby again. 'With him.'

'I guessed that. I'm old, not senile. I know that in the eyes of youngsters these days…' at which point she glanced towards Kirby and Shirley, 'the two go together. You know better, my lad.'

My lad? thought Kirby.

Harold told Edna in detail about where and what they'd been doing. 'That's not good,' she said when she heard about the dead goblin and Harold reckoning it was goblins who had abducted Sarah for Marianne. 'Not good at all. How are they getting through?' She poked Harold again, several times. 'Huh? It's your job to see that doesn't happen.'

This time Harold took a step backwards under Edna's gaze and the barrage of finger-poking.

'Sorry to interrupt this family row,' Kirby said. 'However, one of the reasons I'm here is to tell you that she's turned up.'

Edna paused mid-poke. 'Who?'

'Sarah.'

'I thought it was Susie?'

'No that's her friend.'

'Sarah's friend?'

'Yes, Susie.'

'She went missing as well?'

Kirby rolled his eyes wondering if he was perhaps wrong about Edna after all. He glanced at Shirley who was trying not to laugh. 'No! Stop, take a breath and listen.'

Edna widened her eyes in mock hurt. 'No need to get shirty.'

Kirby scowled.

'Alright I'm listening.'

'Good. Sarah is the girl that went missing. Susie is her friend. Right?'

'Right. Have you got a picture?'

'Of Susie?'

'No, Sarah of course.'

Kirby gritted his teeth, biting back a reply for fear of going round in yet more circles. Instead he took out his phone and, after several attempts and a little muttering, he held it out for Edna to see. 'On the left is Susie. The one on the right is Sarah, you know the girl who went missing and has now turned up.' She snatched it from him. She nodded. 'Marianne's alright. Seen her around, should've guessed.'

Harold shrugged. 'No reason to.'

'Hmm,' Edna said, and with a deft two-finger touch enlarged the image and then scanned across it. 'What about this other girl?'

'Susie,' Kirby said.

'I know that. What I mean is, look at them. Could be sisters or at least related.'

Harold shrugged. 'Marianne only had the one.'

Edna slapped Harold on the arm. 'I said could be.'

'You thinking both of them?'

Edna nodded. 'Maybe that's why they get on so well.' She handed Kirby his phone back. 'They related?'

'Don't think so. We'll ask, but I'm sure Susie'd have said.'

'Hmm…'

'Oh,' said Harold.

'Hmm,' Edna repeated. 'An' both of them here.'

Harold reached across his head with his left hand and scratched at his right ear. 'You think Marianne knows?'

'Must do.'

'Then…'

'Exactly…'

Harold looked at the photo again. 'Can't be, surely?'

'Hmm…'

Kirby waved a hand in between them. 'Excuse me, hello, I'm still here. And if you two are holding back information that might help the police with their enquiries, then...'

Edna turned on him and planted a finger on his right lapel. 'Listen here, Mr Polis man. If we told you everything we think, and you go ahead and put it all in some report, your superiors will trot you down to see a shrink in no time. And before you can say Caractacus, they'll have you in a white van and on the way to the funny farm.'

Kirby opened his mouth to reply but couldn't find any suitable words so closed it again. He glanced at Shirley, who shrugged.

'Well done,' Edna said. 'Very sensible. Listen. I think Sarah and Susie are related and close at that. I'm not saying Susie is lying. She might not know, which then begs the question why? Hmm...'

'So why?' Kirby asked.

'Don't know,' Edna replied. 'You need to find out. You're the policeman,' she added, before darting out of the shop accompanied by the gentle tinkle of the bell. Kirby watched her go and then blend in with all the other grey cardigans on the street.

'If you didn't know...' Shirley said. 'Well, you wouldn't know. And she don't half move fast for... for...'

'Edna,' Harold completed for her.

'She didn't pay,' Shirley said, eyes still on the door. 'And she's still got your basket.'

Harold shrugged. 'She never does and I can always get more baskets.'

Kirby put aside the basket issue. 'And Susie?'

'I think we might need to see her.'

'So do I,' Kirby said, taking out his mobile.

'Susie, hi, Inspector Kirby. Where are you?'

'Whitley Bay with some friends. They thought it'd do me good to get away for a day, enjoy the sun, that kind of thing.'

'When'll you be back?'

'We're not planning to come back till late. Is that a problem?'

'No, no. You enjoy yourself. I'll get round to your place in the morning. Ten-ish?'

'OK, bye.'

Harold looked up as Kirby put the phone back in his pocket. 'Not in then?'

'Whitley Bay, not getting back till late.'

'You didn't ask about her and Sarah, sir.'

Kirby shook his head. 'I don't believe she knows more than she's telling and it's easier to talk about it with her face to face. Also, it's a good excuse to have another look at their flat now that Sarah's back.' He looked at Harold. 'You can come along as well since you're supposed to be my expert.'

Harold nodded. 'In that case I want to go and check something out, and it might be a good idea if you came along. It'll help with your education, as it were.'

'So where are we going?'

'The Metro.'

'The Metro?'

'Yes, I'll get my coat.'

TWENTY-FOUR

....

Harold reappeared wearing his coat. He frowned at Kirby and Shirley as he strode past them. 'Coming?'

'No hat?' Shirley asked with a smile.

Harold took it out of his pocket and rammed it on his head, scowling at Shirley. He harrumphed, and the door to the shop opened with an annoyed tinkle. Kirby and Shirley followed.

'You not going to lock it?' Kirby asked. Harold gave him a look that suggested it was a ridiculous idea. Harold shifted the coat on his shoulders before heading off down Eskdale Terrace. The way the coat moved suggested it was heavier than might be accounted for by the weight of the leather alone.

Kirby sighed.

'You alright, sir?'

'Something I'd forgotten that's all. Too late now.'

Kirby caught up with Harold. 'So this guardian thing, how long's it been going on for?'

'My people have been here long before the streets of Jesmond existed,' Harold said.

Kirby smiled. 'That doesn't say much.' He winked at Shirley. 'You're trying to say you're what, Saxon, Nord?'

Harold gave him a look that indicated he was deeply offended by those suggestions. 'We've already had this discussion.'

'Really? Remind me.'

'I am certainly not any of those incomers, nor the other incomers, the Romans. I am British.'

Kirby put on his best innocent look. 'So what is that, Harold, Celtic?'

'I've told you, British! Brigante if you want to be more precise. Although so called academics like to say they're Celts.' Harold shuddered.

'British,' Kirby repeated to Shirley with a smirk. 'Wait up, Harold,' he said, as Harold strode off down the street, forcing him and Shirley to break into a run. While they did their best to avoid people coming the other way, Kirby noted that Harold walked in a straight line; that people coming in the other direction swirled around him, like waves around a rock, before continuing their journeys. It was as if they reacted to him, rather than saw him.

'So, enlighten me,' Kirby said. 'Why the Metro?'

'You'll see,' Harold said turning into Eslington Road, with the entrance to Jesmond Metro station ahead of them.

Harold strode towards the barrier and people moved aside to let him through. No ticket, no card, yet the turnstile turned.

'Hey,' Kirby shouted, he hated fare-dodgers. Then he remembered he didn't have a card or ticket either. He whipped out his warrant card and waved it at the guard on the gate, as did Shirley. The guard sniffed and let them through. By now, Harold was disappearing down the escalator, two steps at a time. Kirby and Shirley had to sprint to catch up. 'You didn't...' Kirby took a deep breath, 'pay.'

Harold narrowed his eyes. 'We're not taking a train,' he said, as if that should be obvious. At the bottom of the escalator, he headed towards the southbound sign, his heavy footfall echoing around the tiled hall. On reaching the platform, there were two would-be passengers staring at the adverts on the opposite wall.

'I thought you said we weren't going anywhere?' Kirby said.

'No, I said we weren't taking a train.'

'Where else do you go from an underground platform?'

Harold pointed. 'Hopefully through that door.'

'What...' Kirby's voice tailed off as he noticed a door that he'd have sworn hadn't been there a few seconds ago. It was an old, heavy-looking wooden door with three thick metal bands running across it. There were no signs. No "For staff only", or "Keep out".

'I've wondered what was behind there,' Shirley said.

Harold's hand stopped half an inch from the door's peeling green paint. He turned his head and raised the rim of his hat with the tip of a finger. 'You could see this?'

Shirley frowned back. 'Yes, of course. When I lived around here I often took the train into town. I used to lean against it. No one ever seemed to use it.' She shrugged.

'Just wondered what was behind it.' She smiled. 'One day, when there was no else down here, I did have a peek.'

'You actually opened it?' Harold said.

'Well, yes,' Shirley said narrowing her eyes at Harold. 'How else do you think I had a peek? You needn't worry though, I didn't go in. It was all dark and I'm not keen on spiders.'

'Spiders?' Kirby said with a smile. 'The indomitable Constable Shirley Barker afraid of spiders?'

Shirley scowled at Kirby. 'Don't you dare tell anyone at the station.' After a pause she added, 'sir.'

Kirby grinned. 'Your secret's safe with me, Constable,' he said, then added, 'for now.'

Shirley tutted. 'Me and my big mouth.'

Harold pulled his hat down again and shook his head before pushing the door open and stepping through.

'Hold on,' Kirby said. 'So we're going in there?'

Harold took a step back and looked down at Kirby from under the brim of his hat. He gave a long sigh. 'I have a feeling I'm going to regret this, yes. And we're not so much going in as going through.'

'Through?'

'It's one of those gateways I told you about. And that's what you do with gateways, go through them. I want to make sure no one's been tampering with it.'

'As in Marianne?'

'Exactly,' Harold said slapping the door with the flat of his hand and producing a small cloud of dust and green particles. He walked on. Shirley shrugged at Kirby and fell in behind Harold. 'Oh hell,' Kirby whispered to himself and followed. He glanced back to see the two passengers still staring at the far wall.

They were in a narrow passageway with a dull glow coming from the far end, which wasn't that far, only about five metres.

'I don't like this,' Shirley said.

'Why?' Harold asked. Kirby noted that there was now more respect, perhaps a little reverence in Harold's voice.

'Spiders?' Kirby suggested.

'Not just that!' She lowered her voice. 'It's... it's creepy.'

'Oh,' Harold said, sounding disappointed as he took out something from inside his leather coat and stepped into the passageway with exaggerated caution. Harold held his other hand to out stop Kirby getting ahead of him.

'What are you expecting?' Kirby whispered.

'More to the point, what the hell is that?' Shirley said in a louder voice, pointing to Harold's hand that wasn't holding Kirby back.

Harold waved his free hand in the air. 'Keep your voice down, and what does it look like?'

'It looks...' Shirley started before lowering voice again. 'It looks very much like a small crossbow,' she said, trying to put as much force behind a hoarse whisper as she could.

'That's because that's what it is. Believe me, you can't be too careful.'

'Too careful!' Shirley said having given up whispering. 'That's... that's an offensive weapon and you were walking around Jesmond with it for heaven's sake.'

'Shhh...'

Shirley turned to Kirby. 'Sir!' she said in a forceful whisper.

'Why do you think I sighed when we left the shop?'

'You knew?'

For once his superior officer status abandoned him. Kirby felt rather like a naughty schoolboy who'd been caught smoking behind the bike sheds, which he had been, on more than one occasion. 'Yes, well, I...'

'What else has he got in there?'

'Don't ask.'

Shirley registered her displeasure with the pair of them by crossing her arms.

'When you two have finished,' Harold said edging forward. 'For now, just trust me.'

'Trust y...' Shirley ran out of letters and words.

Kirby and Shirley watched Harold creeping to the end of the passage, which as he approached appeared to shimmer. Without breaking his stride and now with confidence, Harold walked towards and into the barrier. He bounced off it and landed in a leather heap on the floor. The crossbow fired and the bolt stuck in a beam overhead with a twang. Harold grabbed his hat, which had been thrown off in the collision and rammed it back down on his head.

'Holy hell,' Kirby said. 'Shirley's right, put that damned thing away before you do some real damage.'

Harold tucked the weapon into an inside pocket. As he did so, Kirby got a glimpse of other "things" and decided not to mention it. He didn't think his dented sense of seniority could survive Shirley's response.

'Hmm,' Harold said.

'Is that what you were expecting to happen then?' Shirley said, leaning against a wall, arms still crossed and foot tapping on the floor

Harold glared at Shirley, whose returning glare could have blistered paint.

Harold retreated to being sheepish. 'Yes, I regularly walk into solid walls, you know, just for fun. You should try it some time.'

Shirley's voice came down a notch as curiosity took over. 'So what should have happened?'

'I should have been able to walk straight through, of course.'

'It looks solid,' Kirby said, feeling it was now safe to enter the conversation again.

'Yes, I know it looks solid. It always looks solid. But… oh, never mind.'

'Safe to say then that someone has been tampering?'

Harold approached the gateway again, this time with more caution.

'So what's wrong with it?'

Harold shook his head and reaching out, touched the gateway with one hand. Under the pressure of his fingertips, multi-coloured ripples spread across the surface. 'It responds to individuals, letting them through and anyone with them for the next ten seconds or so. My guess it's been changed to allow the goblins through and at the same time exclude me.'

'Can you change it back?' Kirby asked.

'Not from this end.'

'I can see a figure,' Shirley said, 'a person, on the other side.'

'Really?' Harold asked.

'Yes. It's a bit fuzzy, definitely a person though.'

'Goran,' Harold said walking past Kirby and heading back towards the door.

'So what now?' Kirby asked.

Harold shook his head. 'I don't know. I think I need to talk to Edna.'

Back on the platform, there were now five people. None of them turned to see them appear, from what as Kirby looked back, was a plain dirty cream coloured wall. Although, if he tried hard and knowing what was there, perhaps… He shook his head.

Outside the station Shirley pointed along the road. 'The girl's flat is around the corner.'

'Close to where the line runs?' Harold asked.

'I guess so.'

'Bit of a coincidence, don't you think?' Harold said turning to Kirby.

'Why?'

'Being near to the Metro and the gateway.'

Kirby shook his head. 'If you say so. Believe it or not, gateways to other worlds are not something we have to factor in to our investigations on a regular basis.'

Harold sniffed the air like a bloodhound trying to catch a scent.

'What,' Kirby asked.

'I don't like coincidences,' Harold said.

'That makes three of us,' Shirley said.

TWENTY-FIVE

....

Harold was tidying the shop, thinking of closing up for the evening, when the bell tinkled. And this wasn't a last minute customer tinkle this was a warning tinkle. Harold glanced up at the convex mirror. It was a tall man with long dark hair. On the surface he looked young, an academic perhaps. However, the sneer as he glanced around the shop betrayed that.

'Hello, Mephisto,' Harold said. 'Wondered if you'd call in.'

'Still here then, Harold,' Mephisto said, his gaze taking in the whole shop.

Harold spread his arms wide. 'As you can see. And as you must have known, you having hidden away not far from here.'

Mephisto grinned. 'Ah yes, needs must and all that.'

'Still couldn't resist the limelight though. All that Youtube nonsense. Once a second rate showman, always a second rate showman, eh.' Harold shook his head. 'A cat, really? And that cheap trick at the end.'

Mephisto sniffed before picking up a mop, which with a faint pop, became a banana. Mephisto smiled and started to peel it.

'More cheap tricks, Mephisto?'

'Cheap tricks, Harold? You've been living one for how many years is it now? All these nice people thinking you're just some dusty old shop keeper. Except now of course that Inspector, what's he called?'

'Kirby.'

Mephisto opened his eyes wider, pretending he hadn't known. 'That's it, Inspector Kirby,' he said taking another bite. 'I think we might have to deal with him when this is all over. Knows far too much.'

'You, Mephisto?' Harold pointed to the banana. 'That's more your style.'

Mephisto threw the half eaten fruit on the floor. 'Careful you don't slip on that, or on anything else for that matter.'

Harold laughed. 'First cheap tricks and now cheap threats. You know, I've almost missed you.'

Mephisto scowled. 'You weren't laughing last time. All those riots. We plundered the magic, fed the flames...'

'And still failed.'

'Not before you and Edna were tearing yourselves apart trying to protect this precious world of yours. And then there's Geraldo and Roberto. Is he still masquerading as that dumb rabbit? Why, Harold? You don't belong here.' Mephisto spread his arms. 'And this shop, what's all that about? Do you actually sell any of this rubbish?'

'Enough.'

Mephisto picked up a tin of floor polish. 'Beats me why anyone would come in here for anything.'

'Buying that?'

'Huh?'

Harold took the tin from him and put it back on the shelf. 'Maybe people like a bit of stability in a fast changing world.'

Mephisto sniffed. 'If you say so. Come on, Harold, these people have lost the way, they don't believe any more. They wouldn't know real magic if it slapped them in the face. Tricksters and illusionists are all they have. They all applaud and cheer even though they know it's a sham. They've shunned true magic and forgotten it even exists, replaced it with a pale, worthless imitation.'

Harold shook his head. 'That's their choice. It's their world. And the magic's still here waiting to be discovered again. What's more it belongs to this world, Mephisto. It's not yours to plunder. That's not right. There has to be balance in all things.'

'Who says?' Mephisto said taking a couple of steps down one of the isles. He picked up a can of sweetcorn which disappeared from his hand. A mouse ran off along the tops of the other tins. He picked up another can.

Harold put a hand on the shelf. 'You can stop that now.'

Mephisto yelped and dropped the can, then licked his fingers. 'Now who's using cheap tricks.'

Harold smiled.

'You won't stop us, Harold. Nor will that interfering old crone, Edna.'

'Us? Mephisto. Harold paused as if thinking about it. 'Of course, you were never any good on your own. You know I'm surprised that Marianne has forgiven you this time.'

Mephisto reached out towards the shelf again before thinking better of it. He turned his attention back to Harold. 'We're a team. She needs me.'

'Only because she daren't turn all Sisillius's misogynistic brutes into stone.'

'It's not only Marianne now though is it?' Mephisto said with a grin. 'We've got help from a native of this world. You know what that means.'

'A young girl, that's a bit low even for you and Marianne isn't it?'

'She's Marianne's daughter.'

'She knows nothing of her mother. Then you abduct her, for what?'

Mephisto laughed. 'Knows nothing. You think so?'

Harold shook his head. 'Even Marianne must know she's playing with fire.'

'Marianne doesn't burn easily as you well know. Unlike others.'

Harold cocked his head to one side. 'What's that supposed to mean?'

'We know all about your little retreat Harold. Those nice people and what's your 'nephew' called, Goran is it?'

Harold grabbed Mephisto by the lapels of his jacket and pulled him towards him until their noses were almost touching. 'Look into my eyes, Mephisto, tell me what you see?'

Mephisto held Harold's gaze. 'Harm me, Harold and who knows what Marianne might do.' Mephisto raised a hand but the look in Harold's eyes made him hesitate.

'Don't even think about it.' Harold said pushing Mephisto away so that he clattered against the shelf behind him. 'If any harm comes to them there are not enough worlds for you and Marianne to hide in.'

Mehpisto stepped out of Harold's reach. 'Words, Harold, merely words,' he said although Harold could see the doubt in his eyes.

Mephisto opened the shop door. The bell gave a single clipped "tink". He pointed a finger at Harold. 'It's different this time, Harold. You'll take my advice if you know what's good for you and keep out of our way.'

Harold laid a calming hand on the bell which still held the echo of a vibration. He bolted the door for the first time in years before making his way into the back room. He took a glass out of a cupboard. On the shelf above he moved aside a dozen bottles of ketchup and lifted down a half full bottle of McCallan Malt whiskey which he kept for special occasions, deciding that sometimes there had to be exceptions. After taking a first sip he took out his mobile.

He smiled as he heard the faint words. 'Damn… blasted thing.' There was pause then a more controlled voice took over. 'Hello, this is Edna. Who's that speaking please.'

'Edna, it's me, Harold. Your phone'll have told you that.'

'Oh, you know I don't hold with these things. Anyway, why're you calling at this time, when Enders is on?'

Harold relayed a shortened version of his conversation with Mephisto.

'Oh,' Edna said.

'Yes, exactly. I'm going to be at the girls flat with Kirby about 10.00am, can you meet me there?'

'No, sorry, Pet. I needs to be seeing someone else. You'll be fine there without me.'

Harold poured himself another drink.

TWENTY-SIX

....

Kirby parked a few doors away from Susie and Sarah's flat at 35 Eslington Road. Not because there wasn't a space nearer, it was just he liked to get a sense of the place, the street. He was outside a neat row of three-storey terraced houses, some of which had been converted into flats. Further up the road were some large double-fronted detached houses, where at one time some of the more well-heeled Victorian citizens of Newcastle had lived. It had seen rougher times as well, then in the last twenty years had come up in the world again. So now there was a mix of the original residents and newer professional types, hence the four by fours with private number plates parked next to ageing Ford Fiestas and Renault Clios. Some gardens were little oases of well-tended calm whereas others were full of straggly grass, verging on the wild. These, no doubt, were favourite haunts for the local cats. There was a rumble on the other side of the road, the Metro. Locking the car Kirby looked around before wandering down the street. Out of the corner of his eye he caught the slight twitching of a curtain, a professional, it hardly moved. He made a note of the house number.

On Susie's doorstep, there was quite a gathering. Harold and Geraldo were standing watching him. To his dismay, Harold had his coat on. Geraldo looked like a walking rainbow in a coat of many colours. He couldn't see Roberto, or that Geraldo had anything he could be in, which he was thankful for. He found the idea of a talking rabbit more than a little disturbing.

Kirby closing on the little chattering group when Shirley arrived. He waited for her as she got out of the car.

'Interesting looking pair?' Shirley said with a grin.

'Yes, I asked Harold to join us. The other one's Geraldo. Come on, let's see what's going on.'

Shirley's eyes widened. 'Oh, that's Geraldo?'

'Yes, but don't get your hopes up, I don't see any sign of the rabbit.'

Shirley tutted.

'Morning, Jonah,' Harold said.

'I wasn't aware I'd issued a general invitation,' Kirby said to Harold.

'I thought Geraldo's expertise might prove useful.'

'Did you?' Kirby noted that he didn't explain what that expertise might be. He assumed magic, which made his heart sink a little.

'And should I frisk you?'

Harold smiled holding out his arms.

Kirby thought better of it, valuing a full set of fingers. 'Has anyone rung the bell?'

Harold reached up and pressed. 'No, we were waiting for you.'

Susie opened the door in a white T-shirt with a 'Students power the future' slogan on it and long, checked pyjama bottoms. However, he knew from his daughter that didn't mean she had just got up and that this was considered perfectly acceptable "around the house" wear.

'I hope we haven't got you up?' he tried anyway.

'No,' Susie said. 'I know that's the traditional view of students, however, I've lots to catch up on.' She looked past Kirby and her smile turned into a concerned frown at the gathering behind him.

'Er, yes, the team. Sorry about that. Shirley, you know. This is Harold and that's Geraldo. He paused seeing Susie's bemused expression as she took in Harold's coat and Geraldo's multi-coloured jacket. They're… er… experts,' he said, avoiding saying what they might be experts in.

Geraldo bowed with a flourish. 'Geraldo the famous magician, mademoiselle,' he said, handing Susie a card that had appeared in his hand. 'You must come to my show.'

'Er, thanks.'

'No Roberto?' Kirby asked as Geraldo walked past him.

'No, Inspector. Roberto is not enamoured with early mornings.'

Thank heavens for that, Kirby thought.

Shirley, who was behind Kirby, tutted again. 'I'd like to have seen him,' she muttered.

Susie led them down the tiled corridor to the back of the flat and into a large open-plan room as the latest fashion in house renovation dictated. The ceilings were higher than in modern houses and the walls were a pale yellow. The sun was streaming in through the glazed rear doors of what Kirby presumed was an extension, lighting the table in the kitchen area on which was a laptop and several books. There was also a faint smell of pine disinfectant as if to dispel another student myth.

'Looks even nicer with the sun coming in,' Shirley said. 'Great place to work.'

'Yes,' Susie said. We're very lucky, although it does feel a bit empty without Sarah around. When do think she'll be back? She is OK, isn't she?'

Shirley smiled. 'Yes, her Dad says she's fine, a bit tired that's all. I'm sure she'll give you a call when she feels up to it.'

'Speaking of Sarah, can I see her room?' Kirby asked.

'It was the first door on the left that you passed coming in.'

'Thanks,' he smiled at Susie.

'Sorry,' Susie said. 'Would anyone like some tea?'

'Splendid idea,' Kirby said.

He opened the door and stood taking it all in. It looked as if Sarah had just left. The bed wasn't made. There was a pair of jeans and a T-shirt on a chair, and a couple of pairs of shoes on the floor underneath. There was a desk and chair under the window, which looked out over the street. A closed laptop and couple of books. It was a little untidy, but not messy, especially when he thought about his own daughter's room.

He held out an arm. 'You two stay here while the Constable and I have a look around first.'

'Well?' he said to Shirley as they entered.

'As I left it the other day. Nice,' Shirley said. 'A definite one up on my first place.'

'Not quite what I was meaning.'

Shirley shrugged. 'Again, can't see anything out of the ordinary, sir. No sign of any struggle or anything. She sniffed the air. 'The only thing I can smell is perfume, if you know what I mean.'

'I do, Constable. And I agree.'

Kirby turned. 'OK, you two can come in.'

Harold entered first and inspected the book shelf next to the desk. 'Some here on the occult, witchcraft and,' he wrinkled his nose, 'vampires.'

Kirby glanced across at Shirley. 'Fiction, popular among the young, so I'm told.'

'Especially girls,' Shirley said. 'Bit after my time though. Can't see it myself.'

'Hmm,' Kirby mused. 'My daughter was into it for a while. It's as if as technology takes over, they want to believe that there is something else, perhaps a little magic in the world...' He paused, realising what he'd said.

Geraldo waved a hand in a theatrical gesture. Kirby suspected Geraldo's whole life was a bit of a performance.

'That's precisely it, Inspector. Millions of young people, how shall I put it, leaning that way, thinking those thoughts, make it more likely.'

'What do you mean?'

'The young,' he said, extending a hand palm up towards Shirley, who shrank away from it, 'are more open, their minds more receptive. So it's easier for them to make, let's say, a connection.'

Kirby put down the photograph of Sarah and her father he'd been holding. 'What, you mean wishing for something can make it happen?'

Geraldo gave a little laugh and rolled his hands as if he was about to make something appear out of thin air. Kirby was even a little disappointed when it didn't. 'No, no, at least not in the way you mean. Think of it, a lot of people all on the same wavelength, as it were, can be a powerful thing.'

'Like the riots?'

Geraldo raised an arm with a finger pointing at the ceiling. 'Exactly! People blamed technology, mobile phones, messaging and the like. However, underneath all that was the power of all those human minds, and influencing them, well…'

Shirley looked up, having been on her knees peering under the bed. 'What, like telepathy?'

Geraldo smiled back. 'There you go, you see. Because you can't touch something or measure it, you're sceptical about its existence.'

Shirley tutted and got off her knees, brushing at her trousers. 'If you say so. Anyway, there's nothing under there,' she paused and sneezed, 'but dust.' She glanced across at Geraldo. 'Unless of course it's invisible, in which case…'

Kirby huffed in response. 'Yes thank you, Constable. Well, have we seen enough?'

Geraldo sniffed twice. 'I almost missed it.'

'It's perfume,' Shirley said. 'Fragrance of the night by Dior, I'd say. Got some myself, although I don't wear it much. I'm sure it brings me out in a rash.'

Geraldo scowled at her.

'What?'

His eyebrows took on a life of their own as they fluttered independently. 'It's,' he held up both hands, palms out, 'yes, definitely the smell of magic.'

'Here?' Kirby said.

Shirley lifted her nose towards the ceiling and sniffed. 'No, I'm certain it's Dior.'

Geraldo went into his matinee crouch and swept an arm around the room. All that was missing was the cloak. The arm paused on the wardrobe. A bit of a cliché, Kirby thought. The arm started moving again, now pointing out of the door. 'A little in here. No, no…' The arm swept out of the room, taking the rest of Geraldo with it.

'I told you he'd be useful,' Harold said as he and Kirby followed Geraldo.

'We'll see.'

Geraldo was at the front door, knees bent and still sniffing. 'Goblin.'

Kirby groaned.

'Do they use Dior as well then?' Shirley asked.

Kirby glared at her.

'Sorry, sir.'

Geraldo ignored them both. 'Yes, I was misled by what I'm guessing is next door's tomcat.' The arm was raised, finger pointing, over his head. 'And!' Kirby's eyes followed, happy to see only a ceiling above him. They followed the arm again back towards the living area. It passed one door and then pointed at a third. 'Aha!'

Shirley tried the handle. 'Locked.'

Kirby wandered into the kitchen with the others trailing behind him. Thankfully Geraldo had straightened up. It seemed his magic-sniffing had been distracted by tea and digestives, both of which he helped himself to.

'Milk and sugar, anyone?' Susie asked.

'Just milk, thanks,' Kirby said, taking the mug from Susie. He was relieved it was what he recognised as tea, not some herbal or scented concoction. He took a sip and smiled at Susie. 'So Susie, the other doors?'

'The one next to Sarah's is my room.'

Shirley poured herself some tea. 'You work in here though?'

Susie shrugged. 'Sarah's is the larger bedroom and mine has no window. Only fair seeing as it's her place. So

I like to work in here and Sarah doesn't mind. Says it means there's always tea on the go.'

'And the others?' Kirby asked.

'The one next to this is the bathroom.'

'And the one next to your room? The one that's locked.'

Susie gave a little shiver. 'The basement.'

'And you don't like the basement?' Harold asked before Kirby could.

'Yuck, no.'

'Why?'

Susie shifted from one foot to the other and back again. 'I know it sounds pathetic, we opened it once and there were,' she glanced at Shirley, '...spiders.'

Kirby tutted. 'Not again.'

'Don't blame you,' Shirley mumbled through a mouthful of biscuit.

'Also, it was a bit, you know... spooky.'

'Spooky?' Kirby said, more because he felt he should be the one asking the questions.

'Don't underestimate spooky,' Harold said.

'I don't,' Kirby said. 'You have the key though?'

Susie opened one of the kitchen drawers and rummaged around inside. Having removed a garlic press and a corkscrew, she produced a key. Kirby was reaching out when Geraldo grabbed it. He waved his other hand over it and opened both palms towards them to show it had gone.

'Nice,' Shirley said. 'Shame the rabbit wasn't here, we could have had the full show.'

Kirby raised his eyes to the ceiling before looking at Harold, who grinned.

'Shall we?' Geraldo said, his arm once again leading the way.

'Does he ever stop?' Kirby asked Harold as they followed.

'Not that I've noticed.'

'I'd still like to see the rabbit,' Shirley muttered.

At the door, the hand-waving was repeated for the key to reappear.

'Ta-ra,' Shirley said.

The key turned in the lock with a satisfying clunk. There was even a theatrical creak as the door opened, which Kirby thought must have pleased Geraldo. Harold leaned in and found the light switch. A single dim, bare bulb cast gloomy shadows. Inside, Susie had been right, there were cobwebs everywhere. Kirby let Geraldo and Harold go in first.

Shirley shuddered, then followed Kirby. 'Come on, Shirley, they're only spiders,' she said to herself, hesitating on the top step and holding her arms close to her sides to avoid touching anything.

Harold stopped on the bottom step which had Kirby bumping into him and Shirley into Kirby. 'Ah, I should have guessed,'

'What?' Kirby said.

'Being so close.'

'What!'

Harold moved across to where Geraldo was crouched next to the far wall.

'A door,' Susie said, from behind them all. It seemed her curiosity had got the better of her own aversion to spiders.

Geraldo stood and spun around in one fluid movement. 'You can see it?'

'Yes, sort of. If I look directly at it, it's just a wall. Then if I kind of look at it sideways, I can see it. Does that make sense?'

Geraldo took four rapid steps across the room, before pushing past Kirby and Shirley to get to Susie, who was still on the steps. He leant his face so it was inches from hers. Susie leant back a little but held her ground. Kirby was impressed.

Geraldo's eyes flickered over Susie's face. 'Hmm…'

'Hmm?' Shirley asked.

'Hmm,' Geraldo repeated, then stepped back past Kirby.

'So are you going to bounce off this one, Harold?' Kirby asked. 'At least this time you aren't holding a crossbow, so you can't shoot anyone.'

Harold frowned back. Geraldo rotated his head towards Harold and raised an eyebrow.

'Temporary glitch, that's all.'

Geraldo went back into a crouch and let his arm take him back to the wall. As he had with Susie, he leant his face inches from it. 'Seems normal.'

'Not in my world, it doesn't,' Kirby muttered.

Harold put his hand on the wall and now even Kirby could see the door. It was old, solid, with an arch at the top and no visible handle, locks or bolts.

'Well I never,' Shirley said.

'So how does it open?' Kirby asked.

Geraldo waved both arms over his head, catching the single bulb as he did so, which sent their shadows dancing around the room. 'Magic.'

Kirby raised a hand to stop the light swaying, one could only take so much theatre. 'I'm not sure I want to ask this, can you open it?'

Geraldo waggled the fingers of his right hand and spread them before extending his arm until they were a few millimetres from the door.

'Was it my imagination,' Shirley said, 'or did that door flinch?'

'Shhh,' Harold said.

Geraldo moved his hand across the door until he got to where you might expect a handle to be. He took a deep breath and waggled his fingers again. Then his hand shot back as if he'd been stung. 'That's a bit nasty.'

'So can you open it?' Kirby asked again.

Geraldo scowled at him. 'I can. Just... just not now.'

'Why not?'

'Because it doesn't want me to. I need to think about it. If I go in heavy-handed as it were I could bring the whole house down.'

'That's as good a reason as any,' Kirby said. He wasn't sure whether to be disappointed or relieved.

Outside, Kirby and Shirley watched Harold and Geraldo head off in the direction of Harold's shop. Harold's coat was flapping in the breeze and Geraldo's jacket seemed to shimmer.

Shirley shivered. 'You know, sir, there are times when I think a career in traffic doesn't seem such a bad idea.'

'I know what you mean, Constable.'

'So what now, sir?'

'I'm not sure, Shirley. At the moment it's as if I'm waiting for things to happen; that I have no control over where this investigation is going.'

'Welcome to the world of a detective Constable, sir.'

Kirby laughed. 'Yes, however, I'm an inspector and I'm supposed to know what I'm doing.'

'You'll get there, sir. You always do.'

Kirby smiled. 'Thank you, Constable. Tell you what, why don't you look into that shop, Mystique, see what you can find out? I didn't exactly get far with the assistant.'

'Sir.'

TWENTY-SEVEN

....

Kirby watched Shirley get in her car and drive off. He looked back at the door to the girls' flat, shaking his head as he thought about the last half-hour or so. 'Actual magic, really?' he said out loud to see if it might make it more believable. When he'd been in the flat and Geraldo had said it, it was almost as if, 'Oh yeah, magic'. Now outside and on his own, part of his brain was suggesting that a chat with a psychiatrist might be a good idea. The curtains of the house opposite twitched.

'I'd think twice about keeping an eye on everything if I were you,' Kirby muttered. 'You might see things you really wish you hadn't.' Heading back to his own car he took his keys out of his pocket. He hesitated, then shoved them back in to re-join the sweet wrappers and walked past. Sometimes walking helped, as if the simple rhythm of putting one foot in front of the other freed the mind.

It was a lovely summer's day and even the breeze was warm, having declined to come from its normal easterly direction for a few days, fancying the south for a change. A hazy sun was shining through high cloud, casting a shadow that led him towards Clayton Road. However, he felt anything but bright himself. A few days ago his life had been a bit weird, even for a copper. That was normal weird, though, just people. And yes, people could be damn weird, look at Medusa Lil for example. However, they were still people. You knew what you were dealing with. Sooner or later people did what, well, what people did. He knew how their minds worked, even the potty ones, especially the potty ones. That's what coppering was all about, understanding people and how their minds worked. And the fact that he understood all that was what made him a good copper. This however? Magic, goblins, secret doors and God knows what else might be lurking behind those doors. This was Jesmond for heaven's sake, where chintz was still alive and well.

He had no idea how this worked. What made these people's minds tick, what drove them. They didn't want the latest in flat-screen TV or the thrill of joy-riding in an expensive car. They didn't want the things they couldn't afford, or even money. At least he presumed they didn't want money. That was it, he didn't know what they wanted. It wasn't as if he could go to the library and look them up, if of course the library had been open, which it wasn't. Anyway, he couldn't just Google them. Actually, when he thought about it, he could of course Google them, although who knows what that might come up with, after all, that was people again. He suspected that goblins and real magical people, whoever they were, were unlikely to be posting or blogging about themselves, with the possible exception of Mephisto.

On Clayton Road, Kirby called in at the newsagent, bought a paper, then crossed the road and opened the door to the coffee shop. His mind worked best when it thought he wasn't looking. In this case, that meant doing the cryptic crossword, or rather trying to do the cryptic crossword. As a detective, he always thought he should be better at them than he was.

In the corner on the sofas was the same group of mums with their four-by-four buggies parked next to them. One of them was bouncing a baby up and down on her lap while still talking to the others. The baby had that concentrated cross-eyed look that said, 'I think I'm going to throw up.' The au pairs weren't there, no doubt scared off by the accusing looks the mums had been giving them.

'Hello, again. Flat white, wasn't it?'

Kirby glanced at all the options chalked on the board. There were too many. 'Er, yes, thank you.'

'Skimmed, semi or soya?'

'Sorry?' The trouble was when he left his mind working on something in the background it was like running a memory-hungry program on a rather slow computer, everything else suffered. 'Er, yes, semi please.'

Kirby took his coffee and wandered towards the same table he'd sat at the day before. At the back, blending in with a group of other grey cardigans, was Edna. She wasn't talking, just listening. He suspected that Edna did a lot of that, and unlike most people she really listened. Forget social media, there was little to beat the grey-cardigan telegraph when it came to finding out what was going on locally. Edna nodded in his direction.

Kirby folded the paper and took out a pen, the free one that came in the mail yesterday with the brochure asking him if was saving for his own funeral so as not to be a burden on his family. He'd looked to see how long the policy ran so that he might schedule his own demise, it didn't say. Clue one down, "One who criticises prison". Anyone who's been there, Kirby thought, but then it's only seven letters.

'One across, the answer's scarlet,' Edna said, looming over his shoulder.

'You start with the down clues,' Kirby said, trying to sound matter of fact, as if he'd known she was there, which he hadn't. 'They're supposed to be easier. They use up their best ones early on.'

'The answer's still scarlet.'

Kirby frowned as Edna sat down. One down, "Mark from a wound girl allows to become red".

'See, mark from a wound, scar. Allowed, let and…'

'Yes, yes,' Kirby said, turning the paper over. 'I don't suppose you've come over simply to irritate me by helping with the crossword. Or at least not the crossword part.'

Edna ignored the sarcasm. 'Find much at the girls' place?'

'That's quick, even for the grey-cardigan drums.'

Edna smiled and nodded towards the back of the room. 'Oh, they're good. Don't miss much that lot. They're not that good though. Harold told me last night.'

'Of course.'

'Did he tell you Mephisto's been to see him?'

Kirby shook his head. 'No'

'Well he has.'

'And?'

'Making threats.'

'Harold strikes me as the sort who can take care of himself. I've seen that coat of his.'

'Harold, oh I'm not worried about, Harold. He was threatening his family.'

Funny, Kirby thought, he'd never imagined Harold as having family. 'Do they live near?'

Edna narrowed her eyes at him in the way that said, 'how can you be so stupid?'

'They're not here,' she said, emphasising the "here".

Kirby sipped at his coffee. 'Then they're a little outside my jurisdiction.'

'Hmm,' Edna said, as if reluctantly accepting the point 'Also, if that numpty Mephisto is making threats, then Marianne's behind them.'

'I take it that's worse?'

Edna sucked in a breath. 'And getting potentially worse all the time she's here.' She sniffed the air. 'I can almost taste it. It's like it's swirling in the air, a vortex that's slowly getting tighter, spinning faster. Magic is like dust.' She waved a hand above her head. 'Out there in space, it's spinning around until it forms clumps, which form bigger clumps, which spin faster and eventually they become something substantial.'

Kirby stared at Edna. 'You been watching that Professor Brian Cox?'

'Might 'ave been.'

'Or of course it could just be the steam from the coffee machines.'

Edna smacked Kirby on the arm in rebuke, with, he had to admit, surprising force. He suppressed a whimper. 'Anyway,' he said, which came out as more of a squeak. 'Anyway,' he repeated, making an effort to lower the tone of his voice. 'It's not good.'

'No, it means Harold could be distracted and he'll want to go back and make sure they're alright; warn them.' She frowned. 'Which means I could end up looking after that damned shop.' Then she brightened up and smiled, gently patting Kirby on the arm this time. 'You should go with him.'

'Me! That other...' He found his throat tightening as he forced out the words, 'other world. Why?'

'So you can see what this is really all about.'

TWENTY-EIGHT

....

'So you still at your father's?' Marianne asked as she and Sarah waited at the entrance to Jesmond Metro station.

'Yes, although I'm going to go back to the flat in the morning.'

'Good idea,' Marianne said. 'And what's he doing now?'

Sarah grinned. 'He thinks I'm in my room "resting" and he thinks he's watching the highlights of today's cricket.'

'Excellent,' Marianne said. 'You're learning.' She smiled at her daughter. 'Nice dress by the way, suits you.'

Sarah returned the smile. 'Roger always said I looked good in dresses, that I had the legs for them.'

Marianne raised an eyebrow. 'Roger?'

Sarah peered at the ground and shuffled her feet. 'An ex.'

'Oh.'

Sarah shrugged.

'Hmm, well never mind that now. They're here. Come on.'

Marianne led the way into the station concourse. She smiled at the man operating the barrier. He smiled back and the gate swung open as a group of about twenty or thirty goblins in grey hoodies came up the steps. Other passengers stood back to let them through.

Outside, the same thing happened as had in the station, people steppingd aside and standing still as the goblins headed out along Eslington Road, dividing into groups as they reached the junction. It was as if people's lives were on hold for a few seconds, which in effect they were. Then again, as in the Metro, they went about their business as if nothing had happened. A few sniffed the air before shrugging and walking on, but that was it.

'Are they necessary?' Sarah asked, wrinkling her nose.

Marianne smiled. 'They have their uses.'

'When you're not around they'll be fighting amongst themselves like the other night. One lot killed and burnt one from another gang down in the Dene.'

Marianne laughed as she set off up the road. 'Yes, I know. I bet that Inspector Kirby had a fine time explaining that one away. And when we're gone, if they fight, then that's fine. The more trouble, the more they stir things up, the better. They'll find their way home eventually. Well, most of them anyway.'

Sarah skipped a few steps to catch up with her mother. 'Sorry Mother, this is twenty-first-century Jesmond, not sixth-century BC or whenever, wherever.'

Marianne looked around at the rather splendid three-storey, Victorian, terraced houses, many divided into desirable flats. 'Oh come on, Sarah, stuffy old Jesmond could do with a bit of stirring up. When I was here, at least it had a bit of life. Walk down these streets then and you could get high just by breathing the air. Now it's all lattes and frappuccinos, kohlrabi and Treviso lettuce and the like. The gods help us from the ambitions of the pretentious middle classes.'

Sarah crossed her arms. 'Yes, well I live here. I like it and I don't see why you have to spoil it.'

Marianne put an arm around her daughter's shoulders. 'Listen, when we've finished, this place can be whatever you want it to be.'

'And your place?'

'Oh, that will definitely be what I want it to be.' Marianne grinned. 'Come on,' she said, increasing her pace behind the now disappearing gangs of goblins.

'Where are we going?'

'The Pub. That's where the entertainment's likely to start. Also, if there's one thing I do miss it's a good gin and tonic.'

Outside the Collingwood Arms, a large group of student-types were sat at some of the benches and tables drinking and chatting. Others were leaning against the stone sills of the ornate windows doing the same.

'Bit early for them, isn't it?' Marianne said.

'It's popular with post-grads and post-docs.'

Marianne rubbed her hands together and smiled. 'Good, good. The more the merrier, eh?'

248

One of the students started to rise as Sarah approached. Marianne glanced across and he froze, knees bent, arm half raised in greeting and a puzzled look on his face. He sat back down and within a couple of seconds was laughing with his friends again.

'Friend?' Marianne asked.

'Roger.'

'Your ex?'

'Uh-huh.'

Marianne studied the young man who now seemed oblivious to them. 'Not bad looking I suppose.'

Sarah half smiled as she stared across at Roger.

Marianne frowned. 'What, you still have feelings for him?'

'He was... is a nice boy,' she shrugged. 'I liked him, that's all. It just... didn't seem appropriate.'

'Yes, well stick with me girl and you can have your pick, believe me.'

'If you say so,' Sarah said, glancing over at Roger again before entering the pub.

Inside, Marianne looked around. 'Well at least they haven't tried to gentrify the Colly too much.'

Sarah followed her mother's gaze. 'I think the new trendy residents, as you might label them, like a bit of authenticity.'

Marianne laughed. 'Authenticity, is that what you call it?' she said, wandering up to the bar. Despite several groups already waiting to be served, the barman approached them first.

'What'll it be?'

'Now that's a trick I wouldn't mind having,' Sarah muttered.

'Two gin and tonics,' Marianne said. 'Oh, and make that large ones.'

'Coming up.'

The barman put the drinks down in front of Marianne with a smile. 'That'll be…' Marianne looked him in the eyes and he didn't finish. Instead he turned to the two men next to her. 'Yes, gents, what'll it be?'

'Mother!' Sarah whispered as they picked up their drinks.

'What? I'm like the queen. I don't carry cash.'

'He's a student trying to work his way through college. I've worked in a bar, that's likely to come out of his pay.'

Marianne's gaze drifted towards an older man at the other end of the bar, also serving customers. The man glanced across at the student, smiled and nodded. 'There, it's settled alright.'

'What is?'

Marianne nodded over her drink towards the older man. 'He's the manager and he's going to give your young barman a raise. How good's that?'

Sarah sipped at her drink. 'I thought you told me magic was not to be wasted on trivia.'

Marianne made for an empty table, put her drink down, sat and then leant back, spreading her arms across the back of the padded bench seat. 'I can feel it gathering,' she paused, rubbing the tips of her fingers with her thumbs. 'It's like a tingling. It's all around me and it's more intoxicating than this gin.' She grinned at Sarah. 'Soon we'll have magic to burn as you kids might say.' She paused before adding with another grin. 'Or even literally.'

Sarah sipped and studied her mother.

'Oh that was good,' Marianne said, draining her glass and then sucking on the piece of lemon. 'Want another?'

'I've hardly started this one.'

'Suit yourself.' Marianne rose from the table. As she did so, she glanced out of the window behind them. 'Forget that, at least for now. Come on, the entertainment's about to start.'

Outside, one group of goblins was trying to distract the students, while others attempted to steal packets of crisps and pints of beer from the tables. At first the students took it as a light-hearted prank, laughing as they snatched their beers away from the group of "kids" in grey hoodies. However, the goblins became bolder, trying to push the students away. There were cries of 'Hey!' and 'Watch it,' as some of the students began to object and push back. Within a few minutes, angry voices were being raised, beer was spilled and glasses were broken. When the manager appeared at the door, scuffles were breaking out between one or two of the students and the goblins, as well as between the goblins themselves.

'Call the police!' he shouted back through the door. His 'Clear off, you lot,' was ignored as the goblins turned their attention to a small group of elderly people at another table. One of the goblins threw his hood back and grinned a grin that almost split his face in half, showing an impressive array of pointy teeth as he did so. A woman screamed as the pensioners moved faster than Marianne suspected they'd done for years, abandoning their drinks, which the goblins now fought over.

'Mother?' Sarah said, her brow furrowed with uncertainty and concern.

Marianne laughed. 'Don't worry. It's at least given them something to talk about for the next year or so.' In the distance, a siren could be heard. 'Come on, perhaps it's time we left. Shame, I quite fancied another G & T.'

TWENTY-NINE

....

Kirby walked out of the back door of his mum's house. She was sitting with her back to him, a mug in her hands. She had her eyes closed and her face raised as if soaking up the late afternoon sun. 'Hello, Jonah. There's some tea in the pot, pet.'

How did she do that? 'Witch,' he muttered as he leant down and kissed her on the cheek.

She laughed. 'You better believe it,' she said, as he went back inside to get himself a drink.

'You left the door on the latch again,' Kirby said, back in the garden and sitting down next to his mum. 'You shouldn't do that, you know.'

She smiled at him. 'It's fine. There's no trouble round here. Mrs Dawson said she might drop in and what with me being in the garden, I might not hear the bell.'

Kirby shook his head. He'd had this conversation with her before and it made no difference. 'Is it OK if I stay here again tonight?'

'That's fine, dear. But you'll have to have the little room. I've got company staying.'

'Oh.'

'Yes, that lady I was telling you about from up the coast. You know, where I stayed after your dad passed away.' Mrs Kirby sat up as if a thought had just occurred to her. 'You could meet her. Nice lady, you'd like her. She's a widower you know.'

'So you said. On second thoughts, I'll go home.'

Mrs Kirby scowled at him. 'Now, Jonah…'

His phone vibrated in his pocket; he'd forgotten he'd put it on silent. 'Sorry, Mum,' he said, standing up and taking it out. 'Kirby.'

'Shirley, sir.'

'Ah yes, well done, Constable.'

'Sir?'

'Never mind. What is it?'

'There's a bit of bother, sir. Seems some teenagers have been kicking off with a group of students and it's escalating.'

'I'm sure we can leave that to uniform, Constable.'

'Er, sorry, sir. It started in the Collingwood Arms and the teenagers have been described as all wearing grey hoodies.'

'I'll be right over.'

Kirby shoved the phone in his pocket. 'Sorry, Mum, got to go.'

Mrs Kirby shook her head. 'Always the same, Jonah. Anything to save you getting on with your life.'

He leaned down and kissed her on the cheek again. 'That's right, Mum. You know me, any excuse.'

Kirby slapped the blue light on the roof of his car and switched on the siren. He was aware of curtains twitching as he accelerated down the road. He hated doing this. He knew some coppers loved it. However, he always seemed to find the idiots that panicked and weaved all over the road when he was behind them, or stopped dead as if he was supposed to drive over the top of them. *Who did they think he was? Batman?*

Rush hour on Gosforth High Street didn't help and now a bus was pulling out. 'Get out of the way!' he yelled, waving his hand across the windscreen. The bus got the message, then a hundred yards down the road, at a pedestrian crossing, the lights had changed. This of course had twenty or more people dithering, some dashing across, some getting to the middle and rushing back, others couldn't seem to make up their minds. One of those little trolley things on wheels, favoured by less mobile elderly ladies, overturned. Potatoes were rolling everywhere, with the elderly owner, now surprisingly nippy, chasing them down as if it was some mad parlour game. There was pushing and shoving and angry shouting, with cries of 'Oi!' and 'Mind me spuds.' Kirby put a hand on his head and groaned, it was like a nineteen-sixties' British comedy film. Sid James started laughing from the passenger seat. He could see the headlines, "Police car on emergency call causes another riot". Finally, he spotted a gap and risked it.

'Sorry,' he shouted, leaving a puddle of mashed potato behind him. Sensing his relief, the siren picked up the pace as he was speeding down the road.

Turning off Clayton Road and heading towards the Collingwood pub, he was flagged down by two uniformed officers.

'What's going on?' he asked, getting out of the car.

'It is all kicking off around the pub, sir, and down towards the Metro station.'

At that moment Shirley came running across. 'This way, sir. I suggest we run down Eskdale and try to get round the back.'

'What happened?' Kirby asked as they set off at a jog with Shirley in front. 'Not sure, sir. One witness reckons this gang of hoodies appeared from nowhere and started attacking people. It's just that at five in the afternoon it was a group of students outside the pub having a drink. Then more hoodies showed up and now they seem to be fighting with each other as well as anyone else that gets in their way.'

'What about Susie?' Kirby asked between gasps, doing his best to keep up.

'I rang,' Shirley shouted, glancing back over her shoulder. She slowed her pace to allow him to catch up. 'She's OK. Said she can hear things going on, shouting and the like, but she's fine. I told her to stay indoors.'

'Good.'

Shirley pointed. 'Look over there, sir.'

Harold was standing on the corner of Lambton Road. Kirby cut across and stopped, hands on his knees, sucking in lung-fulls of breath.

Harold looked round. 'Look like you've been running, Jonah.'

'I... what...I...'

'What's this all about, Harold?' Shirley asked, allowing Kirby to concentrate on breathing.

At the bottom end of the street, a group of what looked like teenagers emerged running towards the Metro station. Behind them were another group.

'Uh, oh,' Shirley said.

The first group stopped and were turning to face the second mob. Both were brandishing small clubs. Guttural shouts and cries were being exchanged while the clubs were waved in the air. Although Kirby couldn't understand the words, it was obvious they were issuing challenges to each other.

'What the hell is going on, Harold?' Kirby said, having got his breath back.

Harold shook his head. 'They'll have been sent to stir up trouble. You know I said that the magic in your world was spread thin, like an even layer?'

'Yes, so?'

'Well it's like it's attracted to strong emotions, fear, fury, all that adrenaline coursing through bodies. Then you can sort of feed off it if you know what you're doing;

harvest it. And there's one person I know who is capable of that.'

'Marianne?'

'Exactly,' Harold said, using a hand to shade his eyes as he peered down the street. 'Although I haven't seen her yet.'

Kirby watched as the two groups of, he hesitated to use the word goblins, for the moment at least, confined themselves to verbal exchanges.'

'But they're fighting each other,' Kirby said.

'Ah yes, unpredictable lot, your goblins. I'm guessing that body in the Dene belongs to one of these groups and they reckon the other lot were responsible.'

'Not something to be settled over a nice cup of tea then,' Shirley said.

Coming from the other end of the street Kirby heard the sound of approaching sirens, and few seconds later three police vans screeched to a halt. Out of each poured half a dozen uniformed officers in full riot gear.

'I guess the chief'll want to nip this in the bud,' Shirley said.

'Wonderful,' Kirby answered. 'All we need.'

The squad lined up and, on command, began their coordinated and deliberate shuffle towards the gangs, shields raised. It reminded Kirby of a Roman re-enactment he'd seen a couple of years ago, except that this lot were wearing shiny boots, not sandals. He half expected to hear the twang of a ballista. The two groups of goblins stopped their forceful exchange of opinions and turned to face the wall of blue closing in on them.

'You've got to get them to stay where they are,' Harold said, waving a hand towards the police line. 'If the goblins feel closed in they'll panic and fight.'

'I'd like to see the arrest sheets,' Shirley said.

'Oh, hell,' said Kirby. 'They've been deployed. So they'll want a result to show for it.'

'Just stop them,' Harold said turning and walking towards the two groups of goblins who for now seemed to have forgotten their differences in the face of a common enemy.

'Come on, Constable,' Kirby said jogging towards the line of blue and Perspex, holding his warrant card high. 'Time to save the day.'

'Let them through,' a voice behind the shields shouted.

After a few moments of sideways shuffling, accompanied by, 'Watch what you're doing with that shield you could've had my eye out' and 'Get off me foot!', a gap opened up.

'Ooh, evening, Dave,' Shirley said to one of the officers as she skipped through behind Kirby. 'Looking good.'

'Er thanks, Shirl,' came the muffled reply.

'Evening, Inspector,' Kirby said, putting on what he hoped was a bright smile with a hint of a casual-yet-business-like manner about it.

The inspector narrowed his eyes. 'What're you doing here, Kirby? Especially getting between my lads and that lot of little... little...'

'Misunderstood group of junior citizens?' Kirby finished for Inspector Carter.

Carter frowned. 'If you say so. Anyway, back to what the hell are you doing here? The rumour mill says you're on something so weird your chief goes right off his Hobnobs if it's even mentioned.'

'I am,' Kirby answered and waited. Carter had a reputation of being a "by the book" copper, something he drummed into those under his command. Which meant he struggled with anything that might be deemed outside the book. Imagination wasn't his strong point.

Carter pointed down the street. 'And who's that idiot in the leather gear running towards those misunderstood junior citizens?'

'He's with us.'

This caused Carter to pause. Kirby could almost hear the cogs grating against each other, like a learner driver trying to find reverse. Carter scratched his head, then stopped when he realised he still had his helmet on. He glanced at Kirby. 'Looks a bit of rum 'un to me.'

'He is, sir,' Shirley said, 'and more than a little, weird,' she added, eyes wide, drawing out and exaggerating the word "weird".

Kirby glanced at Shirley, who had fixed a smile on Carter, willing a whole slot machine of pennies to drop.

'Super's still going to want a report,' Carter said as if still trying to hold onto the book, feeling the need for its comfort, given the direction this might be going.

'Perhaps, sir. However, believe us, he's not going to appreciate the report he'll get if you catch up with that lot,' Shirley said, nodding in Harold's direction, who was waving his arms and shouting at the goblins in their own guttural language.

'So what's that?' Carter asked. 'Some sort of eastern European dialect?'

Shirley's eye blinked under the strain of maintaining the fixed smile. 'Not exactly, sir.'

Carter glared at Shirley and then looked at Kirby, who added his own smile and nodded in Shirley's support. Carter's face contorted and his eyes flickered from side to side as anger, puzzlement and frustration battled for prominence in his facial expressions. After a couple of seconds he bellowed at the line of policemen. 'Right, you lot, stay there. Anyone who moves a muscle will be on traffic duty in the morning.'

He turned back to Kirby. The shouting seemed to have restored his confidence a little. He pointed a finger. 'You better be right, Kirby. Or I'll... I'll...'

'Throw the book at us, sir?' Shirley suggested.

Both Kirby and Carter glared at her.

'Sorry, sirs.'

Carter's pointing finger quivered. 'Well, I'm just saying, that's all.'

'Understood,' Kirby said watching Harold, who appeared to have succeeded in calming the situation and was now shepherding the goblins towards the Metro. He wondered for a second if they all had tickets. Then he groaned. 'Come on, Constable, we're not done yet.'

Over his shoulder he heard. 'Alright, lads, back in the vans. The cocoa's on me.'

THIRTY

....

Kirby and Shirley caught up with Harold.

'At least you persuaded them to stop fighting each other,' Kirby said to Harold.

'For now. I told them they didn't want to see the dungeons and torture chambers you had in this world.'

Kirby tutted. 'Yes, thanks for that.'

Harold turned to him. 'You got a better idea? At least that's something they understand. Your average goblin not having much in the way of imagination.'

'They'd get on well with Inspector Carter then,' Shirley said.

Kirby glanced at her.

'Sorry, sir. Didn't mean to say that out loud.'

Harold smiled. 'It worked anyway.'

'Yes,' Kirby said. 'And let me guess, we've now got to get them back on to the Metro station?'

'So?'

'So? Twenty or more little... little goblins, carrying clubs. Hell, Harold, get them to drop those things.'

'They're Galgans.'

'What?'

'The little clubs, Galgans. They're the traditional weapon of your goblin, often handed down through the family. Centuries-old some of them with the names of their ancestors carved into them. They're not going to just leave them here.'

Kirby huffed and grabbed a sleeve forcing Harold to turn to him. 'You may not have noticed, Harold, that your average Newcastle resident doesn't walk the streets armed.'

Harold raised his eyebrows.

'Alright, with the exception of you and maybe some of those who frequent the Bigg Market on a Saturday night. What I'm getting at is that it's hardly going to go down well when we get to the Metro. Where, given what's gone on here, there are likely to be more police.'

'Sir, we need to do something,' Shirley said as they approached Jesmond Metro station. As predicted, outside were two squad cars with flashing lights. Standing next to them were half a dozen, nervous looking coppers.

The goblins had also noticed them and were casting uncertain and unhappy glances at Harold as they caught up with them.

Harold said something to them and with some reluctance it seemed their clubs, or rather Galgans, were secreted in their clothing.

'They listen to you?' Shirley asked.

'Yes, er… they know me.'

'Know you, Harold?' Kirby said. 'You've not mentioned this.'

'You never asked.' He sniffed. 'Anyway, I've helped them in the past campaigning for er... goblins' rights.'

'There's a thing,' Shirley said.

Kirby shook his head. 'Good for you. However, now we've got to get them back to where they came from and that means getting past those coppers and the barriers.' He looked up at Harold. 'I don't suppose they've got tickets?'

Harold opened his mouth to speak.

'No,' Kirby answered for him. 'So how did they get through earlier without anyone noticing?'

'Marianne,' Harold said.

'Great.' Kirby scanned the approach to the station, half expecting to see the woman standing there. 'So how did she intend getting them back?'

Harold shrugged. 'Didn't care. The more they roamed causing problems the more she'd like it.'

'What, she'd just leave them here?' Shirley said.

Harold nodded. 'Oh, they might find their way back eventually, but not before a few more of them were dead.'

'And God knows what else,' Kirby finished for him. 'Listen, get them to let me through.'

The goblins stopped, and from the shuffling of feet Kirby assumed they were nervous. A number of them were pulling their hoods even further forward and staring at the ground in true teenager fashion, trying to hide their features, for which he was grateful.

As they let him past, one of the six policemen approached. 'Oh hello, sir. Didn't expect to see you here.'

He made a point of leaning over, looking behind Kirby at the group of shuffling grey hoods.

Shirley waved and smiled. 'Evening, Eric. How's Nancy and the little one?'

Eric half raised his hand as if unsure such familiarity was appropriate in the circumstances. 'Er, hello, Shirley. And er, yes fine thanks.'

'Er sorry, sir' the now uncertain, yet more relaxed, sergeant said to Kirby. 'I'm taking it this isn't your normal bag of bother? You being here and all that.'

'No, Sergeant. This is a bit special, if you get my meaning.'

The sergeant glanced at Harold then across at Shirley, who continued to smile at him. 'Sir?' the sergeant said, letting his curiosity get the better of him.

'Yes, Sergeant?' Kirby said in the senior officer tone that said even if it sounded like he was inviting the sergeant to ask more questions, really he wasn't.

The sergeant let his shoulders sag a little. 'As long as you're sure, sir'

'I am, Sergeant.'

The sergeant nodded and turned to the other officers. 'Alright, you lot, show's over. No more overtime tonight.'

'Well done, Constable,' Kirby said as Shirley joined him, appreciating the deft wrong footing the constable had deployed.

'Thank you, sir.'

They watched the officers get back in their cars and drive away, still sporting the blues and twos, he noted. He'd have words about that later. He turned back to Harold. 'Right, any chance you can get them to sort of line up?'

'I'll try. I don't think they'll be too good at it though.'

Kirby smiled. 'Perfect. Oh, and keep them doing that.'

'What?'

'Behaving like teenagers.'

Kirby led his little band up the front steps of the station. He glanced back to see some pushing and shoving.

'That'll do nicely,' he said to Shirley as they approached the ticket barrier.

'As long as they keep those clubs hidden away,' Shirley said.

'Thank you for that thought, Constable.'

Before Shirley could reply a Metro official was taking a step towards them. The man's level of suspicion given away by the pulling down of his cap and the hitching up of his trousers.

'They're with us,' Kirby said, holding out his warrant card. Shirley did the same.

'They'll still need a ticket,' the man said standing on his tip toes, head bobbing as he tried to count the group behind Kirby.

'They've lost them,' Kirby said.

'What, all of them?'

'Yes, all of them. You know what teenagers are like.' Kirby shrugged, then tutted and raised his eyes to the ceiling in what he hoped would translate as a "what can you do?" sort of way. 'Probably eaten them.' Which he thought might have been true if they'd had them in the first place. He gave a little laugh to show he was joking. The man didn't join in.

'What about the old geezer?'

Kirby narrowed his eyes. 'Him as well.'

'And you two?'

Kirby waved his card and said nothing.

'Well I'm not sure about this.'

Shirley pointed back to the entrance. Their group was blocking the way and other would-be passengers were straining to look over their heads to see what was going on. 'Er, I don't think you want them to miss their train and we have to get this lot back, so…'

'Exactly,' Kirby said, putting on his best voice of authority. 'So why don't you open that nice little gate?' He handed the man one of his cards. 'You can always call the station in the morning. Tell you what, why don't you come down and we can discuss it?'

The man pursed his lips as if he'd just sucked on a lemon. 'I'm sure that's not necessary,' he said through gritted teeth as the gate swung open.

Kirby and Shirley stood aside as Harold shepherded his flock through with the minimum of fuss. Although at one point, during a bit of pushing and shoving, there was a loud "bong" as a small club hit the ground and bounced. Kirby pushed the offending "teenagers" through the gap before bending down and picking it up. 'Been playing rounders,' he said, smiling and hurrying to follow the little group towards the stairs down to the platform.

He caught up with Harold at the door that wasn't there. 'Here, take this,' he said, handing him the club.

'Where d'you get that?'

'Never mind,' he said, shoving Harold through the opening after the goblins. 'Just make sure they're all gone... wherever it is they're going.'

'Move along, nothing to see,' Kirby said to a passenger coming down the steps, who gave him a puzzled look. As Kirby glanced behind him, there was nothing to see.

'Well, I think that went as well as could be expected, sir.' Shirley said.

'You mean for containing a potential rioting group of goblins on the streets of Jesmond?'

'Ah yes, I see what you mean.'

Just then, Harold reappeared through the door. 'Well I thought that went as well as could be expected.'

Kirby rolled his eyes. Shirley hid her smile with a cough.

'What?'

'Nothing,' Kirby said. 'Nothing at all. Listen, are there likely to be any more of them?'

Harold stroked his chin. He looked at Shirley. 'Anything being reported?'

'Nope.'

'If there are then chances are they're in small groups. They'll soon lose interest and make their way home.'

'Well that's reassuring,' Kirby said, shaking his head. 'Come on, let's get out of here.' At the top of the stairs the gate was shut again. 'Would you mind?' Kirby asked the official who was trying hard to look the other way. The man opened it without saying anything.

'So kind,' Shirley said.

Outside the station Harold ran a hand through his hair while looking around.

'What?' Kirby said.

'I'm just wondering where Marianne's got to.'

'Why would she stick around?'

Harold sniffed the air like a bloodhound searching for the scent. 'The magic, she'll feed off it. Like caffeine gives you a kick, magic does that for her.'

'And you can smell it?'

Harold nodded. 'It's like a metallic tang in the air. It gets the back of the throat.'

'Sounds more like hayfever,' Shirley said. 'You don't find there's some very magical bunches of flowers, do you?'

Harold scowled at her. 'Just because you can't see it or touch it or shop on Amazon for it doesn't mean it don't exist.'

'If you say so.'

'Now, now, children,' Kirby said setting off up the road back towards his car. 'I've got better things to do than hang around here listening to you two bicker.'

After a hundred yards or so, Harold gave a loud sniff and grabbed Kirby by the arm, turning him round.

'What?' Kirby said.

Harold pointed towards the station. 'Look.'

Approaching the entrance to the Metro was a woman, at least Kirby thought there was. However, every time he tried to focus, it was as if his eyes slid away from her, as if they refused to believe anyone was there.

'There's someone else with her, I think,' Shirley said, squinting as if that might help. 'I'm not sure. It's... it's like I'm seeing a ghost. Not that I'm saying I've actually seen a ghost of course.' She stopped squinting. 'I'm not, am I?'

'Well?' Kirby asked Harold.

'No,' Harold said. 'They don't appear like that. It's one of Marianne's tricks. The only reason we can see her at all is that she might be...' he paused. 'Look, yes. She's distracted. There's someone with her, a girl maybe.' Harold turned his head a little. 'Sometimes it's easier if you use your peripheral vision, as if you're trying not to see them, if you get what I mean.'

'I can't see anything now,' Shirley said. 'Which could of course be because I'm trying not to look.'

'They've gone,' Harold said. 'And I'd swear there was a girl with her.'

'Sarah?' Kirby asked.

'Could have been. I'm sure she had red hair.'

'We could show the staff a photo of her,' Shirley said.

Harold shook his head. 'Trust me, they won't have seen a thing. They'll have opened the barrier, smiled, said hello, then as soon as they'd passed they would remember nothing.'

'Hmm,' Kirby said turning and starting to walk up the road again. 'You think it was Sarah?'

'Couldn't say for sure, but yes it looked like her.'

Shirley skipped a few steps to catch up. 'According to her, she's not seen her mother since she was little.'

Harold frowned as he turned to stare at the station entrance. 'She wouldn't remember if Marianne didn't want her to. Or if she's anything like Marianne and Marianne's been teaching her a few things, she could tell you black was white and you'd believe her.'

'I wonder if she could teach me that trick,' Shirley said, glancing at Kirby.

THIRTY-ONE

....

Walking into the station, Kirby noted the Desk Sergeant had already adopted his bored, "I've heard it all before" expression towards the irate, well-dressed man on the other side of the desk who was jabbing a finger in the sergeant's direction, telling him how ridiculous it was as he'd only parked there for a few minutes. Kirby walked past at the 'And I'll tell you another thing' moment.' He muttered 'mistake' when he heard the words 'to think I pay my taxes…' If you wanted to annoy a Desk Sergeant, that was one of the best. Kirby took the stairs two at a time in an effort not to hear the reply. At the top he was breathing a little heavily when Shirley walked past.

'You alright, sir?'

Kirby straightened up and made an effort to breathe through his nose, which produced a suppressed wheeze. 'I like to run up the stairs that's all, Constable.' He paused trying to catch his breath and patted his stomach. 'Exercise and all that.'

'Hmm,' Shirley said. 'Couldn't help noticing last night that you were a little out of breath.' She smiled at him. 'Might I suggest a gym?'

Kirby frowned, wondering when things had changed so much that constables felt safe in making such comments. 'No you might not.'

'Sir.'

Kirby headed towards his desk.

'Oh, sir!'

He turned. 'Yes, Shirley,' he said smiling and using her name to indicate that he wasn't holding her comment against her.

'The Chief wants to see you.'

The frown returned.

'Is he in, Jane?'

'Yes, he's expecting you, go straight in. Oh and Jonah.'

'Yes?'

'Try not to upset him.'

Kirby smiled back as he knocked on the door then walked in.

'Ah, Jonah, have a seat.'

'Thank you, sir.' Kirby sat and waited for the chief to start the conversation. Nervous, less-experienced officers would often start volunteering information on a matter that the chief had had no idea about. The chief frowned and Kirby tried to look innocent, as if he didn't know the game they were playing.

The chief shuffled in his seat. 'I'm told you were on the scene of last night's riot?'

'I'd hardly call it a riot, sir. More of a series of minor scuffles.'

The chief drummed on his desk. 'Yes, good, good.'

Kirby waited.

'But still, you were there?'

'Yes, sir.'

'So was this something to do with your current... er, investigation?'

'It could have been that I simply happened to be in the vicinity, sir.'

'Could it?' The chief asked, his frown lines smoothing a little.

Kirby tried a small smile. 'If you would prefer it that way, sir?'

The chief studied Kirby for a second, gave a little shudder and shook his head. He gripped the edge of the desk, the frown lines returning. 'No, no...'

'In that case, sir, yes, I did have reason to believe it had something to do with my current investigation.'

The chief found a small pile of papers and began straightening them. Kirby recognised the signs. 'Shall I keep you informed, sir?' The chief looked across at him. 'On the grounds that if I think you need to know?'

The chief nodded slowly, as if to himself, while staring at a line of pens which he now started to rearrange. 'If you think I need to know.' Again he looked up. 'Yes, yes. Perhaps that would be the best way to handle it.' He began nodding again and casting his eyes around the other pieces of desk paraphernalia in front of him.

'Is that all, sir?'

'Yes, yes. Thank you, Jonah.'

'Sir.'

Kirby closed the door behind him and Jane looked up.

'Well?'

'Tea and Hobnobs?'

'I'll get them,' Jane said pushing her chair back.

Kirby wandered into the main office and stared at his desk and the blank screen.

'You have turn it on, sir,' Shirley said walking behind him on her way to the printer.

'So I hear,' Kirby said, gazing down at a brown envelope with his name on it. He'd learnt that rarely was anything he wanted to see delivered in a brown envelope. 'Come on, Constable, let's go and have chat with Harold.'

Parking on Clayton Road, Kirby wandered over to Mystique, which had a sign in the window, "Closed until further notice".

'I stopped by the other day, sir, as you asked,' Shirley said.

'Hmm,' Kirby said cupping a hand against the window and peering inside.

'The sign was up then. No one in.'

'Hmm.'

'About the shoes.'

'Sorry, yes. There was this strange woman looking after the shop when I called in. Herbal tea and jingling bangles. Titania she liked to call herself, although her real name's Jane. Mind you, the whole place is a bit strange so I suppose she fitted right in.'

'I see what you mean, sir,' Shirley said joining him at the window, peering at a rack of floaty dresses and a Buddha, decked with beads.

Kirby moved his head from side to side wondering if he could see a light on in the back. 'Yes, she was away with the fairies half the time. Which is rather appropriate.'

'Sir?'

'Midsummer Night's Dream, Constable.'

'Sir?'

'You know, Queen of the Fairies.'

Shirley frowned.

'William Shakespeare?'

'Oh, I see,' Shirley said in a tone that indicated she didn't.

Kirby shook his head. 'You've heard of Shakespeare, right?'

Shirley's frown turned into a scowl as put her hands on her hips. 'Yes, sir! In the sixth form they even took us to see one of his plays.'

Kirby glanced back at her. 'Oh, which one?'

Shirley let her hands drop. 'Er, dunno. I was more interested in trying to sneak off and get Darren Pugh to buy me a drink at the bar. He was trying to get off with me you see, so…'

'Yes, thank you, Constable. However, as fascinating as your adolescent love life no doubt was, I'm not sure I need to hear about it.'

Shirley blushed. 'Er no. Of course. Sorry, sir.'

'Anyway, it seems Titania ain't there now.'

Shirley rattled the handle and knocked on the door, but there was no response. 'Been a day or two,' she said, pointing to the pile of mail, leaflets for takeaway pizza and the free catalogues that usually went into the recycling unopened.

'So,' Kirby said. 'I'm guessing it closed soon after I left.'

'That's a coincidence.'

Kirby looked at her.

'Suspicious,' Shirley corrected herself.

Kirby smiled. 'Come on, let's go and ignore all the flagrant minor infringements we'll find in Harold's little emporium.'

The bell tinkled its welcome.

'Nice,' Shirley said. 'If you like the faded 1960s' look.'

'I think for Harold that constitutes modern.'

As Kirby now understood it, fifty years or so was only a fraction of the time Harold and his shop had existed. He guessed that if you asked the older locals, like the lady in the coffee shop, they would say that Harold's shop had always been there. What they wouldn't be able to tell you was just how long "always" was.

In front of Kirby was a bucket containing five or six string mops. A hand-written sign said, "Free bar of carbolic with every mop". From the depths of the dusty interior came a detached voice. 'Morning, Jonah, Shirley.' A few seconds later an ancient, inhabited grey cardigan with leather patched sleeves shuffled around the corner.

'Alright, Harold, we can dispense with that.'

Harold grinned and the arthritic, elderly man became a good foot taller, straight-backed and of indeterminate age.

'I don't know why you do it.'

'I have an image to keep up,' Harold said, still smiling.

'And how did you know it was us?'

'CCHV,' Harold said.

'CCHV?'

'Closed Circuit Harold Vision,' Harold said, pointing to the convex mirror hanging in the depth of the shop above the ancient till, which was one of those where the little white flags with the price jerks up when you bang on the keys.

'Ever thought of CCTV?' Kirby asked.

'Nah. No one ever tries to nick anything from me. At least not more than once, and even then they don't get away with it.' Kirby suspected it was true, but refrained from enquiring as to how Harold achieved that on the grounds that he might not like the answer.

Shirley had picked up a can of sweetcorn and was examining the date on the bottom. Kirby took it from her and put it back on the shelf.

'But…' Shirley said.

'I warned you.'

Harold ignored the exchange. 'So what brings you back this fine morning, Inspector, Constable? Some of my enticing bargains?' He added pointing to the mops.

Kirby shook his head. 'Tempting, I admit, although perhaps not this time. I wanted your take on last night and then I thought we might go and pay the girls a visit.'

Harold rubbed a longer finger under his nose as a black cat meowed and arched its back against his leg.

Kirby watched the cat, which stared back with large, green, unblinking eyes.

'Just a cat,' Harold said, as if reading his thoughts. 'Boudica.'

'Boudica?'

Harold shrugged as if to suggest it was as good a name as any. 'You're not going to like it.'

'You don't say. Since you appeared in my life, Harold, I've seen and heard a lot of things that I haven't liked. However, that doesn't mean I can ignore them.'

'Sure?'

'Try me.'

Harold glanced at Kirby and then Shirley. 'Alright, but you really are going to need me now.'

'That's why we're here.'

Harold nodded. 'Let's go in the back.'

'What about the shop?' Shirley said. 'I'd hate for you to miss a sale.'

Harold was already clacking through the bead curtain. 'It's OK, Boudica can handle it.'

"The back", Kirby knew, was part kitchen, part storeroom. Boxes of crisps and toilet paper were piled up together in one corner, along with other boxes that Kirby didn't recognise. Shirley's gaze wandered across the various items of stock.

'No good will come of that,' Kirby said.

'Sorry, sir.'

In the middle of the room was a solid pine table and a couple of chairs that might have a presenter on the Antiques Roadshow quite excited.

'I like what you've done with the place,' Shirley said as she sat, making an effort to focus on the table.

Harold grunted from where he was standing at an old stone sink. He filled a battered kettle which he then placed on an ancient-looking gas stove. Kirby watched Harold turn the ivory-coloured knob and stand at arm's length holding a match. The initial flame leapt about two feet in the air before settling down.

'I'd get that checked out if I were you,' Kirby said.

'Don't worry. We have an understanding. Coffee?'

'Go on then.'

'Why not,' Shirley said before adding, 'as long as it's not out of date by more than a decade.'

Harold reached on to a shelf and took down a bottle of Camp coffee, then spooned the thick brown goo into three battered and chipped mugs he'd taken off a wire draining rack.

'What the hell's that?' Shirley whispered to Kirby.

Kirby smiled. 'Oh, you're in for a treat.'

Harold filled the mugs with boiling water and topped them up with milk from an actual glass bottle.

'Is that semi or soya?' Kirby asked.

'What?'

He took the mug Harold was offering him. 'Nothing.'

Shirley held her mug in both hands and peered into its murky depths for a second before pulling it towards her and sniffing experimentally.

Harold pushed a small bowl with a rose on it in their direction. 'Sugar?'

Shirley shook her head without looking up from her mug.

'No thanks,' Kirby said

Harold took it back and shovelled four heaped teaspoonfuls into his own mug.

The first sip took Kirby back into his grandmother's kitchen. He could see the flowery patterned apron she wore every day, except on Sundays, and smelled the comforting mix of Dettol and boiled cabbage which was always there. The latter was something of a mystery as his grandmother hated cabbage. She said that was because she'd been forced to eat it as a child on account of it being all her dad seemed to grow on his allotment.

Shirley took a sip and wrinkled her nose. 'Jeese!' She took another. 'Actually, it's not that bad. Although not much like coffee.'

'So, Harold?' Kirby said, glancing across at Shirley who was still sniffing and sipping, 'now that Shirley's approved your attempts at alchemy, what's your take on last night?'

'Just the start.'

'I was afraid you might say that.'

Harold sipped and paused, then added another spoonful of sugar. 'I think Marianne was testing the theory, as it were.'

'I thought you said those riots some years ago were the same thing?'

Harold shook his head. 'A crude blunderbuss-style approach, which is why I suspect it didn't work.'

'And this time?'

'Marianne's clever, don't ever underestimate her. She'll have learnt from that and refined whatever it is she's doing.'

'Which is?'

Harold shook his head. 'That sort of magic's not really my thing. Dangerous game.'

'In what way?' Shirley asked.

Harold shifted in his seat. 'You've got to be strong to wield it. Get it wrong and it's likely to consume you. She almost lost control of it last time, which is why I think we haven't heard of her for some time. She's been recovering.'

'So we force her to over-stretch herself?' Shirley said between sips. 'Problem solved.'

'Except that she'd take Jesmond with her and perhaps a good chunk of Newcastle as well.'

'Ah,' Kirby said.

'Maybe…' Shirley paused, then smiled. 'We could lure her over to Blythe and have a go there?'

Kirby frowned at his junior officer. 'Constable.'

Shirley shrugged and stared into her mug. 'Sorry, sir. Just an idea. Two birds and all that.'

'Yes well, I'm the one who'd have to write the report and explain it to the Chief.' He turned back to Harold. 'And Sarah?'

'Part of that refinement is my guess.' He shrugged. 'One to wield the power, the other to act as a safety valve in some way. And Sarah's a child of this world, which may help as well.'

'So Sarah's definitely in on it?' Shirley asked.

Harold shrugged. 'I don't know. She might not realise what she's doing when she's with Marianne and then not remember a thing when it's all over. Although I think that might be bit much, even for Marianne.' He sucked in a breath and worry lines creased his forehead. 'And despite everything, she is Marianne's daughter.'

'Great,' Kirby said, 'two of them.' He drained his cup. 'Come on, I think we'd better get round there.'

THIRTY-TWO

....

Kirby rang the bell. To his surprise, the door was opened by a slim woman with auburn hair, who he guessed was in her mid-forties. 'Er, hello, is Susie in?'

The woman smiled. 'I'm sorry and you are?'

'Quite right,' Kirby said, taking out his warrant card. 'Inspector Kirby. And this is Constable Barker. At the back there is…er, Harold.'

The woman leant to look past him. 'Good to see you, Harold. It's been a while.'

'Oh hello, Connie.'

'Excuse me?' Kirby said.

At that moment Susie appeared, rubbing her hair with a pink towel. 'Who is it, Mum?' she said before looking up. 'Oh hello, Inspector, Shirley, ooh and Harold.'

'I think you'd better come through and I'll make some tea,' Susie's mum said.

'Good idea,' Kirby said following her down the passage. 'Is there anyone you don't know?' he whispered to Harold. Harold shrugged.

Kirby waited while the kettle boiled and Susie's mum made the tea. She joined them in the four seats around the table while Susie leant against the worktop. 'So would someone like to explain?' he said, raising his eyebrows in Harold's direction.

Harold smiled across at Susie's mother. 'Jonah meet Connie, Susie's mum and er… yes, er… Marianne's sister.'

'What! And you knew…'

Harold held up his hand to hold back the torrent that might be heading in his direction. 'Wait. I didn't realise until now that Connie here was Susie's mother. Although, looking at them, perhaps I should have guessed. However, I haven't seen Connie in a long time.'

'So…'

Harold's second hand joined the first. 'Listen, Marianne and Connie are sisters but that's it, I promise.' He looked at Connie, his face pleading for support.

Susie took the opportunity of the pause to get her own, 'Mum!' in. 'That… that makes Sarah and I cousins. And… and… you knew and didn't tell me?'

Connie took a deep breath. 'I know, dear, and I'm sorry. Perhaps I should have said something before now.'

Susie's face, which had been pink, was now a definite explosion-pending, red colour. 'Perhaps!'

'Wow,' said Shirley, 'And I thought my family was dysfunctional.' Kirby frowned at her. Shirley took a keen interest in the pattern on her mug.

It was Kirby's turn to hold both hands in the air. 'If one person could give me a succinct, and I mean succinct, account of what's going on?' He glared at Harold who passed the glare on to Connie.

Connie glanced around the table before focusing on Susie. 'Alright, alright, I might have told you, love, before now.'

'Might? I...'

Kirby held a hand up again. To his mild amazement, silence returned.

Connie continued. 'And it's why, I'm sure, you and Sarah hit it off. I didn't say anything for good reason at the time.' This time she held up a hand to stop Susie's interruption. 'And I'll explain in more detail when there's just the two of us, OK?' In answer, Susie scowled and crossed her arms, although the affected sternness was lost a little due to the pink towelling dressing gown with a cute rabbit, complete with stand-out floppy ears, on the pocket.

Connie turned back to Kirby. 'Yes, Inspector, Marianne and I are sisters, which is one of the reasons I'm here. I wanted to check up on things. Believe me, I'm not part of whatever Marianne is planning and I never will be. And if I can help you I will. We come from the same womb, but that's where our association stops. I know Harold because we all come from the same... the same village, I guess you'd call it.'

'In this other world? A concept I'm still struggling with by the way.'

'I don't know,' Shirley chipped in, 'might explain some of the characters we see around the town of an evening.'

'And the politicians worry about migration from the EU,' Kirby muttered. 'So how many of you are there, and why come here anyway?'

Connie glanced at Harold, who nodded. 'Not many. There's always been some movement of people who know. Most don't, of course.'

'There's a relief.' Kirby looked towards Connie. 'And you? I understand, I think, why Harold's here. No disrespect, why did you come or rather stay?'

Connie studied Kirby for a second in which he felt his whole character was being assessed. She then turned to Shirley whose wide-eyed look of surprise indicated she felt the same. 'I don't know what Harold's already told you. However, like him, I'm trusting you because if Edna hadn't seen something in you that meant she trusted you, you would never have got to Harold.'

Connie glanced across at Susie, who still had her arms crossed, although her face had returned back to a healthy pink colour. 'Our village,' she said, looking at Harold, 'have always known. We are all guardians of the secret, although a few, like Harold, make it their life's work. Your world has chosen to forget us, although we haven't forgotten you. So in many ways we are children of both worlds. We take it seriously, Inspector. How can I put this, our worlds occupy the same place, only in sort of different dimensions, and in many ways they are very similar. Even our histories are connected. However, your world has accelerated ahead and left ours far behind to the point where contact between the worlds, such as Marianne is trying to instigate, may be an inconvenience for you, but disastrous for us.'

'In what way?'

Connie took a deep breath. 'The riots of a few years ago were horrible and not something anyone in their right minds would want repeating. However, repairs were made, people made speeches, a few programs were put in place and, essentially, your world carries on as if it had never happened. However, if Marianne succeeds then the power it would give her would make her unstoppable. Marianne is one of the most dangerous types of people, someone who believes she knows exactly how things should work and that she is the person to make those things happen. Give those sort of people absolute power and… well your own history also has a few examples of that.'

During the conversation Susie said nothing, although her scowl had deepened to what Kirby could see was again becoming a dangerous level. Even the cute bunny seemed to have lost his smile. Susie's foot was tapping. 'And you never thought to tell me any of this?'

Connie cast a pleading look at her daughter. 'Please, Susie, I will explain. In the village, the tradition is that the revelations take place on a person's twenty-first birthday. Perhaps it was silly of me to stick to that and up till now there seemed no harm in it. I would then have taken you to the village and all would have been made clear.'

Susie's foot-tapping increased in tempo. 'But... but... Sarah... and...'

Connie's eyes pleaded with her daughter. 'Please, dear, this is for you and me.'

Susie took a breath and huffed her displeasure before letting her shoulders sag in resignation. She settled for a glare, to let her mother know she wasn't off the hook.

Satisfied that an imminent explosion had been contained, Kirby glanced at Susie and then back to Harold. 'You have all this in common and you still didn't know Susie was related to Sarah?'

'No,' Harold said, shaking his head. 'Perhaps, as I said, I should have guessed.' Harold turned to Connie. 'Mephisto came to see me. They're threatening the village if we continue to interfere.'

Connie nodded. 'To be expected, I suppose.'

'Hang on,' Susie said. 'Does Sarah know all this and about me?'

Connie shrugged. 'It's possible, if she's anything like her mother. I've sincerely been hoping she wasn't, which was another reason for not saying anything. Yet if she is, she would be very adept at making people see and believe what she wanted them to.'

'And is she?' Kirby said. 'Like her mother?'

This time Connie's shoulders sagged. 'As I said, I hoped not. As far as I knew they'd never seen each other since Marianne ran off with Mephisto. But now she's back, I can't believe she hasn't made contact with her daughter.'

'And of course Sarah was missing for that time. And when we found her, all she kept saying was the name Dunstanburgh. Oh, and she did mention men with beards.'

Connie glanced at Harold.

'Yes, I've told him the potential significance of that.'

Kirby turned to Susie. 'Has Sarah said anything else about that day.'

Susie shook her head. 'No, it's as if it never happened.'

'She may not know anything else,' Connie said. 'There again…'

At that moment the door opened and a yawning Sarah came into the kitchen dressed in a T-shirt, pyjama bottoms and flip flops. She smiled. 'Ooh, quite a gathering.' She yawned again. 'Sorry, is there any tea in that pot?'

Susie edged out of her way, although Sarah appeared not to notice. Sarah poured herself some tea. 'Sorry again, I'm going to go back into my room. Got work to do.'

'Before you go,' Kirby said. 'Where were you yesterday evening?'

Sarah smiled at Susie. 'Here, why? Susie'll tell you. I was knackered.'

'She was,' Susie said, looking at her mum as she said it.

Sarah waved a hand and then flip-flopped back out of the kitchen and into her room.

'Was she?' Kirby asked Susie when they heard Sarah's door close.

'Yes, she fell asleep watching some rubbish on the telly in the afternoon and then went to her room. I didn't see her again and I was in all evening. You called remember. Why?'

Harold put his mug down. 'I thought I glimpsed her near the Metro with Marianne. I could have been wrong of course.'

Susie shook her head. 'I'm positive she didn't go out. I would have known.'

'Perhaps not,' Connie said, grabbing her daughter's hand. Susie didn't resist. 'If she didn't want you to.'

Susie looked close to tears. 'Not Sarah, Mum. Please, I'm sure I'd know.'

'Funny,' Shirley said. 'Somehow I believed her as well.'

'You would,' Connie said.

'This is going to sound weird,' Shirley said. 'A second or two before she actually entered, it's like I caught a glimpse of her out of the corner of my eye standing in the doorway. Then when I turned there was no one there.'

Connie glanced at Harold, who raised his eyebrows in answer.

'Great,' said Kirby. 'So what now?'

'Susie, why don't you pack a case and come home with me for a few days?'

'Mum, I'll be…'

'Please, dear.'

'Alright, Mum.' Susie said as she left the room.

Connie glanced at Shirley, then across at Harold.

'I'll help her,' Shirley said.

'And if you don't need me,' Harold said. 'I've a shop to run.'

'That was good,' Kirby said when he was alone with Connie.

Connie shook her head as she stood up and refilled the kettle. 'No it wasn't, Jonah. I don't like doing that, especially to my own daughter. Then again she can be very stubborn,' she smiled. 'Like her Mother. And I didn't want to argue. Also, there's other things she needs to understand that perhaps I should have told her before now.'

Kirby nodded. 'I know what you mean. I have a daughter myself and she takes after her Mum in the same way.'

'I know.'

'Yes, it's… wait a minute. You said, you know?' Kirby narrowed his eyes at the woman who was now filling the teapot again. 'And you called me Jonah.'

Connie laughed. 'Don't worry, it's nothing sinister. I was wondering how long it'd take. I guessed it was you. Alice Kirby's boy.'

Kirby scratched his head while the cogs in his brain whirred. 'Wait, you're the woman who has that place up the coast, a sort of a retreat, that Mum went to after Dad died. And it's you who was staying with her last night.'

'Yes, I see her from time to time when I come into town.' She gave him a knowing half smile. 'I thought you were supposed to be there?'

Kirby shuffled in his seat. 'Er yes, things to do.'

Connie ignored the evasion. 'I like your Mum, Jonah. She's an intelligent and perceptive woman, even if she tries to hide it at times.'

'Don't I know it.'

Connie laughed again.

Kirby nodded. 'And Susie said her Mum lived up there.'

'That's right. So Alice's told me all about you,' she paused. 'And Jeanie, of course.'

'I'll bet she has.' Kirby felt a knot of emotion forming in his chest.

'Don't be cross with her, Jonah. She's worried about you, that's all.'

Kirby forced himself to relax. Then he blushed, thinking about what else his mother might have said. 'She's been trying…' he coughed, 'trying to get me to meet you.'

Connie smiled. 'I know. As I said, she's concerned about you, Jonah.' She glanced towards the door. 'It's a Mother thing.'

It was Kirby's turn to laugh.

'Anyway, admit it, she may be right some times. When this is all, over come up for a few days. Get away from everything. It's nothing "magical" I promise. Simply time to think and reflect in peaceful surroundings.'

Kirby put his head back, then looked across at this woman who seemed all too easily to get past the Mr Policeman screen he hid himself behind. 'You're right. Mum's right, and Anna, I know. So perhaps when this is over…'

She smiled. 'I'll hold you to it.'

Kirby returned the smile as he rose from the table. 'In the meantime I've got to try and prevent mayhem and God knows what else.'

'Trust Harold,' Connie said when Kirby reached the door. 'He's so much more than he first appears.'

'Oh I think I've learnt that already.'

THIRTY-THREE

....

Marianne had enjoyed her early morning walk. The countryside here was tidy, more cultured and soothing than the still wild unkempt nature of her world. Less exciting though, she thought, however that could always change. She marvelled at how the same place could seem so familiar and yet be so different. Even the animals she'd passed in the fields, the cows and the sheep, were so much more... well, domesticated. Perhaps that was it, she smiled to herself, this version of the world was just so much more domesticated. Maybe that's why she'd come to dislike it in the end. Any wildness she might have found was only temporary. It needed a little livening up and if she had her way, which she fully intended to, that's what it would be getting.

She opened the wrought-iron garden gate. As her feet crunched up the gravel path, the air was cool despite the sun. The morning dew still coated the leaves and flowers of the herbaceous border to one side and the small lawn on the other. A vivid pink rose brushed against her leg as if enticing her to smell its sweet fragrance. All so very pretty. How quaint, she thought, typical Connie. A nosy black Labrador came around the corner of the cottage, tail wagging. Seeing Marianne, it stopped and started backing away, emitting a strangled whine as she looked at it. The blue painted front door opened.

'Oh it's you,' Connie said. 'I wondered when I might get a visit.' Connie took a few steps across the grass to lay a comforting hand on the dog which sat shaking, his eyes fixed on Marianne. Under Connie's stroking, he calmed. 'Go on. It's alright, I'll handle this.' The dog got to his feet and backed away a few steps, growling before turning and running back around the corner from where it had come. 'Do you get a kick out that, Marianne? Frightening animals.'

Marianne grinned. 'And some people, Connie. Let's not forget that.'

'So what do you want?'

'That's nice. Can't I just visit my kid sister?'

Connie shook her head. 'No, not you, Marianne.'

Marianne put her hands on her hips, her eyes taking in the cottage. 'Very good, very you. Very boring.'

'Boring? No, it's never that. In some small way I try to help people and that's never boring. Although, it's not a concept you'd be familiar with.'

Marianne fixed her gaze on Connie then smiled. 'It's still there though, isn't it? No matter how much you try to hide it.'

'I don't try to hide it, I choose not to use it. Not like you anyway.'

Marianne spread her arms wide. 'Well, if there's to be no sisterly hugs, how about a nice cup of tea? After all, I've walked a few miles to get here.'

'I didn't ask you to come.'

Marianne smiled. 'And yet here I am.'

Connie shook her head and led the way along the path to the back of the house. 'Tea and that's it.'

Marianne started after her. 'What, I don't get to taste the hospitality of your little haven here?'

Connie stopped and turned. 'Remember, I'm familiar with all your tricks. I know what it could mean if something from inside just happened to slip into your hands.'

The corners of Marianne's mouth turned down in exaggerated mock sadness. 'I'm hurt. As if I'd do that to my own sister.'

Connie headed over to a small wooden table and the two crude benches either side of it. 'No you're not and yes you would. So if you want tea we sit outside.'

Marianne sat. 'Very well. Or is it because Susie's here?'

Connie pointed a finger at Marianne from the back door of the cottage as she stepped inside. 'You will not touch a hair of her head, do you understand me? You will not speak to her or go anywhere near her.'

Marianne laughed and held both her hands in the air. 'Or what, Connie? You'll remember who you really are?'

'I mean it, Marianne.'

Marianne's eyes narrowed. 'Or is it she doesn't know?' Her eyes widened. 'Is that it, Connie, you haven't told her?'

'She knows,' Connie said. 'At least some of it and I'll tell her the rest in my own good time. So you leave her alone.'

Marianne held up both hands up again. 'OK, little sister, I get the message.'

Marianne's laughter followed Connie into the cottage as she was filling the kettle. A few minutes later, Connie emerged with a tray on which were two cups and saucers and a plate of biscuits. She poured the tea, added milk and handed a cup to Marianne, who inspected its floral pattern. 'Oh, very Country Life.'

'You don't have to drink it.'

Marianne sipped. 'At least it's proper tea and not that herbal muck I have to pretend to like in the shop. Ooh, and home-made biscuits, how nice. You are a busy girl.'

'Shop?'

'Did I say shop?'

Connie put down her own cup and scowled across the table. 'Don't play games with me, Marianne. You know me better than that.'

Marianne raised her eyebrows, holding Connie's gaze over the rim of the cup. 'What, you mean you didn't know, didn't guess?' She put down the cup and smiled. 'Of course you didn't. You must be slipping, Sister dear. My little emporium of oddities on Clayton Road. Mystique.'

'That's you?'

Marianne gave a slow nod. 'To my surprise it's actually doing quite well. All those trendy office types seem to go for that sort of junk. Not that I care of course. But it's a great way to stay in touch with what's going on. I see that self-righteous old hag Edna bustling around the streets. Oh, she thinks she's all it and a bag of chips. She has no idea. And then there's that Harold. They deserve each other those two, they really do. And of course the girls pop in from time to time.' She held up her hand as Connie half rose from her seat. 'I haven't touched her, I promise, in any way.'

'But Sarah?'

Marianne's mocking smile hardened. 'She's my daughter, Connie. Don't you think I want to know she's alright?'

'Only if there's something in it for you.'

Marianne placed a hand to her breast as the smile returned, even if it didn't touch her eyes. 'Oh that hurts. Insulting a mother's love like that. You of all people.'

'Don't bring our mother into this.'

'I was just saying…'

'I said don't!'

Marianne paused for a second, then took another biscuit and leant back. 'Actually, these are really good,' she said, taking a bite and brushing crumbs from her jacket. 'You know that policeman came into the shop the other day asking his clever little questions. What's he called, Kirby?

I sent Jane, or Titania as she likes to call herself, out to deal with him. It's impossible to get much sense out of her at the best of times.' Marianne paused for another nibble of biscuit. 'You know his mother of course, don't you? Interesting pair those two.'

'How do you… you can leave them alone as well.'

'Oh?'

'Alice Kirby's a friend, that's all.'

'Hmm. Well Mr Policeman better not get in my way is all I'm saying. Anyone else you want me to stay away from? Just so I know, I'd hate to make a mistake.'

Connie pointed a finger at her sister. 'Yes, there is. Harold told me that miserable wretch Mephisto turned up at his place and threatened the village. They're nothing to do with this, Marianne, so don't go near them.'

Marianne laughed. 'Oh, I love it. You're now playing the concerned child of the village. I thought you'd turned your back on all that, Connie. You were the one who ran away, remember?'

'From you, Marianne. I ran away from you, not them.'

Marianne raised an eyebrow and curled her lips into a half smile. 'And Mother.'

'Only after you poisoned her against me,' Connie said, standing up and leaning over to pick up Marianne's cup, putting it back on the tray. 'Now I think it's time you left.'

Marianne frowned. 'And I thought we were getting on so well.' She raised her gaze to the upstairs window where the curtains, patterned with lilac clematis, were still drawn.

'So how much does she know? How much do you intend to tell her?'

Connie placed both palms on the table. 'I've told you, that's no business of yours.'

'Not everything then?'

Connie scowled at her in reply.

Marianne rose from the bench. 'Well, Sister dear, I'd make it sooner rather than later. The last thing you'd want is her discovering things by accident as it were, isn't it? The damage that could do.'

Connie pointed a finger in the direction of the path back around the house. 'Go.'

Marianne stepped away from the table, taking another biscuit as she did so. 'Fine, I'm going. Just remember we've had this little conversation.' As she turned the corner, Marianne heard Susie's voice.

'Who was that, Mum?'

'No one, dear.'

Marianne smiled.

THIRTY-FOUR

....

Kirby had spent half the morning catching up on the dreaded paperwork. It was taking even longer than normal on account of the amount of imagination and creativity he had to employ in avoiding "sensationalism", as demanded by the super, while giving a credible account of his time. Somehow he reckoned talk of other worlds and magic doors might lead to early retirement, a thought that held his attention in a positive sense for a time. He eventually dismissed it on the grounds that it also might lead to a certain amount of loss of freedom. The chief was also on his back, asking how long this "little episode", as he'd decided to term it, was going to take. The chief was torn between wanting to totally deny what Kirby was working on and his desire not to let it get out of hand; by that he meant he didn't want it picked up by the media.

Kirby got up from his desk and wandered towards the coffee machine, even though his mug was still half full. He paused at Shirley's desk. 'Any reports of Marianne?' They'd had the techies update an old photograph of her and put it out under "missing persons".

Shirley handed him a piece of paper. 'Yes and no, sir. Yes, as you can see from the list, and no, as in nothing remotely credible.'

Kirby glanced at the paper. 'Getting on a boat to go sea fishing off St Ives in Cornwall, what you think?'

'Or the big dipper at Blackpool pleasure beach?'

'Nothing round here.'

Shirley shook her head.

'Well from what Harold's saying she could walk down the street naked and no one would see her unless she wanted them to.'

Shirley's phone rang. 'Oh, hello… uh-huh… uh-huh… no… really?… uh-huh. I'll tell him.'

'And that was?'

'Colin, sir.'

'Colin?'

'Constable Cuthbertson, from Alnwick. You asked him to let us know if anything unusual happened and it has. Mind you, up there I think a balloon on a stick could cause quite a bit of excitement.'

'Yes, thank you for that insight, Constable.'

'Sorry, sir. It's grey hoodies, sir.'

'Our grey hoodies?'

'Well, let's put it like this, they're causing trouble.'

Kirby looked at his watch. 'It's only lunchtime. Call Col… Constable Cuthbertson back while I get my jacket, and tell him we're on our way.'

'Does he know, sir?' Shirley asked as she parked the Focus outside Harold's shop.

'I don't care, he's coming with us,' Kirby said as he got out of the car. Two minutes later Kirby emerged from the shop and held the door. 'Why?' he shouted. 'Because you're the one who professes to know what's going on… what?… no! Leave them behind.'

Thirty seconds later a disgruntled-looking Harold emerged, pulling on his coat. He was about to put on his hat, then decided not to when Kirby opened the back door for him.

'In the back?' Harold asked.

'Let's put it like this, I'm not going in the back of my own car and you're not sitting in my lap.'

Harold shuffled into the back seat with a growl.

'You should get some corks for that hat,' Shirley said starting the car and pulling away.

Harold glared at her in the mirror. 'Don't like riding in the back. I gets car sick.'

'Tough,' Kirby said. 'And you're not going to be sick in my car.'

'Turn left,' Harold said as they approached the end of Clayton Road.

'Why?' Kirby and Shirley asked together.

'We need Geraldo.'

Kirby turned to look back at Harold. 'What? Why? I'm not running some pensioners' day out scheme here you know.'

Shirley stopped at the junction.

Harold leaned forward to poke his head between the front seats. 'If they're in Alnwick, it means there's a gateway nearby and it's not one we know about. I'm guessing it was opened by Marianne.'

'She can do that?' Kirby asked.

Harold shrugged. 'With the power she's taking from this world, it's certainly possible.'

'Great.'

Shirley glanced across at Kirby. 'Er, sir, I've got a white van behind me and in it is a large man with a red face.'

'If the gateway's still open,' Harold said. 'Geraldo just might be able to close it.'

Kirby tutted. 'Left, Constable.'

The van sounded its horn as Shirley looked right to spot a gap.

Kirby glanced behind. The horn sounded again, twice. 'Blues and twos I think, Constable,' he said. 'Oh, and why don't you wait for a really big gap, just to be on the safe side?'

Shirley grinned. 'Yes, sir.'

'Better leave this to me,' Harold said as they pulled up outside the university theatre.

'I'm looking forward to this,' Shirley said a few minutes later when the back door to the theatre opened and Harold emerged.

Kirby glanced across at her as she was rubbing her hands together in anticipation. 'Why?'

'Talking rabbit, sir. Let's face it, it's not something you get to see every day.'

'Thankfully,' Kirby added.

Harold got back into the car along with a grumpy-looking Geraldo.

'They're not going to like this,' Geraldo said, folding his arms and looking out of the side window. 'Does nothing for my reputation.'

'Yes, well funnily enough,' Kirby said, 'neither does having goblins running around Northumberland do much for mine, or the force's for that matter.'

Geraldo grunted in reply. 'Don't suppose there's likely to be any compensation for my loss of earnings?'

Kirby shook his head. 'You suppose right. Tell you what, if you're good I'll buy you an ice-cream.'

Shirley glanced in the mirror before setting off. 'Where's Ronaldo?'

'Doesn't he play for Barcelona?' Harold said as he struggled to find his seatbelt.

'Real Madrid,' Kirby answered. 'Anyway, she means Roberto.'

'Not fond of cars,' Geraldo said, glaring at Harold, whose seatbelt-searching hand had strayed under Geraldo's bottom.

'Sorry,' Harold said.

Shirley glanced in the mirror again, making sure. 'Damn.'

'Anyway he has trouble keeping his mouth shut at times which, as you might expect, doesn't always go down too well. People think I'm taking the p... anyway they don't like it.'

Shirley huffed her disappointment. 'Blues and twos, sir?'

'Perhaps not.'

Shirley huffed again. 'And I thought this might be fun.'

'If you don't watch it, Constable, there'll be no ice-cream for you.'

THIRTY-FIVE

....

As they were pulling into Alnwick police station Constable Cuthbertson emerged, putting on his helmet.

Kirby wound down the window. 'Going somewhere, Constable?'

'We thought they'd gone, sir. Now we've got a report of a disturbance in Fenkle Street. Kids in grey hoodies trying to nick handbags and ransacking a sweetshop. Some of the boys have got them cornered down by the castle.'

'Right,' Kirby said. 'Tell them not to do anything more than contain them until we get there, OK?'

'Sir? The sarge'll want something to show for this.'

'Trust me, Constable, the Sergeant's imagination is going to be severely challenged trying to charge this lot.'

'Sir,' Cuthbertson said in a voice that suggested he felt he was going to get it in the neck from someone, whichever way this went.

'Oh, and tell your boys they're not to get too close, understood?'

Cuthbertson nodded. 'Yes, sir. Nasty little devils, are they?'

'Something like that. I'd give you a lift, but,' he thumbed to the back of the car, 'we're a bit full with...er, expert help.'

Constable Cuthbertson glanced in the back of the car, then across at Shirley, who gave him a broad smile.

'If you say so, sir. I'll get me bike.'

'Go on then, Constable,' Kirby said to Shirley, who grinned and flicked on the blues and twos.

Harold sucked in air through his teeth. 'That's not good,' he said as Shirley turned the car around.

'What's not good?' Kirby asked.

'The sweetshop. All that sugar.'

'What?'

'And the "e" numbers,' Geraldo chipped in.

'So?'

Harold leaned forward, poking his face between the two front seats. 'All that sugar, they're not used to it and with the "e" numbers it's likely to get them a bit hyper.'

You don't say,' Kirby said as they sped down Grey Place.

At the bottom of Hotspur Street, they turned left on to the main road and only made about twenty yards before coming to a halt. If anything, the blues and twos were making it worse with cars trying to pull over where there was no room to pull over, as if being seen to make an effort was enough. Kirby pointed to a road on the right, not far ahead of them. 'Down there, Shirley.'

Shirley pulled out into the wrong side of the road, which was clear until a white van decided to try and take advantage of the car in front, mounting the pavement while trying to get out of the way. Kirby leant out of the window and gesticulated his feelings on the manoeuvre. The van stopped, blocking the road he'd hoped they would go down.

Kirby glanced into the back of the car. 'I don't suppose you two,' he waggled his hands, 'could do anything about this?'

'Such as?' Harold asked.

'I'll take that as a no then,' he said, getting out of the car. 'Back up,' he shouted, waving both hands in the appropriate way at the van driver, who now had his head out of the window looking around him.

Kirby waved his hands above his head. 'Oi, didn't you hear me? Back up.'

Instead of doing as commanded, the driver grinned at Kirby. 'So where's the cameras then?'

Kirby stopped mid-stride, so unexpected was the reply. 'What!'

The driver continued to crane his neck out of the window. 'I heard you was here.'

Kirby resisted the temptation to correct the man's grammar. 'Well that'd be the siren and the flashing blue light, always a bit of a giveaway. Now get out of the way.'

'Is she here?'

Again the man had managed to come up with a response which was outside those that were acceptable. 'Who?'

'You know, Brenda what's-her-name, Vera.' The man grinned again.

Kirby covered the last two steps, whipping out his warrant card as he did so, holding it an inch from the man's nose, causing his head to recoil back into the van where Kirby wanted it. 'Does this say BBC or ITV anywhere on it?'

The driver's face was now turning from pink to red and the hand that had been casually draped out of the window clutched the steering wheel as if he was afraid it was going to fall off. The man glanced in his mirror. 'Er, sorry, there's nowhere to go.'

Kirby leant out and looked behind the van. While the bizarre conversation had been taking place, the car behind had been edging forward as if fearing someone else might take advantage of his original good-citizen attempt to get out of the way.

'Why does this always happen to me?' Kirby muttered holding his card in the air towards the car and motioning it to back up. The vehicle moved a few feet, followed by the van, which provoked a honking from behind. Other cars joined in like a flock of geese in flight trying to make contact with each other in the fog. He wondered for a moment how anyone could think that sounding their horn might improve such a situation. Glancing back, Shirley was giving him the thumbs-up.

'You sure?' Kirby asked getting back into the car.

'Yeah, no problem,' Shirley said while edging past the van and the lamppost on the corner of the road they wanted to go down.

'Watch it,' Kirby said as their passenger wing mirror dipped under the van's mirror with less than an inch to spare. Shirley corrected and a scrunching sound announced that the opposite wing mirror had connected with the lamppost.

'Oops,' she said.

Kirby glared at her while Shirley kept her eyes straight ahead. 'Oops indeed, Constable. That's definitely no ice-cream for you. Now let's see if we can get to the castle with the rest of the car in one piece, shall we?'

'Sir.'

'What happened?' Constable Cuthbertson asked as Shirley got out of the car.

'Don't ask,' she said.

'And do you know that your wing mirror's hanging off?'

Kirby gave Cuthbertson points for agility as he dodged the kick Shirley had aimed at his shins. 'Never mind the wing mirror,' he said, glancing at Shirley while adding, 'for now.' 'What's happening?'

'The boys have just got them cornered near the Barbican, sir.'

'The Barbican?'

'Yes, sir, that's what that bit's called. If you live around here, the castle's just about an annual school visit,' Cuthbertson explained.

'Glad to see your education wasn't wasted, Constable,' Kirby said heading towards it.

'Er, thanks. And, sir, apparently my Inspector is asking why we're not making some arrests. I've stalled him for now, but…'

'Blame it on me.'

Cuthbertson smiled. 'I'll take that as an order, sir.'

Approaching the castle, Kirby could see that a small crowd of tourists had gathered, a number of which were holding up cameras and phones as if this was all part of the Alnwick Castle experience.

'Oh, wonderful,' Kirby muttered. He turned to Cuthbertson. 'You and Shirley, see if you can do something about this lot.'

Cuthbertson headed towards the dozen or so people with his arms outspread as if herding cattle, which Kirby supposed wasn't far from the truth. 'Come on now,' Cuthbertson said, lapsing into police speak in a voice that was a few tones lower than normal. 'Nothing to see here, nothing to see.'

'Yes there is,' someone shouted from the back.

'There's always one,' Shirley said from alongside Kirby.

'I thought you were supposed to be helping him?'

'He's a big lad, sir, and I wouldn't want to cramp his style.'

'You mean this looks like more fun?' Kirby said as they came to four police officers, who were blocking the escape route of what appeared to be six teenagers in grey hoodies, shuffling and fidgeting around each other. He would have said with their eyes darting everywhere, except that thankfully he couldn't see them. He was also thankful that no Galgans were on show.

'I don't think arresting them would be a good idea,' Harold muttered from over Kirby's shoulder.

'Really?' Kirby said without looking back.

The local sergeant glanced across at them. 'Keep an eye the little… the… misunderstood young persons.' he said to the other officers before joining Kirby.

'Well done, Sergeant ,' Kirby said.

'Cuthbertson said you wanted us to hold off, sir.'

'Correct.'

The sergeant cast a wary eye at the crowd. 'Yes well I can't see any of the local press yet. That doesn't mean they're not around though.'

'Quite.'

'Can we make some arrests now, sir?'

Kirby looked over his shoulder to see Cuthbertson still doing his cattle-herding impression as the small crowd edged backwards. He glanced at Harold and Geraldo, who both shook their heads. The sergeant narrowed his eyes and muttered, 'Newcastle types, huh,' as if that explained all peculiarities. 'I take it that's a no, sir.'

Kirby smiled.

'My Inspector's not going to like it.'

'Believe me, Sergeant, he'd like it a lot less if he had to read the charge sheets.'

The sergeant examined Kirby's face, trying to discern further meaning from his expression. However, Kirby was a master of the "giving nothing away" look.

'I hope you know what you're doing.' Seeing a different look, he added. 'Sir.'

'In your own good time, Sergeant.'

The sergeant huffed. 'OK, lads, step back real slow-like. We don't want to spook the little... them.'

With the officers edging away, the goblins saw their chance and, as one, bolted for the gap like ferrets down a rabbit hole.

'My, they can't half move,' Shirley said, 'considering they've only got stumpy little legs.'

'Yes well, come on,' Harold shouted setting off behind them with Geraldo, who to Kirby's amazement also seemed quite fleet of foot.

'Oh hell,' Kirby said, this being the second time in as many days he'd been forced to run. 'Stay,' he said to the sergeant, who looked relieved at such a command. 'Cuthbertson!' Kirby added as he was starting to lag behind the other three. Cuthbertson overtook him as they rounded the corner of the castle wall and headed on to the sloping ground where the castle faced the river Aln. By now Harold, Geraldo and Shirley were fifty yards ahead of him but there was no sign of the goblins. The trio came to a halt at an indentation in the wall. Kirby caught up with them and stood with his hands on his knees trying to catch his breath.

'I really could suggest a good gym, sir,' Shirley said.

Kirby looked up at her. 'If I were you… Constable… I would keep my… suggestions… to myself.'

'Sir.'

Kirby straightened up to see Geraldo with his nose about an inch from the wall. 'So?'

'This is new,' Geraldo said.

'It's new,' Harold repeated.

'Yes, I got that.' Kirby said. 'Running has rendered me a little short of breath,' he gave Shirley a glance that said, 'don't you dare', 'not deaf. I take it this is Marianne's work again?' Harold nodded and Kirby noticed the worried frown creasing Harold's forehead. 'Well?'

'It's not easy,' Geraldo answered for him, 'opening gateways like this. It means she's growing in confidence and in power. Which in turn means she's sucking more power from this world and as she does that the growth of her powers will only accelerate.'

Kirby leant against the wall, studying what to him looked much like all the other stones the castle was built from. 'Oh, whoopy do.'

'Er, sir,' Shirley said, pointing at Cuthbertson, who was listening open-mouthed to his radio.

'Constable?' Kirby said when Cuthbertson had closed his mouth.

'Well, sir, there's reports of a group of men on horseback dressed in furs galloping along the beach at Dunstanburgh golf course. At first some of the locals thought they must be filming or something, except they then made a bit of a mess of some of the greens and fairways.'

'Not all bad then,' Shirley said. Then added, 'Sorry' as Kirby glared at her.

'Connie,' Harold said.

Kirby turned to him. 'What?'

'Embleton's near the golf course. That's where Connie lives and where Susie is as well, since she's visiting her Mum.'

'I'll get the car and bring it close,' Shirley said before sprinting back up the slope with the others following, Kirby walking.

'You'd better squeeze in the back,' Kirby said to Cuthbertson as they approached the car, which already had its blue light flashing.

'Well, I'm not going in the middle,' muttered Harold. 'Not with my back.'

Cuthbertson folded himself into the middle seat in the back of the car with Geraldo and Harold either side. Kirby forced the door shut at the second attempt, amid loud complaints from Harold and Geraldo. 'Right, everyone, comfortable?' Kirby asked as he got in the front seat.

'What do you think?' Harold said.

'Siren, sir?' Shirley asked.

'I think that would be appropriate, Constable.'

'Yee-haw,' Shirley shouted as the front wheels spun and the car did its best to accelerate.

THIRTY-SIX

....

When they arrived, Kirby saw a flashing blue light over the heads of a group of people wearing interesting jumpers, golfers he presumed.

The back door opened and Harold fell out as the internal pressure was released. He took a deep breath as he picked himself up. 'I'm sure my lungs have been squashed.'

'Quit moaning,' Kirby said as Cuthbertson toppled sideways and crawled out.

Kirby ignored the groans and complaints behind him as he and Shirley nudged their way through the multi-coloured throng and angry voices. He could hear a shout, in vain, of 'One at a time, please. One at a time,' from somewhere near the middle. Emerging next to a young uniformed officer, Kirby showed him his warrant card. The officer looked relieved and tried to take a step back, only to jump forward again after a shout of, 'Oi, get your size twelves off me foot,' from behind him. This pushed Kirby nose to nose with a red-faced man with a bushy moustache, who was wearing a tartan hat with a pompom. He wondered if the man was wearing the hat for a bet, but decided it best not to ask. Instead, he held his card above his head, which had the effect of attracting the eyes and silencing the voices. 'Everyone get back please and give us some room to breathe.' There was a bit of shuffling.

'The inspector said get back!' Shirley shouted in a voice so loud that Kirby expected to hear the sound of shattering windows from the clubhouse. It had the desired affect though as the press of golfers around them pushed and shoved to clear a space, no doubt, he thought, in an effort to prevent permanent damage to their eardrums should Shirley vent forth again.

Kirby waggled a little finger in his ear. 'Thank you, Constable.'

Shirley grinned. 'Anytime, sir. I was known as Foghorn Shirl at school.'

'You do surprise me.'

The golfers were now gathered behind the man Kirby had recently been nose to nose with. With a nervous glance at Shirley the man smoothed his moustache and stepped forward. 'You in charge then?' he barked at Kirby.

'And you are?'

The man scowled, making his lush, bushy eyebrows join forces above his bulbous nose. It looked as if the man had a second moustache on his forehead.

Both moustaches twitched. 'Pemberton, Giles, Major, retired. club captain.'

'Excellent. I'm Kirby, Inspector, still very much active.' The moustaches twitched again as Kirby smiled. 'Perhaps we can go inside and you can tell me what's happened.' This produced a harrumph from Pemberton. However, Kirby was already striding towards the door giving the man little choice but to follow. Inside, Kirby picked his way over broken glass to a table with four hard chairs around it. He ignored the sofas and easy chairs on the grounds that he didn't want anyone he was questioning to feel too comfortable. He sat and motioned Pemberton towards the chair opposite him. This produced another 'harrumph'. As the major sat down, there was the sound of crunching glass. A small woman in a black dress appeared next to them, eyes darting between Pemberton and Kirby.

This time, only the lower moustache moved. 'Well?'

The woman shuffled under Pemberton's gaze. 'I just wondered if...'

'Yes?'

'If you might like some tea?'

Pemberton's upper moustache scowled. 'No, Marjorie, I don't...'

'Splendid idea,' Kirby interrupted, smiling. 'And perhaps some for my colleagues outside?'

Pemberton's scowl deepened, but Marjorie seemed pleased. 'Of course, certainly,' she said and scuttled off back behind the bar.

'Now Mr Pemberton...'

'People around here call me Major.'

'Really?' Kirby raised an eyebrow. 'Well I'm not from around here. So, Mr Pemberton, perhaps you could tell me what happened?' Now both scowling moustaches were directed at him. Judging from the depth of the lines on his face Kirby reasoned it was Pemberton's favoured expression.

'I've already told that young pup of yours out there. You only have to look at the greens to see what's happened. Who's going to pay for all this? That's what I want to know.'

Kirby fixed a smile on his face. 'Well I'd still like to hear it from you. It's a police thing. Humour me.'

Pemberton shuffled in his seat and smoothed his lower moustache with a finger. 'If you insist. I was on the ninth with Hughes and Blake. We're all decent handicaps, me off ten and the others twelve and thirteen, so we'd driven down the centre of the fairway and were about…'

What is it with golfers? Kirby thought. 'Perhaps we could get to the horses and the men?' he said, fearing he was going to get a blow-by-blow account of the man's round.

'Ah, yes. Well we'd heard the sound of horses on the beach before we'd finished the ninth and then as we were standing on the tenth tee they came into sight. A whole mob of them, wearing furs and the like. At first we thought they must be some film lot, actors, you know.' Pemberton described how, on seeing them, the men on horseback had veered off the beach and with complete disregard for golfing etiquette, Blake being about to play his shot, had whooped and hollered before riding straight across the ninth green towards them. 'My God, if we hadn't thrown ourselves into a bunker we'd have been trampled. Would have been carnage out there.'

'Really?' Kirby said, wishing he'd witnessed the last bit.

'Damn right. Then they rode straight across the fifteenth green and off towards the clubhouse, making a damned mess of the sixteenth, seventeenth and eighteenth. By the time we got to the clubhouse, some of them were inside. We could hear the sound of smashing glass. Bloody hooligans.' Pemberton wagged an agitated finger towards what had been the display cabinet. 'Look, they've taken the trophies, including the Pemberton Cup for the lowest handicapped round in the club championship. I only presented it last year. Silver-plated that one was.'

'Can you describe them?'

'Well the Pemberton Cup was about two feet tall with…'

'Er no, I meant the men.' The major looked disappointed. 'You can describe what's been taken to an officer later.'

Pemberton harrumphed and reverted to his preferred scowl. 'As I've said, they were dressed in skins and furs. Some had helmets on, others had long hair down to their shoulders, and beards. Yes, big bushy beards. Bunch of weirdo types if you ask me.' His eyes widened as if a thought had just occurred to him. 'Yes, weirdos, perhaps those re-enactment chaps. You know the sort.' He pointed a finger to his head. 'Gone a bit loopy, starting to believe they're the real thing and all that.'

'Yes well,' Kirby said. 'A line of enquiry I'm sure we'll follow up.'

Pemberton smiled and sat up straighter; no doubt, Kirby thought, feeling he'd put the police on the right track.

'Was there anything else?'

'Ah yes, nearly forgot. They tried to abduct Marjorie.'

As if on cue, Marjorie placed a cup of tea, along with a plate of digestives, in front of Kirby. 'Oh yes,' Marjorie said. 'He was ever so big and strong, although he did smell a bit sort of animally, if you get what I mean. Picked me up as if I was nothing. Put me over his shoulder, he did. I never…'

'Yes well,' Pemberton interrupted. 'There was this woman with them and when the brute came outside with Marjorie over his shoulder she screamed at him and thumped him on the arm. He then set Marjorie down and they got on their horses and rode off.' The scowl was back. 'This time, over the first, third and fourth. I ask you, as if they hadn't done enough damage to the course already.'

Kirby looked up at Marjorie. 'Must have been a terrifying experience.'

'Yes, I… I suppose it was,' she said, stroking her hair, which was tied up in a bun, while staring out of the window.

From the faraway look in her eyes Kirby had the feeling she rather wished they had taken her with them. When he looked back at Pemberton's twitching moustaches, he could understand why.

'And the woman?'

Pemberton's moustaches started to quiver, either with fear or excitement, Kirby couldn't decide. 'Oh a wild one, that one. Oh yes.' A finger smoothed the lower moustache as Pemberton's gaze also drifted to the window. 'Long wavy auburn hair and the darkest eyes I've ever seen. Eyes that seemed to see into your soul, like black pits they were. She wore a cloak and underneath a tight black dress, cut low at the front. A fine figure of a wo…' Pemberton coughed as if realising he'd said a little too much. 'Er yes, very… er, wild she was.'

Excitement then, Kirby thought. 'Thank you.' He smiled. 'That was most informative.'

Outside, Harold came over to him along with Geraldo. 'Marianne was with them.'

'So I gathered. I think the old club captain over there took a bit of a shine to her.'

Harold laughed. 'Well he wants to hope she didn't take a shine to him.'

'Oh I don't know,' Kirby said as he watched Pemberton haranguing a person he took to be a greenkeeper. 'I think he just might deserve her.'

'Anyway, they're long gone now,' Geraldo said.

'Where did they come from?' Kirby asked. Geraldo pointed across the golf links to Dunstanburgh Castle. 'Ah.'

'And where have they gone?'

'I think I can answer that one, sir,' said Cuthbertson, who had joined them, along with Shirley.

'Yes, Constable?'

Cuthbertson pointed down the road which led from the golf club. 'There's been a bit of disturbance over at Embleton village.'

'Connie?' Kirby asked, seeing a frown of concern on Harold's face.

'I'm sure she's fine, but…'

'Back in the car then,' Kirby said. Shirley grinned and Geraldo and Harold groaned.

Kirby shook his head. 'Tell you what,' he turned to Cuthbertson. 'For the sake of everyone's comfort, why don't you go back to Alnwick and we'll deal with this?'

'Sir.' Cuthbertson glanced at Harold and Geraldo. 'I'll let my Inspector know there's a specialised unit up from Newcastle on the case.'

Kirby smiled. 'Well done, Constable. You'll go far.'

THIRTY-SEVEN

....

Shirley covered the mile or so to Embleton faster than Kirby thought necessary. The locking of brakes on the loose gravel outside the church earned her a grunt of disapproval. However, he had to admit it did get the attention of all those milling around in the churchyard.

Getting out of the car, Kirby was pleased to see that both Connie and Susie were there. They left a small group, including the vicar, which seemed to be inspecting a number of flattened gravestones, and came over to the gate to join them.

'I'm glad to see the two of you are OK,' Kirby said.

'Oh, they weren't after us. I'm guessing that this is Marianne's way of keeping her boys happy. No doubt they were getting a bit restless and she thought a little plunder would help.'

'Anyone hurt?'

Connie shook her head. 'David who runs the Bell has a few bruises after one of them took a shine to his wife, and he tried to intervene. But it seems Marianne stopped them short of real violence. They took a load of Scotch and brandy, left the gin for some reason, then came across to the church to see what else they could plunder. At first everyone thought it was some joke or a film crew riding through the village. That is until they smashed a few cars with axes and swords.' Connie's gaze drifted down the road to where more people were gathered outside the pub.

'Much the same as at the golf course.'

'There as well?' Connie smiled. 'Sorry, Inspector, I was thinking of how the major would have taken that.'

'Yes, he seemed more interested in the state of the greens than the fact that one of them tried to run off with the barmaid.'

'Marjorie?'

'That's right. She seemed to be a little disappointed that Marianne had stopped them.'

Connie laughed. 'Well it might have put a little excitement in her life.'

At that moment, they were joined by two men, one Kirby deduced was the vicar due to the fact that he was wearing a dog collar. The other was wearing a red face and a nose that shone even brighter. Beneath it was a bushy moustache. Not another one, Kirby thought, this time trying to ignore the eyebrows. 'Gentlemen,' he greeted them and smiled.

The vicar opened his mouth to speak but the moustache got in first. 'About time, let me tell you…'

'Boys,' Connie said in a voice that silenced moustache man even if the face reddened a little more at being addressed as 'boy'. Kirby was impressed. 'Let me introduce you to Inspector Kirby and Constable Barker, from Newcastle. Inspector, Constable, this is the Reverend Green and Mr Pemberton, who's chairman of the village committee.' She smiled. 'I believe you met his brother over at the golf course.'

'Really,' Kirby said, 'Your brother, how... interesting.'

'I would never have guessed,' Shirley muttered.

The vicar's mouth opened again, but he was beaten to it once more.

'So those beggars have ransacked the golf club as well, have they?' The moustache twitched. 'I tell you what, if I could have got hold of my shotgun, I...'

'Might have been in serious trouble,' Kirby finished for him. Pemberton scowled. 'Just as we have laws against people marauding through villages on horseback, we also have laws about the inappropriate use of fire arms.'

Pemberton seemed about to say more when a look from Connie restricted him to a smoothing of his moustache and a loud, 'Pah'.

Kirby turned and smiled at Shirley whose shoulders sagged a little, guessing what was coming. 'Well, Reverend, Mr Pemberton, Constable Barker here will be only too glad to take your statements.' He smiled. 'Won't you, Constable?'

'Nothing would give me greater pleasure, sir.'

Kirby wandered into the churchyard with Connie. Harold was talking to Susie, and Geraldo was inspecting some of the headstones. 'You must teach me that trick.'

Connie smiled. 'Ah yes. I shouldn't, then Pemberton and his brother the major do wind me up with the way they treat everyone as if they were lords of the manor.'

'I can imagine.'

Connie glared across at Pemberton who was now in full flow at Shirley. 'Poor Shirley.'

Kirby smiled as he heard Shirley ask, 'And how are we spelling bumpkin, sir?'

'Don't worry, Shirley's spent a fair few Saturday nights down on the quayside. I'm sure she can handle Pemberton.'

Connie laughed. 'I guess so. Anyway both Pembertons don't like me much.'

'Oh?'

'No, I think they prefer their women a bit more subservient. They've both tried it on with me a couple of times. However, their idea of a chat-up is to treat you like some filly. A loud "What Ho" and a slap on the rump.'

This time Kirby laughed.

'Yes well, they won't try it again I can tell you.'

'I'll remember that,' Kirby said. Connie blushed a little. 'Yes well, er, so what exactly happened?' he said changing the subject.

Connie pointed over towards the village hall and puffed out her cheeks. 'Not much to tell really. They came up there, from what you've said, I guess from the golf course. Then they caused a bit of damage at the Bell and to a few cars before charging over here to the church. They've taken a couple of silver candlesticks. That's about it, apart from the damage you can see here, which is easily sorted.'

'And they weren't after you and Susie?' Kirby said as they were joined by Harold.

Connie shook her head. 'No, as I said, I think Marianne's just giving them a run out to keep them happy. And of course any trouble they can stir up helps.'

Harold told her what had happened in Alnwick.

Connie nodded. 'Ah, testing the water?'

'That's what I thought,' said Harold.

'In what way?' Kirby asked.

'I think you need to be prepared for more trouble,' Harold said.

'Riots you mean?'

Harold glanced at Connie, who shrugged. 'She's building towards whatever it is she's planning. Knowing Marianne, it'll be ambitious and that requires a lot of power. Stirring up a few villagers won't be anywhere near enough.'

'So what are we talking about?'

Harold took a breath. 'Last time I think she bit off more than she could chew. It was too wide, she couldn't control it and if you can't control the power you're trying to release you put yourself in danger. My guess is she'll try to keep it more local this time.'

'I agree,' Connie said.

'What do you mean by local?' Kirby asked.

Harold shrugged. 'Well, they've already tried in Newcastle, so I'm guessing basically Northumberland. Also, it seems that whatever she's planning will be focused around here.' He looked at Connie again. 'So what? Newcastle, Morpeth, Ashington, Alnwick, Rothbury, some of the bigger villages, Berwick maybe.'

'I guess so,' Connie said.

'So when? Tonight?'

Harold shook his head. 'No, not with all that booze they've taken. My guess is in a few days' time.'

Kirby frowned. 'Well, that's alright then. I'll just tell the chief to put the whole of the Northumbria force on high alert for rioting in a few days' time. Without of course being able to tell him exactly why.'

'Sometimes,' Shirley said appearing beside Harold. 'I'm more than glad to be a humble PC.'

'Yes thank you for that, Constable. Was there something you wanted?' Kirby raised an eyebrow at her. 'You can't have finished all the statements already?'

'I've got the most important ones, sir, and Mr Pemberton's, there was no avoiding that. A local is on his way, so I thought he could finish the rest since he's familiar with the place and all that.' Shirley smiled and tried her best to look innocent, then hopeful. 'You know, while we do more of the important stuff, sir.'

'Hmm…'

'Oh and sir?'

'Yes.'

'Er, those who've had cars damaged want to know what they should put on the claim forms?'

'Tell them it's not our area of expertise… and the local police will help them with that.'

Shirley grinned. 'So we can get on with the more important stuff, sir?'

'Yes, Constable.'

'I'm too soft,' Kirby muttered as Shirley went back to a small expectant-looking group.

Connie laughed. 'Tea? My place is not far down the road.' She glanced at Harold and her expression hardened. 'I think we have some serious thinking to do.'

Harold nodded.

THIRTY-EIGHT

....

'So how far is it?' Kirby asked walking along the road beside Connie. Shirley had taken the car with Harold, Geraldo and Susie.

'Half a mile, that's all.'

To his right, across the fields and silhouetted against the skyline, Kirby could see the unmistakable outline of Dunstanburgh Castle. Birds were singing in the hedgerows and the odd seagull was calling overhead. The sun was warm on his face and a faint breeze ruffled his hair. 'It seems so peaceful,' he said.

'It is. I love it here.'

'Sometimes as a copper you forget that most of the world is peaceful, most of the time. With a few exceptions of course.'

Connie shielded her eyes and followed his gaze. She touched his arm. 'Maybe you need to take a break occasionally.'

Kirby looked across at Connie whop was smiling at him. He smiled back. 'You've been talking to my mother again.'

Connie laughed. 'Perhaps. It doesn't make it any less true though. As I said last time, she worries about you,

Jonah, that's all. It's what mothers do. Also, she's a very perceptive lady your mum, not much passes her by.'

'Oh I know that. The "little old lady" routine is just a front. I can't help thinking she would have made a great master criminal.'

Connie laughed again, a joyous sound to Kirby's ears that made him think he spent too much time mixing with people who didn't laugh enough, at least not in the genuine sense.

'I know what you mean. Only there's too much good in your mum for that.'

'Hmm, perhaps.'

'Well we're here,' Connie said turning off the road and heading through a gate on to a narrow track.

Kirby found himself wishing the walk had lasted a little longer. Ahead and on a small rise was a neat double-fronted cottage which sat in the countryside with the calm assurance of belonging. Over the door and across one of the windows a red rose was glowing in the afternoon sun. To one side was a stone outbuilding that appeared to have been converted into two small units. 'Is that for your, er… guests?'

Connie smiled. 'Yes, and I've a room inside for guests as well. The offer's still there. You know, when this is all over, you might like to come out for a few days and we could chat?'

'Chat?'

'You know what I mean.'

Kirby smiled and shook his head. 'I know, mother again. She wants me to talk about Jeanie and everything. Honestly, I'm fine. I miss her of course, but... I'm fine.'

'It couldn't do any harm. And it'd keep your mum happy.'

This time it was Kirby's turn to laugh while holding up his hands in mock surrender. 'OK, OK. After this is over I'll think about it.'

Connie smacked him on the arm. 'Just don't forget.'

'Somehow I don't think that'll be an option.'

Connie grinned at him. 'Come on, hopefully they've got the kettle on.'

In the kitchen, Harold was sat nursing a mug of tea and Geraldo was stuffing cake into his mouth.

'I can highly recommend the cake,' Geraldo mumbled through a mouthful, smiling up at Connie. 'Lemon drizzle, rather splendid.'

'Thanks,' said Connie. 'Did no one think plates might be a good idea?' she added, looking at the crumbs scattered all over the wooden table.

'Ah, yes,' Geraldo said. 'Sorry about that. Didn't want to go opening cupboards and all that.'

Connie shook her head. 'Never mind. Where's Susie?'

Harold put down his mug. 'Outside showing Shirley, er, Constable Barker around.'

She nodded. 'So what d'you think, Harold?'

'I think we need to know more about what's going on.'

Connie took a deep breath. 'So do I.'

Harold sipped his tea. 'You don't need to come, Connie.'

She shook her head. 'I know I've tried to leave it behind, but it's still home, it still means something to me and there are people there that I care about.'

'Still.'

Connie nodded. 'Also, maybe it's about time Susie learnt about where we come from.'

As she said the last few words, Susie came into the kitchen with Shirley following her. 'Learnt about what, Mother?' She frowned. 'So are you finally going to tell me everything?'

Connie sighed and nodded. 'I know, I should have tried to explain it all before now. I'm sorry, it never seemed to be the right time. And it's not like telling you I'm Scottish or something like that.'

Susie's frown turned into a scowl and Connie glanced across at Kirby. 'Apologies, sort of a family joke.'

Susie crossed her arms. 'This is no joking matter, Mother.'

'No I know, dear, I…'

'Whoa, whoa,' Kirby said, banging a palm on the table. 'I am still here and I am the Police Inspector, therefore, at least nominally, supposed to be in charge. So I'll decide who's going where. Or at least I will when I know where it is we, or whoever, is supposed to be going.'

Connie looked across at Harold, who glanced at Geraldo, who contented himself with another slice of cake.

'Well,' said Harold. 'I think we need to go to the other side.' Connie nodded her agreement.

Kirby had a good idea of what "the other side" might be, but thought he'd ask anyway, so he could get his head around it. 'And by that you mean?'

'You know, my other side.'

'I thought that's what you meant.'

'You should come too.'

'Me?'

'Yes, then you'll understand a bit more of what you're up against.'

Kirby nodded. Much as he didn't like the idea, he had to agree that one thing worse than knowing what you were up against, was not knowing what you're up against. Especially when you'd had the chance to find out what it was and turned it down. 'Alright, Harold, you and me then.'

Connie laid a gentle hand on his arm. 'We're coming as well. I'm sorry, Jonah, this is Marianne and nobody knows her better than I do. Also, no matter what I think of it, as I said, it is my home as well.'

Kirby huffed. 'Alright, you, me and Harold and that's it.'

'And Susie.'

'What?'

'Don't worry, she'll be safe, I'll see to that.'

'No... I...'

Susie folded her arms again and gave him the sort of glare that he imagined she'd learnt from Connie.

'Sorry, Jonah,' Connie said. 'It's about time I let Susie see her heritage.' She glanced at Susie. 'And if Sarah's there, Susie might be important.' Susie smiled, her arms remaining crossed.

Kirby gave in, feeling he might as well be seen to agree. 'Fine. So how does this work?'

'First thing tomorrow,' Harold suggested.

Kirby held his jacket open. 'Er, I hate to be practical about this, clothing? I mean I'm hardly dressed for trekking through... well I'm hardly dressed for it.'

'When we get there, you'll need to change anyway,' Harold said with a half-smile that Kirby didn't like the look of.'

'Into what?'

'Something that'll blend in.' There was that half smile again. Kirby was liking this idea less and less.

'And I always have spare underwear,' Connie said. 'You never know what my guests'll forget.'

Kirby was out of practical objections. 'Great.'

'That's settled then. I'll get the beds made up. Come on, Susie, you can give me a hand.'

The pair hurried out of the kitchen before, Kirby thought, he had a chance to change his mind.

Kirby turned his attention to Geraldo, who was still eating cake. Geraldo stopped mid-chew and his eyes widened. 'Not me, no way!'

'Thank heavens for that then,' Kirby said. 'Shirley, you can take the car back and drop Geraldo off while you're at it.'

'Ah, sir!'

Kirby put his head in his hands and then looked up again. 'I'm sorry, Constable, I can't drag you into this. Especially since it's what you might call a little out of our jurisdiction.'

'Begging your pardon, sir, but I am part of this. And what if something happened to you?'

Kirby frowned.

'Alright, sir, nothing's going to happen to you.' She paused and then opened her eyes wide as if a thought had just occurred to her. 'But... I mean, what if it did? What about officers not going alone into risky situations and all that? And... and, who's going to look after you, take notes? Besides, how'll you get back if I've taken the car? Also, my Barry plays five-a-side with his mates Thursdays and then goes off to the pub. So...'

'Alright!'

Whoo, hoo,' Shirley said, rubbing her hands together and jumping up and down like a child on Christmas morning.

'One thing, Constable.'

'Sir?'

'No notes.'

'Sir.' She smiled.

'I suppose I'd better get the bus back to Alnwick then,' Geraldo said, glancing at Kirby and Shirley with a pleading look on his face.

'Good idea,' Kirby said.

'I tell you what,' Shirley said. 'I'll go and help Connie and Susie with the beds.' She also hurried out of the kitchen; again Kirby suspected in case he changed his mind. Kirby got up from the table and grabbed a piece of cake. Taking a bite as he wandered out into the front garden he had to admit, it was rather splendid. He stood staring across at the castle in the distance, wondering what he was doing. He then wondered about his own sanity. Or perhaps this was all a dream, a nightmare? Harold joined him and he concluded that even his mind couldn't dream up all this.

'Don't worry, Jonah. Connie's right about her and Susie.'

'And Shirley?'

Harold smiled. 'I know a thing or two about people and she's a good 'un that one.'

'Great. Tell you what, let's make a real outing of it,' Kirby said watching a seagull ride the breeze over the top of the cottage. He was sure it looked down at him before screeching twice as if to mock him. He glanced across at Harold, who was also watching the bird as it headed back towards the coast. 'Yes, why don't we take a picnic, a rug and lashings of ginger beer while we're at it?'

Harold shook his head. 'I'll ask, but I don't think Connie'll have any ginger beer. We could try the village shop. I don't stock it meself, not much call for it these days. Although out here you never know.'

Kirby waited for Harold to finishing digging before giving him a look that was so black all that was missing was a thundercloud over his head.

'Oh, I see.'

That evening Connie and Susie rustled up a delicious meal of tasty cold beef and cheese, with salad out of the garden, along with some wonderful bread. He'd eaten in some fancy restaurants in his time yet somehow this was as good as it got. There was even a bottle or two of wine. Looking around the table it struck Kirby as strange. Here was as diverse a group of people as he could possibly imagine. Well, a week or so ago that he couldn't have imagined, all sitting together enjoying good food, wine and conversation. Despite whatever might be to come, there were smiles and laughter. When it all boiled down to it, they were all just people, keen to have a good time and get on with each other, delighting in each other's company. Why couldn't it always be like that? It didn't matter where you came from or what you did, most people wanted to have a good time and be happy. However, that was the problem, it was only most people. As he knew only too well, there were people for whom others' happiness was irrelevant, or who were jealous of that happiness, and set out to spoil it. And that's where he came in. It was his job to make sure they didn't, or at least if they did, they didn't get to do it again.

After the meal, Kirby wandered outside cradling a mug of coffee in his hands. The setting sun cast a warm glow over the world, the same warm glow he used to feel when he was on holiday with Jeanie. Although this was far from a holiday. Perhaps it was the wine that made him think of Jeanie and their times away together. He could feel her next to him, sense her smiling, which made him smile in return. He heard footsteps.

'Sorry, sir. Didn't mean to disturb you. Fancied a bit of the good old country air. It's a lovely evening.'

Kirby turned and smiled. 'It's fine, Shirley. I was miles away for a few moments that's all. And yes, it is a lovely evening. Tomorrow it's... I was going to say back to the real world, however, I have a feeling it'll be anything but.'

'I guess so, sir.'

Kirby glanced back, the sound of voices were drifting out of the open door. He frowned. 'Tell me, Constable, what am I?' Seeing the confusion on Shirley's face, he added, 'In the police sense, that is.'

Shirley's expression lightened. 'Oh I see, an Inspector, sir.' She nudged him. 'And not a bad one at that, if I may say so.'

'Thank you. Let's just go with that thought.' He waved a hand to encompass the cottage. 'And what should that mean here, now?'

'Er, that you're in charge?' Shirley ventured.

'Thank you, Constable. I thought it should be the case. However, it's good to be reminded of that fact from time to time.'

THIRTY-NINE

....

When Kirby woke, the sun was creeping past the gaps in the curtains sending three spears of light across the room. He looked at his watch, seven-thirty; that was a change. He lay there for a few minutes thinking how strange and pleasant it was to hear nothing apart from the sound of birds and the odd sheep. No cars or the distant rattle and thump of lorries driving drove down the main road. He got up and pulled back the curtains. Clouds were threatening to hide the sun, and in the distance darker ones seemed to be gathering out to sea, promising rain later.

Each of Connie's little guest rooms had their own bathroom. Having showered, he put on the clean underwear which, as Connie had promised, he found in one of the drawers. She'd even found him a polo shirt that fit. The only problem was that it was pink and he wasn't sure if he wore pink. Jeanie had bought him one or two pink shirts over the years. Eventually she'd given up when they remained in the drawer. They were still there.

Stepping outside, Kirby glanced at the next-door unit. The curtains were open and the lights off, so Harold must be up. Shirley had shared with Susie. Coming from the cottage was a faint and enticing smell of fresh coffee. Being a good copper, he followed his nose.

'Sleep well?' Harold said as Kirby entered the kitchen.

'Ish. It's almost too quiet.'

'I know what you mean.'

'Where are…' he hesitated a moment before adding, 'the girls?' It sounded a little too informal, as if this was some social gathering.

Harold shrugged while lathering butter and jam on a piece of toast. 'Doing whatever it is they do in the morning.'

Kirby dropped a piece of bread into the toaster, poured himself a mug of coffee and sat down opposite Harold. 'So where exactly are we going?'

'To start with, the Whin Sill, near Craster. After that, there's not much point in me telling you because it won't mean anything.

Kirby was in mid-frown when Shirley came in. She was wearing a pair of jeans and a white blouse she must have borrowed from Susie. Her hair was loose about her face rather than being pulled back into her customary ponytail. It struck him that for the first time he was seeing her as a young woman, not just as a police officer. In reality, she wasn't that much older than Susie or his daughter Anna for that matter. Reflecting on that it said something about Shirley's professionalism, and then again perhaps something about his fixation with the job as well. You saw people every day without knowing the real them.

He made a mental note to allow for her comparative youth, well a little anyway.

The toast popped. 'Ooh, toast,' Shirley said, snatching it out of the toaster and starting to butter it.

'Er…' Kirby said, thinking he might need to revise his generous thoughts of a few moments ago.

Shirley stopped with the piece half-way to her mouth. 'Oh, sorry, sir, was this yours?'

He smiled.

Shirley blushed. 'I'll put some more in.' She helped herself to some tea from a pot near the cooker, then sat at the table. 'Nice shirt, sir. Pink suits you. Maybe not in the station though…'

'No, perhaps not. Thank you, Constable.'

Shirley smiled as she took another bite of toast. Susie then appeared with Connie.

'Ooh, toast,' Susie said.

Shirley got up from her seat. 'I'll put some more in, sir.'

When they'd all finished, Kirby helped Connie clear the table of plates and mugs, and stack them in the dishwasher. 'I hope that's alright? I know everyone has their own system.'

Connie smiled. 'It'll do.' She looked at her watch. 'There's a bus a little after nine. It leaves from near the hall, so we need to be away in about fifteen minutes.'

'We could take the car,' Shirley volunteered.

Connie shook her head. 'Er well, we might not come out in the same place as we enter.' She glanced at Harold, who nodded in agreement.

'Oh,' Shirley said. She leant towards Kirby. 'A bus, sir?'

'I know, Constable, the thought of using your actual public transport is a little strange, although I'm sure you'll manage.'

Shirley shuddered. 'If you say so, sir.'

The bus arrived as promised and Kirby found himself the first to get on with the others lining up behind him.

'Family outing is it then?' the driver greeted them.

Kirby wasn't sure what to call it, so settled on, 'something like that.'

'You paying for the lot?'

Kirby glanced behind him at Harold, who smiled back. 'Looks that way.'

'That's five at two pounds forty. Twelve quid please, sir.'

As Kirby took out a tenner and fiddled in his pocket for the two pounds. Harold pushed past him.

'Nice coat, mate,' the driver said. 'Won't it get a bit hot and smelly though?'

Harold stopped and turned but before he could say anything, Kirby was pushing him down the bus. 'Come on, Grandad, let's find a seat.'

'A National Trust shop,' Shirley said hopping off the bus in the car park. 'I like a National Trust shop. Bought a Christmas prezzie for me Mam in one last year and a brolly.'

'Yes, well, Constable, 'Kirby said. 'Remember we're still on duty.' He looked down at his pink shirt. 'Even if it doesn't feel like it.' He turned to Harold. 'So what now?'

Harold pointed to a gate at the far end. 'If we follow the path that'll take us around the back of the Whin Sill.' He grinned. 'Then the fun starts.'

'If you say so.'

They set off across the car park and through the gate. The path took them across a field where a small herd of cows paused momentarily in their chewing to stare at them before returning their attention to the more serious business of grazing. Harold led the way. Connie fell in beside Kirby and the two girls were chatting together behind them.

'Shirley seems a bright, lively girl,' Connie said.

Kirby smiled.

'What?'

'It's funny this morning, for the first time, I saw her as a "girl", not much older than my daughter and not simply a fellow police officer. And yes, she is bright and a good officer. A bit too lively for some perhaps and she might need to watch that if she wants to get on.'

Connie laughed.

'What?'

'Oh, she's not daft. I think she knows where and when to draw the line. She likes you, Jonah. Looks up to you. And admit it, you enjoy the banter as well. Perhaps you see something of your younger self in her.'

Kirby raised an eyebrow. 'Hmm, perhaps.'

Harold stopped and pointed. 'There.'

All Kirby could see was the vertical striations of the rock face and the steep slope in front of it.

Kirby peered again. 'Where?'

'There,' Harold repeated. He strode across the field to the base of the slope and began scrambling up the grass and scree.

At the top, Kirby paused to get his breath back. 'Hell,' he said. 'I didn't see that.' In front of him was an opening about four feet wide and perhaps eight feet high. A cool breeze was coming from the gap, carrying with it a faint musty smell.

'No, well,' Harold said, 'it wouldn't do if anyone could just wander in.'

'We're going in?'

Harold entered the cave and his voice echoed back 'That's the idea.'

With a sigh, Kirby followed him. After they'd gone a few yards, Harold stopped in front of a large wooden door. It looked old, but nothing special. Shirley came to stand beside Kirby.

'Brrr.' Shirley shivered in the cool dampness and rubbed her arms. 'So is that a magic door?'

In the dim light Harold frowned. 'If you want to put it that way, yes.'

Shirley's eyes were wide with anticipation. 'So how do you open it? Is there a magic word?' she held out her hands, waggled her fingers and lowered her voice. 'Open sesame.'

Susie sniggered. Connie smiled and Kirby tutted.

Harold reached forward and grabbed a large metal ring, turned it, then pushed. The door creaked.

'Oh,' said Shirley.

Kirby watched Harold step through it as if it was just any ordinary door. Like Shirley, he was a little disappointed. He wasn't sure what he'd expected, a shimmer perhaps or at least a bit of a sizzle. Then that was TV, wasn't it? Where magic had to announce itself or the audience might not get it. This was real. As the thought occurred to him, he let a nervous little laugh escape. He then wondered if, when you were starting to go mad, you knew you were starting to go mad.

Harold glanced back. 'You alright?'

'As I'll ever be.'

Connie took Kirby's arm, guiding him through. 'Come on, it won't harm you.' Susie and Shirley followed.

Kirby glanced back. 'Er, do you think they should be coming?'

Susie managed to look hurt. Shirley glared.

Kirby held up a hand. 'Listen, this is not a girl thing. It's your safety I'm concerned about. And being a semi-senior police officer I feel responsible for it.' As he spoke, he realised he had no idea what they were going to meet or what that meant for his own safety, which he also took seriously.

'Come on, Jonah,' Connie said. 'We've had this conversation. You'll just have to trust Harold and me on this one.'

'Yes, sorry,' Kirby muttered. 'I keep making the mistake of thinking I'm in charge in some small way.'

'If we're quite ready?' Harold said, pointing into the gloom before striding off ahead. Kirby followed Harold, who delved into his coat and produced his hat, which he proceeded to ram down on his head. Kirby hunched his shoulders in what he thought of as a posture of reluctant acceptance, balled his hands into fists and shoved them into the baggy pockets of his jacket, where they disturbed a layer of sweet wrappers and fluff. Walking along, he admitted to himself that he was so far out of his comfort zone he'd left it behind in the car park.

He didn't like it. He was used to being in charge and here they were being led God knows where, having gone through a door that wasn't supposed to exist, by quite possibly the strangest man he'd ever met. And he'd met some pretty strange ones in his time in the force. What's more, it also occurred to him that yesterday he'd been with another man whose companion was a talking rabbit. What worried him most was that it was all starting to seem normal.

To think it had all started with an innocent pair of shoes left at the side of the road. As a detective you expected the unexpected, however this was somewhat extreme. He prided himself on being a good copper and how he always applied logic to a well-honed instinct. But now? On the one hand he seemed to have thrown away all logic and his instinct was away somewhere with its shoes and socks off, paddling in the surf and eating ice-cream. On the other hand, in the back of the coppering part of his mind, there was the feeling that there was a thread of sense to it all.

Kirby huffed and tutted.

'You alright, sir?' Shirley asked.

'Fine and dandy thank you, Constable.' Now his coppering mind was raising the question of what the hell was he doing? After a moment or two he decided he was following his nose.

'Yes,' he said out loud, feeling that might make it more convincing.

'Sir?'

'Nothing, Shirley.' That's what he was doing, following his nose. Kirby straightened his back and lengthened his stride a little while holding on to that thought as if it was a lifeline back to sanity. His old boss Harry had said that's what you did as a copper, when all else failed, you followed your nose. There again Harry had ended up in the funny farm, talking to the wall. He wondered if Harry had met Harold.

Well he was here now and whatever was ahead was, well, ahead. He pushed the doubts down into his pockets with his fists to join the fluff. Shuffling along what seemed to be a dark, damp corridor, the group had all stopped talking. The only sound was the echoing footfalls of Harold in front of Kirby and the others behind him. They'd been walking for what, a couple of minutes? It occurred to him that there was no obvious source of light yet there was enough of the stuff to see by. Not enough to see more than a few feet, but enough. He studied the walls, old damp brick. However, as he made that observation, they changed to large stone blocks, then a hundred yards or so further on, to rough uneven stones and then to a solid wall of rock. Now he noticed that the light level was increasing. He could see ahead of Harold. A few seconds later, it was obvious they were in some sort of cave that was much larger than the one they had entered by. They stopped.

FORTY

....

Harold had found a convenient ledge and was perched on it staring down the cave to a grey wall of mist which Kirby presumed was the entrance, to what though? 'So where the hell are we?' he said out loud. Harold ignored him; he was waiting for something.

Shirley entered the cave behind Kirby. 'I dunno, you've got to admit it's a bit of an adventure.'

Kirby looked back the way they'd come and could see nothing other than a wall of rock. 'Hmm, sometimes as a copper in Newcastle the most adventure I crave is trying the new guest ale in the local.'

Shirley frowned in reply

'Ssh,' Harold said. 'Stay there.' He pulled his hat down a few more millimetres and crept towards the grey mist.

A man-shaped silhouette appeared. As the silhouette solidified, Kirby noted the man was young. Also, he couldn't help noticing that in his right hand was a seven-foot spear and a long bow was slung across his back and shoulder. This was not quite what you came across often in Newcastle, even in the Bigg Market on a Saturday night.

Knives occasionally maybe, but spears and bows, no. Kirby pushed a reluctant Shirley behind him.

'Goran,' Harold called, striding across to meet the young man. They clasped arms in greeting. 'Good to see you.'

'I got the call,' Goran said. On seeing Connie, he dropped to one knee.

'Hello, Goran,' Connie said. 'You've grown.' She put a hand on Susie's arm. 'This is my daughter Susie.'

Now that Kirby could see him better, the young man was clad in tight leather and had a slim, athletic frame. Having risen off his knee, Goran aimed a broad and warm smile at Susie. Kirby noted she was smiling back in the same manner. 'Heaven help us,' he thought. Goran pointed at Kirby and Shirley with the spear.

'The other-worlders,' Harold said. 'Jonah and Shirley.' Goran nodded.

'Other-worlders?' Shirley whispered to Kirby.

Kirby shrugged.

'Mind you he's a bit dishy, isn't he? Bit young perhaps, still,,,'

'I wouldn't know.' He nodded towards Susie, who was still smiling. 'It seems you're not the only one to think so.'

Harold turned back to them. 'We need to go. And you lot need to change.'

Kirby stared at Harold, while still keeping a wary eye on the albeit now more friendly-looking Goran.

'Before that, perhaps you'd like to tell me exactly where we are, who this young man is and why did he drop to his knees at the sight of Connie here?'

Connie smiled.

'Also, why he's carrying what, where I come from, might be classed as two very offensive weapons? Especially when you said we'd all be perfectly safe.'

Harold glanced at Connie. 'I'm not sure I used those exact words.'

Kirby narrowed his eyes at Harold. 'Alright, let's put it like this, you and Connie led me to believe that before I agreed to Susie and Shirley coming along.'

Harold nodded and puffed out his cheeks. 'Well, Goran is er, let's say, my nephew.'

Goran grinned.

Harold smiled and held his arms out. 'And he and his weapons, among other things, are the reason why I suggested we'd be safe.'

'Hmm… and Connie?'

'Er, can we leave it at she's special for now?'

'OK… and back to where are we?'

Harold grinned. 'Oh, we're in Northumberland.'

Kirby frowned. 'Yes, however, I'm not exactly going to be able to catch the bus back to Embleton and walk into the pub for a pint, am I?'

'No.' Harold looked down at the floor and, finding a dry patch, sat down cross-legged. With a sigh, Kirby eased himself down too. Shirley sat beside him, eyes wide in anticipation. He could tell she was enjoying this. Connie and Susie stood behind them, Connie with an arm round Susie's shoulders. 'Well, as I've touched on before, this is not the Northumberland you know.'

'I think I'd guessed that. So this is it, we're now in that other alternative past? This cave, me, us?'

'Yes.'

Kirby nodded to himself for a second or two in an effort to let his brain accept that it might be true. It was one thing being told that such a place existed when you were sitting outside a pub in Jesmond eating crisps with a pint of IPA in your hand. It was quite another to actually find yourself there.

'I'm still not sure I understand all this, Mother,' Susie said.

Harold's gaze flicked from Kirby to Susie and then to Connie.

Connie gave Susie a gentle squeeze. 'That's why you're here, dear. It's difficult to explain and I wanted you to see it.'

'Come on then,' Kirby said to Harold.

Harold looked up at Connie who took a deep breath and nodded. Harold focused on Susie. 'It's where we, at least your mother and I, come from. As Jonah said, this is the past, although not your past, a sort of parallel past. To be more accurate, around what for your history is the sixth-century BC.'

Susie glanced around the cave, then across to the entrance, where Kirby noticed she let her eyes dwell on Goran. 'Cool,' she said.

'Mega-cool,' said Shirley.

Harold smiled and held out his hands. 'That's the young for you, adaptable.'

Kirby shook his head. 'Moving on. We need to get changed?'

'I don't want you to stick out.'

'As in?'

'Think of someone walking around the Spanish City in Whitley Bay, on a Saturday night in designer gear, wearing heaps of gold jewellery and bragging about how rich they are.'

'As in not being a target?'

Harold nodded. Kirby nodded along with him, as did Shirley.

Harold patted Kirby on the shoulder, then rose and with Goran's help dragged over three large chests. He pointed to two of them. 'Men's, women's. Choose what you like that fits. Take one of the padded jackets as well, it could get cold.'

'Fabulous,' Kirby said pulling out several pairs of leather trousers. He chose the most battered ones he could find. At least they looked rugged rather than the fashionable sort he saw teetering down the high street at the weekend above high heels. After about five minutes,

Shirley, Susie and Connie emerged from the back of the cave. Connie looked as if she had worn this type of clothing all her life, or at least a some of it, which she had of course. Shirley and Susie were admiring each other and themselves, obviously enjoying the experience. Then he reckoned you can get away with most things when you're young. Both girls wore fetching calf-length boots and, tucked into them were leather trousers that hugged the legs. Over those, they wore short leather skirts. They were also wearing woollen shirts and soft leather padded jackets. It all looked as if it could have been made for them by some expensive fashion house. Kirby suspected he didn't quite have the same impact. The trousers were comfortable rather than hugging, which he reckoned would be a blessing for the rest of the party. The shirt too was chosen more for comfort than looks. The waistcoat he liked. Lots of pockets in which he'd stuffed his various bits and pieces.

Connie grinned at him.

'What?'

'Nothing, interesting to see you out of uniform that's all.'

'I don't wear a uniform.'

Connie laughed. 'Yes you do. You just don't call it that. But, believe me, you look every inch the policeman.'

'Hmm, well, I'm not sure how this look would go down back at the station.'

Harold looked them all and down while Goran looked Susie up and down. Harold frowned when he got to Kirby.

'What?'

'Boots,' Harold said. Kirby was still wearing his brown brogues.

'Really?' Kirby said. 'These are pretty sturdy.'

Harold nodded. 'You'll thank me for them.'

'Really,' Kirby repeated, not convinced. He tutted as he unlaced his shoes; in for a penny and all that. He tried three pairs of boots before finding some that fitted. Standing up, he had to admit they did give him the feeling that they could tackle anything. They might draw a few strange looks in Newcastle, although only a few. He was just glad there wasn't a mirror. He had the impression he looked as if he was going to a fancy dress party as a pirate; all he needed was the eye patch and a parrot.

Harold threw them each a small leather shoulder pack. 'Select another shirt or two and some more under... things,' he said, glancing at the girls.

'What?' Kirby said. 'How long are we going to be away?' Harold shrugged. 'I have things to do. I'll be missed.'

Harold shook his head. 'It doesn't work like that.'

Kirby waited. 'What doesn't?'

'Time, how long you're here compared to there.'

'Thanks, that makes it all so clear.' Kirby shook his head and decided not to press it further on the grounds that he was here now and he guessed he wouldn't understand anyway. He sighed and started to stuff some spare clothes into the bag. As did the others, although they were a bit more selective. Connie was ready first, and again she looked as if she was enjoying herself. She turned to help Shirley. As he pulled on his own pack, he watched Goran helping Susie into hers and taking great care over the length of the straps. No one offered to help him, he noted.

'What about our own clothes?' Shirley asked. 'My mother knitted that cardy.'

'They'll be fine here,' Harold said, at which Goran raised an eyebrow. 'Alright, they will probably be fine here.'

'Define probably, Harold,' Kirby said.

Harold shrugged. 'Well, you do get the odd bear around here.'

'Bear?'

'Yes, bears and wolves. You used to have them too until you shot them all.'

'Not personally.'

Harold huffed as if he didn't quite believe him.

'Wonderful.' Kirby had a vision of a bear wandering around in his favourite Loake's brogues. 'Bears,' he grumbled. Before he could grumble any more, Goran interrupted them.

'Harold, time to go.'

Harold nodded.

'You carrying?'

Harold opened his coat. Inside was the small crossbow and three knives. Strapped to his waist was a scabbard. He pulled the sword part way out. It reflected the light with a reddish tinge. Goran grinned.

'What the…?' Kirby hesitated as Harold and Goran turned to him. 'You mean… I asked you… in Alnwick as well.'

'Don't fret, I picked up the sword while you were changing.'

'And the rest?'

'Got to be prepared,' Harold said.

Kirby shook his head. 'What for? You've got enough on you to start a small war. It's Alnwick for God's sake. No one starts a war in Alnwick.'

'Unless it's over a parking space for your four-by-four,' Shirley muttered.

When Kirby turned to her she was taking a keen interest in the stitching of her jacket.

Harold was about to answer again when Kirby glared at him. 'And don't tell me you knew you'd be coming here, wherever here is. When we get back, you and I are having words, or there'll be a couple of rather hefty coppers paying your shop a little visit.'

'Well,' Harold said, trying his best to look hurt. 'This isn't Alnwick.' He waved an arm towards the entrance to the cave, before opening another chest. 'So I suppose we should get you something as well.'

'Me?'

'When in Rome,' Harold said, delving into the chest and pulling out a short sword and what looked like a vicious hunting knife, both attached to a wide leather belt.

'What's Rome got to do with it?' Kirby said, half wondering if this was yet another twist on where they were.

'Just an expression,' Harold said, holding out the weapons and shaking them at Kirby.

Kirby shook his head. 'What the hell am I supposed to do with those?'

'Strap them on,' Harold said. 'It's important to look the part. 'Trust me. You'd look out of place if you weren't armed.'

Kirby opened his mouth only to find he'd run out of words. As far as he was concerned he had already used up a year's worth of trust in the last few days. He took the belt and strapped it around his waist, adjusting the sword so it wouldn't trip him up when he walked. Hell, he thought, this stuff was of more danger to himself than anyone who tried to attack him. He drew the sword half out of its scabbard. To his dismay, it looked as if it had been used and not just for chopping vegetables. There were spots of rust and small notches in the blade.

'Sorry, not the best, I know. Hopefully, you shouldn't have to use it.'

'Shouldn't! Hopefully!' Kirby rammed the sword back in the scabbard. 'Harold, this may be news to you but in the modern police force self-defence training doesn't tend to include sword play.'

He looked up to see that Connie had selected a sword and a longbow, and Harold was handing Susie and Shirley slimmer versions of the sword he'd given him and delicate-looking crossbows. They were both grinning as if Christmas had come early and their respective boyfriends had actually listened to the hints they'd been dropping for the previous two months.

'Why not hand us a couple of hand guns and have done with it?' Kirby mumbled.

'Wouldn't look right,' Harold said, as if that was all the explanation needed.

'Of course,' Kirby muttered. 'Why didn't I think of that?' He shrugged, then straightened his shoulders in a "well here we go" sort of way. 'Come on then, lead on McDuff.'

'Who's McDuff?' Shirley asked.

Kirby shook his head. 'We haven't got time.'

Goran stood alongside Harold, looking out. 'At least it's stopped raining.'

At the cave entrance, the air was clearing. Curls of mist clung to the tops of trees before drifting away to reveal a thickly-wooded landscape for as far as Kirby could see. The smell of rich soil and wet vegetation filled his nostrils. Until now his brain had continued to put up some resistance to being where he'd been told they were. However, peering out he had to admit this wasn't Alnwick, Craster or Northumberland as he knew it. He watched

Harold taking a deep breath, the lines on his face seeming to soften and smooth as a smile appeared.

'So where are we going?' Kirby asked.

Harold pointed. To what, Kirby had no idea. 'Down there.'

He glanced across at Connie, who was smiling. 'Our village.'

'I can't see anything?'

'No you won't.'

'We'd better get moving.' Goran said, looking towards the sun which was a smudged, watery yellow disc sinking towards the horizon. 'The sun'll be gone in an hour.' Kirby expected him to add some warning about being out in the dark. He didn't.

FORTY-ONE

....

Kirby let the others drift ahead of him. Half of his policeman's brain was trying to analyse his current situation, the other half was trying to make sure he didn't trip up and make a fool of himself. He glanced ahead at Shirley who seemed to just accept the situation and even appeared to be enjoying herself. Correction, she was definitely enjoying herself. He shook his head, for him it felt ridiculous and bizarre. Here he was, a Newcastle copper, dressed like an extra from some second-rate TV historical drama, following a man who normally wore a grey cardigan and ran a corner shop. Although he had to admit that in this environment Harold was a different. He'd seen glimpses of it in Jesmond, when Harold put on the coat and became taller, as if the old man routine was a front, which he supposed it was. In this place, Harold's eyes were sharper, his jaw stronger, jutting forward as if leading the way. Without his baggy wool disguise, the man's frame and muscles were defined. Strong and wiry were words that came to mind.

When Goran appeared, Kirby fancied he could see some family resemblance, the same physique, the same shaped nose. They both looked as if they belonged, even if

Harold had a name straight out of a children's book. Except of course that a character from infant literature was unlikely to be carrying a small arsenal hidden in his "longcoat".

Then there was Connie, who seemed equally at home here, which shouldn't be a surprise as apparently it was, or at least had been, her home. His mum had been right, she was a nice lady. She was easy to talk to. She'd make a good copper, he thought. The sort of person you naturally found yourself opening up to. He smiled to himself. He knew he was still carrying mental baggage, that it was time he put it down and left it behind. So maybe he would pay her a visit when this was all over.

Falling behind the others a few steps was Susie. Her body language spoke volumes. Arms folded across her chest, her eyes were fixed on Connie's back.

Kirby caught up with her. 'Don't be too hard on your Mum.'

Susie glanced at him then resumed her focus on her mother. 'Is it that obvious?'

He smiled at her, 'Well, I am a detective of many years' experience.'

Susie returned the smiled. 'Sorry.'

Kirby nodded. 'It's something you don't understand until you're a parent yourself. It suddenly hits you that there is someone whose safety and happiness means more to you than your own. Someone who you'll do anything to protect. That when they're hurt, all you want to do is take that hurt from them and make everything better. You can't always do that of course and that failing hurts you even more.'

Susie put her arm through his. 'You're talking about your daughter, aren't you?'

Kirby nodded. 'When Jeanie died, above everything else I wanted to protect Anna from the world. Then as a single parent there was no one else to tell me I was overdoing it. My Mum said she'd cope just as well as me, if not better. Yet I still…'

Susie wiped a tear from her eye with the back of her hand.

Kirby patted her hand. 'I'm sorry, I didn't mean to upset you.'

Susie smiled at him. 'No, thank you.' She glanced at her mother again. 'I want to be angry with her and sometimes I think I am. I do know she only has my best interests at heart. I only wish she'd told me everything sooner.'

'When is sooner though? Too soon and you would have struggled to cope. For whatever reason, she decided to leave here, live in my world, your world. I'm sure she felt she had no choice.

'I know you're right.'

Kirby straightened his shoulders. 'As a policeman, I'm always right.' He sagged a little. 'However, as a parent I admit that even I make mistakes.'

Susie laughed.

Kirby patted Susie's hand. 'And your Mum's gone one better than telling you about it, she's brought you here.'

'I suppose so,' Susie said, her gaze drifting ahead towards Goran.

'A bit different to the guys at college then?'

Susie glanced at him before focusing on Goran again. 'Just a bit. See how he moves. While we clomp along, his footfall is the merest whisper. He seems to flow over the ground with the grace of a male ballet dancer.'

'I'll take your word for it.'

Susie blushed. 'No, it's more than that. I'm not saying he isn't rather sexy in a rugged sort of way. It's like he was shaped by this land, time, whatever, the same as we're shaped by living in twenty-first-century Newcastle. I get the feeling that as he looks over the landscape, he misses nothing, knows every tree, every animal, sensing anything that might be out of place. Same as you would in Jesmond.'

Kirby looked around them. 'Yes, I see the similarity.'

Susie laughed again. 'You know what I mean.'

Connie turned and looked back at them. 'You two seem to be getting on well.'

'The Inspector and I were having a chat, that's all.'

Connie raised an eyebrow and smiled. 'Really? About what?'

Susie smiled. 'Oh, just things.' She leant into Kirby. 'Thank you, Inspector,' she whispered, then skipped ahead to link arms with her mother.

Kirby watched them, thinking that when he got back he should perhaps have a long chat with his own daughter.

Looking around, Susie was right. Back in Newcastle he had a feel for the place, his instincts analysed and filtered even when he wasn't aware of them doing so. Here those instincts were about as much use as a chocolate teapot. Kirby closed his eyes for a second and then opened them as if hoping he'd find himself back on familiar streets in his beloved brogues. He wasn't, and what's more, he was carrying a weapon, not that he had a clue what he would do with it if they were attacked; he'd probably chop off his own hand. Whenever the debate had arisen in the canteen of whether the police should carry weapons, as it did from time to time, he would ask, 'What, do you think this is the wild west?' In fact he'd said it so often that now all the other officers would chorus it as soon as the subject was raised.

Kirby chastised himself. That kind of woolly thinking got you nowhere. He'd always prided himself that he accepted situations for what they were, not what he wished them to be. He'd seen other officers make mistakes trying to manipulate facts to fit the picture of what they thought a crime should be. No, you formed a hypothesis from the evidence, not try and fit the evidence to your hypothesis. And you got that by walking the streets and talking to people. After all, crimes were committed by human beings. Things didn't steal themselves, knives didn't suddenly decide to poke people. Wasn't that what he kept telling the young detectives as they peered at their screens and searched Google looking for answers?

That's what he was doing here, following the people, so perhaps he was following his instincts after all. He'd always said to expect the unexpected. And this was about as unexpected as unexpected could get, so he was doing that as well. Ahead, Harold was picking his way, choosing paths with the confidence of someone who knew their way around like he did in Newcastle. Kirby smiled, happy that his instincts were back in play.

FORTY-TWO

....

The sun was setting when they entered a village made up of, from Kirby's watching them digging around on "Time Team", twenty or thirty round houses. People stopped what they were doing and others emerged from the buildings. Four large men sporting impressive beards approached them, hands on the hilts of their swords. Kirby's hand also went to the sword at his side although he couldn't think why. He suspected that these men could remove his head from his shoulders while he was still working out which was the pointy end. To his relief all four broke into broad grins. One of them stepped forward and grasped Harold's arm, pulling him into a fierce, back-slapping embrace, which Harold returned with equal vigour. Kirby hoped this wasn't a greeting everyone would get as he wasn't sure his soft twenty-first-century body would survive it. When Connie appeared from behind Harold, three of the men dropped to their knees as Goran had done in the cave. The man Kirby took to be the leader of the group, who looked a little older than the others with more grey in his beard and hair, pulled her into a hug.

'Hello, Oralf,' Connie said.

When they pulled apart, Kirby saw to his surprise that the man had tears in his eyes.

The man wiped his eyes with the back of his hand and started speaking.

'I take it this is your language?' Kirby asked. Harold nodded. 'What's he saying?'

Harold leaned in a little and kept his voice low. 'He's saying, "It's been far too long little sister."'

'Sister?'

Connie leaned forward and kissed Oralf on the cheek and said a few words in the same language.'

Oralf nodded and hugged her again.

When they parted, Connie held on to Oralf's arm. 'Susie, come and meet your uncle.'

Oralf spread his arms wide. 'Surelsia?'

Susie stepped forward to be engulfed in her uncle's embrace. When he released her he spoke again.

'He's saying,' Connie said, 'that you were just a babe last time he saw you, and look at you now.' Oralf laughed and hung an arm around Susie's shoulders as he carried on. Connie smiled. 'And that you'll have to fight off all the young men of the village.' He glanced across at a scowling Goran and laughed again. Susie blushed, which evoked more laughter. Still with his arm around her, he directed a question at Connie.

Susie looked across at her mum. 'He's asking if you know all about them. I told him that we're here now and it's complicated. He knows that.'

'I wish I could talk to him.'

'I know, I'm sorry. Please believe me it was for the best.'

Susie nodded.

Oralf turned to Harold.

'This is Oralf,' Harold explained to Kirby and Shirley. 'The leader of the village and my cousin, sort of, and as you've gathered Connie's brother. Two of the others are his personal spearmen and the taller man at the back is his brother-in-law.'

Kirby nodded. 'Oralf,' he said, holding out his hand and trying not to stiffen in anticipation.

'Joo-nar,' the man said along with a few more words and waving his arm to take in the village. He then grasped Kirby's forearm, at the same time giving him a friendly thump on the shoulder which almost had Kirby off his feet. He was sure to have bruise in the morning.

Shirley looked a little worried as Oralf approached, then relieved as he simply bowed in front of her. He looked her up and down, said a few words, then grinned.

'He said "welcome",' Harold translated.

Shirley narrowed her eyes at Harold. 'That was a lot of words for "welcome"?'

'Er, he praised your fair hair and, er… your beauty.'

'Oh,' Shirley said as she caught the drift of what Harold was saying. She smiled at Oralf. 'Charmed, I'm sure.'

Oralf laughed again and clapped Harold on the back before leading them to the centre of the village.

'What did you say to him?' Shirley asked as she walked alongside Harold.

'I just told him you were spoken for by a mighty warrior.'

'Hmm,' Shirley said, frowning.

'What's the matter?' Kirby asked.

Shirley shrugged. 'Dunno. Just somehow a vision of Barry slouching on the sofa with a beer, a bag of cheese and onion, watching the footy, doesn't quite equate with mighty warrior.'

The round houses surrounded an open central area in the middle of which a fire was blazing, and sizzling on a spit was a whole deer. The smell that drifted his way made his stomach rumble in anticipation.

'Yes, smells good, doesn't it?' Harold said. 'Don't know about you, I'm hungry and fresh venison beats spam fritters or a Ginsters meat pie. First though, we'd better get rid of this lot,' he said, tapping the sword at his side. 'Not very hospitable to turn up at a feast in your honour armed.'

'Alright though in a pub in Jesmond,' Kirby said, raising an eyebrow.

Harold smiled. 'Well, you never know.'

Kirby watched as Connie led the girls towards a small hut, while Harold took him into an identical one a few yards away.

'They were expecting us?' Kirby said shrugging off his pack next to what he guessed was a sleeping mat.

Harold turned to him. 'This is Oralf's world. They knew we were here the moment we left the cave.'

'I didn't see anyone.'

Harold unbuckled his sword. 'Would anyone see you in Jesmond if you didn't want them to?'

'No.'

'There you are then.'

With some relief Kirby let his own sword belt drop to the ground. He glanced across at Harold. 'So what about Connie's parents? I presume her father was head man or whatever before Oralf?'

Harold nodded. 'He was although it doesn't always follow.'

Kirby let the silence develop as he fiddled with his pack. However, this time Harold didn't fill it. 'And?' he asked after a few seconds.

'Ah.'

'Ah?'

Harold put his own pack down then stood and scratched his chin. 'Well, Marianne was always a headstrong girl with bold ideas, shall we say. She had abilities even then and believed she knew how they should be used. When she was fifteen she ran off to be with Sisillius. Not that she had any affection for him; he was a miserable little sod even at that age. However, his father was the most powerful man in the area and Marianne thought she could use him.'

'Well that explains why Connie and Marianne don't get on.'

'Oh, that's not the half of it. You see their father went to take Marianne back and Sisillius's father had him killed. Some say Marianne put him up to it. Sisillius says her father attacked him.'

Kirby whistled through his teeth. 'And was it Marianne?'

Harold shrugged.

'What about their Mother?'

Harold shook his head. 'Dead, or so we presume. She wandered away one day without telling anyone. Hasn't been seen since. Before she went though, Marianne convinced her that somehow it was all Connie's fault.'

'Poor Connie.'

'Yes, well now you know.' Harold put a hand on Kirby's shoulder. 'I didn't tell you any of this, OK?'

Kirby nodded. 'Thank you.'

Harold shrugged out of his coat. 'We'd better get on, they'll be waiting for us.' He had just laid out what to Kirby was a bewildering array of knives on his mat when they heard raised voices. One of those voices was Oralf's and Kirby didn't need to understand the language to realise that he was arguing with someone.

Harold picked up his sword and buckled it back around his waist before stepping out of the hut. Kirby thought about doing the same, then for the sake of everyone's safety decided not to.

Outside, Oralf, Goran and several of his men were standing in front of six men on horseback in breastplates and helmets, blocking their entry to the village. One of the riders, whose breastplate was decorated with gold serpents, removed his helmet. His dark hair fell to his shoulders and despite his young age, Kirby guessed seventeen or eighteen, gave Oralf a glare that suggested the man should be on his knees. Oralf scowled at him and remained on his feet, hands on hips, bearded chin jutting forward in defiance. They exchanged a few more heated words.

'Branion,' Harold whispered, 'Sisillius's brat. Thinks he's it. He's giving Oralf a hard time for perceived insults, feels that Oralf owes him respect. The young idiot doesn't seem to realise that in this world you have to earn respect. He's also insisting that Oralf sends his warriors to fight for his father, his rightful king. Oralf's telling him that he doesn't recognise Sisillius as his king, that he doesn't have a king. As you can imagine, given what I told you, Oralf doesn't have a lot of time for Sisillius.' Harold winced.

'What?'

'Er, he's also told Branion that if Sisillius comes here himself, he'll shove his crown, er… where the sun don't shine.'

Branion's red face told Kirby that this hadn't gone down too well. The young man's hand had reached for the sword at his waist and there was much scraping of metal on leather as weapons were half drawn. For a moment, both sides contented themselves with glaring at each other.

'Looks like I'm on,' Harold said stepping forward. He grinned and opened his arms wide, which attracted everyone's attention and had the effect of lowering the tension a notch. 'Well, look at who else we have with us. Hello, Mephisto, playing at warriors now are we? I see they must have found some children's armour to fit you.'

One of the men on horseback, skinnier than the others, nudged his horse a step forward. The others let their hands fall from the hilts of their swords. Oralf's men did the same. 'Harold, I might have guessed you'd be interfering. And who's that with you?' Mephisto grinned. 'Oh, smells like a policeman, how amusing. What's he going to do, arrest us?' He turned to Kirby and laughed. 'It's alright officer, we'll come quietly… I don't think.'

At that moment, Connie emerged from her hut with Shirley and Susie behind her. The look of disdain and superiority that had been on Mephisto's face moments beforehand was replaced by uncertainty. He glanced at the men around him as if to reassure himself that they were still there. The men's hands twitched towards their swords again. On seeing Connie, they satisfied themselves with resting them on the pommels.

'So, Mephisto,' Connie said, 'Marianne's letting you out on your own and with Sisillius's whelp for company.'

Mephisto's horses nickered and took a step back as if sensing its rider's unease. 'Keep out of this, Connie.'

Kirby whistled through his teeth as Connie stood, hands on hips, and gave Mephisto the sort of look Jeanie used to give him when he'd spilt beer on the carpet. 'Or what,

Mephisto? Why don't you crawl back under the stone you came from and leave these good people alone?'

Mephisto pointed at Connie. Goran snarled, took a step forward and lowered his spear, which had been pointing skyward. Before anyone else could react, Goran flew backwards landing on his back with a grunt. To his credit, he managed to keep hold of his spear. Mephisto's pointing finger was now wagging. 'Tell that boy, Connie, if he tries that again he'll…'

Mephisto didn't get to finish his sentence as his horse reared and he clattered to the ground. It sounded to Kirby as if someone had kicked the bins over. Branion's hand once again strayed to his sword. Until, that is, Connie gave him such a thunderous glare Kirby half expected the young man to get off his horse, slink into a corner and stand there, head bowed until told he could come out again. Instead, he did his best to hold on to the last of his dignity, like a too small towel when trying to shed wet swimming trunks on the beach. He then backed up his horse until he was in the middle of his men. Meanwhile, Mephisto managed to control his own horse and at the third attempt hauled himself back into the saddle. He said something to Branion, who glared at Oralf and then nodded.

'You'll regret this, Connie,' Mephisto said as they turned to leave.

Shirley came to stand next to Kirby as they watched the horsemen go. She puffed out her cheeks and he could sense her relaxing. 'Almost as bad as after a Newcastle-Sunderland game when the pubs shut.'

Kirby smiled.

'I would have stepped in of course, sir, but I didn't think my police whistle and a stern look would have quite cut it.'

'Very wise, Constable.'

They both looked across at Connie who had her arm round Susie's shoulders. Next to them stood Goran looking a little dusty and embarrassed, his only injury his pride. 'Mind you, sir. Next time there's a derby match, perhaps we could get Connie in to help out.'

FORTY-THREE

....

Kirby watched Oralf standing tall in the centre of his men, laughing and slapping them on the back. 'He doesn't seem too bothered by it all.'

Harold shook his head. 'Oh he is. But he's the head man and he needs to put on a show for his people.'

'So what'll happen now?'

'He can't fight them. There's far too many and he knows that. They'll have to move the village.'

'Where?'

Harold shrugged. 'Into the hills. There are forts up there. There may be other communities around that think like him and will join him. If there are enough of them, Sisillius will leave them alone. He won't risk losing men over some insult to his idiot son.'

'And if not?'

Harold shrugged. 'Life's never certain here.' He clapped a worried Kirby on the shoulder. 'Come on,' he said, leading the way to the centre of the village where a crowd was gathering. 'That's another day and here you learn to live in the present.'

When all the village had gathered, Oralf stood and waved for silence.

'Stand,' Harold said.

Oralf spread his arms and started speaking. He then extended an arm in their direction.

'He's welcoming us,' Harold whispered.

Oralf motioned Connie and Susie forward and draped an arm around each of their shoulders. He said a few more words. The whole village then dropped to their knees.

Kirby glanced at Harold.

'Oralf is the leader of this community. Connie is, if you like, the Queen of these people, of their tribe.'

'And Marianne?'

'Ah, yes, well that's another bone of contention.'

'I see.'

'Oh,' Harold said, pulling his shoulders back and smiling. 'Now it's my turn.'

Kirby looked at Oralf, then grabbed Harold's arm. 'Don't say anything I might regret, understood?'

At the mention of Joo-nar everyone bowed in their direction, however at least they weren't on their knees. Harold spoke and they bowed again.

'So what did you say?' Kirby asked as they sat down.

'Only that you're a great leader in your land. A peacekeeper.' Harold grinned. 'Known far and wide for your justice and fairness.'

Before he could say anything else, Kirby was handed a large cow horn. An amber coloured liquid was sloshing around inside. He sniffed it.

Harold leant towards him and whispered. 'Don't smell it, drink it.'

'What is it?'

'Ale… more or less.'

'More or less?'

'Drink,' Harold said, grinning across at Oralf and raising his own horn to his lips. After several impressive gulps, he lowered it, licked his lips and burped. 'Your turn.'

Kirby took a sip.

Harold elbowed him in the ribs. 'I said, drink! You're not some young girl at her first ball with a glass of fine wine.'

Kirby lifted the horn to his lips and followed Harold's example. It wasn't at all bad, or at least it would have gone down well enough in that pub Hugh had taken him to. 'I've had worse,' he said. He hiccupped and then burped. 'Pardon.'

Harold shouted something across to Oralf who raised his own horn in response. Putting it to his mouth, he tilted it back until ale flowed down his chin. Then he belched with gusto, wiped the back of a hand across his mouth, roared with laughter and held the horn out for a refill. Connie, sitting next to her brother, whispered something in his ear and he laughed again as he put an arm around her shoulders.

'What was that all about?'

'I told him what you said, that you'd had worse. However, I did add that you thought it'd taste better after the fourth or fifth hornful.'

'What?'

Harold grinned. 'It's all expected. Like compliments and banter at a dinner party.'

Kirby shook his head. 'Oh yes, dinner party. I'll keep that in mind.'

Kirby could see Harold was enjoying this. He had the look of a Newcastle supporter out on the town after they'd won, which was never good. Harold nudged him. 'Come on, our turn. What do the students sing? Down in one, down in one, down in one.'

'Oh, hell,' Kirby thought as he raised the horn to Oralf in salute. He let a generous amount flow down his chin and on to his leathers reckoning it would do them less harm than it would do him.

As the food was being served and his horn was refilled, he noticed Susie and Shirley being led to the opposite side of the ring by three young women.

'Oralf's daughters,' Harold explained, 'they'll look after them, don't worry.'

'Hmm.' He watched one of them give Shirley and Susie a more delicate, pottery drinking vessel. 'I think they're rather underestimating Shirley.'

Susie smiled and Shirley looked a little disappointed. Another handed them some food on a wooden trencher, while the third stood behind them and started braiding their hair. Shirley shrugged in Kirby's direction before downing her drink in one and holding the cup out for a refill. Oralf's daughter's giggled in response.

'Shirley's blonde hair is something of a rarity,' Harold explained. 'Er, much prized by the menfolk.'

'Really?' Kirby said raising his drinking horn in Shirley's direction. 'As long as none of them try to get familiar with her. I've seen her in action. Not to be messed with that one.'

Harold laughed and nudged him again. 'What?' When he looked, Harold was raising his horn again in Oralf's direction. 'Oh, hell,' he thought.

After eating his fill, Kirby sat there in a contented fug as others, including Harold, danced to the complex rhythms being pounded out by three men on a collection of drums. He mused for a while on how many different sounds you could get out of such simple instruments. He felt an arm brush his shoulder as someone sat down next to him. It was Connie.

'Not dancing?'

'I don't think my version of embarrassed dad dancing would impress them. What do you think?'

'Perhaps not.'

Kirby glanced about him at the happy, rowdy gathering. Leaning back to take it all in, he started to topple and was saved by a strong hand from Connie.

'Steady.'

He gazed down at his drinking horn, which miraculously was full again. 'I think I could get used to this.'

'No you couldn't,' Connie said gazing into the red-hot glowing embers of the fire. 'This is the good bit. The winters are harsh and the people have to be tough to survive. What's more, it can be bloody and brutal. Oh, don't get me wrong, I love my brother and these people. But if they have to fight, they will, as they have done in the past. And when they do some will die. My brother is a kind and in many ways a gentle man at heart, who takes his role as the head of these people seriously.' She peered across at Oralf and then down as she swilled the ale around in her own, more delicate, drinking horn. 'It's his job to keep as many of them alive as he can and that means being in the thick of it when the trouble starts.'

'He looks like he can handle himself.'

Connie smiled and nodded. 'Oh yes, make no mistake on that front. One or two have doubted it, yet he's the one sitting there laughing and drinking.'

'Fish out of water.'

'Sorry?'

'Me. Sure you can wear the clothes, however, that doesn't make you one of them. You on the other hand…'

Connie laughed. 'No, not really. Yes, I can speak the language and fit in.' She shook her head looking around, taking in the people and the huts. 'I've been away too long, grown soft. I like my sofa too much, wine in the fridge and watching the odd TV soap.'

It was Kirby's turn to laugh. He glanced around. 'Still, real men and all that.'

Connie nudged his shoulder with hers. 'Don't do yourself down, Jonah Kirby. Different place, different time. This lot wouldn't survive in your world for ten minutes. They would have no comprehension of any of it. And in that world, you are somebody. Other people look up to you. You perhaps don't always see it. They treat you with a little more respect, even before they know you're a policeman. You have that certain something about you.'

'Huh, like I've seen a lot of that recently.' He threw a small stick into the fire and watched it catch, flames flickering and then dying. 'I have no idea where this is all going, or what I'm doing.' He shook his head.

Connie squeezed his hand. 'You're doing what you do best, Jonah. Like Oralf, you're caring for your people. You're being a copper and a good one at that.' She kissed him on the cheek and then got to her feet. 'And on that note, I'm going to bed. Goodnight, Jonah.'

'Night, Connie.'

She looked down at him, smiling. 'And try not to drink too much.'

'A bit late for that.'

'Hmm.'

Kirby watched her go and wondered how the hell he was going to get to sleep on nothing more than a rush mat. He needn't have worried.

Kirby felt someone kicking his feet. It couldn't be the long-suffering Mrs Kirby; she generally elbowed him. And when had the mattress become so damned hard? He opened one eye. Smoke. He sniffed, smoke. The place was on fire. Both eyes opened wide as fear kicked in. He sat up and immediately regretted it, feeling that somehow although his body had risen, his head was still pinned to the floor. Thoughts of "never again" went through his mind.

His feet were kicked for a second time.

'Ugh?'

After a second or two of indecision, then trial and error, his eyes decided to focus. He recognised Harold, and memories of the night before came trickling back, although they were somewhat vague as he tried to recall the end of the evening. After the ladies had retired, there had been even more drinking. This time accompanied by singing and drinking, he remembered that. And then he remembered there had been lots of both. He sort of recalled trying to get them to join in with "We all live in a Yellow Submarine".

'Come on, rise and shine.'

'I'll give you rise and shine, you…'

Harold raised his eyebrows and tilted his head. Standing next to him was one of Oralf's daughters.

'Sorry', he said before it occurred to him that she wouldn't have understood anyway. The girl held out a drinking horn. The sight of it made his stomach churn.

'Don't worry, it's water,' Harold said as Kirby was about to wave it away.

He took the horn and nodded his thanks. His tongue felt about twice the size it should be and it seemed that the rest of his mouth had been filled with the hide he'd been sleeping on. He took a long drink. 'That's not just water,' he said, resisting the urge to spit it out in front of the young girl.

Harold smiled. 'It's mostly water. Anyway, it'll do you good. Drink it.'

Kirby complied and he had to admit he was starting to feel better. Or at least the feeling that his stomach was on a rocking boat somewhere had subsided. 'What's her name?'

'Er, Dor-ice.'

'Doris?' The girl smiled at the mention of her name. He handed her the horn. 'Thank you, Doris.' She took it from him and smiled again, then blushed and ran out of the hut.

Kirby looked up at Harold. 'Doris?'

'Er, yes, my fault.' When she was born, me and Oralf had a bit to drink and he started asking me about girls' names, you know, where we're from.'

'And you suggested Doris?'

'Yes well, not really. I went through a list and he liked Doris. In our language it sounds a bit like Mountain Stream.'

Kirby shook his head, then held on to it with both hands, groaning.

'Come on, we haven't got time for this.' He threw a shirt at Kirby, who sniffed at it. 'Doris washed it.' He grinned. 'Taken a bit of a shine to you.'

'Really,' Kirby said pulling the still slightly damp shirt over his head. Then Harold helped him to his feet and thrust his sword belt into his hands. Kirby stood still for a second, to make sure his legs would support him, before taking a step towards the entrance.

'Yes. Oralf wonders if you'd like to marry the girl.'

Kirby stopped and held on to Harold as his legs threatened to buckle. He searched his memory for anything that might have precipitated such a suggestion. He wondered if here, perhaps smiling at a girl was enough. 'Er, she's young enough to be my daughter.'

Harold hadn't stopped grinning. 'Not that important.'

'Oh yes, I can see that going down well. Sorry, just off to see my young wife in that other world.' He raised his voice a little. 'Really, Dad, that's nice. Say hello to Doris for me and have a good time. Try not to get maimed or killed, ha, ha' He glared at Harold. 'What d'you think?'

Harold laughed. 'Come on, we've got to be off.'

Outside Kirby's eyes became slits with his brain protesting at the harshness of the sunlight. Someone thrust something into his hands. He opened one eye a fraction wider. It was Goran and the something was a brown hunk of dried meat.

'Eat,' Goran said. 'You'll feel better.' He did, and he did, a little.

When he managed to open both eyes, he noticed Shirley and was standing with Oralf's three daughters. Her hair was braided, and keeping it in place was a decorated leather band. Around her neck were wooden beads she hadn't been wearing the night before. Susie and Connie joined them, and he had to admit that all three looked as if they belonged here.

Harold handed him his pack, which he shrugged on to his shoulders. Goran was already heading out of the village. Susie kissed and hugged the three girls, then skipped along to catch up with Goran. Shirley hugged them as well and then headed across to Kirby while Connie talked to her brother.

'What d'you think, sir?' Shirley asked, patting her hair.

'Very nice. I'm not sure the Chief would approve of the headband and beads mind you.'

Shirley frowned, 'Perhaps you're right. Maybe I'll save them for when I go clubbing.'

'Yes, well stay here for too long and I think "going clubbing" could take on a whole new and more literal meaning.'

As they left, the girls waved and Doris blushed as her eyes met Kirby's. Harold nudged him and laughed.

'Made a friend, sir?' Shirley asked.

'Yes, thank you, Constable. Just remember you're still on duty and your appraisal is coming up soon.'

'Sir.'

It was only as they were leaving the village did Kirby think to ask. 'Where are we going?'

'Dunstanburgh,' Harold said.

'Dunstanburgh?'

'Well, what will be Dunstanburgh. It's not far, see that hill?'

Kirby raised his eyes from the road and squinted into the light in the direction Harold was pointing.

'Over that hill is another hill.'

'You don't say.'

Harold ignored the sarcasm. 'And over that hill is what'll be Craster in a couple of thousands of years in your world.'

'Ah.'

FORTY-FOUR

....

Leaving the village behind, Harold strode ahead and Connie took his place beside Kirby and Shirley.

'Where are we?' Shirley asked. 'Or rather where will this be?'

Connie lifted her gaze to the road ahead. 'How well do you know the area?'

'Pretty well. Visited it in the summer since I was a kid. Used to walk much of it with my Dad, especially along the coast. He loves it'

Connie pointed. 'Recognise it?'

'Looks like part of the Whin Sill.'

Connie nodded. 'Aye, that's Ratcheugh Crag.'

'Near Longhoughton?' Kirby asked.

Connie glanced back towards the village. 'That is Longhoughton, or at least it's where Longhoughton will be. Not that in your time anyone will know. Oh, some people may get a queer feeling as they walk over a patch of ground that perhaps something was here a long time ago. Then they'll shrug and walk on.'

Shirley glanced back over her shoulder. 'What? You mean that these ancient places leave a sort of trace, a memory in the land?'

Connie smiled, then nodded in appreciation. 'Something like that. Although it's not the place, it's the people. There's magic in people. They leave their mark where they've lived, and the land doesn't forget them.'

'But this isn't my Northumberland, my past?'

Connie puffed out her cheeks. 'Yes and no. I know what Harold said but it's not that simple. It's all connected. Think of it more as an alternative.'

Shirley scratched her head. 'Thanks, that really helps.'

The ground rose in a gentle slope before them and Kirby ran his hand through the tall grasses at the side of the track as he pondered on what Connie had said. 'So, are the billions of people in our time still marking the ground? Must get very confusing.'

Connie smiled. 'No, for magic to work, you have to believe in the magic. I'm afraid you lost that many centuries ago. Maybe when I'm long gone someone will walk over where I lived and get a funny feeling.'

'They'll struggle where I live, Shirley said. 'I'm on the fourth floor.'

They fell into a companionable silence for a while. Kirby let his mind focus on the meditative rhythm of putting one foot in front of another. He could hear the gulls calling their raucous cries and every now and then he caught sight of one wheeling on the updraft created by the Whin Sill. He caught a whiff of wood smoke on the breeze and to his left, in a copse of stunted trees, a thin smudge of grey rose before dissipating. He pointed to it.

'Charcoal,' Connie said.

The path ahead narrowed as it continued up the slight incline, forcing them to walk in single file. Passing through gorse and bramble, Kirby appreciated his leather clothing which shrugged off all attempts of the vegetation to snag him. On reaching the top he stopped, taking in the view. Below, the sea glinted in the summer sun reflecting the blue of the sky. The shore was as he remembered it, great slabs of rock with gouges carved by the sea so that it looked like a patio laid by giants. The tide was perhaps half way in, or out of course. In the small sandy inlets, Knot and Dunlin ran from the waves on stick thin legs like frantic clockwork toys, until taking flight, then banking, dipping and weaving together as if bound by invisible wires.

Susie had stopped ahead of them and was shielding her eyes with a hand as she looked up and down the coast. Goran stood next to her, leaning on his spear saying nothing. 'Wonderful,' she said. 'Just perfect,'

'You like it up here?' Kirby asked.

Susie smiled as she glanced towards her mum. 'Very much. I like living in Jesmond and Newcastle, and sometimes you kind of forget. Then when you come back…'

'I know what you mean,' Kirby said. 'There's something about it that soothes the nerves.' He glanced across at Harold. 'A little magic perhaps.'

Harold grinned. 'You're learning.'

'You know,' Shirley said as she too paused to admire the scene spread out ahead of them, 'I think of myself as more of a city girl. I love the buzz and all that. I have to admit though, there is something to be said for this. For a short time at least, you know.' She paused to slap at an insect that had landed on her neck. 'Not that I'd want to make a habit of it.'

'Yes well, come on,' Harold said, glancing across at Goran who raised an arched eyebrow in reply. 'I hate to break this up. We need to get off the ridge. I don't want us to be seen.'

'By who?' Kirby asked.

'Anyone.'

They followed the coast before turning at the headland and walking down towards the sheltered bay that in Kirby's world would be Craster in a couple of thousand years. In his mind, Kirby could picture the harbour wall and the few small fishing boats that were left bobbing in its shelter. He could almost smell the smokehouse where they still produced traditional kippers. They continued down into a wooded area at the bottom of the little valley and then up along where a row of small cottages would be. A mile or so ahead was an outcrop that at the same time was familiar and yet so different. To Kirby's eye it looked naked without its ruined castle, which in his day dominated the skyline.

'Funny, I still expected it to be there. It seems like it's always existed, so permanent.'

Harold nodded, understanding what he meant. 'Someone's there though,' he said pointing to a drift of smoke rising skyward.

'Sarah's there,' Susie said. She shook herself as if a chill breeze had intruded on the warm summer day. Connie put an arm around her and gave her a hug. 'I'm sorry, don't know how I know. I just do.'

'I believe you,' Harold said. He turned to Goran. 'I think we need to cut inland.'

Goran nodded and led them down a narrow track between two thickets of hawthorn with vicious thorns. Again Kirby was glad he was wearing the leather. After a few yards, the way broadened out and he caught up with Harold. 'The girl's there?'

'Susie reckons so.'

'And you believe her?'

Harold patted Kirby on the shoulder. 'Listen, I know you're still struggling with the idea that magic is anything other than sleight of hand and some fancy card trick on Saturday night telly. But here people understand, they believe, and because they believe it remains real. Sarah is Marianne's daughter and old blood. Susie is Connie's daughter who's Marianne's sister, they're linked. Bring them somewhere like this and the magic speaks to them. And because they're not used to it, it might be that it kind of floods into them, awakens things.' He looked across at Connie, who nodded.

'What things?'

'Not sure.'

'That's helpful.'

'The ability to connect with magic is strong in our line,' Connie said. 'Whether you can use it and how might vary. Also, so does how it affects, changes you. Marianne has always been fascinated with its power and that's perverted her.'

'And you?' Kirby asked.

'I've seen what it did to Marianne, even as a child. I didn't want to end up like her.'

'And what about me, Mother?'

Connie gave Susie another hug. 'You'll be fine. You've sensed Sarah because of your emotional connection with her, that's all.'

Kirby studied the pair of them. Something inside him told him they'd both be fine. Connie glanced across at him and smiled.

'Where to?' Shirley asked.

Harold shielded his eyes. 'The top of this little ridge, what in your day is called Scrogs Hill. There's cover up there.'

As they set off again, Connie dropped in beside Kirby. 'Well, well, Inspector, I do believe there's a little magic in you as well. Mind you, I shouldn't be surprised knowing Alice.'

Kirby frowned. 'I don't know what you mean.'

'When we were talking about Susie's connection to magic I sensed your desire to protect. It was faint, however it was there, like a warm blanket.'

Kirby raised a sceptical eyebrow. 'Really?'

Connie laughed. 'Yes, really. In your world the magic is spread because no one believes. So it has little effect for most people. Here it concentrates with those that have an affinity for it.'

Kirby scratched his head. 'I dunno.'

Connie smiled and took his arm. 'Oh, but you do, Jonah Kirby. Because in your world, you use it all the time without realising it.'

'I thought you said it has little effect.'

'I also said, for most people. Yes, it's faint, almost imperceptible, and you call it instinct, following your nose. You ask the right questions that get people to open up to you. You know when something doesn't smell right.'

'That's just experience. Being a copper.'

'Perhaps,' Connie said, letting go of him. 'Come on, we're lagging behind.'

Kirby quickened his pace, tagging on to the back of the group. He studied those ahead of him. Goran was out in front leading. Connie and Harold were chatting, and Susie and Shirley were sharing a joke, heads close together and giggling. He wondered about what Connie had said. Was it possible he was using magic? Was that what instinct was? He shrugged, what did it matter what you called it?

Although he did wonder about taking more interest in horse racing when he got back.

After another fifteen minutes walking Harold called them to a halt in the middle of a ring of scrubby trees. Their tops were bent at almost ninety degrees, away from the sea, testament no doubt to the gales that blew in on the prevailing north east wind in the winter.

'Good a spot as any,' Goran said, slipping out of his pack and helping Susie and Shirley with theirs.

'Now what?' Kirby asked as he sat down.

Harold smiled. 'Don't know about you, I could do with something to eat.'

'Fine, point me in the direction of the nearest burger van and I'll buy.'

Harold indicated to Kirby's pack. 'We can do better than that.'

Kirby undid the thong that secured the flap. Inside were what looked like parcels of leaves. He took one out and peeled away the outer layer to find some of last night's venison. 'Wondered why it seemed heavier. Then again my brain was struggling a little first thing.'

Susie, Shirley and Connie were also delving into their packs and coming up with their own parcels of flatbread and dried fruit and what looked like cheese. Meanwhile, Harold had produced three large skins of liquid.

'Quite a picnic,' Kirby said.

'There are some blackberries back there as well,' Goran said, flowing to his feet, much to Susie's obvious pleasure.

'I'll help,' Susie said.

'They're getting along well,' Harold said lying back with his hands behind his head.

'He's a bit different from the lads she meets at uni that's all,' Shirley said. She grinned. 'A bit exotic.'

Kirby sat picking at the grass. 'Yes, well I've heard of long-distance romances. However, they're normally measured in miles, not centuries.'

'Hmm,' Connie said, her eyes fixed on where the pair of them had disappeared down the slope among the vegetation.

Above them a few crows were riding the breeze. Kirby watched them bank and twist against the mid-afternoon sky. It would be idyllic if wasn't for that fact that he was about two-and-a-half thousand years in the past with a bunch of bloodthirsty, heavily-armed warriors half a mile away. 'So why are we here?'

Harold propped himself on an elbow. 'We need to get an idea of what Marianne is up to. Think of it as a bit of reconnaissance, a stake out.'

'You've been watching too many American cop shows. I don't think we in the Northumbria police force do "stake outs".'

Harold shrugged. 'What then?'

'We keep an eye on things.'

'I'll tell you what she's up to,' Connie said. 'No good.'

'Agreed,' Harold said. 'Then again we've got to understand what sort of no good if we can.'

Kirby chewed on the end of a grass stalk, something he hadn't done since a kid. 'I understand your concerns for this world, Harold. However, my focus is on keeping law and order in mine.'

Harold nodded. 'Understood. The thing is, if we can try to combat whatever she's doing here, that'll help in your world as well.'

'So when do we take a look?'

Harold leaned back and closed his eyes. 'Later, in the evening, just before the sun goes down.'

'Why?'

Harold opened one eye and focused on Kirby. 'Because to get a bit closer I want us to hide in the shadows and for that you have to have shadows to hide in. So chill, man, and let the vibes of this place ease your troubled mind.'

Shirley threw a small stone at Harold. 'So what did you do in the sixties, Harold? Were you into long hair, flower power and all that? Or was it all a blur?'

Harold grinned. 'Wouldn't you like to know?'

Shirley laughed. 'Perhaps not.'

Susie and Goran returned with a small mountain of blackberries. Kirby thought about asking if they'd picked them above waist, or at least dog-height, before deciding that might not apply here. There again, who knew what else might have wandered along this path? He ate them anyway, along with the cold venison and flatbread. As picnics went, it better than soggy sandwiches and a packet of crisps . 'So what now?'

Harold lay back down, hands resting on his stomach and closed his eyes. 'I suggest we all get a bit of rest.'

Kirby huffed. He put his pack behind his head and lay back. He sat up again and removed a few sharp stones before trying again. He glanced across at Harold who was already snoring. He peered up at the sky and was reminded of his daughter. A Simpson sky she would have called it, after the intro to the cartoon series. And it was, fluffy white clouds against the blue. If anything, the blue seemed more intense in this world. He wondered if that was due to a lack of pollution or simply that he never took the time to look. You simply accepted it, the sky was the sky. He'd never considered how enormous it was and how small it made him feel. He shifted his weight and then removed another stone, from under his backside this time. He'd never understood how people managed to fall asleep on the ground, or in deckchairs. It was ridiculous. He believed you needed to be comfortable, warm and in the dark to sleep. One out of three wasn't enough. He yawned.

Next thing he knew someone was poking his arm.

FORTY-FIVE

....

'Hey, sleepyhead, we need to get up and see what's going on.'

Kirby looked up at a human silhouette kneeling next to him. He took a deep, slow breath and focused. It was Connie and she was smiling.

'Back with us then?'

'Sorry, it's so peaceful. Must have nodded off.'

'You don't say. I would never have guessed from the snoring.'

'Sorry.' Sitting up Kirby realised Harold and Goran were gone. The sun was sinking towards the horizon and those shadows Harold wanted were lengthening. He must have slept for a couple of hours. Susie and Shirley were sitting, picking at the last of the blackberries. A mental inspection of his body found several points of complaint where the hard ground had dug in. He rolled on to his knees and then stood up, grunting. It was as if someone had stuck all his vertebrae together. He rolled his neck and there was a definite click. 'Where've they gone?'

Shirley looked across, licking her fingers. 'Gone to do a recce. They shouldn't be long.'

Two minutes later, Harold and Goran reappeared.

'Ah, awake then,' Harold said. 'Sleep well?'

'Define well.' Kirby said, putting his hands in the small of his back, still trying to massage some feeling into his flesh.

'That's the trouble with your lot, soft. All pocket-sprung mattresses and the like.'

'And I suppose you sleep on the floor, or is it a bed of nails?'

Harold grunted but didn't answer.

Kirby smiled. 'Thought so.'

Harold shared out what was left of the bread and meat.

'What did you find out?'

Harold shook his head. 'Not much. Other than they're not there.'

'You mean they've left?'

'No. The horses are gone. My guess is some of them have gone hunting. Others will be paying visits to villages as they did with Oralf. If they're coming back tonight, they'll be back soon.'

'Why?'

Harold gave Kirby a withering look. 'Being as there's little street lighting in the Iron Age and horses don't have headlamps. So staying out in the dark is not such a good idea.'

Kirby returned Harold's withering look with one of his own. 'No, I mean, how do you know they've not just gone, as in not coming back?'

'Ah. The womenfolk are still there and the goblins are hanging around their pens.'

'Pens?' Shirley asked.

'Yes well they're not exactly seen as part of the family, Uncle Goblin and all that.'

'Nice.'

Harold put a hand on Shirley's shoulder. 'This is the Iron Age. And you wouldn't class your average king or chieftain as an equal-opportunity employer.'

'So what now?' Kirby asked.

'We need to get closer for when they return.' Harold shielded his eyes with a hand and studied the setting sun. 'Should be easier now. And Goran made a note of the possible escape routes.'

'Escape?' Kirby said. 'That implies trouble and running for our...' he glanced across at Susie and Shirley. 'Well, running anyway.'

Harold shrugged. 'Just planning for all possibilities. Anyway, let's go.'

'All of us?' Kirby asked, glancing again towards Susie and Shirley.

Shirley raised her eyes skyward and tutted. 'If it comes to the running bit, sir, why don't we put a friendly tenner on who's ahead?'

'We stick together,' Harold said. 'Anyway, if it came to running for our... well you know, my money's on Shirley.'

'Thanks,' Kirby muttered as they set off.

Topping a small rise, Harold held up a hand for them to stop and motioned to get on all fours and head for a gap in the bushes ahead.

'Ow,' Kirby complained as he picked a thorn out of his hand.

'Shhh,' Harold said. 'Sound travels here.'

'Not on its hands and knees though,' Kirby muttered.

Harold tapped him on the shoulder and pointed down the slope. Ahead of them was a large timber and thatch building with smoke rising from a hole in the centre of the roof. There were several smaller buildings surrounding it. Beyond that the land was wooded and stretched into the distance. The smell of cooking and animal dung drifted towards them. While Kirby was watching, several women emerged and a few seconds later the sound of hooves beating on the hard earth announced the arrival of about twenty horses and riders. Harold motioned to get down. 'Let's see who we've got,' he muttered, delving into his pack and coming out with small pair of binoculars.

'Very Iron Age,' Kirby whispered.

'Sisillius is there.'

'Which one?'

'That's him in the middle on the grey. The so-called king, with ambitions above his abilities.'

'Not much of a kingdom.'

'No,' Harold said. He glanced across at Connie who shook her head.

'What?' Kirby asked.

Connie took the binoculars from Harold. 'If you're planning to take a kingdom, you need men and horses, and lots of them.'

'I thought you said others would be going around the local villages recruiting?'

Connie waved a hand ahead of her. 'Yes, but that's not going to deliver anywhere near enough. And there are only buildings there for say what? A couple of hundred?' Harold nodded.

'And how many does he need?'

Connie shrugged. 'A few thousand at least.'

'Perhaps they're elsewhere?'

'Unlikely,' she said, passing the binoculars to Kirby.

Kirby surveyed the scene. 'So that's where Marianne comes in, right?'

Harold shook his head. 'Still need men,' he said, holding his hand out for the binoculars again. 'Oh, look and there's Mephisto.'

'I've been meaning to ask,' Shirley whispered. 'Mephisto? Doesn't sound very Iron Age.'

'Here he's Mathwyn. You might know him better as Merlin.'

'Merlin?' Kirby said out loud before remembering to whisper. 'Merlin?' he repeated. 'As in King Arth...'

Susie was on her feet pointing. 'Sarah.'

At the back of the group, dressed in a deep scarlet robe, was a young girl who from this distance could have been

Susie's twin. Her red hair fanned out behind her and on her head, glinting in the setting sun, was a jewelled band.

Connie gripped Susie's arm. 'And next to her is Marianne.' As she said it, Marianne pulled down the hood that had been covering her face.

'Sarah,' Susie repeated. Harold grabbed at her to pull her down, but it was too late. Sarah had also brought her horse to a halt and was pointing in their direction. Marianne's gaze followed her arm. Kirby staggered. It felt like an earthquake had shaken the ground beneath his feet. Recovering he saw Goran steadying himself on his spear and Harold holding on to a small tree.

'I think it's time we were leaving,' Harold said.

'Sarah,' Susie said again, then collapsed.

'Sorry, Connie, we can't hang around,' Harold said as Connie bent down next to her daughter.

'Fainted, that's all,' Connie said, looking up. 'The magic and the sudden connection was too much for her. Give her a few minutes.'

'I'm not sure we've got a few minutes,' Harold said.

Goran reacted by scooping Susie up in his arms. 'I'll take her,' he said turning and heading into the undergrowth. Connie followed.

'Run?' Shirley suggested.

'No,' Harold said. 'Not yet. Save your energy. Just walk fast.'

'Couldn't you have chosen an easier route?' Kirby said, ducking beneath a bramble that scratched at his face before batting away branches that sprung towards him as Goran led the way, carrying the still unconscious Susie.'

'We could, but then they would have been more horse and rider friendly.'

'Ah.'

'Stop,' Harold ordered a few minutes later.

Goran turned, looking as cool as ever despite his extra burden.

Connie pushed Susie's hair back and laid a hand on her forehead before feeling for a pulse in her wrist. Susie's eyes fluttered. Connie nodded, looking relieved. 'She's alright. It was the surge of magic; she's sensitive to it.'

'Shhh,' Harold said.

Kirby leant on a branch, panting, and watched Harold do something he'd only seen in old cowboy films. He got on his hands and knees and put his ear to the ground. 'Does that actually work?'

'What?'

'That, putting your ear to the ground?'

'It might if people shut up and stopped shuffling around.'

Everyone except Harold gave each other guilty glances.

Harold held his breath for a second or two. 'Listen,' he whispered.

'I can't hear anything,' Kirby whispered back.

'Exactly, they're not following.'

'Perhaps we've lost them?' Kirby whispered again and then wondered why they were whispering if they weren't being followed.

Harold shook his head. 'I doubt it, what with you crashing around like a small bull elephant.'

'So why then?'

'They're a superstitious lot and it's getting dark.'

Shirley grinned. 'What, those big hairy-arsed, and hairy-faced for that matter, men are afraid of the dark?'

'Not of the dark so much,' Harold said, narrowing his eyes and peering around, 'as what might be hiding in it.'

Shirley's grin faded. 'Like what?'

Harold half crouched and peered down the track they were on. 'Creatures… and things that prefer the night.'

'That's right, reassure me,' Shirley said glancing back the way they'd come.

Harold straightened up then smiled. 'Or it could just be they know where we live, as it were.'

Shirley relaxed a notch, then scowled and pointed at Harold. 'You… don't do that again.'

Harold's smiled widened.

'She's coming round,' Goran said as he knelt and put Susie on the ground in a sitting position while still holding on to her.

Susie opened her eyes. 'What happened, where are we?' She then became aware of Goran's arm around her and shuffled in closer, bringing a smile to the young man's face. Connie frowned at her daughter.

'What?' Susie said.

Harold gave a brief account of the encounter with Sisillius, Mephisto, Sarah and Marianne. Susie shook her head. 'All I remember was Sarah. She was in my head, calling to me.'

'And it was her?' Connie asked. 'Not Marianne?'

Susie nodded. 'I'm sure. It was Sarah's voice. She wanted me to join them. For a second it felt as if that's all I'd ever wanted. Then the connection sort of snapped and that's the last thing I remember.'

Connie nodded. 'It seems Sarah has at least some of her mother's talents. Luckily, they're still a little raw.'

'Yes, well,' Harold said, 'let's get Susie away from here.'

'I think getting Susie and the rest of us home might be a good idea,' Kirby added, glancing towards Shirley as he said it. 'And by that I mean my version of home.'

'Agreed,' Connie said.

Harold nodded as Goran helped Susie to her feet. 'You OK to walk?'

Susie held on to Goran. 'Yes, I think so.'

'I'll help you,' Goran said, putting an arm around her waist.

'Thanks,' Susie said, leaning into him.

'Heavens,' muttered Connie. Harold grinned.

'So where to now?' Kirby asked.

Harold pointed off to their left. 'That way, back to the cave. It's not far from here. We've effectively come round in a long loop.'

'Won't they expect that?'

'Perhaps, however, there's more than one. Think of it as a network.'

'Wonderful.'

FORTY-SIX

....

Walking back to the cave only took an hour or so. The moon cast just sufficient illumination for Kirby to pick his way over the ground. He was, however, glad that Harold and Goran appeared to know where they were going in the dark because he didn't have a clue. By the time they arrived, Susie was fully recovered, even to the point where she was managing without Goran's arm around her all the time. Inside, Harold lit a couple of torches which cast enough light to enable them to change back into their twenty-first-century clothes. To Kirby's relief his brogues were still there and in one piece.

'I was thinking you might need some protection,' Harold said to Connie.

'From what?' Connie said.

'If Marianne was aware of Susie, then she also knows you were there as well. And that you have a good idea of what's going on.'

'So what are you suggesting?'

'That Goran stays with you.'

'Hang on just a minute there,' Kirby said glancing at the smiling Susie. 'I'm not sure I want to be responsible for someone wandering around rural Northumberland who wouldn't look out of place in a Lord of the Rings film.'

'Hey, listen,' Susie said, 'stick him in a pair of jeans and a T-shirt and no one would suspect a thing.'

Harold nodded. 'That's what we've done before.'

Kirby turned to Harold. Goran was behind him smiling. 'Before?'

'When he looks after the shop. If I have to go away or I fancy a bit of a break.'

Kirby shook his head. 'He does what! And does he have a passport or any form of ID?'

'Er, no.'

'So effectively, he's an illegal immigrant.'

Harold shrugged. 'Is he? I mean he is British. He's still technically from here...'

'...just not the same historical time,' Kirby finished for him.

'Hmm,' Shirley added. 'I don't think that's actually breaking any laws from what I can remember.'

Kirby threw his hands in the air. 'Funnily enough, I don't think anyone has seen the need to legislate for the possibility of immigration through time travel.'

Harold huffed. 'Exactly.'

'Wonderful. It'd be a first, I'll give you that. And more than a little difficult to prove without freaking out all the authorities concerned.'

'How are they going to know?'

'I think the spear and bow might arouse some interest. What do you think?'

Harold now had his hands on his hips. 'Look, it's not as if he's going to go down the pub with them.'

'Well, that's alright then. I'll simply…'

'Boys!' Connie said. 'It's nice of you to be concerned, but Susie's staying with me, at least for now. If it's Marianne we're worried about, then sorry, Goran's not going to be much protection.'

Susie frowned and Goran looked disappointed.

'What time is it?' Connie asked when they were back on the other side, their side, and walking to the car park and the bus stop.

Kirby looked at his watch. 'Seven-thirty, why?'

'Well, if we get a move on we'll catch the last bus.'

'Bummer,' Shirley said. 'The National Trust shop'll be shut. I like a National Trust Shop.'

'Me too,' Susie said. 'I could do with another of their shoulder bags, mine's seen better days.'

Kirby looked at them. It was as if the last twenty-four hours hadn't happened. That they hadn't been to an Iron Age village with real fur-clad warriors carrying spears and swords which could do serious damage. You'd think they'd been to some re-enactment day and that the "warriors" from the "village" packed up at five o'clock to go for their fish and chips. Then on Monday they were back to being accountants or shopkeepers.

When they arrived at the bus stop, the bus was pulling in. The door opened and the same driver who had brought them here smiled out at them. 'Had a good day?' The others piled on past Kirby, leaving him to pay again, he later realised. 'Careful, Grandad,' the driver called out to Harold. 'There's no rush.'

Harold muttered something guttural that Kirby didn't catch. The driver grinned.

'That saved us a walk,' Connie said as the bus was pulling away and Kirby sat next to her.

'Hang on, the driver said "had a good day?"'

'Yes, well, you get that in the country. People are a bit more chatty.'

Kirby frowned. 'No I mean day, as in today, as in we'd only been there for the day.'

Harold poked his head between them from the seat behind. 'I told you, it doesn't work like that.'

'As in?'

'Well, you weren't in the same time period, were you?'

'No, so?'

'Well there you are then.' Harold smiled and sat back.

Kirby may have quit physics after O-level, but even he knew that did not constitute a credible answer. Then again he wasn't sure he could cope with one that did, so he left it at that.

Back in the kitchen of her cottage, Connie sat at the table relentlessly stirring her tea despite not taking sugar.

'What?' Kirby asked.

'I don't like it.'

'Could be the milk,' Harold said, sniffing at the bottle. 'How long have you had it?'

Connie scowled at him. 'Not the tea. Marianne. I know what she's trying to do. She wants to use Sisillius to carve out a kingdom, her kingdom. However, she hasn't anywhere near enough men from what we've seen.'

Kirby put his own mug on the table. 'You said she was trying to recruit from the villages?'

'Even so, she'll be way short of what she needs. Those other chieftains have men and lots of them. If they gang together against a common enemy, as it were, Sisillius's meagre band wouldn't stand a chance.'

Kirby helped himself to a chocolate digestive. He was half way to dunking it when he saw a questioning frown from Shirley. 'Er, perhaps she's curbed her ambition. Settled for a bit of raiding and pillage and all that.'

Connie shook her head. 'No, not Marianne. Those raids were only to keep the men they've already got happy. She'll have promised them plunder. Also, if she doesn't keep them occupied, they'll fight amongst themselves.'

'If she's got the magic, can't she just... I don't know, magic a victory?'

Connie tutted. 'What, like turn the other army into frogs or hit them with bolts of lightning?'

'Er, something like that,' Kirby muttered, sensing he was on dodgy ground.

Connie patted his hand and gave him the sort of look he felt she might give a five-year-old. 'It doesn't work like that. You still need men, warriors. You can view the battlefield, see where your enemy are, create illusions, bring down walls, spread fear. However, when men are standing toe to toe slugging it out in a shield wall, you'd be just as likely to turn the whole battlefield into two armies of frogs, even if that were an option, which I'm pretty sure it isn't. Also, whatever virtues frogs have, fighting doesn't rank high among them.'

'Could be fun to watch though,' Shirley said. 'I mean, thousands of frogs trying to battle it out with little swords and helmets and stuff.' She blushed as the others turned to stare at her. 'Sorry, must stop thinking out loud.'

'So what then?' Kirby asked, turning back to Connie.

Connie glanced over to Harold, who shrugged. 'Wait?'

'And you're convinced she's still going to try and pull magic from this world with all that goes with that? Even if we don't know what she's going to do with it?'

Connie frowned. 'I'm afraid so.'

'But not right now?'

'No. She has to act soon though.'

Ignoring Shirley, Kirby dunked his biscuit. 'Well, if something occurs to you, let me know.' He turned to Harold. 'Or if there's is so much as a twitch in the ether, or whatever it is, I want to know. Understood?' Harold nodded. 'However, for now I think we'd better be going.' He turned to Shirley. 'Come on, Constable, before you have a chance to share any more of your invaluable insights.'

'Sir.'

FORTY-SEVEN

....

'Well it all seems very quiet now, Jonah.' The chief beamed at Kirby. 'Nothing's happened for a few days. No more reports of teenagers running amok or those idiot re-enactment people tearing up golf courses on their ruddy horses.'

'Yes, sir.'

The smile faded. 'You don't seem happy about it, Jonah?'

'I don't think we've heard the end of it, sir.'

The chief twitched and started rearranging his pens, lining them up on one side of his blotter. 'No? And what makes you think that?'

'Er, my experts, sir.'

The chief relocated his pens to the other side of the blotter and lined them up there. 'That'd be like the expert with the long leather coat with suspicious-looking bulges under it and the hat?'

'Yes, sir.' Kirby smiled. 'The hat's from John Lewis,' he added, thinking a bit of normality might help ease the tension.

'Really?' The chief nodded as if wondering how much of what he knew to admit, even to himself. 'Things get back to me you see, Jonah,' he said in a tone that Kirby interpreted as him wishing they didn't.

'I understand, sir.' Kirby took a deep breath, realising that any tension easing he'd achieved would now be reversed and then some. 'At some point, sir, I might need back-up to ensure things don't… er, escalate.'

'Escalate!' The chief's hand spasmed, sending two of the pens skittering across the desk. One landed in Kirby's lap. He smiled and placed it back on the desk.

'I just need access to some of the units, such as in Alnwick and the like. And for them to know I'm acting with your authority, sir.' He paused. 'That way we can hopefully contain it.' The chief's fingers were now drumming on the desk and he wasn't making eye contact. Kirby tried again. 'We might even be able to keep it out of the press, sir. Avoid any sensationalism.'

The chief nodded clenching and unclencheing his fists. 'Avoid sensationalism, yes, yes.' He looked up at Kirby and took a deep breath. 'Very well, Jonah. I'll make sure they know.' He narrowed his eyes and pointed a shaking finger at Kirby. 'No sensationalism remember. Sensationalism would not be good for any of us.'

'No, sir.' Kirby tried what he thought was a reassuring smile as he stood. The chief's hand twitched again and more pens ended up on the floor.

'I think tea, Jane,' Kirby said, closing the door behind him.

'On my way.'

Walking back to his unit, Shirley appeared and fell in beside him. 'How'd the chief take it, sir?'

'As well as could be expected.'

Shirley sucked in a breath between her teeth. 'Ooh, that bad then?'

'Yes, Constable. However, at least we can count on support when we need it.' Kirby paused. 'Not that I have any idea what support we'll need, where or even for that matter how much use it might be.'

Shirley smiled. 'At least it's something, isn't it, sir?'

'Well I suppose whenever it happens, whatever it is, we might be able to use it to keep the press out of it.'

'The press, sir?'

'Yes, to get that commitment I suggested that we'd avoid any sensationalism.'

'Oh, what, like reports of fur-clad warriors brandishing swords riding over a golf course and scaring the locals?'

'That sort of thing, Constable.'

Shirley pulled a lopsided 'oo er' sort of face. 'I hear that a career in security isn't all that bad, sir, even if it does mean working nights a lot of the time.'

'Thank you for that, Constable.'

Shirley smiled. 'Always glad to help. So what now?'

'I think we need to catch up with our favourite shopkeeper.'

The bell tinkled and Kirby caught a flash of grey among the shelves near the back of the shop.

'Afternoon, Jonah, Shirley.'

Kirby glanced at Shirley who didn't even smile at the mention of his Christian name, so that was progress at least. He watched her hand moving towards one of the tins on the shelf next to them. It stopped an inch away. She frowned and let her hand drop.

'Well done, Constable.'

'Goes against the grain though, sir.'

Kirby smiled. 'The greater good and all that.'

'If you say so, sir.'

They walked down one of the aisles, stepping over what Kirby assumed was supposed to be a display of, but looked more like a pile of, cloths and dusters. There was a sign on top, "Buy two get one free".

'Someone could trip over that,' Shirley said when Harold appeared.

'That's the point, can't miss them then. And they feel guilty so they tend to buy.'

Shirley frowned. 'Isn't that a bit underhand?'

'It's called marketing.'

Kirby put a hand on Shirley's arm before she could dig herself in deeper. 'It's two days now, Harold, and nothing. Not so much as a minor misdemeanour.'

Harold scratched his head. 'I know. It's worrying.'

'You, Enda or Geraldo sensing anything.'

'Nope, not so much as a tremor.'

'Perhaps she's given up,' Shirley said. 'Realised she can't recruit enough men and so there's no point.'

Harold shook his head. 'Not Marianne, you heard Connie. No, this is the calm before the storm.'

'And I think the storm clouds have started building,' came a voice from behind them. Kirby's heart leapt and Shirley yelped as she stepped on the pile of cloths and dusters, kicking a few across the floor.

Harold raised a hopeful eyebrow.

Shirley scowled at him. 'Forget it.'

Kirby put a hand to his chest as he turned to be greeted by the most hypnotic pair of eyes he'd ever come across. 'Heavens, Edna, don't do that. And how the hell did you come in without sounding the bell, some sort of trick?'

Edna grinned. 'Was already here, idiot.'

'Oh.'

'Yes, well as I said, I think it's starting.'

'What's starting?' Shirley asked.

'Whatever Marianne has in mind.'

'We've had no reports of…' just then Shirley's radio chirped. She stepped over the cloths and turned away to answer it. She listened 'Uh-huh,' she said glancing back at Kirby and shaking her head. She put the radio back in her pocket. 'Hexam, groups of teenagers shoplifting and…' it chirped again. 'Morpeth this time.'

At that moment the shop bell gave a frantic, urgent tinkle. It was Geraldo. 'It's started.'

'We know.' They chorused.

'Oh.'

'You lot better get going then,' Edna said.

'Where?' Kirby asked.

Edna grabbed him by the sleeve and dragged him outside the shop. The rest followed. She pointed to the north where storm clouds were, literally, building. 'Them's not natural.'

'Rothbury now, sir,' Shirley reported.

Kirby looked at Harold. 'Dunstanburgh?'

Harold nodded. 'Got to be.'

'How long have we got?'

'Couple of hours maybe. Depends on what she's planning, how much power she needs.'

'Blues and twos I think, Constable,' Kirby said opening the car door. Harold and Geraldo got in the back. 'What about you?' Kirby said to Edna, who'd stayed on the pavement.

'Nothing I can do to help there. I'll keep an eye on things here.'

Kirby slammed the car door. Shirley switched on the lights and siren and, in a plume of grey smoke from the tyres, took off up the road. On reaching the dual carriageway outside Gosforth, Shirley put her foot down as cars pulled over to let them through. Kirby glanced behind. Harold seemed at ease as Shirley threw the car around a van that dithered in front of her. Geraldo on the other hand was wide eyed with fear, staring out of the window at the world flashing past them. His knuckles were white, gripping the handles of a leather bag he had on his lap.

'What's in the holdall?' Kirby said, noticing it for the first time.

There was a rustling from inside the bag, which bulged and rocked. Then the zip flew back with a loud "zzziippppp" noise. A voice called. 'I am. And I've had enough of being thrown around like washing in a tumble drier.' Following the voice, a pair of long white ears poked their way out to be followed by a pink nose and then the rest of the head of what was unmistakably one cross-looking, scowling white rabbit.

The car veered towards the central reservation and then twitched as Shirley brought it back under control.

'Constable!' Kirby shouted, holding on to the dashboard.

'Sorry, sir. It's not every day you meet a talking rabbit.' She smiled. 'And a crabby one at that.'

Roberto scowled. 'You'd be crabby as well, young lady, if you'd been stuck in a bag and then thrown around like a ball at a children's party.' He then wiped a paw over his ears. 'What's more, the rabbit has a name, it's Roberto. And you are?'

'Keep your eyes on the road, Constable,' Kirby said while watching Shirley's eyes flicking to the mirror every few seconds. He turned back to Roberto. 'This is Constable Shirley Barker.'

'I take it she's trained to drive this vehicle at speed?'

'You bet,' Shirley said as the road cleared and the speedo climbed past ninety.

Roberto looked up at Geraldo, who was still clutching the bag for comfort. He tutted. 'Well, let's see if we can get there in one piece.'

FORTY-EIGHT

....

As they pulled into the Alnwick police station car park, Constable Cuthbertson came running out to meet them. Kirby wound down his window.

'Sir, it started kicking off here about half an hour ago and now there's reports of disturbances coming in from all the surrounding villages, fights in pubs and...' Cuthbertson glanced to the back seat of the car. His jaw moved a couple of times, but no sound emerged.

'Look at me, Constable.' Kirby said.

'I, er...' Cuthbertson's eyes were once again drawn to the rear of the car.

'On me! Constable.'

Cuthbertson blinked rapidly several times and shook his head before focusing on Kirby.

'Now carry on.'

'Er, yes, sir. As I was saying, pubs and supermarkets and the like, wherever there are large groups...' he glanced to the back seat again.

'Constable!'

'Sorry, sir. Yes, it seems wherever there are large groups of people. There's even a report from an old people's home out on the Rothbury Road. Although to be fair, it's not the first time.'

'Right. Your inspector should've received word from the chief that I'm to be given all the assistance I need, yes?'

'Yes, sir. Although we're a bit stretched dealing with what's going on in the town. He reckons he can spare you a couple of squad cars worth, that's all.'

Kirby glanced at Shirley, who shrugged. 'Right, well get them moving.'

'Where to, sir?'

'Dunstanburgh.' He pointed at Cuthbertson. 'Constable, I want one of those cars in Craster and one on the road in from Embleton. If nothing else, they're to stop any press and general gawpers.'

'Gawpers, yes, sir.'

'Great,' Kirby said as they were speeding north out of the town with the two squad cars following.

'There again,' Shirley said. 'I'm not sure what use a group of flat-footed country bumpkin bobbies would be anyway, sir. If anything, the fewer who witness whatever is going to happen the better.'

'Hmm, you might have a point.' He glanced back to Harold, Geraldo and Roberto. 'Equally, I'm not sure what you and I and this motley bunch will be able to do either.'

Harold shrugged in reply.

'Great,' Kirby repeated.

The further north they drove, the darker the sky became. What had been growing clouds became an unbroken blanket of claustrophobic, turbulent grey, oozing menace. Approaching Embleton, thunder rolled across the sky, booming over their heads. Lightning pitched the countryside and buildings into stark monochrome for a few seconds at a time. On the skyline, the castle lay beneath the dark centre of the swirling mass of cloud. When they turned on to the access road, a gust of wind bent the trees away from the castle and buffeted the car. Shirley was edging the vehicle up the track, when the engine began to stutter. The lights flickered, and the windscreen wipers decided it was time for a bout of frantic waving. The siren increased in pitch until it hurt their ears and had dogs for miles around howling. The blue lights blazed for a few seconds before exploding with pops that sounded like gunfire. The car's engine stopped with a final forlorn wail from the siren. Shirley tried to start it again.

'Dead, sir.'

'My God, it's like Close Encounters,' Kirby said.

'Sir?'

Harold "ner, ner nered" the iconic notes. 'The film, from the nineteen seventies, you know.'

Shirley motioned with her hands 'Oh yes, the mash potato mountain. I never quite got it myself.'

'Well…' Harold started.

'I think this can wait, don't you?' Kirby said, pointing towards the castle and getting out of the car. 'I guess we walk from here.' He wandered back to the squad car, which had come to a halt behind them. 'Don't let anyone past this point,' Kirby said to the driver, who was now out of the car and standing transfixed by the light show illuminating the castle. It was as if the lightning was bouncing around inside the walls. 'Did you get that?'

'Yes, sir. No one past this point,' said the officer, who looked relieved he wasn't being asked to go up to the castle.

'I'll come with you, sir,' Cuthbertson said. 'Sort of a local representative.'

'Fine,' Kirby said.

Harold and Geraldo led the way.

'They gets some wild storms out here,' Cuthbertson said, leaning towards them to be heard over the thunder and the sound of the wind, which was rising with every step they took, 'but I've never seen anything quite like this, sir.'

'I know,' Shirley shouted back. 'It's magic.'

'Well it's different, I'll grant you. Although I'm not sure I'd go that far.'

'No,' Shirley said, grabbing Eric's arm in excitement and shaking it. 'No, I mean it really is real magic.'

'Constable,' Kirby said in his best reprimanding voice.

By now they were all leaning, heads down into the wind which was whipping at their clothes. Shirley pushed a lock of errant hair out of her eyes. 'Sorry, sir, don't you think he should know? At this point, it's a little difficult to hide.'

'Fine,' Kirby said trying to button his jacket.

'Know what?' Eric said, clamping a hand on to his helmet to prevent it being torn from his head.

'Like I said,' Shirley shouted. 'Magic.' She pointed towards Geraldo. 'And he's a magician.'

'What? Like we get up there and he entertains us with card tricks and the like? Or is he going to saw you in half, Shirley?' Eric glanced around. 'Or perhaps this is being filmed and he's going to do some David Blaine stunt and make the castle disappear.'

Shirley slapped Eric hard on the arm.

'Ow! Don't start that again.'

'Listen, you big oaf. I mean, like real Gandalf-type stuff.'

'Yeah right.'

Shirley pointed towards the castle as a huge gust of wind brought them to a halt and bolts of lightning danced around the broken turrets of the castle's gatehouse. 'What do you think that is?' As she said it, three purple streaks of electricity arced out into the sea. The air crackled and clouds of steam rose into the air.

Eric stopped and stared up at the castle. 'I have to admit that's a good one.'

'And that's not the best of it,' Shirley said. 'You see the magician guy's holding a bag?'

Kirby groaned, then he thought on top of everything else it hardly mattered. Anyway, in the howling gale Shirley didn't hear him.

'Yeah,' Eric said.

A sudden gust made Shirley stagger and she grabbed hold of Eric's sleeve. 'You saw the big white rabbit, right?' she said in a lull.

'Uh-huh. Why's he brought his rabbit with him? It's not as if he's got his top hat.'

Shirley shook her head. 'That's not just any white rabbit. It's an actual talking white rabbit called Roberto.'

Eric leaned towards her and raised his voice. 'Sorry, I thought you said talking rabbit.'

'She did,' Kirby shouted. 'And she wasn't kidding.'

Eric stared at the bag, then back at Shirley.

'Honest, cross my heart and all that. And you heard it from the Inspector.'

'What the hell,' Eric said, shrugging then shaking his head, which almost caused him to lose his helmet. He clamped it to his head again before battling on into the mounting tornado that was intent on sending them back down the lane.

At the entrance to the site, they all stopped as if wondering who was going to pay or had their National Trust card on them.

Kirby turned his back on the castle and leaned against the fence, which was still gamely resisting being flattened. 'What do you reckon, Harold?'

The brim on Harold's hat, which Kirby noted was now tied under his chin, flapped up and down. It almost poked Kirby in the eye as he leaned in closer. 'I don't know. I can't see anyone. They must be inside.' He paused as another sudden gust buffeted them all. 'I suggest we don't go in there.'

'Don't worry, I had no intention of trying to arrest anyone at this point. So what's this all for?'

Geraldo shook his head glancing back at the castle, then joining the huddle so he could be heard. 'I've never seen so much magical power in one place. Marianne must be incredibly strong to keep it all here. It's got to be very unstable. Anything could happen.'

'Maybe the castle walls keep it focused?' Harold suggested.

Geraldo shrugged. 'Possibly.'

'So much for expert help,' Kirby said.

Shirley's radio crackled. She held it between herself, Kirby and Eric, and they leant towards each other until their heads were almost touching. 'Sir… ? Two… eople, wo.. n says she kno…o."

'Who is it?' Kirby shouted so loud that Shirley and Eric pulled their heads back.

'Say… er… ame… onnie.'

'Let them through.'

'Orry… ot?'

Kirby tried his best idiot constable voice. 'I… said… let… them… through.'

'Es…ir.'

FORTY-NINE

....

Connie arrived with Susie. They were both wearing Barbour jackets. Sensible, Kirby thought.

'Hello, Jonah,' Connie said turning her back on the raging wind in an effort to be heard. 'Harold, Shirley. And Geraldo, Roberto with you?' Geraldo's bag, which he'd put on the ground, moved in response. Connie looked down. 'Hello, Roberto.'

'Connie,' replied a muffled voice from the bag.

'Oh my,' Eric said to Shirley. 'I still thought you were kidding about the rabbit.'

'So what do you reckon she's up to, Connie?' Harold asked.

'Nothing good.'

'I think we'd got that far,' Kirby said, then smiled at Connie. 'Sorry.'

She put a hand on his arm and returned the smile. 'It's fine. I still have no idea what she's up to.' She glanced over her shoulder at the fireworks going on behind them. 'With all this magic gathering in one place, whatever it is, it's going to be something big.'

'So what's she waiting for?'

Connie shook her head. 'The right time, whenever that is. Also,' she paused as yet another sudden gust had them taking a step back. 'Also, it's one thing gathering all this magical energy, it's another fashioning it into something you can use.'

'Look,' Susie said, pointing to the main entrance of the castle. Emerging, silhouetted against the flashing light show illuminating the inside, were men in helmets holding swords in the air. The wind dropped a couple of notches while the clouds grew darker and more foreboding, boiling over the castle. The two broken towers reached skywards as if ready to collect whatever forces were about to be unleashed. Electricity ran up the warriors' blades and arced between them casting a ghoulish blue glow over the faces of the figures in front them.

Kirby felt static in his hair causing it to stand up better than any gel some of the junior ranks used.

'Ow!' Shirley shouted dropping her radio, which sparked and sizzled as it hit the ground.

Kirby motioned her and Susie to get behind him and Eric, not that he had any idea what use they'd be if these men decided to charge. Connie stood next to him.

'Tactical retreat?' Kirby suggested.

Harold shook his head. 'Look, they're forming more of an honour guard.'

Connie turned to her right and pointed.

'What?' Kirby asked.

'I've called for back-up and it looks like they're arriving.'

'Oralf,' Harold said, grinning. 'And he's managed to bring a few friends with him.'

Out of the gloom appeared several hundred men on horseback looking equally as ferocious as the warriors outside the castle.

'Oh hell,' Kirby said. 'I'm now going to be responsible for a pitched battle.'

'Should we do something, sir?' Shirley asked.

'I appreciate the thought, Constable. However, once again I don't think they're going to respect your police whistle and a stiff talking-to.'

'Good point, sir.'

Oralf and his men drew up into a line about a couple hundred yards away from the castle. They drew their swords and started beating them on their shields. At the same time the men either side of the entrance to the castle shuffled aside. The wind dropped to no more than a breeze as two women strode into view: Marianne and Sarah. Both were wearing long red cloaks, which fluttered behind them.

Kirby let go of the post he'd been holding on to. 'What now?'

'I suspect this really is the calm before the storm,' Connie said as two men came to stand between the women in red. One was resplendent in highly-decorated armour, a long scabbarded sword slung across his back, the other was a tall skinny man also in a red cloak. Unlike the women's, his hung limp.

One of the women stepped forward and smiled across at them. 'Well, well, Connie. Just couldn't keep away. And Harold and Geraldo, how nice. You've even brought your daughter to see her auntie. Oh, and is that your pet police inspector?' She laughed. 'What are you hoping he'll do? Arrest us all?'

'Huh,' Shirley said. 'I didn't even get a mention.'

'I'd take that as a plus point, Constable,' Kirby whispered.

Marianne carried on. 'And what about that ragtag army, Connie? Are you expecting them to die for you? Because that's what'll happen. If not here, then when we get back. You know me, little sister, forgiveness never was a strong point of mine.'

Connie took a step forward. Kirby put a hand on her arm to restrain her. She patted it and then removed it. 'You always did like an audience, Marianne. So what now? I know you're ambitious. You still need men though, and despite this little show you haven't got enough.'

Marianne laughed again, 'Oh, that's exactly why we're here. You'll see.' Marianne led the two men, who Kirby recognised as Sisillius and Mephisto, along the castle walls toward the seaward side on their left. Sarah stayed with the men at the entrance to the castle.

443

Kirby and their little group followed along the line of the fence.

'What's holding all that power in place?' Harold asked Connie.

Connie shook her head. 'I don't know. It can't be an easy thing to pull off.'

About half way along Marianne stopped and smiled, turning her attention to her daughter. Back in the entrance Sarah, a shadow against the eerie glow that now filled the inside of the ruin, raised her arms and threw back her head. Sparks flew from her fingers. Increasing in intensity, they merged into a single stream of energy which after a few seconds began to pulse as if it had a life of its own. Electricity crawled over the walls, occasionally sparking skyward or setting fire to a tussock of grass, which sizzled for a few seconds before subsiding to a dull orange glow.

Marianne now turned towards the sea, on which there was no swell, not a ripple; not even the smallest wave disturbed the patches of sand. The last seagull took off with an angry caw. They watched as a mist rose from the water several hundred yards from the rocky shore. It was thickening and swirling when Kirby thought he heard rhythmic splashing. It was faint, but growing stronger.

'No,' Connie said. 'No, no, no, no!'

'What?' Kirby asked. Connie pointed out to sea. staring across the unmoving water, tall dark shapes were emerging from the fog. The heads of enormous beasts, dragons, were shrugging off the damp blanket of mist.

Oralf's men backed their horses a few steps until Oralf barked a command and they stopped. After a few seconds it was obvious these huge heads were made of wood and painted in crude, garish colours with bared fangs and bulging, ferocious eyes. These were the savage looking prows to large wooden ships and in those ships were savage men. Drifting across the calm sea they heard the dull thud of the drums beating in unison, accompanied by the splash of oars. Kirby didn't need his O-level history to tell him that these were Danes, Vikings.

'She can't do this,' Connie shouted.

'What's she doing?' Kirby asked.

'She's reaching into the past, yet another past.' Connie shook her head and glanced across at Harold who was standing open-mouthed. 'She's forced gateways, disrupted nature. She's interfered with the fabric of time and space. Nothing good can come of this.'

'You don't say,' Kirby muttered as he too stood transfixed at the incredible sight of fifty Viking long ships heading to the shore of Northumberland for the first time in a thousand years.

Connie clambered over the fence. 'No, no,' she shouted. 'You can't do this, Marianne. This is wrong on so many levels. You've no idea what impact this might have on our world, this world and their world for that matter.'

'Too late, Connie,' Marianne said, pointing out to sea and grinning. 'They're here and they're coming with me.

I've freed them from their nightmare. They were stuck forever floating on an endless sea, banished from their own lands. I found them and agreed to release them. They think I'm a goddess, Connie. They're mine. These are the warriors who will win me everything. What's more, they will breed me more warriors. There are no limits to what we might achieve in our world, this world, any world.'

Connie took two steps towards Marianne before she fell to her knees, gasping for breath. Kirby vaulted over the fence before he too found himself on his knees. He crawled over to Connie.

'Foolish man,' she gasped.

'I'm a copper,' he said, managing a half smile. 'Sworn to protect.'

They both glanced up. Marianne's attention was now on the ships. The steady beat of the oars were bringing them closer to shore. Kirby could hear the faint shouts from the thousands of men in the boats, no doubt eager to begin the pillaging and other things they were renowned for. He glanced back to make sure Shirley and the others were still in one piece, at least for now. They were all standing as if in a trance watching the potential tide of destruction wash up towards the shore.

At Geraldo's feet the leather bag opened. Out popped two white and pink ears, followed by the rabbit's head complete with twitching nose. Kirby laughed; he couldn't help himself, it was all so incongruous. Roberto hopped out of the bag and through the fence. He stood on his hind legs sniffing the air and watching the boats as he ran both paws over his long ears, which sprang to attention in response.

'Uh-oh,' Connie said.

'What?' Kirby asked as, finding he had recovered some of his strength, he pushed himself to his feet. He held out a hand to Connie.

'I wouldn't want to spoil the surprise,' she said standing, watching and still holding on to Kirby's hand.

They watched together as Roberto hopped across the grass, all the while growing in size. When he was about three feet tall, the image of a giant rabbit was replaced by that of a small man. Small, broad-shouldered and carrying a sword that was nearly as tall as he was, together with a round shield. The "small man" strode across the field, growing all the time until Kirby reckoned he was over seven feet tall. What's more, the sword which he was now unsheathing had also grown in proportion, which made it pretty big.

'Oh,' Kirby said.

'No!' the big man roared.

'Woo hoo,' Kirby heard Shirley shout from behind them. 'Go, Roberto!'

Connie leaned into Kirby. 'Meet Ronnelfus, a.k.a. Roberto.'

FIFTY

....

Marianne now turned her attention to Ronnelfus, or Roberto, it didn't matter. Lightning flickered from the castle walls into her outstretched hands until she was encased in its dancing blue energy. Her cloak stood out behind her and sparks seethed like electric snakes in her hair. After a few seconds she unleashed the gathered power towards Ronnelfus. A split second before it hit him, he held his sword out towards her. The bolt wound itself around the weapon and his arm, seething and writhing with barely contained malice. With a grunt, he swung the great sword in a wide arc, hurling a now white-hot ball of lightning at the nearest ship, which exploded on impact. Kirby pulled Connie into him and instinctively covered his head with his other arm. But instead of debris and bodies being thrown into the sea and crashing on to the shore, the boat winked out of existence as if it had never been there.

'What?' Kirby said, staring at the still calm sea where the boat had been only moments before. 'Sorry,' he said when he realised he was still holding on to Connie.

'That's alright. It's just it was never meant to be here. It's the magic that's holding them and as soon as the tie was broken, it was pulled back to where it came from.'

'That's good, right?'

'Yes, he needs help though,' Connie said as Harold and Geraldo joined them with Shirley. They watched Marianne hurl two more bolts of fizzing energy at Ronnelfus. The first he parried with his shield and another ship disintegrated and disappeared. The third caught him more on the arm, causing him to stagger to his knees. They could see Marianne was breathing heavily with the effort she too was expending, then as Ronnelfus was pushing himself to his feet with his sword, she took aim again. She was raising her hand to deliver another blow when Kirby heard a loud "twang" near his left ear. Marianne's arm flew back and the shaft of lightning seared skywards tearing a gaping hole in the black shroud over their heads. For a second, a ray of sunlight bathed them before the clouds closed over, as if embarrassed at having allowed the intrusion.

'Good shot,' Shirley called.

'For once, Harold,' Kirby said. 'I'm glad you ignored my suggestion not to come out tooled up.'

Marianne howled, more in frustration than pain, and the small crossbow bolt stuck in her hand burst into flame.

'Er, sir,' Shirley said. 'I hate to be the bearer of bad news, however, I think we've rather reminded her we're here.'

Geraldo and Harold came to stand beside Connie. 'Get behind us,' she shouted to Kirby.

'I told you I'm sworn to protect.'

'Well, you can't protect anything if you're a smouldering heap of cinders. Look, we know things and stand a chance at sorting this, you don't.'

Shirley grabbed Kirby by the arm and dragged him back. 'No disrespect, sir, I don't think a tweed jacket and stout brogues are going to offer much resistance to what she's throwing around.'

Marianne raised both arms above her head and flexed her fingers as if manipulating the colossal charge building between her hands. Then with a scream that would have shattered windows if there'd been any, she unleashed a bolt of white menace at them. Connie, Harold and Geraldo threw up their own hands, managing to deflect the crackling ball of lightning over their heads. Half a mile behind them a hedge burst into flames accompanied by the communal bleating of sheep trying to find cover.

Connie pointed to her right where one ship, ahead of the main fleet, was close to the shore. 'They can't be allowed to land. If they do, there's no turning this back.' Ronnelfus had also spotted the danger and was surging into the glassy water to meet them, roaring his challenge as his boots sent plumes of spray into the air. Oralf responded by lining his men up on the beach ready to charge.

Kirby ducked as another bolt of pure energy hurtled towards them. Again it was deflected, and again trees and bushes were incinerated to the noisy alarm of the unlucky sheep. This time Connie, Harold and Geraldo staggered, holding on to each other for mutual support. Kirby could hear their ragged breathing. Harold's coat was smouldering in places. It seemed his John Lewis hat was made of less stern stuff as the top ignited.

Harold wrenched it from his head and began stamping on it. 'Damn, I liked that hat.'

'And there's me saving wine corks for it,' muttered Shirley.

Meanwhile, Marianne was gathering herself again.

'We can't keep doing this,' Connie said, hands on knees, sucking in air. She glanced back at Kirby. 'Remind me to get fitter if we get through this.'

Kirby was about to smile when he spotted Marianne throwing her arms forward again. 'Duck!'

All five of them threw themselves to the ground, and with a hiss of static the fiery ball flew over their heads. Another chorus of plaintive bleating signalled its landing. To their right, a clash of swords announced that the first of the Vikings were off the ship. Ronnelfus, up to his thighs in water, had already dispatched three of them and the others were hesitating as the sea hampered their movement.

'What now?' Kirby asked.

Connie shook her head, pushing herself upright. Marianne was also catching her breath when Susie's voice rang out.

'Sarah, Sarah, please don't do this.'

They turned to see Susie walking up the incline to the gateway in which Sarah stood, arms out, head back at an unnatural angle. Her feet were several inches above the ground as purple lightning held her, swirling around her body. Sisillius's men stared at Susie approaching, making no attempt to stop her.

Connie rushed towards the gate, followed by Kirby. 'Susie, no!' Connie cried.

When they got there, Susie was standing a few yards from the maelstrom that centred around Sarah. Sarah's eyes were closed and her whole body was vibrating, her skin alive with writhing spears of crackling blue energy.

'Sarah please, it's me, Susie.' Susie took another step forward. Eric was behind her, holding on to his helmet. Connie waved him back.

Connie approached her daughter from behind. 'Susie, listen to me, stay there.'

Susie held a hand out behind her. 'No, Mother, stay back. Sarah's the key, I know it. She's my friend and now I know she's also my cousin. This is not her. This is Marianne's doing.'

By now Marianne was only a few yards away. She glared at Susie and then screamed at Connie. 'Get her away now, or you're all dead,' She glared at Mephisto, Sisillius and the men with him. 'What are you waiting for, stop her!' Those men nearest Sarah glanced at each other and then at the ball of energy surrounding her, which appeared to be losing some of its coherence, its stability. They stepped back.

'Cowards,' Marianne screamed.

'Susie!' Connie called.

452

'No, Mother. If Marianne wastes any of her energies she fails. And she knows it, look.' Susie pointed seaward without taking her gaze from Sarah, whose head had returned to the vertical. Sarah's eyes opened, focusing on her friend. Out to sea the mist that had announced the arrival of the Viking ships and had since been dissipating as they came closer to the shore was thickening again. The ships furthest out to sea were being gathered into its gloom, the splash of their oars and the cries of their warriors fading.

Marianne had also seen what was happening. Her uncertainty was clear as she hesitated, eyes darting between the ships and Sarah. For a few seconds she switched her attention back to the shoreline, focusing on the mist which retreated once more. However, on turning back to Sarah it began rolling in again. Kirby could see the panic in her eyes, the indecision, the growing fear and with it her faltering resolve. Her arms were shaking as she reached out and took a step towards Sarah. She stopped, beaten back by the forces that still consumed her daughter. 'Sarah, concentrate, we're nearly there. It's almost ours. We can't lose it now.'

'Sarah,' Susie called, edging closer. 'You don't have to do this. This is not who you are. Come back to us.'

'Stop her,' Marianne screamed again. Several men now unsheathed their swords. Before they had taken more than two steps, they were writhing on the ground covered in a tracery of sparks. Their clothes smoked and ignited in several places. The men screamed and rolled in an attempt to put out the fires. Their discarded swords were consumed in white hot scabbards of heat which left puddles of molten metal on the ground. The rest of Sisillius's band shuffled away fearing that the same punishment would be dealt to them.

Marianne now turned her attention to Mephisto. 'Mephisto, you coward, this is everything we've worked for. Do something, you miserable excuse for a man.' Mephisto didn't move.

Sarah gazed at her mother, wide-eyed, as if seeing her for the first time. She then focused on Susie. She raised her hands in front of her face and for a few seconds stared at the light and energy that weaved across them and surged from her fingertips. She flexed her fingers and her gaze followed the lightning trails arcing from them into the fabric of the stone.

'Sarah, it's me,' Susie said, holding her hands out towards her cousin.

Sarah smiled in recognition and let her hands drop to her sides. The aura that had surrounded her faded. A final few sparks skittered across the ground as if looking for holes to crawl into. And then Sarah dropped to her knees, her head sagging forward. Her body was shaking and her chest heaving as it sucked in air. Susie ran forward and threw her arms around Sarah, pulling the now frail-looking girl into a protective hug. Eric followed and stood over them as if he felt he had to offer some form of protection.

'No!' screamed Marianne. Ignoring her daughter and Susie, she ran past them both and into the castle. The warriors who had at first formed a proud honour guard now ran in fear of their lives. They swarmed past Susie, Sarah and Eric without even a glance in their direction, following Marianne into the castle.

Cries of alarm could be heard coming from the boats. The unrestrained mist rolled over the ships as if resenting having been held back it was greedy to reclaim them. Ronnelfus backed out of the water. The boat in front of him, which only moments before had been disgorging terror, was sucked back out to sea. The garish and ferocious-looking carved dragon at its prow dissolved into a monochrome outline before it too was engulfed in the deadening blanket of grey. Oralf and his men backed up the shore, not wanting to get too close to the rabbit-turned-giant warrior. Finally, job done, the fog itself retreated. A seagull swooped down with a plaintive cry, skimming the surface as if reclaiming its territory. The flat sea left behind began to pulse. Swell rose and fell, and once more waves rolled up the beach.

'Is that it?' Shirley asked.

'Perhaps not quite,' Harold answered. 'Look.'

The gloom around the castle was dissipating, and here and there patches of blue could be seen through the cloud, shafts of sunlight spotlighting the ground. However, over the castle itself a cumulus of concentrated darkness was rising, mocking the weakness of the dissolving clouds which surrounded it. Rising higher and higher its anger grew, pushing against the constraints that held it. Thunder boomed overhead and every few seconds lightning left jagged after-images in the eyes as it illuminated the ruin from within. They could hear the shouts of alarm from the men who were now trapped inside the fortress, in the eye of their very own terrible storm.

'What the…' Kirby started. He didn't finish. He couldn't find the words to express what he was seeing.

'Susie, get out of there,' Connie shouted. Eric picked Sarah up in his arms and he and Susie ran back to stand beside Connie.

The castle was rebuilding itself. Stones were appearing one by one as if it were a giant Lego set. Kirby half expected to see some enormous hand reaching into the earth and plucking them from the ground before placing them on the walls. The two gate towers reformed in front of his eyes. Already the one to their left was complete, even including a flag which now flew horizontal in the wind that once again shrieked around the site. Time-ravaged walls were rebuilding, wind and water scoured stones were once again pristine.

'How?' Kirby managed when he finally got his voice to work again.

Connie stepped beside him and gripped one of his hands in hers. 'It's sort of the same trick, just different.'

'That's clear then.'

Connie ignored Kirby's sarcasm. 'She's reaching into the past. Reversing time.'

'I thought that had failed with the ships?'

Connie shook her head. 'That was so much more difficult: spread too wide and over water. It's why she needed Sarah to hold it all together. This she can concentrate in one place, it's embedded in solid ground making the connection easier. It's earth magic and we are children of the earth.'

'Why?' Kirby asked, staring at the now complete and magnificent testament to the skill of those medieval builders. In answer, there was a deep rumble and what sounded like a great burp erupted from the earth. The castle vanished.

'Oh.'

'Some trick,' Harold said.

Shirley tutted. 'That's torn it.'

'Er,' said Eric. 'When I said that thing about David Blaine, I never imagined…'

Within seconds the dark and angry clouds lost their venom, folding in on themselves, leaving behind wisps of white fluffiness. The sun bathed them with its late summer warmth as if nothing had happened. Sea birds called overhead and behind them the sheep were once again bleating in contentment. All was a scene of serenity and peace, except Dunstanburgh Castle which had graced the ground in front of them for nearly eight hundred years was no longer there.

Kirby walked up to where the castle had stood, while Connie helped Susie and Eric with Sarah who was still unsteady on her feet.

'How is she?' Kirby called back.

'Physically OK,' Connie said. 'Just drained and shaken. Nothing a cup of tea and a good meal won't cure. I'm not sure how much she understands about what's happened. Full realisation of that might take a little longer to get over.'

'You think she didn't know what she was doing?'

Connie shook her head. 'Some perhaps, then knowing Marianne, not the full extent. She warped her mind and shaped her thoughts.'

'Her own daughter?'

Connie shrugged as she and Susie led Sarah away.

Kirby looked around him. All that was left was a complex of trenches he assumed went down to the bed rock, marking where the walls had been. He stood, hands on hips, scanning the site. Nothing, not a single stone. He bent down and picked up a metal box. It was a collecting box that had been set in one of the walls. It rattled with a few coins.

'It didn't belong,' Harold said from behind him.

'The castle did,' Kirby replied, 'here. So, where's it gone?'

'The other side. It'll look quite something. No one'll have seen anything like it.'

'Oh well,' Kirby said with a huff. 'As long as someone's happy then.'

Harold shrugged. 'It may help to attract warriors to her cause. Or then again it may scare the hell out of them.'

Kirby shook his head. 'Sorry, Harold. I know you, Connie, Geraldo and Roberto, er Ronnelfus, did all you could.' As he spoke, Ronnelfus – now Roberto again – hopped across the grass towards them. Apart from a long scratch down one ear he was little the worse for wear. Along the beach Oralf and his men held their swords above their heads and waved a salute as they headed back towards Craster and the Whin Sill. Kirby just hoped they gave the village a wide berth. The last thing he needed was pictures of them all over social media creating more sensationalism. He glanced around and realised that when it came to sensationalism, pictures of a few hundred armed warriors on horseback were the least of his worries. He smiled. It was almost funny… almost.

Shirley bent down and started scratching Roberto between the ears, which brought a sigh of appreciation. She looked down. 'Er, so tell me, I mean why a rabbit?'

Roberto peered up at her. 'Suits my personality.' It was hard to tell if a rabbit was being sarcastic or not.

'Of course. Obviously. Silly me.'

Shirley stood up and turned a full circle, looking at where the castle wasn't. Next to her, Roberto was on his hind legs doing the same. 'Well at least no one got hurt, sir.' Shirley paused. 'Well at least not seriously. Unless you count those Vikings, some of them might have, I suppose,' she said, again glancing down at the white rabbit next to her. 'And in some ways they don't count, at least not here. That's almost a miracle in the circumstances. Got to be worth something that surely, sir?'

'Yes, Shirley, that has to be worth something.' Kirby stood, hands in pockets, still staring at the now empty patch of ground. He'd been here, seen it happen and was still struggling to believe it.

'Er, sir?'

'Yes, Constable.'

'Forgive me for asking, sir. How are we going to explain this one?'

'Good question, Shirley. Any thoughts?'

'Other than I'm glad I'm not the senior officer, sir?'

'Yes, other than that one, Constable.'

'Earthquake?'

'So where's all the debris?'

'Followed by a tsunami?'

'Which only took away the castle, leaving no other evidence of itself behind?'

Shirley squinted out to sea where the sun was now glistening off the gently rolling water. 'It was incredibly powerful and very localised, sir.' She paused, scratching her nose. 'Rare I know. Maybe even the first ever recorded.' She smiled and nodded, pleased with her suggestion.

'Hmm.' Kirby pondered this for a second. 'And when all those experts from the university arrive and start poking around, what then?'

Shirley held her arms wide to take in the castle-vacated patch of land. 'What can they say other than it's clearly gone? And of course there's no such thing as magic is there, sir?'

'True, true.'

Shirley smiled wider as another idea struck her. 'Or perhaps the Chinese or the Russians took it?'

'Overnight?'

'I bet they could, sir, if they really wanted to. They brought a huge ship or ships, took the castle apart then sailed off with it.'

'Ships that no one saw? And why?'

'Stealth ships, sir?' she shrugged, smile fading. 'And because they can. I mean it's the sort of thing people would think they might do. You know, just to prove something. Or maybe the Government secretly sold it to them?'

'I can't see any government owning up to that.' Kirby laughed. 'However, I applaud your imagination, Shirley. Come on, I could do with a cup of tea.'

'And cake, sir?'

'Definitely cake, Shirley.'

FIFTY-ONE

....

Kirby sat in front of the white-painted cottage under the clematis and rose arch. The sweet scent from the few remaining blooms drifted down, adding to his feeling of peace and contentment. The sun was doing its best to find gaps in the clouds and illuminate a final autumnal flourish of colour in the garden. It really was chocolate-box idyllic, or at least it would be if it wasn't for one thing. Nursing his second mug of coffee, he looked out across the fields and towards the coast, still seeing what wasn't there. It was as if his mind refused to accept what had happened and insisted on painting the castle back into the scene.

The "experts" had swarmed all over it. They'd taken measurements, prodded and probed, but after much head-scratching had failed to come up with a plausible theory. The best they could do was to say that this was the result of some, as yet, unexplained natural phenomenon. That was based on the reports and mobile videos of the storm that had raged over the castle at the time it disappeared. A local disturbance of the Earth's magnetic field caused by, or causing, a local quake of some sort, they said. Shirley had got that far. The fact that there was no debris of any kind and that everything else was as it had been before, was ignored.

Some even postulated that the castle had never existed: that it was the result of a mass hallucination that had persisted through history as a result of peculiarities in the local geography which played with people's minds. The only problem with that theory were the thousands of photographs.

After a few weeks the experts slunk away as if embarrassed at their inability to find any valid explanation.

The press had also turned up in force, of course. However, to the chief's and super's relief and delight, any possible role of the Northumbria police force was way down the list of targets for theories, exposes or potential blunders. Thankfully for Kirby, there were no pictures of him or any other copper on the scene. Nor were there any of Viking ships or fur-clad warriors. At least he'd succeeded in that. Also, since there were no reports of suspicious men in a white van seen near the scene at the time, there was nothing like that for the police to be unsuccessfully looking for. And not even the press could connect the extremely localised thunder and lightning storm with any incompetence on their part.

Some newspapers went down the "taken by the Russians" route, again as speculated by Shirley. He half wondered if she'd missed her vocation. They then blamed the Government, MI5 and/or MI6 for not knowing and preventing the theft of a national treasure. Although they never explained why the Russians might want a ruined thirteenth-century castle from the Northumberland coast.

Kirby's personal favourite was provided by The Sun with the headline "E.T. Takes Castle Home". By linking it to aliens they were of course, unwittingly, closer than anyone else, except they were pinning it on the little green men variety. Their theory was that these aliens were collecting exhibits for some galactic theme park. The lifting of it did at least explain why there wasn't a single stone left. The thunderstorm was apparently to hide their castle-stealing ship. Although Kirby did wonder why if you had the technology to cross half the galaxy, your chosen method of disguise was a thunder and lightning show that attracted everyone's attention for miles around. Also why Dunstanburgh? Why not Bamburgh or Alnwick? Surely they were far superior prizes? After a few days of speculation and producing ever more weird and wonderful experts, the press went back to their usual diet of lurid celebrity revelations.

All this had, of course, been a boon for the local B&Bs, guesthouses, pubs and the tourist industry in general. For a couple of weeks, even the smallest, dampest little room was going for five times the normal fee, even in the height of what passed for summer. And ironically, far more people were flocking to see the castle now that it wasn't there compared to when it was. "Nowt so queer as folk," as his dad had been fond of saying.

Connie joined him on the seat.

'I don't think I'll ever get used to it,' Kirby said.

'I know what you mean. It was part of the landscape, solid, dependable, a reminder of the past.'

He nudged her with his shoulder. 'Can we get it back?'

Connie shrugged. 'It's possible. I mean magic took it away, so I'm sure sufficient magic could bring it back. Not that I know how that would be done. I'm not sure anyone does. Perhaps not even Marianne, even if she could be persuaded, which I don't think she could.'

'Really?'

'No,' Connie shook her head. 'Marianne did that in a fit of rage. Rage and anger are powerful emotions, and powerful emotions can unleash powerful magic.'

'Remind me not to make you angry then.'

Connie laughed. 'Anyway, how would you explain it? It disappearing is bad enough. A sudden reappearance?'

'Hmm, to borrow from Shirley's imagination, maybe the Chinese or the Russians, who really did take it in the first place, had a change of heart. Or lots of behind-the-scenes diplomatic negotiations and all that.'

'Yes, well don't hold your breath on it coming back any time soon.'

Kirby nodded and drained his coffee. 'Pity.'

Connie held out her hand. 'Finished?'

Kirby smiled and handed her his mug. He turned back to the view as Connie went inside. The cry of a herring gull overhead caught his attention and he watched it swoop and glide on the breeze as it angled its flight over towards the Whin Sill. The birds didn't seem to mind the castle not being there. After all, it was just a heap of stones, and life was going on quite happily without it. Yet for Kirby it was as if a piece of his childhood had been snatched away, and he suspected that feeling would echo for so many people brought up in the area; a feeling of deep, almost spiritual loss.

Part of him felt he'd failed even though, as Shirley had pointed out, no one had been hurt, at least not in this world, apart perhaps from a few sheep. And who knows what havoc Marianne would have wrought in that other world if she'd succeeded? Although he suspected she wasn't finished with her ambitions as far as that was concerned. Still, there was nothing he could do about that. That was part of the reason he was here, to try to accept everything. That he really had done all he could. That sometimes things happen that even a copper, or especially a copper, has little control over.

His mum had badgered him to take the break, telling him that it'd do him good, that it'd be good for his soul. She was right of course, not that he would tell her that, and not that he'd needed much persuading either.

He was wondering whether a third mug of coffee, along with a go at the crossword, would be appropriate when the creaking of the gate on its rusty hinges made him look up. 'Uh-oh,' he said to himself. He smiled. 'Hello, Susie.'

Susie smiled in return, curling a strand of straying auburn hair behind an ear. 'Oh hello, Inspector. You decided to take that break after all?'

'Yes, something like that.'

'Yes, well Mum can be very persuasive. Doesn't take no for an answer.'

'So I'm discovering.'

'Anyway, are you enjoying yourself?'

'Er yes, thank you.'

'Good,' Susie said. 'Mum inside?'

'Yes.'

Susie stepped inside the cottage and Kirby abandoned thoughts of another coffee, at least for now, as he listened to the conversation drifting out of the open door. Part of him thought he shouldn't listen, but then he was a copper and a lifetime's training in professional eavesdropping was hard to ignore.

'Hello, Mum.'

'Oh, hello, dear. Staying long?'

'I thought I might have a weekend away from the city and uni, why?'

'No reason.'

'If the Inspector's in the spare room, I can always take one of the units.'

'No, no, that's alright, dear. You can have the spare room.'

'Oh, Mother, you've not made the Inspector stay out there, have you, when there's only the two of you?'

'Er… no dear.'

'Then how come the spare room's fr…'

Kirby waited as the couple of seconds passed. He held his breath. He could almost hear the cogs turning before…

'Mother!'

Kirby decided now might be a good time to have a look at the garden, water a few plants, pull up a few things, like weeds, out. Well maybe not that, that could get him into trouble. His phone rang. At home in Cramlington he struggled to get reception, unfortunately here it was perfect.

'Hello, Shirley.'

'Hello, sir, having a nice time?'

'Yes,' he said, glancing back to the cottage door. 'At least I was.'

'Sir?'

'No, I am, thank you.'

'That's good, sir. That's very good. I'm glad. Yes, excellent.'

'Constable?'

Shirley cleared her throat. 'Ahem. Er, sir. You remember Lily "Medussa" Johnson a.k.a. Diamond Lil?'

'Yes, Constable, she's not easy to forget.'

'Well, sir, she's escaped from remand.'

'Escaped? She must be well over seventy and she suffers from arthritis. So what, she made her getaway on a mobility scooter and they couldn't catch her?'

'Well you see, sir, she was in an open prison and they didn't think. As you say, she's getting on a bit and they kind of left it er... open.'

Kirby sighed. 'Don't tell me the press have got hold of it and sensationalised it?'

'Yes, sir, they're calling it the "The Snake Escape" and "Anna Cond 'em".'

'But she's not called Anna.'

'Apparently it's her middle name, sir.'

'Brilliant.' Kirby shook his head: you couldn't make this up. 'Does that need me? Just make sure the chief has a good supply of Hobnobs.'

'Sorry?'

'Never mind.'

'Em...' there was that throat clearing again. Kirby waited. 'Actually, sir, that's not really why I called. I thought I'd lead you in a bit, gentle-like, seeing as you're on your hols an' all.'

Kirby took a breath. He didn't like where this was going. 'Very thoughtful, Constable. Go on.'

'You know the wall?'

'I guess we're talking Hadrian, not garden?'

'Ha, ha. Yes, sir, very funny. But you're right.'

'Of course I know it. Don't tell me that's gone now?'

'Ha ha, again, sir.' This time the laugh was forced and a little on the hysterical side. 'Ah, no. Although I can see where you're coming from.'

'So?'

Shirley gulped.

Here it comes, thought Kirby. 'Out with it, Constable.'

'Er… people are seeing Romans, sir.'

'What, like re-enactment types?'

'Er… no, sir, like real ones. Or at least what they're saying are the ghosts of real ones.'

'Ghosts, Shirley! Since when did we believe in ghosts?'

'I know, sir, and before a couple of weeks ago I would have thought that as well.'

'Still, Shirley, ghosts? People reckon they see all sorts of nonsense. That doesn't mean we have to believe them.'

'Yes, sir, I know. This time though it's lots of people and, what's more, they've filmed them on their mobiles.'

Kirby's heart sank, literally, he felt it this time. He was sure it was pressing on his bladder.

'And, sir.'

'Go on.'

'One of those who filmed them was the Chief's daughter. They were all on a family day out at Housesteads.'

'And don't tell me, the Chief was with them?'

'Yes, Sir. Saw it all.'

'Wonderful.'

'And that's not the best bit.'

'There's more?'

'Yes, sir. They took the chief's mother's Labrador, Angus.'

AUTHOR'S NOTES

....

Thanks for reading Inspector Kirby and Harold Longcoat. Having got to the end I hope you've enjoyed this book. If you have please leave a review on which ever site you purchased it from. Also on Goodreads if you're a member (if not it's a great place to discover new authors). As a self-published author reviews are so important and always greatly appreciated.

If you visit my author site at www.martynfiction.com you can find out more about me and my work. There is also a collection of thirteen short stories of the weird and wonderful available for free!

When they've recovered from this adventure, Kirby, Shirley and the rest will return in the near future taking on the might of the Roman army along Hadrian's wall.

As for the story's setting, Northumberland is where I grew up. I also spent, or misspent, my university years in Newcastle. It is indeed a magical county, although perhaps not quite in the sense explored in this book, but who knows? It is a land of wild hills, mile upon mile of deserted sandy beaches, incredible wildlife and of course it is packed with history. The castles of Alnwick, the ancestral home of the Percy family and Dunstanburgh, featured in these pages, do of course exist. There are also many other castles dotting the region that are well worth a visit. And yes despite Marianne's best efforts Dunstanburgh is still there. Like Shirley and Colin I recommend the mile or so walk along the coast from the pretty little fishing village of Craster. You can park in the carpark where Kirby and the rest set off for their journey into the 5th century BC. Last time I visited there was indeed an excellent National Trust shop.

Most of the places I use in the book do exist, or at least they did at the time of completion, although I may have taken some literary licence with their exact locations for the sake of the story. The exceptions are Harold's shop, although there are similar establishments, and the other shops and cafes I refer to. However, the Collingwood arms can be found. There is one place whose name I have changed for reasons that will become evident in the next book. However, it's true identity will be obvious for anyone who knows Newcastle and if you don't it won't make any difference to your enjoyment.

Again, thank you for reading.

Ian Martyn

ABOUT THE AUTHOR

Hi, I'm Ian Martyn, I live in Surrey in the United Kingdom. One long hot summer as a teenager (they were all long hot summers then, weren't they?) I visited a friend's house. Her Dad had a collection of sc-fi and fantasy paperbacks. The covers looked great. I picked one at random, started to read and I've been hooked ever since. You can find more about me and my writing on my web site: www.martynfiction.com.

Also by Ian Martyn:

Ancestral Dreams: The Return
Project Noah
Bleak – The story of a shapeshifter.
Bleak – the first mission (a 10,000 word novelette). Now free on Amazon

Collection of short stories:

Dancing With The Devil - Thirteen science fiction and fantasy short stories of the weird and wonderful is available for free from my web site at www.martynfiction.com

Printed in Great Britain
by Amazon